I0659494

## ABOUT THE AUTHOR

IAN MCHUGH's first success as a speculative fiction writer was winning the short story contest at the 2004 Australian national SF convention. Since then he has sold stories to professional and semi-pro magazines, webzines and anthologies in Australia and internationally. His stories have won grand prize in the Writers of the Future contest, been shortlisted five times at Australia's Aurealis Awards (winning Best Fantasy Short Story in 2010), reprinted in Australian year's best anthologies, honourably mentioned for world year's bests and appeared in the *Locus* and *Tangent Online* annual Recommended Reading Lists. He graduated from the Clarion West writers' workshop in 2006.

Ian lives in Canberra, Australia and is a member of the Canberra Speculative Fiction Guild.

*Angel Dust* is his first story collection.

# ANGEL DUST

# ANGEL DUST

# IAN McHUGH

T℘ Ticonderoga
publications

*To Mum & Dad*

*Angel Dust* by Ian McHugh

Published by Ticonderoga Publications

Copyright © Ian McHugh 2014
Introduction copyright © Kaaron Warren 2014

*All rights reserved. Without limiting the rights under copyright reserved above, no part of this publication may be reproduced, stored in or introduced into a retrieval system, or transmitted in any form or by any means (electronic, mechanical, recording or otherwise) without the express prior written permission of the copyright holder concerned. Page 293 constitutes an extension of this page.*

Designed and edited by Russell B. Farr
Typeset in Sabon and Optimus Princeps

A Cataloging-in-Publications entry for this title is available from The National Library of Australia.

ISBN 978-1-925212-03-7 (limited hardcover)
     978-1-925212-04-4 (trade hardcover)
     978-1-925212-05-1 (trade paperback)
     978-1-925212-06-8 (ebook)

Ticonderoga Publications
PO Box 29 Greenwood
Western Australia 6924

**www.ticonderogapublications.com**

10 9 8 7 6 5 4 3 2 1

*My thanks to Russell and Liz for the chance to have a book with my name on the front, to Kaaron for her encouragement and inspiration, to Sheila, Scott and Mike for their kind words, and to them and all the other editors who have found a place for my stories in their books and magazines. My thanks to my friends, to the KSPers, the CSFGers, the FWORians, my CW'06 classmates, Les and Neile and all the teachers at Clarion West and at WotF and elsewhere whose time, effort, wisdom, encouragement, critique and friendship has helped my writing (and me) to flourish. Thanks (and apologies) to all those who have found their way into my stories. Thank you to Angie, for taking my hand that day, and not letting go. Thanks to my family, for being my friends as well. Thank you to Cora and Finn, for being the bright suns that my world spins around.*

# CONTENTS

# Introduction

## Kaaron Warren

Ian McHugh is a writer with a vivid imagination who has the rare ability to transfer that imagination to the page.

He's like a traveller, a travel-writer, who visits these odd places (great collapsing houses, a beautifully rendered Australian outback) and comes back home, changed and able to share all he's seen in a way that makes us feel we have travelled there ourselves.

Along the way, he draws emotions from us like tears. There's the sadness of "The Wishwriters' Wife", a simple-seeming fairy tale depicting a once powerful love and what happens when that fades.

There's the humour of "Apricot Finds a Treasure", I think my favourite story in the collection, an exploration of discovery, wit, story and loneliness in a perfectly drawn world.

There's the frightening "Cold, Cold War" which is what it says, an action packed, well-described, vivid new take on the plague story.

McHugh holds thrall over it all, his control powerful over words and imagery.

Reading this book is like reading an ethnography of new worlds. One story, "Extracted Journal Notes for an Ethnography of Bnebene Nomad Culture" does exactly this, with a level of detail so clear, it seems strange the Bnebene don't actually exist.

He builds all his landscapes like this. In "Bitter Dreams", a story full of Australian themes and geography, with a beautiful rendition of the country town, he produces a murder mystery that reads like a mutated "Boney".

McHugh has the great ability to create places so real and new that it feels as if we inhabit them. In "Sleepless in the House of Ye", relentless worms terrify those living in great dying houses. These whiskered creatures struggle weakly as their world falls, bringing an emotional tug to the reader.

In "The Tax Collector of Rhuin", the first of his Rhuin tales, he talks of cultures lost, laughed at, dismissed.

There is a sense of melancholy or sadness running though many of these works. Loss of life, love, respect, culture. Worlds dying. An emptiness, a lack. And yet the stories are filled with life, and there is the occasional glimpse of hope.

That hope can be found even in "The Canal Barge Magician's Number Nine Daughter", what I would consider the darkest of the stories, with awful details revealed matter-of-factly, such as the belt made from the mummified foetuses and umbilical cords of Number Nine Daughter's sisters.

The Ornomagnen people appear again here. There are many narrative threads running through this collection, with the Rhuin people, the golem, the Green Christ and the Ornomagnen people, as well as a recurring angel or angel-like imagery.

McHugh enjoys these worlds he's created, returning to them time and time again.

He has a beautiful touch with words, a nice turn of phrase, a clever way with imagery. From the titular story

"Angel Dust", we have wonderfully surreal imagery, where people burst 'apart into clouds of copper bees' and cobblestones turn 'into clumps of poppies'.

In "The Beetle Road" breath plumes and metal rings. This wonderful story is about the building of a railroad, resonating with the history of all railroads and attendant worker abuse and death, exploring what lies beneath the surface of humanity in all its forms and addressing racism, judgement and the arrogance of privilege.

He has control of character also, so that these creatures seem to live, to be real.

In "Once a Month, on a Sunday . . . " he gives us a fully imagined and voiced protagonist with understated simplicity. Again, there is a sense of ending, of entropy, of helplessness.

Yet there is hope in McHugh's vision. There is love, deep love. Familial, or sexual, or maternal. There is the idea that as long as we love each other, even if the world ends it has all been worthwhile. The lovely "Almost Angels" is positive, uplifting, with some wonderful imagery.

Ian McHugh is indeed a travel guide, but he is more than that; he invites us to live in the places we visit, and makes us feel as if we've always belonged there.

*Canberra*
*October 2014*

# The Beetle Road

"Josaiah!"

Mr Kneebone's voice sounded like he was just the other side of the tall boulder that Josaiah crouched beside. Further away, he could hear fainter calls of "Master Hollanbosch!" and "Young sir!" Mr Kneebone was the only one of his mother's men who had the status to address Josaiah by his given name.

A three-foot-long metallic beetle—a 'bugger', as the workmen called them—crawled around the side of the boulder and peered up at him with its blank, bulbous eyes. This one's carapace was like polished silver. Josaiah could imagine it as a master tinker's clockwork, rather than a living thing. His own distorted face looked back at him from the bugger's reflective forehead.

This one had no harness, embossed with spells of binding, to hold its wings shut. Not one of his mother's railroad builders, then. It was bigger, too, than most of those at work on the railhead, he thought.

The beetle waved its antennae at him.

"Yes, you're very impressive," he told it. "But not what I'm looking for."

He sighed, even though there was no-one but the bugger to witness it and ask him why.

"Just a glimpse," he said to the jagged peaks that reached up on all sides, bare except for their threadbare shawls of snow. His breath plumed in front of his face. It was a sunny day, but the warmth didn't reach into the shade. This high in the mountains, the air was too dry and thin to hold any heat.

"Josaiah!" It sounded like Mr Kneebone had moved a little way off.

They had been searching for him for some time. Josaiah sighed again. It was probably time to give himself up—damn it all, anyway, all he wanted was to see one of the fair folk.

"Just one would be enough," he said to the bugger.

It trundled past his feet. Josaiah had to look away when it stepped into the sunlight and turned back to face him again. Purple afterimages danced in front of his eyes.

He straightened, dusting off his knees and the seat of his pants, and stepped out of the boulder's shadow as well. The sun was fierce enough to prickle his shaved scalp.

"I'm over here."

Mr Kneebone's head snapped around. His nostril slits flared. Josaiah had spent enough time in the company of saurimen to recognise irritation in his expression. Kneebone tipped back his head, filled his throat sack with air and boomed, "I found him!"

His fixed Josaiah with another reptilian glare, stepping up onto the shelf of rock between them and stalking across. The whip-like tip of his tail lashed from side to side behind his legs. "Your mother wants you," Kneebone growled.

His painted bamboo vest rattled as he hopped down beside Josaiah. Like all the human rail workers, Josaiah had thermals on under his moleskin coveralls, with the addition of a sheepskin coat over the top. Kneebone was naked aside from his vest, gunbelt and the brass codpiece that covered his cloaca, getting sun on as much of his skin as a lizard's dignity would allow. His skin was tattooed with sauriman ideograms over the cardinal energy points of his body—joints, arteries, palms, brow, below his earholes, nostrils and eyes and, under his vest, his vital organs.

Mr Kneebone's inner eyelids half-closed, the equivalent of a human's brows drawing together. "Looking for fairies again, *luusthas?*"

"The fair folk are real," said Josaiah, hotly. The mountains were supposed to be infested with fairies, but all they had found were the damned beetles.

Kneebone snorted. "Come along, *luusthas*. She'll be impatient."

Josaiah fell into step behind him, grinding his teeth. 'Moonchild', the nickname meant—the sauriman term for a dreamer and a fool. There was a loud buzzing and the silver bugger launched itself past them. Josaiah stopped to watch it labour skywards, bright as a falling star that had changed its mind.

A deafening bang, close at hand, almost jumped him out of his skin. Reflexively, he clamped his hands over his ears.

Mr Kneebone stood with his pistol held two-handed in front of him. He thumbed the hammer back, squinting down the revolver's sights. A moment later, with a dissatisfied grunt, he eased the hammer off again. "Should've brought my rifle."

"God's bright hearth, man!" Josaiah cried. "Why are you *shooting* at it?"

Mr Kneebone showed him a mouthful of pointed teeth and re-holstered his pistol. "Come."

&#10038;

From high up on the side of the cutting, Josaiah could look down on the whole railhead and work camp. Smoke drifted gently from the funnels of the two matte-black steam engines, idling quietly until the next section of track was laid for them to crawl forward. Even from a distance, Josaiah could read the huge, brass runes of warding and containment riveted onto the boilers of each engine. In front of the foremost and smaller engine were lined the dormitory coaches, where the human engineers and sauriman overseers slept, and the more luxurious sleeper coach Josaiah shared with his mother.

Behind the rearmost and far larger locomotive was the long train of flatbed trucks, loaded with wooden sleepers and sections of iron track, high-sided tub wagons full of crushed rock and, at the very back, the food vans. Alongside the tracks by that furthest end of the train were lined the white tents of the human work crews.

The labourers themselves were up at the railhead: swinging their hammers to nail down the newest-laid tracks, raking the new rail bed, laying sleepers. Others worked back along the train, lowering sleepers and tracks from the trucks.

All around scuttled bright metal buggers—reds, blues, greens and purples alongside others coloured gold, brass, silver, copper and gunmetal. In pairs, they carried sleepers and rail lengths, laid across the padded tops of their work harnesses, up to the work crews. Singly, they carted sacks of gravel for the rail beds, only their single-toed feet visible beneath their loads. Under the watchful glares if the sauriman overseers, they swarmed all over the rubble pile left by this morning's detonation, clearing aside the loose rock.

At least today the buggers were working again. Recently they had been going slower and slower, which had put his mother in a foul temper.

'The Mundinovan Transcontinental', she called her railroad. 'The Beetle Road', the work crews had dubbed it. The newspapers had taken to the latter name, after a journalist and photographer had come up to see the work, two supply trains ago. Josiah had been very pleased with the picture of himself that they had used for their front page—swinging a hammer, with his shirt off and his coveralls rolled down to the waist like the workmen. The only blemish in it was that they hadn't cut Kneebone's ugly mug out of the frame.

Unusually, today there was a third locomotive lined up at the rear of the supply train, just a small engine with a single, roofed wagon behind it. A party of workmen, with an escort of sauriman guards, was walking up beside the trains, carrying a large iron-bound wooden box on four stout poles.

"What's that?" Josaiah asked.

Mr Kneebone didn't answer.

Josaiah followed the sauriman down the slope to the end of the cutting. At the foot, he wrinkled his nose at a group of crows, bickering over the carcasses of several dead buggers. Kneebone and the other saurimen typically tossed any unmoving buggers, dead or not-quite, upside down at the side of the worksite for the birds to clean up.

Josaiah averted his eyes. When he was small, his mother had taken him on a tour of one of her manufactories. He had been shocked to see children as young as himself at work on the assembly lines, shocked by their hollowed-out faces and the news that they worked there ten-hours a day, six days in seven. Since then—until his mother dragged him up into the mountains for the building of her thrice-damned railway—he had assiduously avoided any further contact with the actual work that underpinned his mother's vast wealth, lest it spoil his enjoyment of his good fortune.

"They should be called a squabble of crows, not a murder," he said to Mr Kneebone's back, seeking refuge in drollness. Once again, the sauriman didn't deign to answer.

Josaiah tried a put-upon sigh. Kneebone just pointed ahead, to where Josaiah's mother was talking with—or rather, at—her clustered engineers. Mrs Hollanbosch had her head shaved the same as Josaiah and all of the human workers. Unlike Josaiah, she had done it voluntarily. Lice, was the reason, and for Josaiah's mother pragmatism trumped dignity. Josaiah was still in mourning for his chestnut curls, for which so many girls in Delphi had professed lasting fondness. He had argued for a protective amulet. "It simply wouldn't be as effective," had been his mother's final, definitive word on the matter.

No other well-born woman could have done any such thing without a scandal. Mrs Hollanbosch didn't even wear a scarf or hat. Even worse, on the railhead she habitually wore a gun belt and holstered pistol, slung mannishly low on her hips. At least, Josaiah reflected, she hadn't gone so far as his cousin Winsome and given away her lady's dresses for a man's pants. Yet.

His mother looked up as Mr Kneebone approached, Josaiah trailing behind. Kneebone jerked a thumb over his shoulder. "Chasing fairies again, missus."

All of the other men addressed Josaiah's mother as 'Mrs Hollanbosch' or 'Milady', as befitted her status. Mr Kneebone had been with her since before she *was* Mrs Hollanbosch.

Her expression when she shifted her gaze to her son changed, if anything, even less than Kneebone's had but, for Josaiah, the cues were even clearer.

"Gentlemen," she said to the assembled engineers, "you have your instructions. Be about your business."

Hearing the edge in her voice, the men retreated with muttered 'Milady's and much forelock tugging.

"Thank you, Mr Kneebone, that will be all."

"Right you are, missus."

"Walk with me," she said to Josaiah.

He slouched into step beside her. The box from the third train was just reaching their sleeper coach. Kneebone had gone ahead and was now supervising the operation of manhandling it aboard. All of the buggers nearby had stopped to watch.

"What's in the box, Mother?"

A sauriman overseer came along, whacking and kicking the buggers back to work.

"You were supposed to be supervising the detonation this morning," his mother said, "In the not too distant future, this will all be yours." *Dead buggers and brain-dead factory brats*, Josaiah thought with distaste. *Marvellous.*

"You're not a child anymore, Josaiah," Mrs Hollanbosch continued. The edge in her tone suggested that she had read his thoughts in his expression. "You must cease acting like one."

As they passed the sleeper coach, Josaiah peered over the shoulders of the men to get a better look at the mysterious box. It wasn't just bound in iron, it was enveloped in etched magic seals—seals comprised of sauriman ideograms, he noted.

"Josaiah," his mother snapped. "Look out there."

He obeyed. 'Out there' was the vista of gradually descending peaks through which they had already brought the rail. The thread of it could be seen in places, wending its way between the mountains. Their present elevation was such that he could glimpse the dark humped backs of the distant foothills.

"It isn't simple ego that has driven me to build your father's fortune to the extent that I have," she said.

*Nonsense*, thought Josaiah. He suspected that his mother viewed even he as no more than an extension of her own ego.

"Everything I have built will be yours," Mrs Hollanbosch continued, "including this, the means to transport the wealth of a continent—of the *world*—from one ocean to the other."

*Yes, and if this railroad doesn't pay off, there won't be anything for me to inherit at all.* Aloud, he said, "I've heard that they're making another attempt to find the north passage." His friend Corvin had even talked, if only to impress the girls, of joining the latest expedition to try and map an ice-free route between the maze of islands to the continent's north.

His mother's eyes flashed. "The north passage is a fiction. There is no path between the islands because the mainland extends all the way to the permanent ice. The only sea passage between the Occidental and Oriental Oceans is a sixteen-thousand mile round trip south."

Josaiah didn't pursue the point. With so much of his mother's considerable wealth—and his inheritance—invested in the railroad, it was in his interests for the search for a shipping route in the far north to be proven fruitless. He had only raised the matter to try and deflect her from the forthcoming lecture about his responsibilities.

"Your cousin Winsome," she went on, "is bringing the railroad up to meet us from the other side of these mountains. *She* has grown up."

"Dear Winsome," Josaiah murmured—Cousin Winsome, who like his mother hadn't let a dearth of cock and cod get in the way of her chosen career.

His mind wandered while his mother talked on. What was in that box, that neither his mother nor Mr Kneebone would even mention for long enough to tell him to keep his nose out?

Secrets, he reflected, knowing better than to sigh while his mother was talking, were such a tedious business.

He brooded over it all afternoon, sulking his way through his nominal responsibility to supervise the afternoon's rock blasting and clearing.

At dinner, which was taken in the sleeper coach with his mother and Mr Kneebone, he asked again about the box, now resting on a coffee table in the small lounge area outside his mother's sleeping compartment.

"Look, Mother, what is inside that?" he demanded. "You lectured me today about growing up. Well an important part of growing up is having the opportunity to prove myself trustworthy with secrets."

His mother continued on with her meal as if he hadn't spoken. Kneebone gulped down a slice of rare meat—unchewed, in the sauriman fashion—and fixed Josaiah with his flat reptilian stare.

Mrs Hollanbosch put down her fork with a click. "You can prove yourself by accepting that this secret is not yours to know." She arched her brows, holding his gaze. "We *can't* tell you. Answering your question would weaken the spells."

Josaiah looked from her to Kneebone in amazement. "What a load of superstitious nonsense!" He threw down his knife and fork and pushed back his chair. "Have it your way, then. I shall see for myself."

He rose with every intention of marching over to the box and doing just that. He got halfway there before Mr Kneebone caught him, grabbing him across the throat and kicking his legs out from under him to unceremoniously dump him on his back. The breath whooshed out of Josaiah's lungs.

Gasping, he stared up at the sauriman in disbelief. Kneebone had threatened him with an imaginative range of violent acts over the course of Josaiah's life, but this was the first time he had ever actually done more than cuff him about the head or twist his ear.

"Mother! Did you *see* what he just did?"

Mrs Hollanbosch regarding him calmly while Kneebone stalked back to the table and resumed his seat. She picked up her napkin and dabbed at the corner of her mouth before speaking.

"It's locked, anyway, Josaiah," she said. "Come back and finish your dinner."

☀

He slept fitfully that night and awoke in darkness. The coach was silent. His thoughts went immediately to the iron-bound box, at the opposite end of the coach.

What was in it, and why would his mother and Mr Kneebone not even talk about it? To test him, plainly—to see if he could let the matter rest. He didn't believe for a moment that his mother actually subscribed to that old sauriman superstition about loose talk compromising the efficacy of magic spells.

He was tempted to pad down to the other end of the coach and take a peek—or, at least, find out if it was indeed locked. But not with his mother and her preternatural senses in the next room. And not after her complicity with Kneebone's frankly shocking display at dinner.

The thought of getting out of bed in the cold triggered an urge to urinate. The coach's built-in drop toilet was in the ensuite off his mother's compartment. There was a chamber pot under the bed—which he would have to empty himself, ugh!—but he recognised well enough the jiggly feeling that would need to be worked out before he could get back to sleep. At home, he would have tickled whatever girl was sharing his bed that night into sufficient wakefulness to service him with sex. Here—unless, again, he wanted to clean up after himself—he would have to walk it out.

With a sigh, he swung his feet over the edge of the bed and rummaged around in the dark for yesterday's socks and his boots. He grabbed his coat from the peg and shrugged into it on his way out.

The cold night air bit straight through the legs of his thermals and snuck up under the hem of his coat. Josaiah shivered and headed for the latrines. His unlaced boots crunched on gravel. Beetle cages stood a short distance from the track, the buggers piled on top of each other inside. Every so often there was a faint rustling as one of them shifted position, causing a cascade of adjustment.

The engineers' carriage was dark, as were the windows of his mother's sleeping compartment. Red light showed around the shutters and doors of the carriage Mr Kneebone shared with the other saurimen. What his mother saved in food by employing lizards, Josaiah reckoned, was more than made up for by the extra coal they burned to keep their braziers going all night. Not to mention that they were next to useless if the weather turned both cold and cloudy.

A bugger stood in his path. In the moonlight it was difficult to distinguish its colour, other than that it was pale. Josaiah was surprised to see it outside of the cages. Then he saw that it had no harness.

"You again," he grunted. "Kneebone shooting at you wasn't enough to keep you away, then?"

There was a ripple in the air, as of something translucent being shaken out, and suddenly a girl stood in front of him. She was as tall as he was and clad in a dress of some shimmery, reflective fabric that clung to the curves of her hips and legs in a manner that made Josaiah's jaw drop open. Her long, pale hair glittered, dancing snakelike around her head and shoulders although there was no breeze to speak of. There was a hint of gauzy wings in the air behind her shoulders.

Not a girl, Josaiah corrected himself in amazement. *A fairy.*

He gazed into her dark-in-dark eyes. Her face was the most perfectly beautiful visage he had ever seen. He blinked. He could see through her, as if she was made of smoke.

Was she a fairy or a ghost?

She spoke, then, her voice a whisper that seemed to come to him only partly through his ears.

*Help us. Free the queen.*

And then she was gone. Only the bugger remained.

Josaiah stared at it.

The bugger lifted the two halves of its carapace and spread its wings. It buzzed up off the ground and hovered in front of Josaiah's face, dark eyes only inches from his. Then it rose higher, and launched itself into the night.

"No, wait!" he belatedly thought to call. "Come back . . . "

An instant later, red light spilled across the ground where Josaiah stood. He blinked up at Mr Kneebone, standing in the doorway of the sauriman coach. Speaking of preternatural awareness of Josaiah's comings and goings.

"*Luusthas*, what are you doing out?" The lizard man's voice slurred, the cold making him sound like he was drunk.

"Going to take a leak."

Kneebone peered into the dark but didn't step down from the coach. "Who were you talking to?"

Josaiah spread his hands. "Who do you see?"

Mr Kneebone glared at him suspiciously. "Get back to bed."

The door slammed shut and Josaiah was left once again in moonlit dark.

Slowly, with a sick feeling in his stomach, he turned to look at the bugger cages.

"Oh, Mother, you've outdone yourself this time."

✸

The fairy girl haunted what remained of Josaiah's sleep. He dreamed that she came to him in his bed. When he reached out to touch her translucent skin, he felt not the pliant warmth of human flesh but the unyielding smoothness of beetle chitin. When she touched him in return, he felt the crawl of clawed beetle toes. He awoke in a sweat, half expecting to find his bed full of bugs.

Her face stayed with him when he closed his eyes again. *Help us. Free the queen*, she had said.

Said, and then turned back into a silver bugger. Was there a fairy's spirit trapped inside every beetle forced to labour on his mother's railroad? Josaiah felt queasy, thinking of all the dead and dying the overseers had tossed aside for the crows.

He stayed in bed in the morning, pleading a headache and the possible beginnings of a cold—a result, he told his mother, of his over-exertions the day before. As expected, this final embellishment infuriated her enough that she just slammed the door, rather than berating him.

When he heard Mr Kneebone's voice in the lounge compartment next door, he slunk out from under the covers and pressed his ear against the thin dividing wall.

"I told you, we should not have brought her here," Kneebone was saying.

"You saw how they were working," replied Mrs Hollanbosch. "It was necessary."

"*Luusthas* was out of his bed last night, and there are mountain folk about. Unharnessed. There was one nearby when I found him yesterday. Might have been a young queen."

"Did you kill it?"

"Flew away."

A pause. *A young queen?* Josaiah thought.

"I do wish you wouldn't call him that." Josaiah was annoyed to hear that his mother sounded more amused than outraged by Kneebone's use of his insulting nickname. "It doesn't earn him respect with the men."

"*He* doesn't earn respect with the men," Kneebone retorted.

There was another pause, then his mother murmured, "He'll grow up," quietly enough that Josaiah barely caught the words through the wall.

*Grow up?* Josaiah thought. *I'll show you grown up, mother. Where are all the fair folk, eh, mother? Well, I know. And I know what you've done.*

❖

Knowing what his mother had done was one thing. Knowing what to do about it was quite another.

Josaiah thought hard while he stalked around the railhead, the former an unaccustomed exertion for him and his presence on site an unaccustomed surprise to the human and sauriman work crews. Were the beetles watching him too? Certainly, wherever he went there seemed to be at least one pair of beady black eyes fixed on him. Was that normal? He couldn't decide.

So, he thought, his mother had enslaved the fair folk of the mountains to help build her railroad and, somehow, turned them into beetles. It *had* to be the fairy queen in the warded box outside his mother's sleeping compartment—presumably also trapped in beetle form, given the size of the container. Josaiah had never heard of such a curse—some black sauriman art from the islands, it had to be.

Many people back in Delphi had said to his mother that the fair folk wouldn't tolerate the building of a railroad through their territory. Most of those people, it was true, had never ventured further West than Bridge City, but this, evidently, was his mother's response. It was, he had to admit, elegant to the point of genius.

Would releasing the queen from the box lift the curse? The silver fairy certainly seemed to think so, and Josaiah knew enough about magic to know that it hinged on such simple principles.

But should he release the fairy queen? If he released the fairies, would they immediately wreak their vengeance on his mother and all her workmen? He didn't particularly care for any of the men—human or sauriman—but he didn't want to be responsible for their deaths, either. And if he released them, surely the fair folk would indeed block the completion of the railroad. Given how much of her own wealth his mother had sunk into the project, that would be the end of Josaiah's own inheritance. He had no desire to be poor or—horrors!—to have to work for a living.

The silver fairy's beautiful face swam in front of his eyes—that and the perfect curves of her breasts, hips and thighs, so clearly visible under her sheer dress. An awkward pressure built inside the front of his pants as he walked. Certainly, she would be grateful to be released from the curse. Perhaps she might even offer him a hero's prize. He adjusted his crotch. Now *that* would be a story to take back to his friends in Delphi.

But even if he did decide to release the fair folk, there was the matter of the lock on the queen's box prison, the key to which he frankly had no idea who, of his mother and Mr Kneebone, had in their possession.

And Kneebone seemed to be following him everywhere.

When the lunch bell rang, Josaiah joined the general exodus from the railhead down to the camp. He infiltrated himself amongst a party of tall Hillevionese engineers and then, as they passed by the idling locomotives, ducked into the gap between the two engines and out onto the other side of the track. Walking quickly, while trying not to look like he was in a hurry, he set out along the supply train, glancing casually about now and then to check that Kneebone hadn't followed him.

The sauriman would expect him to head up into the surrounding peaks, as he had on his previous excursions. Instead, with a last look to confirm that he wasn't watched, Josaiah stepped off the embankment outside the end of the cutting, and down among the pine and spruce trees of the forested valley below. He bounded down the slope, skidding now and then on the loose, dry soil and needle litter. When he was out of sight of the train, he stopped.

Panting for breath, he looked around. Would she find him down here? He could only hope. He found a fallen trunk to sit on and perched nervously, more than half expecting Kneebone, rather than the silver fairy, to turn up and take him back to camp.

It wasn't long that he had to wait, and she came to him in her fairy form, rather than as the silver beetle. His heart tripped. She seemed less ghostly in daylight, more solid, although still drained of colour.

She stopped a short distance away. *Will you help us?*

"I don't know how," he blurted, and kicked himself mentally.

*Release the queen*, she said. She moved closer and, seated as he was, he found himself at eye level with her breasts as they gently rose and fell. With her clinging dress, he barely had to exert his imagination to envision her unclothed. The compression of his stiffening cock was compounded this time by his seated pose.

"It is not so simple . . . " he began.

*You will be rewarded.*

His mouth was suddenly too dry to speak. He tried to work some moisture around his teeth with his tongue. "What's your name?" he croaked.

*My name?* she seemed confused by the question.

"I'm Josaiah."

She lifted her head, sharply, and looked up the slope towards the train, then returned her black-in-black gaze to Josaiah. *I will reward you.* She reached out a slim arm and brushed his lips with her fingertips.

Then she vanished. Her disappearance was so abrupt that Josaiah almost fell off his log in surprise. The silver beetle launched itself into the air and buzzed off between the tree trunks.

Josaiah stared after it in stupid amazement. His lips burned from the touch of her fingers. Her touch had felt like electricity—like the sting of those static devices they showed at carnivals for a penny a try, that made all the girls squeal. His erection was excruciating.

He heard footsteps coming down the slope. It was Mr Kneebone, a long rifle cradled in his arms. The sauriman stopped by Josaiah's log and regarded him for a moment, his tail whipping back and forth behind his legs. With a dissatisfied growl, deep in his throat, Kneebone lowered himself to sit beside him.

"Well?" said Josaiah, truculently, when Mr Kneebone didn't immediately speak.

"She shows you what you wish to see, *luusthas*," he said. "It is an illusion."

"I don't believe you," said Josaiah.

The sauriman shrugged, a human gesture. "What you see is different to what I see."

"Oh? And what do you see? Just an ordinary bugger, I suppose," said Josaiah. "Don't lie to me, Kneebone, I know what you and Mother have . . . "

Kneebone bared his teeth in a growl, silencing him. The sauriman composed himself, flicking an imaginary speck of dirt from the barrel of his rifle with a thumb. "What I see," he began, in a faraway voice. "Ah, *luusthas*, her neck frills, they are red like blood, full of the heat in her. Her tail is long, the longest I have seen, and its tip quivers, just so."

He gave a little shiver, then grinned broadly at Josaiah—another imitated human gesture, but this time done deliberately for its horrible effect.

"I don't believe you," said Josaiah. "That can't be true." But his eyes were hot and his stomach tight with doubt.

※

He followed Kneebone back up to the camp and returned to supervising the work at the rock face. *Could it be true?* he wondered, watching the bright metallic beetles heaving and hauling at the rubble. Were the fair folk really nothing more than these buggers, playing tricks?

But she had *touched* him. The thought of it still tingled his lips. How could that be, if she was just an illusion? And how could she show him one illusion and Kneebone another, both at the same time?

*No*, he thought. *It can't be.* Kneebone was lying, trying to deflect him.

A sauriman snarl caused him to turn. One of the overseers was carrying an exhausted beetle away from the rock wall by its hind legs.

"Hey!" Josaiah strode over to the surprised sauriman. He grabbed the beetle and slapped the sauriman's hands away. "Leave it."

The sauriman's nostrils flared angrily, but he backed away.

Conscious of the eyes suddenly fixed on him—human, sauriman and beetle—Josaiah carried the worn out bugger to the side of the railhead. Its legs collapsed loosely underneath it as he set it down. This one's carapace was a fiery red. Josaiah ran his hand over the smooth chitin.

He looked around. His mother and Kneebone were back towards the trains, watching. On an angry impulse, Josaiah pulled out his belt knife and with several sharp strokes, sawed through the harness binding the beetle's wings.

The bugger didn't move. Its antennae remained still. It was dead.

Josaiah's eyes filled with tears. Another dead fairy. *Damn you, Mother.*

He wiped his face. This couldn't go on.

※

He was shocked when, after dinner, his mother put down her napkin and said, "You'll be confined to your quarters from now on. When the supply train goes back for fresh materials, you will return to Delphi."

Protests queued up on Josaiah's tongue. All useless, they remained unspoken. With as much dignity as he could muster, levelly meeting both his mother's and Mr Kneebone's eyes, he rose from the table.

"If you don't mind," he said. "I'll use the latrine before I retire."

She examined him closely before replying, searching his face for some hint of deviousness. He gave her none. "Very well," she said. "Mr Kneebone will accompany you."

Without waiting for the sauriman to follow, Josaiah turned and stalked to the door. Outside, the temperature was already dropping.

He walked passed the beetle cages, with the buggers piled inside, out into the deeper dark by the latrine pits. He roved his gaze over the steep sides of the cutting, searching for the lip above. Would she be there? Was she watching? If she was, would she know that he was now a prisoner?

Mr Kneebone's footsteps crunched behind him. By the time they reached the latrines, the sauriman's feet were dragging slightly with each step. *Slowing down,* Josaiah thought. In the cold, he could probably overpower Kneebone.

Did he dare?

And to what end? To escape? He was hardly dressed or equipped to survive alone in the mountains. To free the bugger-beetle-fairy queen? Even if he ran back to the coach his mother was there and she had a gun.

Would she shoot her own son? Absolutely. Probably only in the leg, but she wouldn't hesitate to put a bullet in him to stop him. And even if she didn't, the box was still locked and he didn't have a key.

What if he took Kneebone's gun? Did the old lizard have the key?

He glanced over his shoulder. Mr Kneebone was a couple of yards behind him, turned half away to look back at the train. There was activity around the sleeper coach. Josaiah swore under his breath. A quartet of saurimen were unloading the box. His mother was silhouetted in the doorway.

Mr Kneebone turned back to him. "You going to piss, or not?" His words slurred.

Biting back a terse retort, Josaiah turned back to the task at hand. Sour-smelling steam rose in front of him. He hoped the silver fairy wasn't watching now.

Where were they moving the queen to? The sauriman dormitory coach, he thought. It had to be.

What was he going to do now?

❂

He barely slept and was already up and pacing his sleeping compartment when Mr Kneebone arrived with a breakfast tray. Kneebone looked him over, but didn't comment. Josaiah pointedly ignored the tray until the sauriman had left, locking the door from the outside. Only then did he sit down on the bed and tuck into his meal.

At least they were still feeding him.

A rough sawing sound caught his attention. It sounded like it was coming from underneath him. He listened. It *was* coming from underneath him—from under the bed.

Josaiah set the tray aside and knelt to peer beneath the bed. The carpet was moving, something pushing it up from below. Quickly he pulled the bed aside, then rolled back the carpet.

There was a ragged hole in the floorboards. The silver beetle clung to the underside of the coach, peering up at him as it delicately brushed wood splinters from its mandibles with the tips of its antennae. Josaiah sat back and it climbed through the hole.

Almost immediately, the silver fairy stood before him.

Josaiah held up a hand. They show us what we want to see, Kneebone had said. "Show me yourself as you really are. Don't try to fool me, if that is what you are doing."

She stared at him for a moment. Then she vanished again and the beetle stood before him once more. Josaiah had to look away, his heart aching with a sudden painful intensity. He re-gathered his composure. "Your queen has been moved to the sauriman coach."

*Yes. It is guarded outside, but not within.*

Josaiah looked at the beetle unhappily. It was a different shape to the others, as well as larger, he noticed abstractly. Its back seemed flatter and its head more bulbous. "How do you know?"

*I watched, listened. You must help. Open the box.*

"Must I?" Josaiah folded his arms. "And how am I supposed to get there in daylight without being seen?"

*Under.*

The hole the bugger had come in through was big enough for him to pass. "But then what? Even under the train, I'll been seen easily."

*Guards will see only what they wish.*

The words were close enough to Kneebone's to leave Josaiah feeling like he'd been kicked in the gut. He gave a bitter laugh.

"Here," he said to the beetle, "have some salt to rub into my wound." The bugger just stared at him, antennae waving slightly. "Why should I help you?"

*We die.*

Josaiah swallowed. He waved a hand at the hole in the floor. "Lead on, then, if you will."

❋

The silver bugger was true to its—her?—word, although when it said "under" the train, Josaiah hadn't realised it meant that they would go along clinging to the undersides of the coaches. His arms burned from holding himself up, the blood pounded at his temples.

It made perfect sense, of course. They were far less conspicuous that if they had been on the ground, and therefore it must have been far easier for the beetle to works its mental deceit. Knowing it hardly made the journey more comfortable, though. Josaiah's fingers were cramping long before they reached the sauriman coach at the other end of the train.

The scaled legs and tails of a pair of sauriman guards flanked the space where the sliding door was on the side of the coach. Josaiah dropped down with a gasp between the coach's rear set of wheels, where he would be sheltered from view, even without the bugger's illusion. The pain in his fingers was excruciating when his flexed them. His legs had fared well enough, but the muscles of his arms and torso felt like they were on fire.

"Now what?" he said. "If you try making a hole in the floor, the guards will hear."

*There is already a hole.*

Josaiah looked around. "I don't see a . . . " But he did. The dormitory coaches had squat toilets that were left as open drop holes when the train was moving. In the work camp, they had buckets underneath for night soil. It would be tight, but Josaiah would probably fit through one of the squat holes. The night soil bucket for the saurimen hung close by, under the end of the coach. Josaiah shuddered.

The silver beetle watched him in silence. He sighed. "Well, I guess I'm committed now, aren't I?"

Holding his breath and averting his eyes, he took down the bucket and set it aside. He peered up through the hole, half expecting to see the open cloaca of a squatting lizard, about to crap on his face.

The coast looked clear. The bugger crawled up through the hole ahead of him. Gingerly, Josaiah gripped the edges of the hole. Fortunately, saurimen were more fastidious defecators than their human counterparts. He got his head and one arm through, then squeezed the other arm and shoulder up. He almost wedged as he tried to get leverage to pull himself the rest of the way through. Then he was up and crouched inside the coach.

It was stiflingly warm. A rough curtain separated the squat hole from the rest of the coach. Cautiously, Josaiah pulled it aside far enough to peer around. A scaled hand grabbed him by the hair and wrenched him forward.

Josaiah sprawled heavily on his front. Tears sprung to his eyes and his hands came away bloody from his stinging scalp. A foot caught him hard in the ribs and knocked him over onto his back. Mr Kneebone stood over him, ragged bits of Josaiah's hair sticking out between the digits of his clenched fist. In his other hand he had a pistol.

"Should have chained you up, *luusthas*," he said. "I said so to your mother. Said it would keep you out of trouble. Keep you safe. Said you would not leave well enough alone, otherwise."

Josaiah backed up on his elbows and heels, dragging his backside over the boards. Mr Kneebone stalked after. The curtain flapped behind him. The sauriman whirled.

For an instant, Josaiah glimpsed the silver beetle, then something seemed to boil out of the stove-lit gloom of the coach. He had an impression of darkness and lightning.

Mr Kneebone evidently saw it much more clearly. He staggered back with a wide-mouthed hiss of terror and tripped over Josaiah's legs. He fell. The pistol bounced between them, Josaiah grabbed for it, missed. Heart in mouth, he scrabbled after it.

Mr Kneebone was swearing and spitting, realising he had been tricked. Josaiah's hand closed on the barrel of the gun. Kneebone was rising, going for his belt knife. Josaiah pushed himself up and swung the pistol. The butt connected between Mr Kneebone's eye and ear. The sauriman's limbs jerked spastically.

He caught himself on one hand, raising the other in defense. Josaiah knocked it aside and hit him again, this time on the base of the skull.

Kneebone collapsed bonelessly, like a puppet with its string cut.

Josaiah sat back, chest heaving. Mr Kneebone didn't move, except for his tail, which twitched a rapid tattoo on the boards.

"Is he dead?"

*Release the queen*, said the bugger. *Free us.*

Josaiah looked around. The warded box stood on the floor at the end of the coach, past the folded sleeping nets of the saurimen. His eyes fell on the brass locking plate on the front of the lid.

*Free us!*

The words had a compulsion to them that jolted Josaiah into motion. He had to fight to hold himself still long enough to think. "Stop it!" he said. "Stop!"

The pressure in his mind eased.

Gingerly, he reached over to the pouch hanging from the side of Mr Kneebone's gunbelt, loosed the ties and felt inside. He gave a little, hiccupping laugh of relief, holding up the key, etched with ideograms, for the bugger to see.

It watched expectantly as he rose and walked over to the box. He knelt and slotted the key into the lock, then paused, struck by a moment of doubt. As far as he had come, was he doing the right thing? Releasing the buggers would ruin his mother—and him.

Something struck his mind, pummelling the last of his resistance. His arm jerked, his hand turned the key. The box lid swung up.

Inside was a beetle. Its carapace was as metallically polished as any, but blue-black in colour. It was at least as large as the silver beetle, filling the box, and the difference in its proportions from a normal bugger was even more marked. Its bulging head was fully a third the length of its body.

Darkness exploded out of the box. As he sailed backwards through the air, an odd, clear little part of Josaiah's mind reflected that if the buggers' alternate forms were indeed illusions, they were damned solid ones.

Daylight smacked into his eyes as the roof and walls of the coach exploded up and out. He hit, bounced, gasping and winded and with barely enough wit to curl into a protective ball as bits of coach roof rained back down.

The hail of debris stopped. Cautiously, Josaiah raised his head.

The mountain queen towered above him, twenty feet tall with blue-black skin. It was impossible to tell where her black robes and black mane of hair started and finished as they both billowed and whipped around her.

A sauriman's rifle cracked. Where the bullet went, Josaiah didn't see, but the queen raised an arm. The guard was lifted into the air. He cried out, struggling in the invisible grip, then vanished in a pop of greasy smoke. All around, the enslaved buggers were bursting the harnesses that bound them and rising, fearsome figures of bright metal. Human labourers and engineers sprinted away past the parked trains. The queen swept an arm after them. Her long fingers made grabbing motions. In quick succession, a dozen men at the back of the fleeing crowd were picked up and reduced to greasy wisps.

The silver fairy stood at the queen's side, dwarfed by her but far taller, now, than Josaiah. She was all silver, except for her eyes, and no more resembled a human girl than a sauriman did.

"Stop her!" Josaiah cried. "Let them go!"

The silver fairy looked down at him. *Why?*

*You!* the queen thundered.

Josaiah's mother stood at the centre of a huddle of her saurimen, shoulder to shoulder with their weapons pointed outward. A pathetic last stand.

The queen raised her hand again, flicked her fingers. The saurimen were flung to the ground. Forefinger and thumb pinched together. Josaiah's mother was lifted from the pile. The queen shifted her grip and Mrs Hollanbosch let out a snarl of pain.

"No!" Josaiah cried. He leapt up, the world spun around him and he fell off the side of the coach. Desperation got his feet back under him. He staggered sideways, arms raised, trying to put himself between the queen and his mother.

The terrible figure paused, peering down at him.

"Please."

The only sounds were the receding shouts of the fleeing human workers.

Josaiah turned his attention to the silver fairy. "Please. Don't make this my reward."

For a breathless moment, the queen didn't move. Then she tipped her head towards the silver fairy. Her gaze didn't leave Josaiah, and neither did the silver fairy's, but he was sure some communication passed between them.

The queen straightened. *So be it.* She opened her fingers. Josaiah spun to see his mother fall. He lunged, thinking somehow to catch her, got a flailing forearm across the mouth for his trouble and ended up sprawled in the dirt beside her. He scrambled up, reaching out to try and help her to her feet. She slapped him away.

*Leave our mountains,* said the queen, *and you will be spared.*

Josaiah's mother raised her voice. "What of our people on the other side of the ranges? How will they know?"

*They will be told.* The queen swept a hand towards the west. *One comes.*

Josaiah had barely more than a heartbeat to wonder what she meant. With dizzying suddenness, the queen vanished. The black beetle rose into the air. The drum of wings was deafening as all of the other beetles followed at once. The sunlight caught their many coloured metallic shells.

Josaiah fell to his knees. He looked for his silver fairy, wondering if perhaps she might linger, just for a moment to say goodbye. He was unsurprised to find the place where she had stood empty. He thought perhaps he could pick her out, flying near the queen.

*Ah, well,* he told himself, *you wanted to see fairies.*

Something struck him hard between the shoulder blades, knocking him onto his face in the dirt. He rolled, hurting and bewildered, and saw his mother, holding one of the guards' rifles, the butt towards him.

He watched the gun as she swung it around, the muzzle wavering in his direction. Her jaw worked and he thought she might be too angry to even speak. Then she choked out, "You are not my son."

She swayed for a moment, as if she was going to fall. The gun slipped from her fingers. Then she turned away. There was a catch in her first step but she didn't stumble. Her stride steadied as she marched away.

Josaiah heard her barking orders to the surviving saurimen. A quartet hurried over to the exploded dormitory coach. He watched them clear the rubble off Mr Kneebone and, after a brief check, fashion a makeshift stretcher from a couple of broken posts and a sleeping net. Josaiah lay his head back down on the ground, squeezing his eyelids shut on sudden tears.

His mother raised her voice again, calling the workers back to the train. A short while later, he heard the chug of the locomotives building steam, followed by the squeal of brakes unlocking and steel wheels beginning to turn. He pushed himself up to his knees and watched the trains pull away.

There was a moment when he might have run and leapt aboard the wrecked sauriman coach, but he couldn't find the strength in his legs. She really meant it, he thought, numbly. He was no longer her son and she was abandoning him without a backward glance.

In short order, Josaiah was left alone. The buggers were gone from view. A few crows hopped about the worksite. The mountains looked down from all around.

A laugh bubbled up from his chest. It passed as quickly as it came.

"Just one fairy," he said, "would have been enough."

He sat a while longer, then slowly, painfully, picked himself up and staggered down to the work camp. He found an abandoned rucksack and took it into the kitchen tent to begin filling it with food. He was just buckling the straps, trying think of what else he would need—blankets, coat, was there anything else?—when he heard the crunch of gravel outside.

Hooves.

He burst out of the tent, startling the horse so that it almost bucked its rider. The rider pulled its head around, wheeling it until it settled. Josaiah stared.

The rider was just as surprised once she calmed her mount enough to look at him properly. "Josaiah?"

"Winsome?"

His cousin was dusty and filthy, her shirt stained yellow with sweat inside her open coat. Her eyes were shrouded with the dark bags of someone who had gone without sleep. Dried foam caked the corners of her horse's mouth. Its legs trembled as it stood.

Winsome raised an arm to encompass the abandoned camp. "Where is everyone? Did you get the news already? Why are you still here?"

"News?" he asked, baffled.

"They found the north passage."

*The north* . . . He thought his legs might give out. *All for naught.* He could have just left it all alone, could have not been left behind.

"Josaiah? What happened here?"

He ran a hand over his face, uncertain whether to laugh or cry. "I let the fairies go."

Her jaw dropped slowly open. "Oh, Josaiah, you . . . "

"*Luusthas*," he finished.

"You *luusthas*," she agreed. The corners of her mouth twitched as she shook her head. "Oh, Josaiah."

"Well," he said, taking a deep breath. "Mother's on the train, so you won't catch her. Your horse looks like it's ready to drop, and so do you, if you don't mind my saying. I can offer you food and shelter, if you wouldn't mind giving me a ride in the morning."

She considered him from under the wide brim of her hat, lips pursed. For a moment he thought she would decline. Then she nodded. "I expect you'll need me to cook, too, won't you?"

He tried to look abashed, but his relief wouldn't let him.

She dismounted and tossed him her animal's reins. "You can at least look after the horse."

He hesitated. She watched him expectantly. "People died, Winsome."

She nodded. "Go see to the horse, *luusthas*," she said. "Then you can tell me about it."

# ANGEL DUST

It was a day when autumn's bitter rain swept in off the strait. It rinsed the filth from the streets and beat against the black tower that rose from the heart of the city's sprawl.

In the plaza before the tower's gate, a pair of statues stood on man-high plinths, rendered from the same black stone as the tower and overgrown with climbing briars. A female figure and a male, they wore the long-bodied forms of the race of Avalae, the city's first masters, and had the high-domed skulls and small round ears, set low behind the jaw, distinctive of that vanquished folk. The statues reached, left-handed, towards each other, as though they longed to cross the space between, their unseeing gazes locked together. The woman's outstretched arm ended in a stump above the wrist.

Had the statues ears to hear, they would have known the cry of dismay that arose from the ghettos, below.

The angel was returned.

Always in the past, the angel's homecoming had been greeted with joy, and the ears of the city dwellers had pricked up to listen for the strident chorus of the returning songships. But on this day, as copper sunshine found the gap between horizon and clouds, there arose no triumphant song from the harbour. Had the statues eyes to see and legs of muscle and sinew to walk among the people, they might have seen the faces that turned up to watched the angel's passage, tight with worry, and they would have marked his course, erratic as a butterfly's, the beat of his grey swan wings laboured and inconstant.

"Where is the fleet?" the people whispered. Their whispers turned to wails, when they saw the scant dozen ships that limped into port, and heard the mournful dirge they sang.

The rest would not return, the statues might have heard the sailors say. They were burned or sunk, along with the armadas of Melkurr and the Gil-Gadin. Melkurr was defeated, its capital sacked, and the sheikdoms were falling one by one.

From their plinths before the gate, the statues could have watched the angel battle to reach his tower roost. Were their eyes acute, they might have seen the trail of blood that mingled with the rain, and seen that, as it fell, it turned to glimmering dust.

Had the statues walked the city streets, they might have witnessed the wonders where the dust alighted. Cobblestones turned to clumps of poppies. Some grew legs and scuttled away. Downpipes turned to twisting vines, or pythons that insinuated themselves through the windows of the houses. A colony of pigeons grew arms, and minds that thought, and plotted war against the rats and starlings who raided their nests. People who were touched by the dust burst apart into clouds of copper bees, or turned inside out, for golden-boughed trees to spring from their quivering guts.

The angel slumped gratefully over the high balustrade of his refuge. Had the statues chanced to look up, they would have seen a last drop of blood turned to dust as it fell.

✦

Her eyelids fluttered. She heaved a raw breath, then another. For a long time, that was all she did, her new mind aflood with the sensations of her body, and all the memories of things she would've seen and known, had she always had eyes to see, ears to hear.

Centuries of days and nights overlaid the deserted plaza, harvest dances and winter stillness, the red crackle of solstice bonfires and the smoke and clamour of war. Changeless, through it all, was the petrified stare locked on hers, stone fingers always reaching, never touching.

She swayed, wincing as the briars that wreathed her hooked their barbs into newly soft skin. She shifted her arms, to extricate herself, and cried aloud when she saw the flat stump that ended her left arm above the wrist.

A memory swam to the surface, of Yng'finail Reavers fighting the beast-headed slave warriors of Avalae, a massacre dance of iron blades on bronze, swirling about the plinths. A wild-swung halberd struck her wrist, splinters showering the wielder. She remembered the fractures spreading through her arm, as the temperature fell and rose in the nights and days and weeks that followed, until, with a crack one frosted morning, the hand tumbled from her wrist.

Her gasps became sobs. The briars stabbed her anew. Moving

slowly, whimpering at every tear of her skin, she freed herself from their embrace and shoved the mess of vines from her plinth. She sank down into a crouch, and shivered in the cold rain. The sounds of the restless city assailed her, disorienting. She crept her toes forward until they found the edge of the plinth, and clung there, vertiginous and confused.

A flicker of lightning caught a glint of wet stone in the edge of the briar patch. With a yell, she leapt from the plinth, powered by muscles that did not know, yet, how to properly obey command. Hip, hand and stump met the cobbles. She lay, winded and gasping, staring up into the rain at the black silhouette of the tower that filled half the sky.

When the breath had found its way back into her lungs, she rolled over and crawled to the spot where she'd seen her severed hand. She cradled it, cold and unfeeling against her breast.

Her gaze strayed up, to the statue of her mate, like her hand, still etched in stone. He was all but featureless in the gloom. Higher still, to the balcony that marked the angel's roost, where the mages of Avalae had summoned their fabulous winged beasts to take them hunting, once upon a time. She saw in her mind the angel's latest, agonised return. The tower gate was closed, and there were no windows in its face to show if light and life existed within, except the balcony, and it was dark.

A hand gripped her arm, hard fingers bruising new skin. A rough voice said, "'Allo, lovely." Sniggered.

She twisted, lashing out blindly with her stone hand. Her ears rang with memories of screams cut short, terrible sounds of fright and injury in the shadows at the plaza's edge.

The man retreated, cursing loudly, cradling a forearm bruised, at least, or fractured.

She registered an answering shout from across the plaza. Another man, or several, she didn't wait to see. Clutching her stone hand to her chest, she fled.

She ran down well-lit streets, where the private guards of the well-to-do nervously eyed the first nervous citizens ascending from the city below to come demand the angel's counsel. All stopped to stare, amazed, at the naked woman who sprinted past.

At the foot of the hill, the streets grew darker. She heard the grumble of larger crowds ahead. She slowed, clutching at the stitch in her side, and turned from the main avenue. The cold air burned her lungs, her legs shook and her uncallused heels ached from pounding on the cobbles.

The doorways along this street were alcoved, the frontages colonnaded with the long bones of giants, the doors themselves shrouded in shadow. Blankets spilled into the rain from one, nearby. Shivering violently now, she crept over and reached with tentative fingers. She began to tug at the wet hem of the topmost blanket, then abruptly withdrew her hand. There was a body underneath the covers. She waited, but there came no cry of protest.

She tugged on the blanket again, gathering it into her lap, ready to flee at the first sign of movement. Her hand touched an outflung limb. The flesh was cold.

She drew the first blanket around her shoulders and dragged the remaining covers from the corpse. Bundling them to her chest, she crept to the next alcove along the street. She wrapped herself as tightly as she could, tucking her legs against her chest and pulling the blankets over her head, holding them closed with her single hand. After a time, her shivering stilled and she felt something approaching warmth.

She slept, and her dreams were filled with the black stone features of her mate.

❖

Consciousness returned slowly. The clatter of hooves punctured her dreams, then the creak and crack of a cart following, the tap of passing feet, random snatches of conversation. With a start, she came fully awake.

She raised her head to peer beneath the blanket's fringe, blinking against the morning light. The rain had ceased, but the clouds remained heavy. The street was filled with people.

Most were Yng'finail, the city's current masters, red of skin and silver-pale of eye and hair. Slight figures wove among them, coal black skins stark against white robes and shining gold-in-gold eyes—Gil-Gadin—she had seen their like beneath the angel's tower. A trio of brown-skinned warrior women stalked past, their spiny manes held erect, open vests displaying the scars left by severed breasts.

Others in the crowd were stranger and less human. She remembered them, the cruelly fashioned playthings of the Avalae. Folk with the furred heads and naked tails of rats, scuttling on four limbs or two as the need took them, their eyes the glowing gold of

Gil-Gadin. A hairless Yng'finail, pushing himself awkwardly along on a serpent's coils. A gargoyle leaning on a cane, too old to fly anymore, her once powerful wings twisted with arthritis, copper feathers tarnished green.

All of them, human and less so, had an agitation about them. They moved with a step more hurry and a nervous indecision, both, that on a different day might have been absent. Tempers were quick as people got in each other's way. But only threats and curses were exchanged. It seemed no-one had the stomach for trading blows.

A rumbling beat penetrated the hubbub. It resolved into the sound of dozens of feet—booted, hoofed or clawed—treading in not-quite-unison. A company of soldiers marched by, their armour an irregular assortment of lamellae and baked leather, only a handful with helms of any kind, the rest in felt caps or bareheaded. The weapons on their shoulders made an ugly forest of mismatched steel.

"And what's this, cluttering my step?" said a deep voice, startlingly close.

The door had opened behind her. A cassocked figure filled the frame. Blue human eyes glared down at her from a horned bovine face. Sparse hair covered a hide as thick and dimpled as citrus peel. She had seen his kind stand like colossi on the last day of Avalae, as Yng'finail Reavers slaughtered their lesser brethren around them, until weight of numbers and iron blades brought them down, too.

"Be gone," the minotaur said, lifting an arm to strike backhanded.

She scrambled back, shaking her good arm free of her blankets. She raised the stone hand in warning while she got her feet under her. The minotaur's eyes widened as she retreated into the sunlight.

He followed, raising his hand again, but palm outward this time. "Wait."

But she was already running. A carthorse flapped its neck frills in warning as she skipped in front of it. She ducked the half-hearted swipe of the carter's crop and pushed on through the crowds.

The cobbles were cold and slippery wet, her feet bruised and aching from her running the night before. She soon slowed to a hobbling walk. She had no direction in mind, no knowledge of the city beyond the plaza where she had stood. She passed terraces of shops and houses walled with brick and stone and black iron plate, others roofed in bright canvas to resemble the sails of ships. Others still, grown of living trees woven tight together.

She let the pedestrian tides carry her where they would, until her attention was arrested by the aromas of a pie seller's stall. His wares were heated over a bed of coals in the iron belly of his spider-legged cart. Her stomach knotted painfully as she watched a man walk away with a steaming pastry. She sidled closer, wondering if she might snatch a pie and run.

She noticed a boy staring at her, narrow-eyed and blunt nosed, a younger, leaner version of the pie seller. He tapped a leather cosh meaningfully against his thigh.

Downcast, she retreated, and walked on.

She passed a golden tree, growing in the centre of the thoroughfare. Beneath it, a trio of hook-beaked gargoyle men confronted a party of soldiers with axes. A gargoyle woman knelt between them, wailing and tearing at her breastfeathers.

The black tower loomed above the rooftops. She turned towards it. Her pulse quickened as she ascended the hill, a twinge of fear as she remembered the man she had injured the night before.

Reaching the plaza, she saw that her anxiety was needless. A mob had gathered before the angel's keep, demanding entry. Soldiers watched them, but made no move to intervene. No-one had any attention to spare for her.

She stopped beneath the petrified figure of her mate. His features were opaque with the sun behind him. She stretched up, but his outstretched hand was too high for her to reach. She pulled aside the briars that covered his foot and ran her fingertips over the shape of his toes. The stone was as ungiving as the severed hand she clutched against her belly.

A loaded cart arrived, and people started piling wood for a bonfire. She cleared a nest among the briars, on the side of her mate's plinth that faced the tower. She sank down and curled her limbs around the hollow misery of her belly.

❀

She started from a torpid daydream, of her mate smiling, his stone visage turned to flesh, his fingers grasping hers.

The minotaur looked down at her.

She levered herself up, fumbling for her stone hand. Panic made her clumsy, and she dropped it in the briars at her feet. With a yelp, she bent to grab it.

"Be still," the minotaur said. "I'll not hurt you."

She paused, warily, the stone hand half raised. He gazed at her in silence for a time, then his blue eyes shifted to look at the male statue.

"How did this come to be?" he asked.

She opened her mouth, struggling to shape a response. Although she understood him, like a small child, she lacked the skill to form words of her own. She pointed to the grand balcony.

The minotaur gave a bovine snort and took her by the wrist. Dragging her along in his wake, he marched towards the tower.

A few, braver or more angry than their fellows, still beat at the gate with mallets and staves. The blackened iron seemed to drink the sounds of their blows into itself. The hammerers fell back at the minotaur's arrival. He raised his fist, muttering beneath his breath, then struck the door, three times. With each blow a boom like the striking of a gong echoed inside the tower.

For a time, there was stillness. Then a postern cracked ajar within the surface of the gate and an Yng'finail head peered out. The man's hair was yellowed with age and his skin a jaundiced orange. His pale eyes blinked and watered in the daylight.

"We seek audience," said the minotaur.

The old man licked his lips. His eyes flickered to the minotaur's companion, still caught by the wrist, and back again.

"Forgive me, m'lord," he said. "There'll be no audience today."

He began to withdraw, but the minotaur raised a hand to stay him. "When?" he asked.

The man started an answer, thought the better of it and stuttered to a halt. "I cannot say."

He shrank back as the minotaur leaned towards him. "If he is hurt, I might aid him."

The old man's eyes went wide. He stepped back abruptly through the door and shut it behind him.

An angry mutter passed through the crowd. The minotaur sighed.

"Go to your homes," he said, and turned on his heel. He let go her wrist. "Go."

She stared at his broad back as he strode from the tower. The hammerers closed again towards the gate. She struggled free, buffeted and bumped, and hurried after the minotaur. She tugged at his sleeve to stop him.

She pointed to the male statue.

The slump of his shoulders was answer enough. He said, "Only he who gave life to you can give it to your mate. I cannot help."

She fought with her tongue. "When?"

The minotaur glanced back at the tower. He shook his head. "Come back tomorrow, and see." The pocked skin around his eyes was tight, as though something pained him. "Come. I will see you fed. You can bed in front of my hearth. Cassiann, is my name."

She looked back over her shoulder, at her mate in his cloak of briars. Her gaze travelled up the black face of the tower, to the balcony, silent to the entreaties raised below.

They returned to his house. He had to duck his head to fit through the door, and remain stooped, inside, so as not to scrape his horns on the ribs of the ceiling. Inside, a wooden bench stood along one side of the hall. The door of the front room was open, the room lined with shelves of jars and vials and tins, every one labelled in meticulous script. A high table with an ornate set of scales stood in the centre and, to the rear, a padded couch and scale curtain to pull around it.

He was an apothecary, Cassiann said, and when it was plain she did not know the word, explained that he healed people with magic and medicine. He led her down the hall to the kitchen and parlour in back. He pointed to the stairs, leading up to rooms where he slept and studied, and showed her the larder, the lavatory chute and the water pump. He tossed a fresh log onto the hearth, set out a bowl, and cloths, for her to wash herself, should she wish. Then he said he had customers to prepare for, had missed appointments already. He closed the hallway door, and she was alone.

She wriggled back in the seat of his solitary chair, so that her feet dangled clear of the ground. Her stone hand was cold beneath her living palm. She stared into the flames that licked inside the hearth. Her stomach grumbled, but her hunger lacked the urgency it had before.

Presently, she heard voices, the minotaur's and another, higher in pitch. She listened for a while, idly trying to discern their words. Her gaze wandered around the room, settled on the staircase, then up the curve of the wall to the joists of timber and giant ivory that crossed the ceiling.

She slipped down from the chair.

The lowest stair creaked beneath her foot. She crept quietly up, across the small landing at the top and into the bedroom. She padded past the long bed, to the window that opened over the street. The panes of polished leviathan scales let in light, but revealed only the murkiest outlines of the world beyond. She examined the latch, gave it an experimental tug. The window swung outward. She pushed it open.

Cool air brushed over her face and arms. She leaned her elbows on the damp sill and gazed up at the dark tower, high on its hill. She saw a black stone face, and fingers reaching for her own.

❋

She awoke early the next day, in the dull red light of the coals in the hearth. Her mate's face faded slowly from her mind's eye.

Cassiann was already in his surgery, mixing powders. He paused when she appeared in the doorway. "I hope I didn't disturb you."

She shook her head.

The minotaur returned to his work, tipping a measure of pale green powder into a jar already half filled with white. He stoppered the jar and shook it vigorously to mix the powders together, then placed the jar on a shelf. His hand lingered. He seemed to be gazing at something other than the shelves in front of him.

"It is a lonely thing, to be unique," he said, suddenly. "My people's shaping occurred elsewhere in the realms of Avalae. Our nation holds the islands to the west of here. It has been a long time, since I was forced to leave them."

He fell silent again, ordering the ranks of jars. He stopped, faced her. With an abrupt stride, he closed the gap between them. He reached out, jerkily, to touch her cheek. "My people were made to adore those whose shape you wear," he said.

His fingertips were dry and smooth. He traced the shape of her ear, the rapid pulse that arose in the side of her neck. His hand paused at her collarbone, then slowly eased the blanket from her shoulder.

Carefully, she stepped backwards through the doorway. The minotaur hung his head. His outstretched fingers curled back into his palm.

"Forgive me. I did not think I would be so overcome."

She fled, out into the morning fog.

The greyness was disorienting, and she stayed close to the buildings as she hurried along. Her heart thumped against her ribs—terror at what he might've done during the night, had his compulsion overcome him sooner.

The top of the hill was clear of the mist. The black tower stood stark against the chill blue sky, unrelieved by the bright sunshine.

The buildings at the plaza's edge stuck up like jagged teeth, the city beyond them lost beneath a white blanket of cloud.

Yesterday's near-riot had become an encampment. Handcarts and wagons did service as sleeping shelters. Would-be supplicants hunched around cookfires. There were soldiers among them, now. A delegation of Reaver captains camped closest to the gate.

She rubbed her mate's frigid toes.

The Reaver captains thumped on the gate and hollered up to the angel's balcony. The tower remained silent. The captains argued briefly among themselves, and several left with their men.

A cloud of copper-coloured bees buzzed around her head. She watched them dance patterns in the air. A starling swooped, scattering the cloud. The bird alighted on her mate's outstretched arm. One beady eye met hers. A bee struggled vainly in its beak. The rest buzzed about erratically. The starling flapped its wings and was gone.

"Bet you're hungry, eh?"

She jumped. And Yng'finail in mismatched conscript armour held up a torn loaf of bread, just out of her reach. Her stomach grumbled.

"Need to agree on a price first, love," he said. "It's not coin I have in mind, you understand."

She backed away, only to bump into a second man.

He sneered. "Too good for the likes of us, eh?"

She cried out and swatted at him with her stone hand. He caught the blow on the shoulder of his cuirass, cursing. His companion grabbed her arms from behind. The man she'd struck pulled back his fist and punched her in the mouth.

She tasted hot metal and salt. Pain radiated from her crushed lips. They took her by an arm each and began to drag her away. She struggled feebly, dazed from the blow.

The man to her left punched her under the ribs, driving the air from her lungs. She sagged, gasping.

She heard a sharp enquiry. A Reaver captain had risen, over by the tower gate, and stood watching them with hands on hips. His scrutiny was enough to make the two men falter. Their grip on her arms slackened.

She wrenched free. They shouted after her as she tottered into a run. One of them started to pursue, but a bark from the Reaver captain stopped him. Only their curses chased her from the plaza.

She didn't run far. The press of traffic soon forced her to slow. She found refuge in a doorway alcove. Gradually, her pulse slowed, her panic settled.

A memory floated to the surface of her thoughts, of festival dances beneath the tower: Avalae twirling in silk and gauze, each the focus of a ring of ecstatic slaves, competing for their masters' attention with the energy of their dancing. Every so often a slave would be chosen, and their masters would lead them by the hand through the black tower's gate.

She paused, thinking of cold and hunger, curled in her nest of briars and not knowing when the angel might open his gate. She thought of the men who'd seized her today, of the one who'd first found her, and thought of what might have happened had the first man been more wary, or had the Reaver captain not taken an interest.

She weighed the price of Cassiann's roof and hearth. *Made to adore those whose shape you wear,* he'd said.

❖

She found his door unlocked, the apothecary speaking to a patient in his surgery room. He faltered, as she went past down the hall.

She perched on his tall chair, until she heard the front door shut, and Cassiann came into the kitchen.

"Our angel keeps his tower closed, then," he said.

She nodded.

Heart hammering, she placed her hand on his belly. She slid her fingers downward, felt him quicken. He grunted and caught her wrist. He touched a finger to her battered lips, questioning. She held his gaze, resolute, for the long moment that he stared.

He swept her up and carried her up the stairs.

He was gentle, but hurried. She cried out in pain when he entered her, wound her one fist in his cassock and buried her face against his chest as he thrust between her thighs.

Afterwards, she felt between her legs, found the blood there. She wiped her fingers on the bedsheet, and for a long time couldn't sleep.

When at last she did, she dreamed of her mate. He stood with his back to her, and no matter how fast she ran around his plinth, his face remained stubbornly turned away.

❖

She awoke to find Cassiann kneeling beside the bed. His mouth was agape, his eyes squinting half shut. She realised he was smiling.

He held up a plain-spun dress. "I got these for you." He showed her a felted cloak and sheepskin boots.

"And this." He held out his palm. Across it was draped a simple wire necklace. Twined in its grasp was a small black orb.

Hesitantly, she reached out and touched it with her forefinger.

"It's a pearl," he said, then shyly: "I thought it a good name for you, since you lack one."

Her eyes felt suddenly hot. She tried it out, under her breath, "Purr."

"Here."

He held the wire loop to her throat and clasped it behind her neck. She held the pearl between her fingertips and let him nuzzle at her neck, as his arms came around her.

✦

Snowflakes greeted her when she pushed the window open. The street was clogged with wagons and handcarts and families afoot. A flock of gargoyles flew low over the rooftops, bearing infants and bundles of trinkets. Soldiers passed along the traffic jam, dragging men and boys from the line.

She felt the boards beneath her feet shift with the weight of Cassiann's tread. His hand clasped her shoulder. He peered down into the chaos below.

"Come," he said.

He tarried only long enough for them both to dress. She had to run to keep up with him as the minotaur ploughed through the press. She tucked her stone hand into the crook of her stump and hooked her fingers through his.

She felt a guilty relief when he turned downhill instead of up. She'd lost count of the days since she'd last gone back to the tower. The guilt she felt, standing beside her mate's plinth, touching him, had been too much to bear. She'd taken to lingering at the edge of the plaza, just long enough to see that the gate remained closed, and to drink in the sight of her mate. Then she'd stopped doing even that.

Cassiann's hurried pace brought them quickly to the harbour, emerging onto the waterfront near the city's arsenal.

The songships, few that survived, slept in a row, hulls bumping gently together as they rocked on the tide, their figureheads with faces bowed, arms folded across their wooden chests. They awoke a bitter longing in her, who would awake from their stillness, where her mate would not. But the songships were guarded by soldiers in armour and helms of good steel. She averted her eyes from their unfriendly regard, and hurried after Cassiann.

Further on, the docks became crowded. Gil-Gadin dhows lined the piers. Quar-Akech was fallen, were the words on many lips—the last of the sheikdoms, these ships escaped from the jaws of the invading fleet. Cassiann stopped to question some sailors. "Grahodden", she heard, in regard to the conquerors, and "Uiggrahodd", from whence they came, terms she did not know but she heard the fear and hate they owned when spoken.

These dhows were not staying, save a handful of battered warships. People on the docks shouted their bids for passage to the crews. A few were allowed to board. Other merchantmen were readying to flee as well, offering refuge on their decks for a price. A pair of Melkurran triremes remained aloof, their crews of flat-chested warrior women treating the goings on about them with stoic indifference.

All along the harbourfront, soldiers were fortifying buildings and barricading streets. Cassiann led her past one such barrier, through a gap left just wide enough to allow foot traffic, past an angry carriage driver and his passengers, arguing with soldiers who wanted to divert them two streets over.

The minotaur did not speak until they were back inside his house. He went straight into his surgery and started filling a long wooden case with jars. She put her stone hand on the bench beside the scales and watched.

"The city will fall," he said. "If the angel will not come from his tower, the city's mages will not suffice to turn the invaders back. I must flee while I can. The Grahodden slaughter magic users in all the realms they conquer. And those who rule in Uiggrahodd have styled themselves as gods, and tolerate no other shapings of men, so I am doubly damned."

He stopped his packing and took her flesh hand in both of his. "Come with me. We'll take the East Road, through the mountains. Winter will not have closed the passes, yet."

She looked into his human eyes, sincere in his inhuman face. She thought of her mate, still stone, and the angel in his tower—and her hope, the same—alive or dead, she did not know. And though she could form its sound upon her tongue, she could not bring herself to say the word, "Yes."

Cassiann withdrew his hand, and smiled, sadly, insomuch as his face allowed. He rummaged in the pockets of his cassock, and placed on the table beside her stone hand the key for his house, and a drawstring purse that clinked, full of coin. She knew, then, that he had expected no different answer.

She followed him about the house as he gathered food and a few small, precious things. He tied them in a bundle and slung it from his shoulder, then stood, his head bowed beneath the ceiling, and looked down at her once more.

He brushed his fingers on her cheek. "Live, Pearl," he said.

He turned away abruptly, and strode down the hall. He scooped up his case of medicines as he ducked to get through the front door, and was gone.

She sat alone for a while, touching the key, and the purse, and her stone hand. Then she too, went to the larder, and made a bundle of food. Upstairs, to find a blanket to supplement her cloak. Then she picked up the key and the hand from the table and went out, locking the door behind her, and up the hill, to wait for one last time.

Most of the crowds had fled. The tower gate stood unscarred by their efforts. She stroked her mate's petrified ankle, gazed up at cold stone features, male mirror of her own. She cringed from the disdain she saw there.

Her fingers strayed to the black pearl at her throat as she lowered herself into her briar nest.

After a time, the wind brought the brave chorus of the songships, leading the war fleet out to meet the enemy. She heard the song disintegrate, before it faded, into the bitter laments of the dying. She twisted to peer around the plinth's edge. In the spaces the streets made between the buildings, she saw galleys beaching outside the city walls.

Too soon, the sounds of battle reached her ears: the clatter of steel and the hoarse shouts of officers rallying their men, the whine of killing spells and the wails of the injured.

She remembered those sounds, covered her ears with hand and stump, unwilling, yet, to abandon her mate, as the last diehards fled the plaza. Defenders ran past, few of them armed. Arrows cut some down. A rat-headed soldier dodged around the plinth, barely an arm's length away, and sprawled, a white-feathered shaft between his shoulder blades. He reached out, to drag himself onward with his fingers. He spat blood and shuddered violently, his jaw smacking the cobbles, and was still.

A rock smashed into the tower's face. Another followed, then a barrage. She screamed in terror. Missiles lit with magic were tossed among the stones. They spattered on impact, their fires eating gouges in the tower's face. Some fell short. A rock hit the cobbles only yards away, showering her with splinters of stone.

It was too much. With a howl, she broke from the shelter of the plinth. A spinning rock bounced in front of her. She tripped and fell. Her stone hand slipped from her grasp. She watched helplessly as it arced to strike the cobbles, broken pieces skittering apart.

A fireball detonated near her mate's plinth. Its flaming offspring rained around her. She thrashed and rolled as the magic flame ate through her cloak and into tender flesh beneath. Sobbing and wailing, trailing embers from her hair, she fled.

She ran through streets already littered with corpses, houses already aflame. Hulking figures loomed out of the smoke. She reached Cassiann's house. Mad with fear and grief, she gave no thought to the key tucked into her waistband. She sat, moaning more than weeping, rocking herself back and forth, in the alcove before the door.

✸

In time, she calmed, but remained where she was, shocked and numb, feeling keenly the absence of the cold weight from her lap.

Ash-blackened snow began to fall. People slunk past, hollow-faced and cowed, snowmelt leaving streaks of soot on their faces. Others emerged from the houses, to ask where they were going.

"They've brought our angel from his tower," was the reply.

Her heart thudded. She joined the flow. The snow settled as slush, soaking through her boots and freezing her toes. Only those of fully human shape were abroad. Which others who survived had gone to ground.

She got her first clear sight of the city's conquerors, squads of Grahodden soldiers guarding the intersections of major streets. They were huge men, Cassian's size, and as burly, with skins like brown citrus peel. Their bulk was made greater by the cloaks of mottled feathers and fur caps they wore against the cold. In their fists they gripped halberds and glaives with cruel curved blades.

She stumbled past the ruined barricades that had walled the harbour. A great throng was gathered on the waterfront, its focus a gigantic quinquereme, pulled tight against the wharf. The bare masts of other war galleys filled the harbour, a skeleton forest through swirling snow.

The crowd was packed tight, but she threaded through, crawling in the slush when she could find no other way, desperate to see the angel. A voice rang out, unnaturally amplified, but she did not know its language. She wriggled between the last few rows of legs, heedless of the curses and kicks she earned. She tucked her burning cold fingers beneath her cloak and peered past the kilted thighs of a Grahodden soldier.

The angel knelt in the centre of a wide semi-circle of clear ground, the crowd held back by a ring of halberd blades. A wooden block was set before him, and a basket. A giant Grahodden stood over him, stripped to the waist to reveal the slabbed muscle beneath his pocked hide, a headsman's axe in his hands.

The angel's back was bowed, his complexion drained from Yng'finail red to leprous yellow. Shudders wracked his limbs. His grey swan wings drooped behind him, broken and roughly plucked.

Gazing down at him from the rail of the ship sat three lords of Uiggrahodd. They wore the heads of Grahodden folk, but outsized. Their bodies were those of lions. One raised a prehensile paw, a black talon springing from the thumbtip.

The headsman pushed down the angel's unresisting neck, then stepped back and took a grip on his axe.

The moment dilated. The thumb turned down.

The crowd groaned and surged at the soldiers' line. The Grahodden kept their discipline, laying about the rioters with the butts of their weapons as they closed ranks.

Like a rabbit breaking from cover, she sprang past the soldiers' legs and dashed across the space. Deep voices bellowed behind her.

She skidded to her knees in front of the angel. Holding hand and stump before his face, she shaped a word: "Please."

The angel raised his head, looked at her through a veil of filthy feather-hair. Grey eyes, half-mad with pain, stared into hers. The brows above them creased, as he recognised the shape of those his Reavers had vanquished, generations before. The frown cleared, eyes widened, as he perceived the stuff of his own self that animated her.

"Please," she said again.

His cracked lips worked. An incantation. A string of blood-flecked drool fell. She caught the precious spittle in her palm, closed her fingers around it as the headsman's boot came up under her ribs.

She balled around her hurt, rolling away through the slush. Rough fingers caught her hair and dragged her by it. She gritted her teeth against the pain, clutching her hand against her chest as she felt the phlegm become dust. She saw a halberd silhouetted against the sky.

A voice rose above the melee, a roar of command. It came from the ship. The command repeated. The soldier who held her lowered his weapon. Again, the sphinx spoke, and the noise of the crowd stilled.

The soldier jerked into motion, towing her backwards across the cobbles. The angel was forced down again. The axe rose, fell. The basket rocked. The broken body flexed, a pump of blood from the severed neck. A gasp and a sigh from the crowd. The tattered wings folded limply around the corpse.

The soldier deposited her at the feet of the mob, delivered a casual thump from the butt of his halberd as she found her feet. She averted her face from wondering eyes, pushed past the front rows, moving then in the roil of the crowd, toward and away, the collective beast suddenly lacking its head. She kept her fist pressed tight against her.

She trekked alone up the hill to the tower, past splintered doors and smouldering frames, Grahodden soldiers and defenders' corpses already vanishing under drifts of snow. The black tower's gate hung twisted on its hinges, rent aside by magic, the stone face a mess of scars. Soldiers leaning in the shelter of the arch glanced at her, and away, dismissive.

Her mate was gone from his plinth. Only the stumps of his legs remained. Her stomach convulsed, she dry-retched. The dust in her palm felt like ash.

She crossed the space to the plinth at a faltering run, tripping once but catching herself, the ground turned unsteady beneath her. She slowed, had to force her feet to take her around the plinth, visions of her hand shattering on the cobbles replaying before her eyes.

She heaved again, this time with a sob of bittersweet relief. Her mate lay on a bed of briars, broken off whole above the knees, his left arm raised plaintive to the sky. Scars from magic fire pocked the length of his right side, a finger gone from the hand and his ear ruined in the mess along his neck and jaw. She sank to her knees beside him.

She caressed his undamaged cheek with her stump. Her fist ached, closed tight around the angel's dust.

Her hand shook as she held it over his chest.

She lowered her arm.

Unbidden, her stump brushed the necklace at her throat.

"Pearl," she whispered.

She wondered where Cassiann was, if he was safe.

Her clenched fingers began to cramp in the cold. Snowflakes drifted down. Her gaze fell on black stone shards, still lying where her stone hand had slipped her grasp. She looked at the broken stumps of her mate's legs. Could she do it to him? Bring him into this world, a cripple?

Could she not?

*Made to adore him.*

But did that mean she had no choice? Cassiann had made a choice: to leave, and live, when his compulsion would have bid him stay with her and die. His choice must have hurt him, but he had made it even so, and he was better for it.

*The East Road*, he'd said. *To the mountains.*

But did she want to follow? Did she need to? Her gaze fell on the soldiers, over by the tower gate. What better did Cassiann offer but a measure of gentleness?

*Live*, he had bid her. She touched the roll of her waistband, felt the key still there.

Pearl bent and touched her lips to cold stone. She tasted the salt warmth of her own tears. Gritting her teeth against a cry, she pushed herself away, and up.

With unsteady steps, she walked from the plaza.

Glittering dust trailed from her fingers. Poppies sprang from the cobbles in her wake.

# SLEEPLESS IN THE HOUSE OF YE

"Some of us will have to stay awake," Ghei said. "Some of us will have to take *koy*."

A chorus of hissing reverberated around the chamber.

Poe quivered, hearing the words she'd been dreading. She held her belly with both hands, feeling the heat of the hundreds of embryonic spawn growing there. To take *koy*—summer's drink—as a sire, and avert the change of life for another year was one thing. To take it now, already female and with spawn in their bellies, was ruinous.

Ghei stood defiantly against the tide of disquiet she'd caused, her neck stretched up, ears fanned wide. It was Ghei who'd found the gap—the snowdrift forming where the clean lines of the walls dissolved into the jumbled echoes of the rubble pile, where the stair used to be to the House's upper levels. Ghei had brought the worm she found in the drift to Poe and Chyu. It had been as long as her hand, its movements frantic, responding to Ghei's heat, mouth petals opening, its muscular tail flailing as it sought purchase.

"The gap might not get any worse," someone ventured.

"What if it does?" came the response.

"It's bad enough already," said Poe.

A sneeze echoed. The air in the birthing chamber was acrid, ventilation for the oil heaters largely blocked by the House's fall. A handful of dams had already lain down beneath the vaults furthest from the door—mostly those who had been injured when the House fell, whose spawn had grown faster, since. Their bellies were mounds of cool, slowly pulsing life amid cold and withered limbs, the growth of the spawn inside them suspended until spring.

Those who remained awake huddled between the pillars, a sprawl of warm bodies. Their expirations made a shimmer of evaporating heat above their heads. Many were not far from taking the last sleep themselves, anonymous in the dark with ears drooping limply beside their faces. Munk—their languid, voluptuous Munk—slumped between Poe and Chyu. She was all but gone, her temperature starting to dip towards sleep.

"We must build a barrier to block off the corridor," someone said.

"Have we the strength among us to raise the stones?" came the reply.

"We will build it with timber," a third voice said, after a time. "There are crates in the store rooms, furnishings we can salvage."

Chyu stirred herself to answer that folly. "Useless. The worms will go through timber as fast as they'll eat through your belly."

"The ice is still moving," added Ghei. "It's dragging the wall outward."

Worms always got into a wintering House, eventually. Under normal circumstances, it was only those tiny enough to slither through the wire grates on the drain holes in the walls, high and low, that let in the spring melt and, later, let the water out again with its cargo of wriggling spawn. That was a different matter to the risk they faced now: that the breach would let in worms of sufficient size and in enough numbers to consume the sleeping dams in entirety, along with all the spawn inside them.

Poe listened to the agitated movements of her sibs. Her whiskers caught the increased blood flow in their faces, although it was difficult to read expressions clearly with their ears gone limp. Only Chyu and Ghei had their ears fanned, displaying patterns of hot veins.

Poe saw, again, the strongest of the dams of Ye as they shuffled away across the snow in a double file, burdened with packs and furs and the bellies that swung between their legs. Their tails, wrapped in puttees, dragged behind them. It was a cruel parody of the departure of the sires in autumn, waving their tails jauntily as they strode away down the long pier—vanished under the ice, now—to the ships that would bear them north.

The questers had left at dawn, beneath a clear sky, a day's march to the House of U, Ye's nearest neighbour. The very strongest had towed sleds behind them, loaded with tents, in case the weather turned. Ong had led them off, with a wave to which Poe had briefly raised her own tail.

Munk had squatted between Poe and Chyu as they watched the questers go, her head low between her shoulders. Already, her skin was bleaching from maroon to cream, its texture turning horny and inflexible. Munk's neck was so thin it seemed remarkable that it could still bear the weight of her skull.

"I smell snow," she'd said.

Chyu had found amusement in that, snorting through flared nostrils. She'd scooped up a handful of the stuff to toss at Munk.

"Of course you do," Poe had said.

The blizzard had blown up that afternoon. It was still blowing three days later. Poe and Chyu could've easily gone among the strongest dams, to U. Both of them had taken *koy*, in the summer— just a little, not to delay the change a whole year, just enough for Chyu to remain a sire for a month after Munk changed and Poe for another month after Chyu.

They would have gone, if Munk were not already so close to sleep. They had no way, now, to know the questers' fate, whether some part of Ye's spawning was secured at U.

"I will stay awake," Poe said.

Whiskers and ears turned her way, but she had attention only for Munk and Chyu.

Munk could barely raise her head. "We're supposed to take the last sleep together," she whispered. Poe stroked her drooping ears.

"Someone has to, love, and I am the furthest from sleep," Poe said, more calmly than she felt. "I've sired many spawn. More this year, in you and Chyu."

Munk's ears twitched. She pushed her head against Poe's touch.

"Then I will take *koy* with you," said Chyu.

Poe hissed, then again to emphasise the strength of her denial. "You mustn't."

"It is enough that you and I will survive in Munk," said Chyu. "I am of Mha, not Ye. My clan is not threatened. I will stay awake with you."

Poe recognised well enough from the tone of Chyu's voice and the set of her ears that her mind was made and it was useless to argue.

"I, too, will stay awake," said Ghei, across the chamber. The erratic pulsing of her ear veins, plain from across the chamber, belied her brave words.

"Three is enough," said Poe, into the quiet that followed.

❀

The koy was in the small upstairs larder, still secure in the half of the House that remained standing. The main larder had been a level lower, on the fallen side. They had to dig their way up to the surface from the ground-level doorway, an exhausting task with only three of them capable of making any meaningful contribution.

They went in the middle of the day, amid the long shadows, the sun rising bare handspans above the northern horizon. Their eyes watered in the light, unused for days inside the darkness of the tower. Poe's gaze was drawn upwards, to what remained of the House of Ye, a blurred silhouette against the sky. The blizzard had buried most of the wreckage of the other half. She wished— again—that they'd done more, in summer, than quarry stone for the House's renovation. But no-one had thought the weight of the shifting ice would bring the old House down so soon. Not this winter, they'd all said.

They struggled slowly up the steps to the larder, Ghei had to pause and catch her breath before the top.

Once inside, they found the glazed clay jugs of *koy* nectar easily. Chyu prised the waxed stopper from one while Ghei upturned an empty crate and lined the three beakers she'd brought on top of it. Poe clicked her tongue, swiveling her ears to gauge the stacks of crates, sacks and jars and cloth-wrapped bundles of salted meats piled in the shadows.

"We'll have to move all this downstairs," she said.

Chyu poured and they squatted silently around the crate.

The speckling of pallor across Chyu's skin was stark in the light from the open doorway, its advance evident even in the few days they'd waited inside for the blizzard to blow itself out. Poe could see the same effect on her own bare hands, and feel the emerging roughness there. Ghei's colour was already more cream than maroon. They'd all lost mass from their limbs, necks and tails. Some of it would come back, Poe supposed, after they took the *koy*, and their bodies re-absorbed the aborted spawn.

She reached out, hesitated, withdrew her fingers from the beaker in front of her. She sat back on her tail and hind legs.

Chyu stroked the ridge of Poe's spine between her shoulders, her hand a dull weight through the thickness of Poe's clothes. Poe tried to lift her ears in response. The tips were numb, dead weights of limp skin.

Opposite, Ghei gripped her cup and tossed the contents down her throat, gasped and coughed. Chyu did the same and gave a sob as she slammed the beaker back on the crate.

Poe raised her beaker and drank. The *koy* was thick, oily and milky at once, tasting of bitter sap. She gagged, managed to keep her lips closed, swallowed.

The pain started in earnest within the hour. The other dams stroked them while they kicked and trembled, lying on their sides in the birth chamber. Ghei thrashed so violently that she had to be held down to prevent her from injuring herself. By morning the three of them were recovered, if feeble. Ghei was weaker than Poe or Chyu.

✸

Poe clucked her tongue, ears scanning the corridor for movement, her whiskers extended to catch any rogue trace of warmth. She clasped a snow shovel ready in her hands. The shuttered oil heater on the floor played havoc with her whiskers, but it attracted the worms and they'd found it a more reliable method than scouring the corridors for the faint telltales of the intruders.

Her whiskers caught a hint of something at the edge of the heater's radiance. She swiveled her ears. A worm, somewhat longer than her hand, inched towards the heater. Poe raised the shovel and brought down the flat of the blade with a clang.

She cried out in surprise at the rumbling boom that echoed through the House's surviving chambers. Dust settled from the ceiling.

"Another fall!" she heard Ghei cry.

"Chyu!"

Poe hurried, as fast as she was able, to the outer door and up the ramp to the surface, stumbling dizzily as afterimages danced in front of her eyes. She found Chyu staring up at the remains of the tower, a bag of flour cradled in her arms, not far from where the steps to the larder had been. The stair itself was gone. Its fall had brought the larder down with it. Broken vessels and spilled foodstuffs were visible among the toppled stones.

Poe touched Chyu's arm. Chyu turned her head briefly to brush whiskers, but didn't speak. Ghei panted up beside them.

"Oh, no."

After a while, Poe said, "We need to check what damage has

been done downstairs."

Fortunately, there seemed to be none. They all three walked from end to end of the lower levels, clicking their tongues, ears focused to scrutinise the gaps between the building stones. The birthing chamber remained secure, dug into bedrock, and the breach at the end of the corridor appeared no worse.

Their food stocks were another matter.

"Not enough," said Poe, as they regarded the depressingly small stack of crates, jars and sacks that Chyu and Ghei had brought down to the fuel store, where they'd decided to see the winter out.

Chyu sat back on her tail. "Perhaps for two."

"Perhaps. Not for three."

"One of us could go to U instead. They'll have food enough."

"Go and bring it back?" asked Ghei.

"And stay," said Chyu. "I'm not of Ye. I'll go."

Poe hissed gently. "Two of us will go to U and bring back food. As soon as we have the strength."

❋

"You will see spring again," said Munk. "Flowers." She rested her head on Poe's thigh. Chyu's tail curled around her shoulders.

"Perhaps."

Munk shifted, searching for them with her whiskers. She lacked the strength to lift her head. Poe and Chyu dipped their faces close to Munk's and into the field of her failing senses.

"I would like to smell flowers again," said Munk.

"Yes."

For a while, Munk just breathed. Then she said, "You will see the spawning. All the little ones swimming."

*And then what?* Poe wondered. *Will we have our ending in the summer? Or will we see another winter, and go north? Will it matter, when we've ruined ourselves and no spawn of our wombs will ever eat our flesh?*

Munk was still. Chyu made a small keening noise. Hiccups of grief rose in Poe's throat, that she would not soon be following, that no renewal would come from her own passing.

❋

"Expect us back before two more dawns," said Poe. "If we're not, you'll have enough food to get you through."

Ghei followed them up the ramp to the snow surface. She cut a forlorn figure, so heavily swaddled she could barely walk. Poe and

Chyu weren't much more mobile, with thick puttees bound around their limbs, necks and tails, and their bodies swathed in twotoe furs. The two of them had regained enough strength that they were able to raise their tails from the ground again when they walked. They were still thin, though, the mass in their bellies dissipated rather than redistributed back to their extremities.

The cold burned Poe's nostrils and whiskers and made her eyes ache.

"You *will* be back," said Ghei.

If they weren't, she would have enough food, but would she have the strength, alone? Poe and Chyu were thin, but Ghei was emaciated, the maroon of her skin reduced to a mere webwork around blotches of horny pallor. At least the worms getting into the House had, thus far, remained relatively small.

"We'll be back," Chyu agreed.

Poe brushed her whiskers across Ghei's, before raising her scarf over the lower half of her face. She and Chyu waddled out onto the snow, dragging their sleds behind them.

Chyu raised an arm to indicate direction. Southeast. Poe looked back, at Ghei still huddled at the top of the trench. The ruined House of Ye loomed black with dawn's paleness behind it.

❖

Their long shadows swung across in front of them as they walked, the sun's disc barely clearing the northern horizon before it started to slip back down again. As its setting coloured the snow pink and mauve, Chyu exclaimed and pointed, away to their left.

A silhouette protruded from the surface. It looked like tattered cloth over a frame of ribs or poles. *A tent.* Poe's ears flattened as she followed Chyu, at the possibility that they might find her sibs from Ye, overtaken and overwhelmed by the blizzard.

It wasn't a tent, she saw with relief, but the remains of a large chrysalid. Even broken and mostly buried, it stood as high as their chins. Of the creature that had slept inside it, there was little left to see, just a few splintered long bones sticking up from the snow.

"Twotoe," Poe guessed.

"Big worm to crack open a chrysalid that size," said Chyu.

Poe shut her eyes and scanned the snow underfoot with her whiskers. Only the rapidly fading residue of their own tracks disturbed the uniform chill below. The worm was gone, or at least dug too deep to detect, no doubt off in pursuit of its smaller brethren

— 69 —

that would've gathered to its kill.

Poe thought of Ghei, alone at Ye, and hoped the breach in the outer wall remained small.

They walked through the night. The moonless dark caused Poe's eyes and whiskers to compete for attention. She moved at once over a silver landscape with the stars sweeping the sky above, and through a void of utter cold all about.

It was almost dawn again when they reached the House of U—a squat blankness against the aurora, with half its height buried under the snow. They had to dig to uncover the uppermost of its doors.

Poe lifted the bolt and rolled the door aside. "Ahoy, the House of U," she called. "We are Poe Ye and Chyu Mha from Ye."

There was no answer and no movement from within.

"All asleep," said Chyu.

Poe pushed inside. They paused to unhitch themselves from their sleds, letting their senses adjust to the deeper darkness. Chyu emerged as a mass of bright heat at Poe's side.

They descended into the lower levels of the House, clicking their tongues to get a clear map of the unfamiliar layout. U was built differently to Ye, and newer, its base wider, with its stores all a level above bedrock, divided by the straight stair and a balcony landing.

Movement echoed below. A dam's warm bulk shuffled into range of their whiskers, bowed double with the weight of her belly.

"Who's there?"

"Poe Ye and Chyu Mha from Ye."

"I am Suun U, last to sleep here. I would welcome you better, but I am too weak to climb the stairs."

"Then we will come to you," said Poe.

Suun U touched whiskers with them when they had descended, then pulled back and said, "What brings you to U, so late?"

Cold trickled beneath Poe's furs. "Did our sibs not come here?"

Suun hissed softly, plainly mystified.

Chyu said, "Ye has fallen. The ice shifted around it and cracked the House's walls. Ong Ye led the strongest dams to U."

Suun hissed again, louder. "When?"

Poe whispered, "Weeks ago." She felt the keening rise in her throat.

❂

They loaded their sleds with salted and frozen meats, dried fruits and sacks of flour and grain, thanked Suun U and ate with her, then left her alone with the sorrow they had brought.

The aurora rippled across the southern sky. The northwest horizon was not yet beginning to brighten when they shut the doors of U and went back out onto the snow.

The journey home was slow, with their sleds burdened and both of them near exhaustion. The snow around was unblemished except for the tracks they had left the day before. Poe wondered where beneath it the blizzard might have buried the dams of Ye, how close they had come to U before the storm defeated them.

They might've lost their way, she told herself, and found another House instead. She imagined her sibs far under her feet, the worms gathering to feed.

✸

Ye had been in sight again a long time before it struck Poe, stumping along, that something wasn't right. It took her longer still to realise where the feeling of wrongness came from: the House's broken silhouette had changed shape.

"Chyu!" she cried. "There's been another fall!"

Chyu hissed, perceiving the disaster for herself. They picked up their pace as best they could, with their weary legs and heavy sleds, so tired they couldn't lift their tails.

They abandoned the sleds at the top of the ramp, clambering past a fall of stones to reach the door.

"Ghei!" Poe shouted, flinging open the door. "Ghei?"

Her tail curled in horror. The floor was littered with worms. Some of them were as thick as her tail.

"Ghei!"

The nearest worms turned slowly towards them, responding to their movement and heat, spreading the four petals of their mouths to show their teeth. Poe bellowed and stamped, cracking carapaces. Chyu swept the corridor with her tail. Worm chitin clattered against the walls.

The door of the fuel store stood ajar. Poe shoved it wide, clucking her tongue urgently to hear what was inside. The stove was cold. No warmth radiated from the still pile of blankets beside it.

With dread certainty, Poe flung aside the blankets. Worm tails writhed in agitation at the disturbance.

With a howl, Poe grabbed the largest with both hands and dug her fingers between two rings of chitin. The worm shivered, but didn't release its hold, its front end buried in Ghei's midriff.

Chyu caught Poe's shoulder. "Too late."

Poe shook her off. She heaved, trying to tear the chitin from the worm's middle.

"Poe! I need you!" cried Chyu. Metal clanged on stone.

With a final, futile wrench, Poe released her grip.

Chyu swung the snow shovel again, severing a worm's head from its tail. The tail thrashed and convulsed in the doorway. Its fellows pushed past, heedless, mouth petals gaping.

Poe clicked her tongue, searching for a weapon. She found an icepick. "The birthing chamber," she said.

They cleared the doorway with pick and shovel, then hurried back past the open outer door and down the slope of the corridor, kicking smaller worms out of the way, slashing and stabbing at the largest as they passed.

Worms covered the half dozen sleepers nearest the entrance of the birthing chamber. Poe went past them, scanning her whiskers low over those lying further back. Only a few worms had penetrated any deeper. She kept going until she reached Munk. Chyu was close on her heels. Together they examined Munk's sleeping body from end to end, plucking a handful of small worms free of her cool flesh.

"What do we do?" said Chyu, when Munk was clean.

"We'll have to clear them," said Poe. "All the way back to the breach. We'll dump the carcasses down here for the spawn to eat in spring."

She started to work cleaning the smaller worms from on and around the sleeping dams. Chyu dismembered the larger ones with the edge of her shovel. The chamber echoed with the flat clang of iron on stone. Poe plucked and crushed until her fingers cramped with fatigue. Some of the dams were completely cold, the life sucked from their bellies.

*Too late*, Poe thought in dismay, as she used her pick to prise free the mouthparts of the worms Chyu had severed. *Too late.*

They rested when they were done, squatting on tripods of legs and tail and leaning on the handles of their tools. Poe's limbs shook. She plucked a small worm from her calf and Chyu a couple from her tail. Poe wound her tail around Chyu's. They sat in a daze, listening to the worms crawl towards them. Chyu swept at them halfheartedly with the shovel.

"Some of them are cold," said Poe.

"But not all," said Chyu. "Not all, love."

She stood. Her tail trembled as she tried to hold it off the ground. Poe heaved herself up.

Worms always congregated around the Houses in winter, searching for gaps in the stone, the tiniest slipping in through the drains, the rest preying on each other while they probed the House's defences with mindless patience. Poe had never imagined there'd be quite so many. She kicked the broken carcasses down towards the birthing chamber. The ring of the shovel blade striking the floor drilled into her head.

The density of worms had thinned by the time they worked their way back to the fuel store. They dragged Ghei into the corridor and cleaned the worms from her. Poe felt queasy, handling the shrivelled husk, from which no new life would emerge in spring. Ending without renewal. Extinction. The same awaited she and Chyu.

"What a waste," whispered Chyu.

Poe began to sob, wracking hiccups that burst from her nostrils. They dragged Ghei down to the birthing chamber and left her there, among her sibs. The most they could do was ensure her flesh would feed the next generation, not the worms.

There were few of those remaining in the last stretch of corridor, from the fuel store to the blocked stairs. Poe and Chyu cleared them quickly.

"Mother Mha," Chyu breathed when they reached the stairs.

The snowdrift filled the entire corridor. The tower's second fall had torn the outer wall completely away. An enormous worm lay halfway out of the snow, its girth greater than the length of Poe's arm. A ripple passed along its body and it lurched another handspan clear of the drift.

Chyu began to growl. Her cry rose in volume and pitch as she brought the shovel up to her shoulder. She stabbed it at the worm like a spear. The blade hit chitin and slid along until it found the seam between two plates. The worm swung towards the assault.

Poe struck the ice pick into the worm's other side as Chyu withdrew for another lunge. Its mouth petals flared, revealing rows of hooked teeth. Poe retreated and the worm made another lurch forward. Chyu struck again, and again to little effect. With Poe's next blow, the ice pick penetrated the worm's armour and stuck. Its jerk of pain wrenched the handle from Poe's grip. She flung herself clear of its thrashing.

Her foot kicked something metallic. *The oil heater*!

"Chyu, keep it busy!" she cried.

Chyu slapped the worm's mouth petals. They contracted sharply.

Poe fumbled about on the floor. Her fingers grasped the flintlock lighter. She flicked it frantically to get a spark onto the burner's wick. The wick caught.

Chyu hacked at the worm's side. It's mouth flared and Poe flung the oil lamp into the open maw. The petals snapped shut. The worm swung violently sideways, knocking Chyu from her feet. It flexed upward. Its front struck the roof and Poe heard the crack of splitting stone.

"Chyu!" Poe scrambled to drag her clear. The worm crashed back down. Stones came with it, and ice. The ceiling yawed and tumbled.

❂

"Eat."

Chyu opened her mouth to accept the strip of dried meat. She chewed slowly. She shifted awkwardly, her splinted leg stuck straight out beside her.

Poe pressed close beside her beneath the blankets, sharing warmth. She slipped another strip of jerky into her own mouth.

"Poe?" said Chyu. "How long until spring, do you think?"

"I don't know. I haven't been outside to see." Poe wondered if she would know even if she did go outside. Would the stars and the faint, brief glow of the sun, no longer cresting the horizon, tell her, when she had never wintered in the antarctic before?

"What are we, Poe? We are not sires, the change has come to us. We are not dams, we have no spawn in our bellies. What are we?"

Poe thought it over. "Sleepless," she said at last.

"Sleepless." Chyu's snorts of laughter became sneezes.

❂

Poe awoke in darkness. She lay a while, listening to the quiet, then, painfully, she got to her feet and tottered to the door. Reflexively, she picked up the snow shovel, with its bent and dented blade.

It took her two attempts to open the fuel store's door. Once she had, she paused, listening again, to an unfamiliar sound. Tinkling. She waited for the noise to stop or change. It didn't.

Tinkling. Dripping.

Running water.

"Chyu!" she cried. "Chyu. Chyu Mha! Water! It's spring."

She turned, confused, when Chyu didn't respond.

❀

Poe left Chyu's corpse where it was. She abandoned the shovel, too, but out of habit stomped on the couple of small worms in her path as she crossed to the outer wall. Her feet splashed through icy water in the centre of the corridor. She bent to examine the drain holes at the base of the wall. Snowmelt flowed across to the low centre of the floor and down the shallow slope.

Poe limped along the wall. Light showed around the edges of the outer door. She got it open in several short drags and had to lean on the frame and rest for a minute afterwards. She pushed up the trench through drifted snow and over fallen stones, almost reaching the top before she stumbled, unable to go further. She blinked into the dawn's glare, her eyes watering in the brightness.

"Spring," she breathed. But a long time yet before the snow was gone and there were flowers on the ground, even longer before the sires sailed south, following the summer.

She stayed there, half fallen, and watched the red bright disc rise clear of the horizon before falling once more from sight. Melted snow began to seep through her cloaks. With difficulty, she got herself up again and back inside.

When she recovered her breath, she returned to the fuel store and dragged out Chyu's body. A few paces at a time, she followed the tinkling water downwards.

The floor of the birthing chamber was already under a film of water. There were tiny worms in it, but that no longer mattered. The spawn were growing in the wombs of their dams. They would eat their way free, and then the roles of predator and prey would be reversed.

Poe wondered if she could last until the ships returned. She exhaustion answered for her. It was doubtful the sires would never know what had been done after the House's fall. It didn't matter—enough that the spawning was saved.

She dragged Chyu past her sleeping sibs, to Munk. Painfully, Poe lowered herself between them. She stroked their cold faces. Chyu, lost to life; Munk, with new life soon to burst forth.

She wondered what extinction would feel like, and felt a sudden stab of fear, now that it was upon her. Would it hurt, or would she slip away, unknowingly, as though into sleep? She rested her head against the slight warmth of Munk's belly. In there, was her rebirth. She listened to the tinkling water.

Her mind drifted.

❈ ❈ ❈

# THE WISHWRITER'S WIFE

In the days when fairies were still to be found in the world, and wishes could come true, there lived a wishwriter and his wife. The wishwriter was a clever man, but plain, and born with a twisted back that made him stoop. His wife was beautiful, gentle and generous, and she loved him just as he was.

The wishwriter was happy, for this was just as he had wished. His wife contented herself that her husband, too, was gentle and generous, and it did not hurt her to love him.

The wishwriter made his living because no matter how many fairies came into a person's possession, they could only ever have one true wish. A wish could only be for a single thing; a person could not wish for fame *and* fortune, or a beautiful palace *and* a handsome prince. It could not be an infinite thing—eternal youth or a purse that was always full of gold—or even too large a thing, or the wish would not bind and take.

"It is important for the wish to bind," the wishwriter said, touching his wife's cheek, "otherwise it might fade, or simply vanish.

"And that," he said, "would be heartbreaking."

His wife showed him a smile, and wondered what it would be like to not be bound.

"And a wish cannot make more wishes," the wishwriter said, always pleased to show off his expertise. "So if a person has more than one heart's desire, and many do . . . " He spread his hands with a self-satisfied grin.

" . . . they will come to a wishwriter," his wife obliged.

It was the wife's role to greet her husband's clients, and to flatter and fuss over them while—usually—the houseboy ran to fetch the wishwriter from his club or the baths or the gaming house. Then, once he had snuck in the back door and up the servants' stairs, she would take the clients up to his study, where the wishwriter would now be ensconced behind his desk, his features shrouded beneath a scholar's hood.

"It all adds to the air of mystery," he told her, "which is very important in this line of work."

The wishwriter's wife was fascinated by the many heart's desires of the people who sought her husband's services. One day, she might open the door to find a woman clutching a breadbox, inside which was the fairy she had caught raiding her pantry. The woman would tell of her husband, who could no longer ply his trade as a woodcutter since an accident that cost him his arm, and she wished for him to be whole. Yet at the same time she herself was barren and longed for a daughter. Then the wishwriter would send her away for a week, and when she returned he would give her a tiny scroll on which was written: "I wish, I wish, I wish to find at home my delighted husband holding aloft our infant daughter with his two strong arms." The woman would speak the wish, and the fairy would give up its magic and its bright tiny life to make the wish come true.

Or the wife might discover a young boy waiting on the step, who in desperation had traded his father's precious violin to a fairy trapper. The boy's father had been a great composer, but was now deaf, and the boy wished for him to be able to hear and make music again. At the same time, the boy felt himself a disappointment to his father, for he had not inherited his gift for music and, what was more, his father would certainly be furious when he discovered the loss of his violin. After a week, at the appointed time, the boy would return and read aloud his wish, which said: "I wish, I wish, I wish for my father to hear me playing skilfully on the new violin that is the equal of the one I traded." Then the fairy in its little brass cage would turn to sparkling dust, the dust would become his wish, and the boy would race joyfully home clutching his new violin.

The wishwriter always sent people away for a week, although it rarely took him as long as an hour to piece together their various desires into a single wish.

"Most people could write their own wishes," he confided to his wife, "if only they thought a little."

But of course most people did not, and so the wishwriter would send them away for a week. For although he was gentle and generous he was also clever, and knew on which side his bread was buttered.

He did always strive to write their wishes as well as possible.

"But in truth," he said to his wife, "the precision of the words does not matter so much. Wishes are not fickle things, as long as a person does not get too greedy, and provided the wish is expressed in a single clause."

So the wishwriter and his wife lived comfortably and even grew quite wealthy, for he wrote wishes for rich as well as poor. If his customers had no gold or silver, he would take payment in goods or kind—a winter's supply of chopped firewood, or a gift of music lessons for his wife. Sometimes, during the breeding season, a lucky person would come with two captured fairies and offer the second to the wishwriter as payment.

Whenever this happened the wishwriter would smile and gesture to his wife and say: "I have but a single wish, and it is already true." But he would take the fairy, for fairies were as good as money, especially to a wishwriter.

His wife would stare at the tiny being in its cage. She, too, had come to have a single wish.

For as the wishwriter had grown older, his cleverness had become arrogance and conceit. He had also grown fat, as a result of enjoying his comfortable life. He had developed jowls and a substantial paunch. His muscles had become slack and his skin blotchy. His stoop had turned into a hunch. But he did not care for any of these things, for his wife remained beautiful, even as she aged, and he knew she must love him just as he was. He did not consider that his wife might be troubled.

Although, of course, she had no choice but to love him, still she longed for him to be more like he once had been, and not as he had become. And in her secret heart, she longed not to be bound at all. But as her husband had told her, a wish could not make more wishes, and so the heart's desire that grew within her remained inside and unsaid.

And as the wishwriter grew older, he also developed a sickness of the mind. Subtly at first, then more and more noticeably his moods became erratic. He grew prone to fits of passion and anger, wild tantrums that boiled up from nowhere. He was no longer gentle and generous. His gift for writing wishes deserted him, and people began to take their business elsewhere.

Because his sickness was of the mind, the wishwriter could not see it for himself, and blamed others for their fickleness. His wife tried to bring him healers, but he drove them away with insults and curses, and accused his wife of betrayal and trying to do him harm. She bore his unkind words in silence, for she knew his mind was no longer his own, and she continued to care for him as best as he would allow. But, although she could not help but still love him, she also began an affair with a younger man from the town, who was gentle and generous as her husband once had been.

The last healer that she tried, an alchemist of some note, accepted her apologetic offer of tea, after he too had been driven rudely from her husband's bedside. He watched her pour with shaking hands, then sipped from his cup and offered words of small comfort: "It is unlikely that medicine could have helped him, anyway. Such is often the case with diseases of the mind."

They sat in her husband's study, a room of strong sunlight and deep shadows that reminded her of the wishwriter as he once had been. From a hook by the window hung a fairy in a brass cage, the last of those with which her husband had been paid when he was still well enough to work.

The alchemist gestured to it. "A wish might save him."

The wife looked longingly at the fairy and her eyes filled with tears. She shook her head.

"Ah, of course. You have had your one true wish already," he guessed.

She whispered, "No."

A small frown creased the alchemist's brow. "A cure for your husband is not among your heart's desires?"

*No*, the wife answered, in the deepest part of her heart. She drew an unsteady breath and looked at the alchemist directly. "A wish cannot make more wishes," she told him.

He stared at her. A look of comprehension crossed his features, and with it a touch of compassion. He reached out, his fingertips making fleeting contact with the back of her hand.

"It will be done soon," the alchemist said. "He will not last much longer."

She smiled at him through her tears, and gave him the fairy for payment, despite that it was worth far more than his fee. Even in those days, they were becoming rare.

The wishwriter's health continued to decline. His wild moods diminished and he became increasingly idle and withdrawn. His wife continued to care for him as he lost the ability to meet even his own most basic needs. Still she loved him just as he was—she could do nothing else—and she reminded herself that he had always been gentle and generous to her before his sickness, and he had given her a good life. And, whenever she could, she found comfort in the arms of her townsman, whom she could not love, but who she fancied she might, had she the choice.

Eventually the day came when the wishwriter could not even rise from his bed, and his wife knew that his time must be near. She wrote a letter to her young townsman, bidding him farewell and telling him she believed she would have loved him, had the choice been hers. She gave it to a street urchin to deliver, for she had let the servants go, months before.

Then she sat by her husband's side and waited for Death to come and claim him. As the wishwriter breathed his last breaths, his face eased and his wife thought she glimpsed something of the man he once had been. She grieved for that man, and grieved that he had been gone from her so long before. And she grieved that he had bound her to him, had not given her a free heart when he wished her into being and set himself the task of earning her love.

Quietly, without fuss, Death stole into the room, and the wishwriter breathed no more.

His wife felt relief then, even as she wept, that at last his madness and her misery were at an end.

Her tears did not last long. A calm settled over her. She looked inside herself and found her heart free and unbound. She breathed in, deep. Then out. Motes of sparkling dust rode on her breath, only a few at first, thickening to a cloud as the long sigh went on. As the cloud grew brighter and more dense, so she dimmed and faded.

When only the cloud remained, it swirled about the room until it found the open window. Out it went, riding the breeze. The motes scattering, unfettered at last, and quickly to fade.

# THE TAX COLLECTOR OF RHUIN

Sarheic looked around the room, kitchen for both shop and family, while the baker counted out his taxes at the table. The baker's wife and two children, sitting together by the hearth, returned his scrutiny. The children's eyes were wide, the wife's expression cool. Sarheic was accustomed to both reactions, here and elsewhere.

He was less accustomed to the spark of resentment he saw in the woman's face, or the momentary, snarling curl of her lip when her eyes flickered to the piles of coins and promissory notes on the table.

Less accustomed, but becoming more so. And disturbed by it, in the expressions of good Rhuinish folk.

The faces of the woman and her offspring were pinched, their limbs gaunt beneath threadbare clothes. Sarheic remembered them being plump, the youngest child as a fat baby rolling on the floor only a year ago. The baker had the bruised eyes and creased brow of one who slept too little and worried too much. That, too, disturbed Sarheic.

He cleared his throat. "I used to like the little cakes you would make. I am disappointed that you stopped."

The baker froze.

Silence, for a moment, then the wife answered, spitting words, "Can't afford the quality of flour to make them with anymore."

Sarheic turned his gaze back to her and watched the rest of it die, unspoken, on her tongue. *Snake*, she had been about to call him, used as an insult, and perhaps another epithet or two to go with it.

Her husband hissed at her. He bobbed his head to Sarheic. "Beg pardon."

Sarheic raised a hand briefly to dismiss the apology. He could forgive the woman her ignorance. The snake remained somnolent, curled in the pit of his belly.

He probed again, more directly. "Your children's clothes have holes."

Once again, it was the wife who answered, "Only so many times you can darn worn-out cloth." Her tone was less sharp this time, wariness taking the place of venom.

"Hard to afford new," said the baker, apologetically.

"Business is poor?"

The man licked his lips. He threw a look at his wife and flinched from her scowl. He swallowed. "Business is as good as ever, truth be told."

"But . . . " He knew the answer already but had a need, that he could not adequately explain to himself, to hear someone else say it.

Again, the man glanced at his wife and again he flinched. "Taxes are higher than they were."

"Too high," snapped the wife. "When they don't leave a man enough to feed and clothe his own."

*Too high*, Sarheic added silently, *when so much of it goes now into Ornomagnen coffers and too little remains for the strength and wealth of Rhuin.* He was aware of his fists clenching, his heart beating a little faster while he re-examined the notion that had planted itself in the fore of his thoughts over the past few days. The baker and his family all seemed to hold their breaths. Sarheic inhaled through his nose, taking in the smells of warm bread and woodsmoke and the baker's anxious sweating.

The snake was alert now, deep down, but he didn't need it for this.

He exhaled slowly and unclenched his fists. "Perhaps," he said, "you have miscounted."

"I . . . " the baker began.

Sarheic leaned over the table, resting his weight on his hands and staring at the baker until the man met his gaze and held it.

"You would have fought in the war," he said. There was only one war that needed no name, the *victorious* war, when the Rhuinish host had ravaged their way across Ornomagne a generation before, sacking cities and crushing every army sent against them.

The baker blinked. He shook his head. "I didn't. Got one leg shorter than the other. Army wouldn't take me."

Sarheic straightened, hiding his disappointment. "You should check your books. I will return tomorrow."

The baker stammered incoherently for a moment, before managing a strangled, "Yes, sir. Thank you, sir."

With a nod to the dumbfounded wife, Sarheic took his leave.

*A right decision*, he thought, pausing outside. It felt good, but where did it leave him? A tax collector who encouraged good folk to cheat their taxes? To cheat an *Ornomagnen* overlord, though, and keep Rhuinish wealth in Rhuin.

Someone bumped into his back, hard.

"Watch where you're standing, fool."

Rough fingers caught his arm. Sarheic allowed himself to be turned, even as the snake rose up inside.

His assailant took a step back before striking what he evidently imagined was an aggressive posture. Sarheic looked him up and down, aware of the snake looking out through his eyes. The boy was Rhuinish, but wearing a wide Ornomagnen cavalier's hat and roll-topped boots. The rest of his attire was similarly Ornomagnen frippery and he wore a narrow duellist's sword at his hip, but no pistol.

"Got something to say to me, Snake?" the boy said, resting his hand on the pommel of his sword.

*A bluff, rather than a genuine threat*, Sarheic thought. *His rodent face will be matched by a mouse's heart*, added the snake.

"Apologise," the boy demanded.

*Unlikely, you mannerless turd*, from the snake. Sarheic could feel its anticipation, its eagerness for him to turn it loose.

The boy's friends jeered. Sons of minor nobles or well-to-do merchants, Sarheic surmised, with fathers in possession of both Ornomagnen connections and clever accountants. *Soft-handed, soft-headed tadpoles.*

Sarheic considered. There were four of them, and he was presently unarmed. *Easily rectified*, the snake pointed out. But to kill or seriously wound them—even under provocation—would certainly cost him his job. He hadn't yet decided for certain that he no longer wanted it, having kept it his whole adult life, save for the interlude of the war.

He decided to forgive their ignorance. The snake subsided, disappointed. Like the baker and his wife, they knew him only as Sarheic the tax collector. His nickname had stayed with him but they did not remember how he came to have it.

*Remind them*, hissed the snake, hopefully.

*Hush,* he told it.

He remained silent, with his hands by his sides.

He saw the boy's Adam's apple bob, his confidence faltering in the face of Sarheic's impassiveness. An Ornomagnen youth would have drawn his weapon, taking it for further insult, but these children were only play-acting.

"Bah!" said one of the others. "Leave him. He's not worth the trouble. Old fool's not even carrying a sword."

The first boy sneered. "Go crawl back under your rock, Snake."

He hawked and spat at Sarheic's feet.

"Coward," added one of his friends.

Crowing triumphantly, they swaggered on their way. Sarheic looked down at the gob of phlegm on his boot, briefly reconsidering his forbearing attitude.

*Yes!* cried the snake. *The thrice inbred little smears of infected snot!*

It took some effort to subdue it, this time.

*Ornomagnen poison,* he thought, continuing on to his next appointment. Sooner or later one of those boys *would* draw steel and would kill or be killed over something equally as petty as a bump in the street. His eyes followed a trio of genuine Ornomagnen cavaliers as they went striding past, swords at their hips and pistols across their chests, watched honest Rhuinish folk scurry out of their way. *They* were the sort who would kill over a wrong look— *had* done, no doubt. Who would slaughter those Rhuinish boys for trying to emulate them.

Barely two years had passed since the Whelp who sat on the throne at Neic-ap-Nagh had sold away the land and pride of his people to the son of the very king his father had humiliated only a generation before. Sold, for the price of a minor Ornomagnen princess and to give his heirs a secondary claim to a foreign throne. Sold, all that every Lord of Rhuin before him and every able Rhuinishman had fought to preserve with blood and iron and every ounce of will they had. Sarheic found his fists clenching again.

The snake lurked in the depths, wide-awake still.

He watched a pair of young women totter along the street, faces pale from lack of air, barely able to breathe in their ridiculous corsets, necks corded with the strain of holding upright their enormous, piled wigs. A copper golem followed a mercer in the opposite direction, its arms loaded with bolts of cloth. Sarheic's gaze alighted on a beggar squatting at the side of the street. What dignity was there left for simple working folk when merchants could purchase alchemical slaves—powered by *Ornomagnen* magic—instead?

Barely two years, and all the absurdities of Ornomagnen dress and manners and their golems and their imbecilic honour code were seeping into the blood of Rhuin like poison. What honour was there in threatening an unarmed man? What absurdity was it that compelled men to duel to the death over the most trivial and imaginary slights?

But what was there to do about it? *I know*, volunteered the snake. What, when the lords of Rhuin had quickly realised the Whelp's treachery could enrich them, as well?

Although, Sarheic thought, not all the lords were happy, if rumour were to be believed. His eyes turned to the dark-walled keep that cast its afternoon shadow across the city streets. If rumour were to be believed, then Lord Tibuir was most displeased that Rhuin was now a mere fief of Ornomagne.

If.

Sarheic wondered. Old Tibuir was nothing if not a politician—a thief among thieves. It could well be that Lord Tibuir was himself the origin of the rumour, while at the same time he happily pocketed his share of proceeds from Ornomagne's ever more blatant robbery of his countrymen.

The robbery in which, Sarheic noted sourly, he was himself complicit.

❖

"I cannot pay," wailed the man, middle-aged and soft without being plump. "The taxes are too high and we are too poor."

Tears streamed down his cheeks. Sarheic looked past him through the door of the apartment. It was high enough, at the top of a four-storey block, for its windows to catch the afternoon sun. A very old woman dozed in an armchair positioned to catch the best of it. She coughed, but did not appear to wake.

"My mother is very sick," the man said, following his gaze. "I can barely work because I have to take care of her. There is barely enough money for food. The taxes are too high."

Sarheic felt a knowing calm descend over him, knowing now what to say in response. Six more times that day, he had repeated the offer he had made to the baker. Six more times, it had been greeted with the same wondrous disbelief as the baker and his wife had shown. Only twice had he withheld the offer, once for a fat moneylender and the other for an Ornomagnen alchemist.

He looked at the soft man until he stopped speaking, "Perhaps you have miscalculated."

The man slapped his hands to the sides of his face. "No, no, no," he moaned. "It is all correct, the taxes are just too high. There will be too little left for food, too little for my mother's medicine."

Sarheic blinked at the unexpected response. Was the man an imbecile? He leaned forward, bringing his face closer to the distressed fellow's and waiting until the man met his gaze and held it. "Perhaps you have miscalculated."

Faintly, the other shook his head. "No." His lip trembled. "The taxes are just too high."

Sarheic bit down on an exasperated retort. The snake was with him immediately. *Have you brains or a smashed ham stuffed into your skull, you miserable oaf?*

Sarheic drew back, perplexed, holding the snake in check, and considered while the fellow stood quivering with emotion. He could hardly tell the man outright to cheat on his taxes, but what was he to do if the fellow was too dense to bridge the gap himself? At a loss, he said, "I will return tomorrow. Think on what I have said, and tomorrow we shall see what is to be done."

"Tomorrow will make no difference . . . "

"*Tomorrow*," Sarheic said, and the snake had more than half control of his voice.

The fellow flinched as if struck. Then he nodded, his head bowed, seeming to deflate as he did so.

Sarheic descended the stairs slowly, deep in thought.

He had to collect *something* from this quivering blancmange with his sick mother. But could he, in good conscience? But then what if he did not? If not him, then some other collector, some collaborator or—worse—some *Ornomagnen*, would come instead and demand the full amount. Perhaps a night's sleep would allow the fellow to think more clearly.

"Snake," he heard a woman's voice mutter as he stepped out into the flow of pedestrian traffic on the street. He turned to see as he started walking, but could not identify the speaker. Several people returned his gaze with the same resentment he had seen in the baker's wife.

Sarheic met their stares mildly, allowing the snake to see with him, and forgave them their ignorance.

He could have come home hailed a hero. Sarheic the Snake, who had bested every champion the Ornomagnen had sent against him—all bar one. But how many men could say that they had duelled the Ebony Man and lived? And he *did* defeat the Sycamore Man. Who else alive could say that they had beaten one of the Solitary Men?

But he hadn't the temperament to be a hero, and so Sarheic the Snake had become Sarheic the tax collector once more.

He smirked to himself. *Sarheic the Snake, hero of Rhuin.*

※

That evening, as the last of the sunset lingered on the horizon and the tea houses along the street were filled with conversation, Sarheic climbed up from the balcony of his modest apartment and sat on the roof of the building to watch the stars.

*A good day's work*, he thought. *A just day's work.* Tomorrow held a pleasant anticipation. But his thoughts kept returning, disturbed, to the soft man with the sick mother, a fly in the ointment of his good mood.

Shouts disrupted the hum of voices below. Sarheic peered over the edge of the tiles. Soldiers pushed between the chairs of the teahouses. Rhuinish soldiers, in the uniforms of Lord Tibuir. Their faces were turned upwards as they jostled the teahouse patrons. One briefly aimed his musket, provoking cries of consternation from the people around him. Sarheic followed the gun's aim to the rooftop opposite.

A man-shape danced along the peak of the roof and sprang lightly across the gap to the next building. Man-*shaped*, but barely the size of a cat. The snake observed with a predator's hungry interest as the figure slid across the steeper tiles of the next roof, passing through the spill of light from a garret window. It was a porcelain doll, Sarheic saw, raffishly dressed.

He watched it scamper away into the night, the noise of its pursuers receding after it.

*A golem*, he thought. *Ornomagnen*, said the snake.

He turned to look in the direction from which the doll and its pursuers had come. The black silhouette of Lord Tibuir's keep, dotted with lamp-lit windows, loomed against the night sky.

※

There was a new rumour about on the streets the next morning. An Ornomagnen spy, a golem disguised as a child's toy, had been discovered in the private suites of Lord Tibuir's family but had escaped. Tibuir's Hound had left the city in pursuit during the night.

Sarheic listened with half an ear while he walked along, biting into the little cake the baker's wife had given him. Perhaps the earlier rumours were true, he thought, and Lord Tibuir had indeed been plotting rebellion. What would happen now, he wondered?

He slowed when he neared the address of the soft man and his sick mother. A crowd was gathered in front of the tenement building, city watchmen with quarterstaffs holding them back. With a sinking feeling in his gut, Sarheic pushed his way through to the front.

The bodies still lay where they had landed, on their sides, the son embracing his mother. Sarheic looked up at the balcony four storeys above. His vision went red. The snake took over the beat of his heart, filled the space behind his eyes, filled his muscles, his ears.

"Damn you," it hissed with his mouth. "Damn you, you pox-addled cretin. You *dunce*. You grub, you . . . you *centipede*."

*Why didn't you listen?* Sarheic wailed, inside.

A sergeant of the watch had noticed him and sauntered over. "You have an interest here, tax collector?"

The snake stared at him.

"Man left a letter," the sergeant continued, jaw jutting with resentment. "Said he couldn't pay his taxes and still care for his mother."

Sarheic wrested enough control back from the snake to say, "I was here yesterday. I . . . " He stopped, suddenly uncertain of what he had been about to say. That he had offered the dead man the chance to cheat his taxes? To keep enough back for food and his mother's medicine?

Something struck him in the back. The snake whirled him about in time to slap aside another thrown horse turd.

"Snake!"

"Ornomagnen stooge!"

A man stepped out from the crowd, burly and half a head taller than Sarheic, dressed in the sleeveless tabard of a porter that showed-off his tattooed biceps. He thrust out a meaty hand to push Sarheic in the chest. It was too much.

He let the snake have its way.

The snake caught the porter's fingers and twisted, then brought the heel of his other hand up under the big man's elbow. The joint snapped with an audible pop. The porter screamed. The snake hissed.

"*Stooge*, am I?" it bellowed. "Stooges, all of you! Curs! Lap dogs! Sitting open-mouthed beneath Ornomangen arseholes to lick up their shit and swallow it as it falls." Spittle sprayed from Sarheic's lips, but the snake had him and he didn't care. "*Rhuinishmen* lived here, once. Not curs. Not sheep. Not *rabbits*, to be kicked and fleeced and skinned and butchered for meat!"

The crowd fell back as the snake stepped forward, propelling its jibbering captive by his broken arm. A watchman barred his path with his quarterstaff. The snake took it from him, one handed. Sarheic remembered just in time that the man before him was Rhuinish, and an honest servant of the city to boot, and the snake only dented the idiot's pot helm rather than braining him.

The faces around Sarheic were suddenly wide-eyed with fear. Only now did it occur to them *why* he was the only tax collector in the city who went about his business alone and unarmed.

The sergeant said something but the snake wasn't hearing words and so Sarheic could not either. The crowd parted, jostling each other aside for him to make his way through.

"Spit on you, I say!" And the snake did, catching a woman on the front of her blouse. "Spit on you. And should you dislike it, then look behind your sheep's fleeces and your rabbits' tails and your dogs' lapping tongues and find your Rhuinish hearts."

It kicked its prisoner in the back of the knee and let him fall.

There was a breathless quiet as Sarheic strode away, broken by the whimpering of the porter over his broken arm.

Two heartbeats.

Three.

Four.

Then a shout, as the mob discovered easier targets within its own number. Young fools dressed up as Ornomagnen, perhaps. A roar followed, punctuated by screams, then a pistol shot. Sarheic didn't look back, could barely see ahead past the haze of red that clouded his vision.

❖

He went first to the baker's, threw the purse with startled man's taxes onto the shop counter and told him to hide it. Then he went home and climbed onto the roof of his building and let the snake boil and rage through him while the rioting raged below.

❖

The Ornomagnen quarter burned that night.

By morning, both the riot and the flames had guttered. Sarheic was just Sarheic again. The snake had run its fury out and was coiled once more in the shadows of his belly. A pensive stillness settled over the city. Lord Tibuir's troops were out in force, patrolling alongside the city watch, but no word came from the keep.

Sarheic climbed down to his apartment, ate and drank and used the chamber pot, then he went back up onto the roof again, and brooded.

Life filtered back onto the streets over the next few days, but not normality. Sarheic came down to the teahouses and listened to the few voices at the tables around him, and the new rumours their words carried. Lord Tibuir was going to stand and fight, and all the lords of Rhuin alongside him. The other Rhuinish lords were against him, and Tibuir had already fled. Tibuir was dead. Tibuir was alive. Tibuir's Hound had pursued the golem spy into Ornomagne.

This last caught Sarheic's attention and he followed that thread. The golem had help, the rumours said. An Ornomagnen magician. A Rhuinish traitor. The golem was really the Ebony Man in disguise—that one Sarheic dismissed as fantasy, for how could such a detail possibly be known to rumourmongers?

Discontented, he got up to walk. The rumours swirled around him as he went. The golem had slipped the grasp of Tibuir's Hound. Ornomagnen reprisal was inevitable, Tibuir's city would be sacked. Sarheic's wandering brought him across lines of people with children and belongings loaded onto carts and barrows and bullocks and their own backs, waiting to pass through the city gate. Others were boarding up windows and doors. Sarheic saw men standing guard with old blunderbusses and halberds and even hunting bows. Near the Ornomagnen quarter, he walked over the broken shards of smashed clay golems, stepped around the twisted wrecks of their copper brethren. The snake took it in with silent satisfaction.

He found his own name following him among the rumours, as men who'd fought in the war dredged up memories they thought they'd forgotten. Sarheic the Snake had started the riots, the rumourmongers said, and driven the Ornomagnen from the city. Sarheic the Snake, who beat the Sycamore Man, who had slaughtered half the sons of the Ornomagnen nobility in the war, until they sent out the Ebony Man as their champion.

At the city wall, he found press-ganged workers under guard of Lord Tibuir's troops, building scaffolds and cranes to mount cannon on the battlements. The walls, dating from an era before artillery, would not last long under bombardment of Ornomagnen guns. The soldiers looked Sarheic over but left him unmolested.

More rumours drifted into the city. Tibuir's Hound had failed in her pursuit of the spy, and fallen. Ornomagne had despatched an army to put down Lord Tibuir.

The other Rhuinish lords intended to stand aside.

The city gates were closed. Sarheic retreated to the teahouses and sat among the few old men still there, then to his balcony when the pressgangs started hunting for men to stand the walls. Others came from Lord Tibuir's court, dressed in courtiers' finery and escorted by horseguards. Sarheic ignored their hammering on his door and climbed up onto his rooftop.

Later, he listened to some soldiers talking while they loitered among the empty tables below, their voices overloud in the stillness. A golem—an Alabaster Man—had been caught at Neic-ap-Nagh and destroyed. An Ornomagnen assassin, sent to kill the Whelp who sat on the throne of the Lords of Rhuin.

Sarheic climbed up to his rooftop to think. An Alabaster Man. All the Solitary Men he had ever heard of, the one-of-a-kind golems who could outfight and outrun and outthink a man, were made of wood. He ran through them in his mind. The Sycamore Man, who he had himself defeated and destroyed. The Ebony Man, most famous of them all—

*We would win, the next time*, grumbled the snake.

Sarheic ignored it and continued his train of thought. The exploits of the Hickory Man were also well renowned. He recalled hearing of an Aspen Man getting dismembered and burned during the war. Ironwood, Oak, Cedar, Willow . . . He thought that the Ornomagnen had made new Sycamore and Aspen Men . . .

*Alabaster?*

Sarheic looked towards the keep where Lord Tibuir was ensconced, and wondered.

※

The Ornomagnen army arrived by river.

Sarheic stood up on the peak of his roof and watched them disembark in the distance across the fields. Sailing ships and steam barges lined the waterway. The troops flowed ashore like a multicoloured tide. There were a *lot* of troops. He caught flashes of sunlight on domed metal that could only be the brass carapaces of war golems. Cavalry raced out in both directions to encircle the city.

The Lord of Rhuin would be coming to their aid, Sarheic heard among those others who had climbed up to see. The Whelp, incensed by the attempt on his life, would march from Neic-ap-Nagh and the other Rhuinish lords would flock to his banner.

*Wishful thinking,* Sarheic thought. Even if it were true, they would surely come too late.

The snake bestirred itself, *Unless . . .*

A slow smile spread across Sarheic's face. What did it matter if help came in time, or late, or not at all?

He knew this game.

He pulled off his shirt and dropped it on the tiles. The breeze raised gooseflesh on his bare skin.

He looked around and spied a man with a glass to his eye nearby.

"May I have the use of your telescope?"

The fellow looked at him, lips apart and tongue touching the roof of his mouth to say "no". His eyes widened as he took in the serpentine tattoos coiled around Sarheic's upper arms and across his chest. He thrust the glass into Sarheic's hand.

Sarheic raised it to his eye and scanned the assembling army. Sure enough, there were the officers with their plumes and capes and embroidered jackets—astride their horses at the front, as honour dictated. He handed back the glass.

"Thank you."

He went down to his rooms and rummaged under the bed until his fingers found the hard shapes of his pistol case and his sword. He dropped the sword, wrapped in a tattered yellow duellist's flag, onto the bed while he primed and loaded the pistol. Then he thrust the pistol into the back of his belt and picked up the sword. He shook it free of the flag, then held the scabbarded weapon out at arm's length, letting his right hand remember the weight and feel of it. He let the snake uncoil inside, controlled, filling his belly and his chest, heating his muscles with the anger that he had nursed at a simmer over the days since the suicide of the soft man and his sick mother. He felt the heat rise up his face.

Sarheic the Snake drew the sword.

❉

"Open the gates!" he bellowed. "I have business on the other side."

The officer in charge, a boy with more pimples than whiskers, swallowed nervously. He tore his eyes from the bared blade and duellist's flag, but they fixed instead on Sarheic's tattoos and he stammered as he said, "The gates are closed. All citizens are to remain in the homes unless required to . . . "

His eyes finally found Sarheic's and he trailed off.

"I have business outside," said the snake.

The boy started to protest again, but with a screech the gates began to open. He whirled, shrieking at his men up in the gatehouse. Sarheic strode past and out through the widening gap.

The boy's impotent shouts trailed after him as he marched down the road towards the Ornomagnen army. Where the road veered aside, he struck out directly across the crop fields and garden plots that bordered the city. His boots sank into the tilled soil.

*Rhuinish soil,* the snake reminded him, stoking his rage. *An enemy army stands on Rhuinish soil.*

The Ornomagnen had advanced to the range of their artillery, which had been wheeled to the fore of the assembled regiments. The army's generals would be at the rear. Drawing closer, he saw a company of flanking cavalry point him out and held up his duellist's flag for them to see. Their officer raised a hand to stay his men. Sarheic turned his attention back to the artillery in front of him. After a moment, a rider broke from the cavalry company and disappeared around the side of the assembled infantry.

The snake drew Sarheic's mouth into a smile. The rigid discipline of the Ornomagnen was their greatest weakness. It was a rare officer who would show initiative if it took him beyond the scope of his orders.

Sarheic spied an artillery officer riding along behind the line of guns. He adjusted his course to intercept the horseman. A short distance in front of the guns, he paused to thrust his sword point down into the earth, and continued on with only the flag in his hand. The artillery crews watched him warily, throwing uncertain glances at their officer.

He let the snake have his voice.

"You there!" it cried, in Ornomagnen. "You maggot-infested afterbirth! I see from your seat that you have never ridden so much as a pig before today, and I see from your face that your mother was ridden by a pig as other women are ridden by their husbands."

With that, Sarheic turned his back, exacerbating the ridicule of the snake's words tenfold, and marched back to his sword. He tossed the yellow flag on the ground at his feet. The artillery officer hadn't moved. His face was grey, his expression aghast. His men had all stopped their work to stare at him. Slowly, he turned his head to look back at the mounted infantry officers arrayed in front of their troops. To a man, they sat in stony silence. The artillery officer faced Sarheic again, then very slowly dismounted.

He handed his cape and hat to one of his men, fumbling for a few moments at the cape's toggles. Very slowly, he walked out to where Sarheic waited. The man's fingers shook as he rested his hand on the pommel of his sword.

"Apologise," he said, then as an afterthought, "You Rhuinish dog."

The snake smiled and lifted Sarheic's sword. "Squeal for me, piglet."

With a cry of outrage, the Ornomagnen drew his sword and took up his guard. His stance was abominable, feet too wide apart and his balance off. Sarheic could have pushed him over with a poke in the chest.

He waited for the Ornomagnen to attack.

The man didn't move. The snake lowered his sword, still smiling. Sweat sprang out on the Ornomagnen's brow. The snake let Sarheic's smile grow wider. "Are you a man, or a hamster?"

At last, the Ornomagnen could stand it no more. With a yell, he lunged.

The snake deflected the attack and danced backwards. The Ornomagnen pursued, hacking in wild terror. The snake continued to retreat, making it appear as though Sarheic was only barely defending himself. The Ornomagnen pressed desperately.

The snake drew the fight out, always retreating, never attacking, until exhaustion began to make Sarheic's opponent too obviously clumsy. Then, trying to make it look more happy accident than skill, it batted the other man's sword up out of the way and ran him through the guts.

The Ornomagnen's eyes bulged, his face purpling. He let out a mewl as Sarheic withdrew his blade, and collapsed in a ball around his wound.

Sarheic walked away a few paces, to plant his sword in the dirt once again and scoop up his flag, an invitation to the artillerymen to come and collect their vanquished leader. After a short pause, a group of them scurried out and pick up the groaning officer.

The snake strode after them, back towards their lines. The unarmed Ornomagnen gunners seemed transfixed as it marched between the cannons. It stopped, posing Sarheic with hands on hips, and surveyed the Ornomagnen army.

A large group of officers on horseback trotted into view around the flank of the army, their ranks signified by elaborateness of their brocades and the enormity of their feathered hats. One wore the patterned cloaks of an Ornomagnen magician.

*Ah, the generals*, the snake whispered to Sarheic. *Too late, alas.*

It pointed suddenly to an infantry officer nearer at hand, in front of a squad of ape-like brass war golems. The fellow jumped in his saddle.

"My son!" the snake cried. "You must be my son, for you have my noble Rhuinish features. I think I remember your mother, and her drooling slug of a husband." It spread Sarheic's arms wide. "How pleased I am to have given her an even finer gift than one night of joy with a real man between her buttocks. Although quite how you were born, I am uncertain, since up her arse is the only way I took her."

Once again, Sarheic strode away.

With his superiors watching, this one rode after Sarheic, cursing and spewing threats. The snake kept his back to the fellow until Sarheic reached his sword. It turned him, letting the man hear it laugh as it dropped the flag. There was no easier way to provoke an Ornomagnen than to insult his womenfolk.

The infantry officer leapt from his horse and half-ran to confront him. He had his sword drawn and pointed before he cried, "Apologise!"

The snake bared Sarheic's teeth and replied in Rhuinish, "Not on your life, you syphilitic goat molester."

The man knew enough of the language to know that he was being insulted again. With a wordless bellow, he attacked.

This one was a better swordsman, but not good enough. The snake toyed with him, slicing him over and again until in futile rage the Ornomagnen overextended himself. The snake drove him to his knees, stepped back and lopped off the fellow's head. There was silence from the Ornomagnen lines.

Breathing heavier this time, Sarheic planted his sword in the ground.

Turning, he saw that the game was up. An infantry squad had been brought forward of the cannons. The senior Ornomagnen general had ridden with them, his magician alongside.

"Will you shoot me down, then, like the Rhuinish cur I am?" the snake demanded, waving the duellist's flag. "Or will your spook melt my bones where I stand?"

"I remember you, Snake," said the general. "You were at Pierrendeaux."

*Or perhaps not quite up yet*, the snake purred.

"We *sacked* Pierrendeaux," it replied.

"My wife and daughters died there," the Ornomagnen replied.

*No indeed*, the snake hissed, *not quite yet*. It chuckled, and Sarheic laughed with it. "Ah, yes," it said. "I could not tell your daughters from your dogs, so I had them all before I killed them."

The general's hand went to his sword, but he stayed himself.

"Will you have your lackeys shoot me then, old man?" said the snake, although the general was plainly little older than himself. "Have you flea-hearted, nasty little flecks of lint no champion among you who dares to face me?"

Surprisingly, the general laughed. "As a matter of fact," he said, "we do."

He glanced at the magician, who smiled nastily and turned to beckon behind him. A figure came forward, man-shaped and man-sized and dressed in bright Ornomagnen livery, but sculpted in wood. Sarheic felt a little thrill from the snake that he thought might've been fear. The golem moved as smoothly as a man and carried a sword in its left hand. The Solitary Men, the hardwood golems, were all left-handed. Its eyes were faceted blue jewels.

"I know you, Sarheic the Snake," it said.

Sarheic tossed down the duellist's flag and took up his own blade. "I would know your name, golem, before we fight."

The golem replied in Rhuinish, its wooden lips barely moving with the words, "I am the Oak Man."

They circled, swords held on guard. The golem's feet sank more deeply into the earth than his own, Sarheic saw. *It's heavy*, he thought. *That'll make it slow*, replied the snake.

*We brought a hammer with us, for the Sycamore Man*, Sarheic reminded it.

"I ended the Sycamore Man," the snake said. "I fought the Ebony Man and lived to tell the tale."

"The Ebony Man defeated you," said the golem.

"Yet here I am," said the snake. "Are you as good as he? Or are you a clumsy oaf like the Sycamore Man?"

The golem attacked. Its swordplay was a blur of feints and strikes but, as the snake had predicted, it was ponderous on the heavy ground. The snake retreated easily.

Sarheic had given a great deal of thought, during the war, to how he might best defeat one of the Solitary Men. There was little point striking its torso or limbs, except perhaps at the smaller joints. To do so would only blunt his sword. The pistol in the back of his belt was useless against it and there was no question of him wearing it down.

The head was the only part of it that was not solid timber, housing as it did the golem's animating spells. When he had fought the Sycamore Man, he had battered its head apart with a long-handled mallet, while he duelled it with his sword in his other hand. He had tried the same approach to the Ebony Man. It hadn't worked because the Ebony Man was simply too good.

*Should have kept the hammer*, Sarheic thought. *Should have thought of it today.*

*Then we must be daring*, the snake replied.

The golem attacked again, and this time the snake stood its ground and fenced for a few blows before again retreating.

"You are better than the Sycamore Man," said the snake. "But not the best of your kind." *Not as good as us.* It was the timber that made the difference. The magic stuck better to some woods than others and there could only ever be one of each at a time.

The Oak Man didn't reply, but feinted a couple of times, driving Sarheic back. Its gemstone eyes and lack of visible muscles made anticipating its attacks difficult, but this was compensated for by its slowness on the heavy ground.

*The head*, said the snake. *A sword will do the task as well as a hammer.*

It was right, but the golem knew that as well as Sarheic, and this time he didn't have a second weapon to counter the its attacks. *Daring*, the snake reminded him. *It is only almost as good a swordsman as us.*

It attacked, circling, forcing the golem to turn awkwardly to defend itself. The snake found an opening and hacked at its head, leaving a deep groove above its jawline, at the cost of a slash across Sarheic's shoulder.

He retreated but, when the golem pursued, the snake attacked again.

Once again it created an opening in the Oak Man's guard, catching its head a glancing blow just above the scar of the first. Again Sarheic came away with an injury of his own, this time a shallow cut to his ribs beneath his sword arm.

Twice more, they came together with similar results. Hairline cracks radiated from the gouge that the snake was chopping in the side of the golem's head. But Sarheic was bleeding heavily. He would begin to weaken sooner rather than later.

The Oak Man attacked with a flurry of overhand blows. The snake defended, making it turn again. It switched its point of attack and the snake closed in, leaping sideways to avoid its sudden lunge. It didn't quite. The golem's swordpoint pierced Sarheic's flank instead of skewering him through the guts. Sarheic felt the point come out of his back. The snake caught the golem's wrist, trapping its blade, and hacked furiously at its damaged head. The golem staggered and grabbed for Sarheic's sword with its right hand, fingers jerking spastically.

It twisted its sword and wrenched it out sideways. Sarheic cried out in pain and staggered away. He pressed his left hand to his side, trying to hold the wound closed. His guard wavered, then dropped, and he had to lean on his sword to stay upright.

The whole left side of the Oak Man's head was smashed in, crazed with dents and cracks. Its left eye was out. It swayed, and for a moment Sarheic thought it might actually fall. But then it raised its sword again.

Painfully, Sarheic straightened as well as he could and lifted his guard. He steeled himself as the Oak Man advanced.

It struck. The snake rode the attack, then transferred Sarheic's sword to his left hand and whirled, exposing his back but banking on the golem being slow to adapt when surprised.

It was.

The snake's blow landed. The Oak Man's head came apart. The brassbound scroll that animated it tumbled out, bouncing off its shoulder and landing on the grass.

The golem teetered, off balance, then toppled like a felled tree.

Gasping, Sarheic managed somehow to stay on his feet. He

stabbed his sword into the ground and leaned on it as the fury of the snake drained out of him. He turned to face the Ornomagnen host.

He was surprised to find they were no longer watching.

The general had his sword out, waving it about while he bellowed orders. Around him, the artillery crews heaved frantically to drag their guns around. The infantry regiments were turning their formations, some of them already charging along the riverbank. Sarheic heard a distant popping, then a rising shriek—cannon fire! Gouts of earth and bits of men exploded among the Ornomagnen troops.

Warships sailed down the river towards the Ornomagnen transport fleet, smoke and flashes of fire spitting from their bow guns. Further upstream, troops poured ashore from steam barges.

So, Sarheic thought, the Whelp had come in time after all. The battle on the river was lost in clouds of smoke as the warships came alongside each other, the pop-pop-pop of their broadsides blending into a continuous crackle. Sarheic watched the Ornomagnen cavalry race to intercept the Rhuinish landing force.

No-one in the Ornomagnen army was paying any attention to the lone man at their backs.

*Now,* the snake urged. He began to move towards the Ornomagnen lines in a crippled sideways shuffle, holding his injured side. The general had held his post among the artillery while his command staff raced hither and thither. Sarheic pulled the pistol from his belt and cocked it, holding it close to his side. Still no-one paid attention to him.

He was a few paces from the general when the man turned. He started to spit an oath, wheeling his mount to put the horse between himself and the raised pistol. Sarheic fired.

The ball hit the general low in the chest. He grunted and slumped around the wound, coughing blood.

Sarheic ran.

Yelling in pain, clutching his side, he sprinted as fast as he could. Muskets cracked behind him. One shot struck him high on the shoulder blade, another in the back of the thigh, making him stumble. He recovered, snatched up his sword on the way past, and kept running.

A dark mass between him and the city resolved itself into a line of charging horsemen. Lord Tibuir's horseguards were at the centre, in their polished helms and breastplates. To either side, it seemed to Sarheic, Tibuir had got every man in the city ahorse who could sit a saddle. Sarheic saw men in infantry uniforms and the tabards of the city watch, others in plain clothes waving axes and cleavers instead of swords and spears.

He stopped. Seeing nowhere to go, he planted his sword. An officer of the horseguards signalled and the line split. Sarheic saw foam on the muzzles of the horses, the grimaces of their riders. The horses thundered past on either side, close enough to whip his hair.

There were infantry racing after the horsemen, a distance away yet. Painfully, Sarheic began to limp aside from their line of charge. He watched the cavalry crash into the Ornomagnen artillery, sweeping aside the gun crews and the few infantry who had rushed to protect them.

Slowly, leaning on the hilt of his sword to stop himself from falling, he sat down.

❉

The battle was still raging when Lord Tibuir found him at the improvised open-air surgery set up just outside the city gates. At the river, the remains of the Ornomagnen force was fighting a ferocious rearguard action while they evacuated to their surviving ships.

"Sarheic the Snake," Tibuir said, looking down at him with dark, hooded eyes. His words were slightly slurred and he carried his right arm tucked close against his side. The right side of his face was slack and smooth. "I remember you."

"And I you." Sarheic didn't attempt to rise from his cot. He saw the outrage on the faces of the lord's flunkeys, and decided to forgive them their ignorance. The snake, well sated, did not even register its disappointment.

"I heard that an Alabaster Man was destroyed," Sarheic went on, "attempting to assassinate the Whelp."

Tibuir's lips twitched at the use of the young Lord of Rhuin's nickname. "I heard the same."

"I have only ever heard of the Solitary Men being wooden," said Sarheic.

"I assume it must have been a new kind," said Tibuir. His expression and tone gave away nothing. His entourage were less successful in disguising their hostility and dismay.

Sarheic nodded. "I suppose it must have been."

"You beat another one today."

"Yes, an Oak Man. He was better than the Sycamore Man, but not as good as the Ebony Man."

Lord Tibuir chuckled. "You will never be a hero if you deprecate yourself so, my friend."

Sarheic allowed himself a smile. *Sarheic the Snake, hero of Rhuin.* "No," he agreed, "I will never be a hero."

"We have a need for heroes," said Tibuir, serious again.

Sarheic gestured at his bandages. "I think I am done with fighting, for now."

Tibuir's brows quirked. "Then what do you wish for instead?"

Sarheic had been thinking that over. "If your taxes are fair and just, and go to the strength of Rhuin, then I will collect them for you."

Lord Tibuir laughed aloud. He waved his good hand to encompass Sarheic's various injuries. "Then why this?" he asked. "Vanity?"

Sarheic shrugged, unsure himself. For Rhuin? Not entirely. For his own affronted sensibilities? Perhaps vanity *was* closer to the mark. "For a soft man," he said, eventually, "who would not listen, and his sick mother."

Tibuir regarded him for a moment, then snorted. "So be it, Sarheic the tax collector."

# COLD, COLD WAR

*Russia, 1921*

There was a tower at Petrovsk. A monstrous, broken-topped spike like the one the Allied forces had found at Astrakhan. Having to look up, even flying at two thousand feet, past the upper wing of his Avro biplane to see its top made Masaru dizzy. He groped for the small lump of the embroidered *omamori* amulet hanging from a cord around his neck. The other Avro, painted blue like his, followed as he banked into a wide downward loop, the Australian woman for once holding her proper station off his right wingtip.

Masaru peered past the struts and wires between his biplane's wings, trying to take the sight in. The tower's proportions were such that it upset the perceptions and seemed to distort the flat landscape around it. Its base was a madman's helter-skelter ziggurat, made of impossible stone blocks the size of townhouses, that cut a swathe across the city's snow-covered grid of tenement blocks and terraces between the Caspian shore and the abrupt incline of the escarpment to the west. From the ziggurat's peak, the ragged-toothed tower reached up to a dark stain of cloud fixed in the sky directly above.

Just like at Astrakhan.

Impossibly huge though it was, this tower was barely half the height of the one there. The realisation brought Masaru back to his proper senses. Why the difference?

He turned his attention to the city below. There was smoke coming from the ruined medieval fortress on the escarpment. There were more fires in the town itself. As at Astrakhan, stones from the tower lay scattered among the buildings, with ruin all about them as if they had fallen from its peak. The dome of the mosque, miniscule in the shadow of the impossible edifice, was cracked open like an egg.

Red Bolshevik flags flew above the fortress. As Masaru and Edie swung low overhead, smoke puffed from the mouths of artillery pieces along the wall. Dirt and snow burst amidst a swarm of figures labouring up the slope. A pair of tanks crawled alongside the troops. White banners bearing the two-headed Imperial Russian eagle identified the attacking force.

Masaru shook his head. Even with that tower in their midst, which made the rival Russian forces looked like ants warring in a man's shadow, and even with shape-changing monsters running loose in their country—*hordes* of them, like those the Allied forces had driven at such cost from Astrakhan—still the Reds and Whites would rather fight each other.

There were red Bolshevik and white Imperialist flags scattered too, among the roofs of the city's buildings. There were many more in different shades of blue, with the common populace aping the colour chosen by the Allies to declare their newfound neutrality in the war of Red and White. As the biplanes circled, bright blue banners unfurled from the twin minarets of the shattered mosque.

Masaru's loop took him away from the tower and the battle at the fortress towards the port and the Allied airfield. There was no sign of conflict on that side of the town. Indeed, both the port and the airfield seemed deserted. Masaru was disturbed to see that there were no vessels at the wharf, no planes parked at the airfield. He saw no movement near either. The queasiness returned to his stomach. Petrovsk airfield was base for two R.A.F. fighter squadrons and a large Allied garrison. Where were they?

For the umpteenth time since they had flown out of Astrakhan, he scanned the sea to the east, hoping to see the ships of the Allied fleet already on their way north from Baku, bringing reinforcements for the next big push, inland along the Volga. The water was clear of anything but patches of floating ice, all the way to the horizon. He could feel the bulge of the dispatch wallet inside his jacket, with the urgent demands from the field commanders at Astrakhan for those extra divisions. Edie carried an identical set of papers—the normal contingency. One plane, at least, usually got through.

He checked his rear left quarter, where her Avro was wobbling from side to side, out and back again, rather than holding a steady line at his wing. Masaru felt a surge of irritation. The woman flew like an undisciplined child kicking its heels. He still couldn't believe they had given him a *woman* for a wingman. And an uncouth, irreverent, barely-civilised Australian adventurer woman at that!

Abruptly, it occurred to him that she wasn't waggling her wings idly. He realised his fist was bunched, about to punch the cockpit wall. Masaru took a slow breath, then throttled back to let her come alongside.

She flew in close enough that he could see her shivering. Her scarf only covered her neck, and her cheeks were chapped raw, her lips a pale purple-blue.

She pointed down at the airfield, then raised both palms. Should they land? Masaru chewed his lip in indecision. His eyes were drawn back to the tower, as by a magnet. He did not want to land anywhere near that monstrosity.

Finally, Masaru nodded. They had no choice in the matter, regardless of his fears. Even with its added fuel tank where the trainee's forward cockpit normally was, the Avro's range was barely three hundred miles. Astrakhan to Petrovsk was over two-thirty, and it was another two hundred or so from Petrovsk to Baku. The dispatches had to get through to Baku.

It seemed a forlorn hope that the Allied garrison wouldn't have taken all the fuel stores with them when they abandoned their base. If they hadn't, it meant they must have left in haste, perhaps even under attack, and then who knew what might be lurking down there. Swearing softly to himself, he pushed the Avro's stick forward to begin his descent.

No-one emerged to meet them as Masaru taxied across to the airfield's fuel shed. Leaving the engine running, he lifted himself up to perch on the back lip of the cockpit and looked around. The maintenance hangar stood open, the shadows within cavernously empty. Beyond the hangar, the door of the dispatch office was propped open against the wall. Nothing moved inside.

There were footprints and tyre marks all over. The snow was thin enough that the matted, frozen grass underneath showed through in the tracks. A refuelling car was parked nearby.

His eyes were drawn once again, unwillingly, to the tower, and up higher to the dark stain of cloud above it. Never had he imagined that such things could exist in the world. It reached up higher than any structure built by man. Impossibly high. The ragged tops of both towers and the scattered stones at their feet made it appear that they had been broken off, somehow. But by what means had either of them been built at all? Where had the stones come from, and how?

And what was the link between these towers and the monsters— *Changelings*, as the Russian peasants called them—that had been emerging from Bolshevik territory for the past year?

Once again, his hand was drawn to the *omamori* at his chest. His sister had given him one for protection against injury the first time he went away to war as a young man. She had sent him a new one every year since. He had always kept his promise to wear them, but mainly as a reminder of her. The tower's baleful presence prompted him to wonder if he should write to ask her for an amulet to protect against supernatural harm, instead.

Edie's biplane taxied up beside his, the throttle cut and the propeller winding down. She was already out of the cockpit, hopping nimbly down onto the wing and hanging one-handed from a convenient strut, one foot swinging carelessly. Before the plane had stopped rolling, she jumped lightly down, her boots crunching on the snow.

Masaru ground his teeth in exasperation. *Circus pilot*, he thought. He had heard she had been a wing walker in an American flying show before she'd come to Russia. He reached down to close his Avro's throttle. His ears rang as the roar of the engine wound down.

"It's quiet," Edie said, sauntering over. "Where is everyone?" She took off her flying cap. Blonde curls spilled around her face, caught by the wind.

*Arrogant.* Like most Allied personnel, Masaru kept his own head shaved to avoid lice and the threat of typhus they carried. He said, "What use are you if you break your leg performing childish stunts? We have a mission."

Her face registered surprise, then she put her fists on her hips, ready to argue.

"We will not dally here," Masaru continued. He jumped down on the opposite side of his plane. "You stand guard."

He paused before walking over to the refuelling car and stooped to examine the tracks in the snow more closely. The uppermost prints were still crisp around the edges. Perhaps as recent as the day before. He stamped across to the refuelling car, trying to work some feeling back into his legs. The stillness of the buildings—

that should have been bustling with pilots and ground crew—was oppressive, the quiet broken only by the distant thud of artillery fire from the fort. Masaru undid the button of the holster at his hip, trying to ignore the nervous crawling sensation at the back of his neck.

The drum on the tray of the refuelling car sounded full when he knocked it and, for a miracle, the car's engine turned over on the third attempt. Masaru gave it a bare handful of seconds to warm, then drove over to park between the biplanes.

Edie had wandered off a short distance. She was at least treating the situation seriously enough to have her revolver in hand. But when Masaru turned around again after filling her Avro's tanks, she had her jacket off and overalls down around her calves, squatting bare-arsed in the snow to piss.

He averted his eyes quickly, his face heating. He cocked his fist at the fuel car door, stopped himself. Then, ever so carefully, he pressed his knuckles into the cold metal.

Small arms crackled somewhere in the city, not far away. Masaru drummed his fingers impatiently as the fuel poured into his auxiliary tank. Two fighter squadrons and a garrison of British and American infantry had been based here. Where had they gone?

Done at last, he drove the refuelling car clear of the planes and tramped back across the snow.

"Edie!" he called.

She looked his way, shrugging herself back into her jacket, and raised an arm to point. "There's someone over there, outside the fence."

"More reason for us to leave now," Masaru said, not bothering to hide his impatience.

"He's wearing flying clothes."

"What?" Masaru looked.

Sure enough, there was a lone figure outside the wire mesh of the airfield's perimeter fence, facing them. Even at a distance, it was clear he was dressed as a flyer—leather cap, high boots, wool-collared leather jacket over padded flying overalls.

There was something odd about the way the stranger stood, though—his shoulders hunched unnaturally, as if pulling too-long arms up into his jacket sleeves. His legs seemed strangely bent above his boots. Masaru squinted at the stranger's grinning face.

*"Changeling!"*

The monster sprang forward. Inhumanly long forelimbs thrust from its sleeves. It bounded, ape-fashion, towards the fence, cackling like a hyena.

Masaru scrabbled for his sidearm.

The Changeling leapt at the fence, bouncing off the top of the wire and landing with an explosion of powdered snow. It charged, mouth split open from ear-to-ear to show needle teeth and a lolling black tongue.

Edie raised her pistol two-handed and fired. The monster yelped, rolling. Masaru was amazed. A hit! Then it was up again, whooping and giggling, skittering side to side as it continued its charge. Edie fired again and missed. She held her ground, tracking its approach with her revolver.

Masaru dashed forward, raising his own weapon as the monster sprang. He shoved in front of Edie and fired into its chest. The impact of the bullet sounded like a hammer striking wood. The Changeling was flung squealing backwards. Masaru was aware of Edie swearing. The Changeling thrashed its limbs to right itself and leapt at him again. Masaru aimed his pistol, too slow. A cloven-hoofed forelimb knocked it aside. He threw up his arms to protect himself, and the monster sank its teeth into his hand.

For a moment they braced, arms and forelimbs locked. Masaru stared into its eyes, pinprick black pupils ringed by red and orange bands. Its breath on his face smelled of hot metal. There was nothing left of the man it might once have been. Edie stepped around him, put her pistol to the monster's temple and pulled the trigger.

The blast was deafening. The Changeling's head snapped to the side, and stayed there. Its eyes glazed, and it slithered limply to the ground.

Masaru's ears felt stuffed with cotton wool. He stared in horror at his lacerated hand. The Russian peasants had named them Changelings after the hideous fairy children of their folk tales. The Reds' Plague, the Whites called the affliction, the result of some germ or chemical cooked up in the Bolsheviks' vile scientific experiments. Contagious, virulent as rabies, they said.

Edie called something, but he couldn't make out the words. He cast about for his pistol, spied it in the snow a few yards away, and staggered over to scoop it up.

"Stop!" Edie cried as he began to lift the gun to his head. She smacked his wrist with the barrel of her pistol, sending shooting pain up his arm. His gun tumbled from his grasp once more.

He stared at her in shock. How could she think of stopping him?

"You won't become one of them," she said. "It's not contagious."

He raised his injured hand for her to see, then waved it at the dead Changeling. "That was a man once!" He saw himself turning into another leering monstrosity, shook his head violently. "I will not—"

"It was never a man!"

"Then where do they come from?" he demanded.

Her mouth opened, shut; answers started and discarded.

*The tower,* Masaru thought. From that mad tower. But how? And where had the towers come from? His gaze was drawn up to the immobile patch of darker cloud above it.

"I don't know," Edie said, at last. "But I've seen men bitten and they have not changed."

Masaru had, too—men injured in the bloodbath outside Astrakhan. Days later, still strapped to their hospital beds, they remained men, begging to be released from their bonds. But that didn't mean they wouldn't change. Who knew how long it took? Most soldiers who were bitten killed themselves or were shot by their comrades. He imagined his body corrupting, his mind falling into madness.

He lunged for his pistol. Edie kicked his knee, knocking his leg out from under him. Masaru went down with a yell. Edie scooped up the gun and backpedalled clear of him.

"Enough," she said.

"Then *you* do it," he spat, getting to his feet.

"Who's waiting for you?" she asked, abruptly.

He scowled at her, confused by the question.

"Who have you got at home?" she said. "A wife? Children?"

Affronted by her presumption, he drew himself up. "I have a sister. She has children."

"You provide for them?"

"Their father was a soldier," he said, stiffly. "He died in Manchuria."

"And what will happen to them if you shoot yourself?"

Masaru remained silent.

There was a rolling boom from the escarpment—another salvo of artillery fire.

Edie held up his gun. "Can I give this back to you, now?"

Sullenly, he nodded. She tossed it onto the snow in front of him.

"Stay out of my way next time. I don't need you to save me," she said. "Come on. There'll be more of them, and we're stuffed if they turn up in numbers before we get airborne."

❄

The wind at five thousand feet was burning cold. Masaru pulled his scarf up closer to his goggles. His legs were going stiff, his backside already numb from the cold and sitting in the cramped cockpit.

With a grimace, he forced the fingers of his injured hand to flex. Edie had doused the wound with gin from the bottle she kept in the cockpit of her plane, before binding it with a strip of cloth torn from Masaru's shirttail. It throbbed abominably, the fingers stiff with cold and swelling.

The injury to his pride from being saved by a woman—a *gaijin* woman—felt almost as painful as the injury to his hand.

The fingers of his good hand twitched towards his neck. He hesitated, then grabbed at his scarf and pulled it loose. He opened the collars of his jacket and flight suit to get at the cord around his neck. Holding the flying stick between his knees, he wrapped the cord around his injured hand and gripped the *omamori* in his palm, clenching his fingers painfully around the little embroidered parcel. Through the swelling and his fleece-lined glove he could not even feel the wooden tokens inside, written with the prayers his sister had bought for his wellbeing.

Was Edie right? Or was it just his own cowardice that had allowed her to convince him? The thought of becoming one of those . . . *demons* was just too much to bear. Why would the Changelings' affliction be known as the Reds' Plague, if it was not a contagion?

He pushed down his doubts.

Even if Edie was wrong, he told himself, he had time to complete the mission before the Plague took him.

Their flight ceiling had lowered even further, the clouds darkening overhead. Lightning flashed from time to time deep within, although the thunder was lost in the engine's roar. *Just an ordinary storm.* He hoped it wouldn't break before they reached Baku.

The peninsula should soon be in view, where stood the ancient Azeri capital, surrounded by its sprawling acres of oil wells, their pumpjacks nodding like a thousand iron birds dipping their beaks for water. Masaru squinted into the distance The clouds seemed to deepen and darken even further, funnelling closer to the ground. Lightning stabbed earthward. One *hell* of a storm, Masaru corrected himself.

There seemed to be a steep-sided silhouette, like a child's drawing of a mountain, rising up to meet the descending storm. Masaru felt a deeper chill than the frigid air. He tried vainly to peer harder, uncertain if it was a trick of the gloom. Was their heading too far west, flying into the foothills of the Caucasus rather than skirting their eastern fringe?

He started to turn in his seat, to signal to Edie, hanging too far back behind his left wing. Some fighter pilot's sense made him glance up. Gargoyle shapes plummeted towards them from the clouds like stooping hawks. Masaru saw red eyes and shark-toothed grins.

Instinct took over. He kicked at the rudder pedals and shoved the flying stick forward, banking and diving at once.

A Changeling flyer shot past, folded bat-wings rippling behind its back. Another whisked by, missing the Avro's fragile wood-and-canvas wingtip by barely a yard as Masaru kicked the other way. He held the turn, risking a flat spin and putting the biplane into a roll instead.

Then he was clear and looping around to find Edie. The Changelings were opening their wings like parachutes, some still above, some below, arresting their dives then flapping heavily as they began to manoeuvre. He spied Edie roaring towards them. The muzzles of her twin Lewis guns flashed. Changelings shuddered under the impact of the bullets. Masaru watched, expecting her to pull up, then cried out in dismay as she flew straight through the middle of the flock.

"Stupid *gaijin* . . . " He turned harder, bringing his own guns around to bear.

A Changeling dipped its wings and smashed into the side of Edie's Avro. The impact knocked her into a spin and sent the Changeling tumbling earthward. The rest of the flock charged after her as she fought to regain control of her plane.

Masaru opened fire, strafing the Changelings. He saw bits of them come apart like splintering wood where the bullets struck. A couple fell with shredded wings. One glanced off the centre of Edie's top wing as she righted herself.

Edie ducked and put her Avro's nose down, diving to gain speed and escape. So she had listened to *someone*, at least, Masaru thought. It was always the first lesson the veteran pilots tried to drum into the new recruits: "If you get into trouble, put your nose down and dive towards friendly lines." He stood his own plane on its tail and soared over the top of the flock, then came around and aimed himself after her.

They left the Changelings quickly behind, the creatures' straight-line wing speed no match for even an old Avro.

Daylight peeked under the clouds near the western horizon, lighting one side of the biplanes a pale gold. Masaru's heart was still thumping furiously in uncomfortable discord with the plane's vibration. Ahead, against the dark clouds of the storm, he could see clearly the mist of fine droplets that trailed from Edie's top wing, catching the light. The impact of the second Changeling had cracked her main fuel tank.

He shot her a glare, willing her to turn and see his anger, but she was staring fixedly ahead.

The protests of his injured hand demanded his attention. He had flown two-handed during the dogfight, not thinking. He pulled back his flying glove to find fresh blood seeping through the bandage. Somehow, he had dropped the *omamori*.

He twisted sideways, trying to spot it in the foot-well of the cockpit. Swearing, he held the stick between his calves and groped around blindly on the floor. The plane lurched sideways as he bumped the rudder pedals. *Flying like that bloody woman.* He couldn't feel a thing through his gloves. He swore again and thumped the inside of the fuselage.

Lightning flashed across the storm ahead, illuminating the tall silhouette within. Masaru had no doubt, now, what it was.

❖

"*Shinjirarenai*," he heard himself repeat, as they swooped in over the city of Baku. *Shinjirarenai*, over and over. *Unbelievable.* He understood, all of a sudden, these Westerners who exclaimed "My God!" when all other words failed them.

Gigantic stones swirled down out of the clouds, riding on a tornado wind at the centre of the city. Each came to rest with mad precision on the tower's ziggurat base, building the tower ever higher. Tinier objects tumbled among the gently falling stones. Changelings, in their thousands, falling slowly from the clouds.

Below, in the city, gunfire crackled in a vast, ragged circle around the base of the tower. Buildings and streets exploded from bombs or artillery fire.

A few stray raindrops pattered against Masaru's flying goggles. He wiped them clear. His course had brought him close enough to the tornado to see the faces of the Changelings riding the whirlwind down, and see that they were attired as peasants and labourers, soldiers and businessmen. He saw policemen and nurses and even a robed Orthodox priest.

Close up, strange ripples of light encased the spinning storm, like a film of oil on water—a skin, almost. A barrier.

Masaru looked up, through the centre of the storm. His mouth fell open in simple, stupid awe.

At the top of the tornado, there was a hole in the clouds and, through it, another tower—a mirror image of the one below. Its peak pointed downward, ever diminishing as its stones detached themselves to join the cyclonic dance. Changelings swarmed across the inverted ziggurat base and flung themselves into the whirlwind. Around it he glimpsed a land of cracked desolation, upside-down in the sky.

Something peppered the side of the tornado, leaving spots of brightness in its sheen. Lightning crazed outward from the spots. The tornado lost its shape where the lightning ran. Building stones crashed into each other. Changelings plummeted until they passed the unstable section and the whirlwind caught them again and slowed their fall once more.

Out towards the edge of the city, Masaru spotted the muzzle flashes of heavy artillery. Seconds later, more bright spots flared on the side of the tornado. It wobbled again.

He swooped down for a closer look, not checking to see whether Edie followed. A howitzer battery was arrayed at the edge of the city's large airfield. Masaru saw only Red banners as he passed low overhead, saw nothing but red flying anywhere. No sign of Allied blue, nor the Star-and-Stripes or Tricolore of the Americans and French who had dominated the city.

Where had they gone?

He caught the flash of a searchlight from the airfield, throwing sparks of light through scattered sheets of rain, and banked instinctively. The expected anti-aircraft fire didn't come, though. Masaru peered downward once more.

The searchlight crew were using the light to signal. *Land. Fuel. Help. Land . . .*

He looked up. Edie was circling directly above. His Avro was almost out of fuel. Her situation with one tank holed would be even more desperate.

Where else would they go, besides? And what might they find if they did?

Masaru put the nose of his plane down, coming around to land.

❀

The front lines were very close to the airfield. A continuous rattle of small arms fire was punctuated by the *crump* of explosives. A squad of riflemen jogged towards the biplanes, slipping in the half-frozen mud as they fanned out to surround them.

Masaru pulled down his scarf and stood up slowly in his cockpit, his hands raised. His vantage gave him an excellent view of the howitzer battery. In front of them was a row of machinegun nests. The barrels of the machineguns were unusually elevated, even more steeply than those of the artillery pieces behind them.

Masaru saw why a moment later.

From the rubble of the nearby streets, Changelings launched themselves high into the air on grasshopper legs, over the machinegun nests. The machineguns opened up, shooting all but one of the creatures out of the air. The survivor landed in the middle of a howitzer crew. Masaru saw blood spurt even from a distance. An infantry reserve rushed to intervene. The rest of the gun crews kept to their tasks. Masaru was struck by the discipline of the Bolsheviks, far superior to anything he had seen from their White Russian rivals.

A rifleman called out, beckoning him down from the plane.

Masaru's feet squelched into the mud when he hopped down.. Freezing liquid seeped through the loose stitching at the toe of his right boot.

"You speak Russian?" the squad leader said with a thickly Turkic accent, while another soldier relieved Masaru of his sidearm.

"I do," Masaru confirmed. Carefully, he lowered his hands. "Where is the Allied fleet?"

"Gone." The man indicated with a crooked finger that Masaru should walk with him. Others closed in behind, making refusal an undignified alternative.

About half the soldiers wore some item of military clothing, either scavenged from the Whites and Allies or because the men themselves were deserters. The rest of their garb was civilian. They were all bedraggled, as from a downpour that had ended only minutes before. Their only other commonality was the red Bolshevik star that each man wore, and even this appeared without uniformity on caps, shoulders, and breasts.

"How long ago?" Masaru asked.

"Two days." The man tapped a cigarette out of a crumpled packet and rummaged for matches to light it. Finding none, he left the cigarette in his mouth anyway. It sagged damply. "The French and American garrisons evacuated overland when the Curse fell on the city, yesterday. Fortunately, the Baku Commune was already poised to launch the Revolution and we have stepped forward for the defence of the People."

Masaru barely heard the rest of the man's answer. *Two days since the fleet sailed.* But that would have had them arrive in Astrakhan before Masaru and Edie had left.

So where were they?

Edie's escorts converged with his and herded her in beside him. Her face was smeared with the spray from her holed fuel tank, with outlines of cleaner skin left by her flying goggles and cap.

"What you did was reckless," Masaru said. "The mission always comes first. The dispatches must get through."

Her eyebrows shot up in disbelief. "You came back for me, too."

With a snort, he looked away.

After a moment, she asked, "Where's the fleet?"

"The fleet sailed two days ago," he said.

"Then they should have reached Astrakhan before we left."

Masaru nodded. "Where else would they have gone?"

"*Ask* him," Edie said, gesturing at the squad leader.

Masaru felt his face heat.

"Turkmenistan," was the reply. The soldier gestured with his unlit cigarette. "They sailed east, for Krasnovodsk."

"Why would they go to Krasnovodsk?"

"There is a tower there, too."

Masaru slowed. Of course there was. The soldier behind him gave him a bump with his rifle butt.

"Where are you taking us?" Masaru asked.

"The Comrade General wishes to speak with you."

❋

The Bolshevik general was a remarkably young Russian wearing round-framed spectacles, with the furrowed brow and pale complexion of an academic. He was hatless, his dark hair plastered across his skull. He stood with a mixed group of equally young Russians and Azeri a distance back from the howitzers, observing the effects of their bombardment. Mist rose from the group's sodden shoulders in the chill air.

"If I had twice as many guns, I could bring that tornado down," the general said, in English and without preamble. "As it is, this," he gestured at the battery, "is hopeful at best. Planting a sufficient quantity of explosives where the tornado touches down would also work, but our line is under too much pressure to consider such an attempt."

He turned to examine first Masaru and then Edie through partly fogged lenses. If he was surprised to see a woman flyer, he did not show it. "Your dispatches, please."

Masaru and Edie reluctantly drew the oilskin envelopes from inside their jackets and handed them over. The general flipped open one and briefly scanned the pages inside. With a grunt, he handed both envelopes to one of his aides.

"So, you have come from Astrakhan." He took off his spectacles and produced a handkerchief from his pocket. He squinted and waved the kerchief vaguely in the direction of the tower in its spinning storm. "The Astrakhan tower was stopped by the Red Army before it was fully complete. As was the tower at Petrovsk, which you have no doubt seen." He wiped his glasses and put them back on before smiling primly. "At Astrakhan and Petrovsk we had more artillery."

Masaru thought he had seen some of the guns that brought down the tower at Petrovsk, bombarding the White Russian forces on the escarpment above the town.

The general went on, "However, since then, much of our strength has been drawn away from the Caspian sector by the Imperialist offensives in the Ukraine." He paused and peered intently, first into Masaru's eyes, then Edie's. "I need you to bring the Allied fleet back from Krasnovodsk. We lack the necessary strength here to prevent this tower's completion, and once it is made, we will not contain the Curse here for long. We have sent messages by fishing vessels, but we do not know if they have succeeded."

"The Curse?" Edie asked.

He flashed another neat little smile. "Rasputin's Curse," he said. "*That.*" He pointed as another wave of leaping Changelings were shot to pieces by the crews in the machinegun nests.

Masaru said, "Our mission is to bring urgent reinforcements to Astrakhan. The Allied command there suspects that Volgograd has also fallen to the . . . Curse."

"'The Reds' Plague', you meant to say." The general chuckled. "Interesting, is it not, that each side blames the other?" He pushed his spectacles firmly onto the bridge of his nose, sobering. "Volgograd did fall, yes, but that outbreak was contained. The situation here has become most urgent. *This* is our war now— Bolshevik or Imperialist, Russian, Turk, American, British, French, Japanese. The Whites have not yet accepted this new reality, but I believe your Allied commanders have begun to do so. I have no aeroplanes. I have no pilots to fly yours. You must bring the Allied fleet back here."

Masaru chewed the inside of his lip, almost hypnotised by the rising tower. *Invaders from a land in the sky?*

"Masaru?" said Edie.

"Please understand," said the general, "I do not have the luxury of patience while you wrestle with your decision." He turned to his aides and barked an order in Russian. It was relayed and a soldier hustled up, towing a boy of nine or ten by the collar of his jacket. The general pulled out his sidearm and touched the muzzle to the child's temple.

Masaru blinked, unable to grasp for a moment what the man intended to do.

"Agree, or I will shoot this child, and I will continue to shoot children until you do agree."

"You can't!" Edie cried.

Masaru met the general's wide-eyed stare. He saw unhappiness behind the man's fogged spectacles, and desperation. He looked down at the child's terrified, helpless face. The general must have sent his men to prepare for this when they first spotted the biplanes. Masaru drew himself up to rebuff the threat.

"Stop!" Edie said. "There's no need."

Masaru's teeth clicked shut.

She caught hold of his sleeve. "The Allies can't afford for Baku to fall, either."

He shook his arm free of her. But she was absolutely right. Azerbaijan was the Allies' lifeline to Persia and the Black Sea. Most Allied reinforcements and materials funnelled through here, and Baku's oil was critical.

Masaru let his anger go in a long breath. Stiffly, he inclined his head to the general. "We will do it."

"Very good," said the general, holstering his gun with—Masaru saw—evident relief. "One of you will remain here, the other will fly to Krasnovodsk." He signalled to an aide, instructing the man to have one of the Avros refuelled.

"Her plane has a damaged fuel tank," said Masaru, in Russian. "It will not reach Krasnovodsk."

The general and his aide both nodded, and the aide rushed away.

Masaru said to Edie, "You will take my plane."

She flushed. "I told you, I don't need you to—" She swore at him as he turned away from her.

He set his shoulders as a squall of rain and sleet blew across the airfield. The freezing touch of the drops stung his bare cheeks. Another volley from the howitzer battery struck the spinning storm. Masaru watched the purple cracks run across the tornado's surface. *Not enough*, he thought. The Changelings would surely break through the Bolsheviks' perimeter soon.

*They need a bigger explosion . . .*

The world seemed to slow around him, the noise of the battle dimming in his ears.

He turned to the Bolshevik general. "Would an aeroplane loaded with explosives be sufficient to collapse the storm?"

"What?" Edie exclaimed.

Masaru ignored her.

The general's eyes roved over his face. The man nodded slowly. "It could work." He nodded again, more firmly, and gave a little bark of laughter. "It *would* work."

Masaru's injured hand throbbed. "Then load the damaged plane with as much explosive as it will carry."

Edie gaped at him in frank amazement, her hair hanging in damp ringlets around her face. The general gestured to another aide and repeated the instruction in Russian.

"You can't do this." Edie gripped Masaru by the arm.

He shook her off again. "One of us *has* to do it," he said. "Can you think of another way?" He let her lack of an answer hang between them, before continuing, "It is the only way. If Baku falls to the Changelings, then what?" He pointed skyward. "If that hole stays open, then what?"

He was surprised to see moisture on her eyelashes. Not rain, he thought. Then she blinked and looked past him, towards the tower, and he wondered if it had been imagination.

"What will happen to your sister?" she asked.

The question struck hard. Masaru sought refuge in dignity. "She will understand. It will be an honourable sacrifice. She will be proud."

"Like she was of her husband?"

A vision of his sister, grieving, swam before his mind's eye. Proud, certainly. And broken-hearted.

Edie's eyes were on him again, watching his expression intently. "Can she feed her children with pride?"

He shouldered roughly past her, meaning to stride away. Unthinking, he lifted his hand to his chest. His steps faltered. For a horrible, panicked instant, he didn't understand why he couldn't feel the *omamori* through his flight overalls. Then he remembered. Still in his cockpit, he hoped.

"There *is* another way," she said.

He rounded on her, barely maintaining his self-control.

"I could do it." She held up a hand to forestall him. "No, listen. I can line my plane up with the tornado. If you bring your plane up underneath mine, I can climb down onto your wing and get clear. My plane will hold a straight enough course without me at the stick."

Masaru was shaking his head before she had finished speaking. "Not possible."

"I've *done* it before," she said.

"It is not—"

"Not for me to do? It's my plane with the holed tank, me who went through the middle of those flyers. Remember?"

Masaru could feel the pressure of his answer in the back of his throat, unable to get out. He stared at her helplessly, this *gaijin* woman who had faced a charging monster with a steady aim, who had dived unflinching through a flock of the things, guns blazing. If she were a man, would he still reject her idea in favour of his own suicide? Could he really be rendered a coward by it just because she was a woman—a *gaijin* woman?

He teetered, caught between two answers, both of them true.

She grabbed his good hand, squeezed hard on his fingers. "*We* can do this."

He stared. Then, slowly, amazed at himself, he nodded.

A breathless rifleman ran up. "Comrade General, it is done."

Masaru started in surprise. His head felt light. So soon?

The general had been observing their conversation. He looked from Edie to Masaru. "I wish you good luck," he said, offering his hand to each of them. "If you succeed, you will save many lives. If you fail . . . " He shrugged. "Well, one of you should still be alive to fly to Krasnovodsk." He paused a moment, then added, "Do not fail. We cannot hold them if you do."

Masaru accepted the general's grip. Edie had already set out after the soldier, back towards the Avros. Masaru started to call after her, then paused. To say what? He hurried to catch up, his thoughts still unsteadily awhirl.

Lines of infantry trudged across the airfield through the mud and slush, herded by crack-voiced NCOs. These men were already exhausted, filthy and bloody, siphoned from other parts of the frontline to shore up the defence here.

A company shuffled wearily past in front of Masaru and Edie. A trio of tattered stragglers caught Masaru's attention. Their gaits were even more lurching and uneven than those of the men they followed, peaked caps pulled low over their faces.

Wounded, was his first thought. But . . .

"*Changelings!*" he cried. "The Curse!"

The monsters' heads snapped up.

"Changelings!" The warning was echoed across the field.

The Changelings' torsos popped suddenly inwards, broken blades of ribs piercing their clothes. The creatures snapped off a blade in each hand. Two of them charged at the soldiers now converging on them.

The third came straight for Edie and Masaru. Did they *know*, somehow? How could it be possible?

Masaru's hand went to his holster. He saw Edie do the same, both of them remembering in the same instant that their pistols had been taken. Their escort stood between them and the Changeling. It closed too fast, knocking his rifle aside as he fired. The soldier fell, clawing at the bone blade jutting from his neck. The Changeling snapped off another rib.

Masaru threw himself at the monster's midriff. The impact was like diving into the trunk of a tree. The Changeling stumbled, feet slipping. A blade scored Masaru's flank, ripping his flight suit. He tangled his legs between the monster's knees, toppling it forwards.

He scrambled on top of it, holding it down as the Changeling thrashed, crushing its face into the mud with his hands.

"Go!" he cried to Edie. "Go!"

She sprinted for the planes.

The Changeling bucked, throwing Masaru off. It sprang to its feet with a snarl. A volley of bullets staggered it. Masaru lunged into the mud after the fallen escort's rifle. He scooped it up, rolling onto his back and firing just as the Changeling pounced. The bullet carved a path up the middle of its face. With a shriek, it flipped its bone blades point-down to impale him.

Soldiers barrelled into it, hacking with bayonets, axes, and cavalry swords. Masaru curled into a ball, trampled and kicked as they charged over the top of him. The Changeling was dragged under by the frenzied attack.

An engine roared into life.

With a yell, spitting mud, Masaru pushed himself to his feet and raced towards the parked Avros. Edie's plane was already rolling, with a hasty collection of sacks, cases, and rolled tarpaulins lashed to its fuselage. She hadn't bothered with her flying cap. Her blonde curls whipped around in the draft of the biplane's prop.

Masaru glimpsed her pale features as she looked his way. He couldn't see her eyes behind her goggles.

The Avro accelerated. It bunny-hopped once and wobbled clumsily into the air.

Masaru sprinted for his own plane and scrambled up into the cockpit, yelling for the soldiers standing guard around it to spin the prop.

The biplane roared into the air. Edie was looping around, lining up for the long run in towards the tornado. Masaru flew to intercept her. His heart hammered. Could they really do this? Or would Edie end up making the honourable sacrifice in his place?

Winged figures dropped from the clouds towards Edie's plane. Masaru cried a useless warning. At the last instant, the other Avro jerked aside, barely avoiding the first wave of attackers. Masaru watched Edie dodge and weave, the Changeling flyers swarming around her, as he raced to help.

He started firing as soon as he was in range and kept the trigger down as he tore through the middle of the flock. He banked hard and went back through for another pass. His Avro jolted violently, a Changeling colliding with the fuselage somewhere behind him.

He glanced back, expecting to find half the tail missing and was amazed when he couldn't see any damage. Facing forward again, he was just in time to dodge another plummeting flyer, slamming his plane onto its side. The Changeling's claws tore strips of canvas from his top wing as it tumbled past.

Then he was clear of them and chasing after Edie.

Her plane was badly battered, trailing black smoke. A wing flap bobbed about uselessly behind her bottom right wing, dangling from one hinge that was still attached. Masaru wondered if the Avro would still hold its course without Edie at the stick. The whirlwind loomed in front of them, frighteningly close.

Masaru brought his biplane up underneath and to the left of Edie's, easing his top wing as close to her bottom wing as he dared. Edie leaned over the side of her cockpit, gauging his position, then started to hitch herself up out of the plane. The Avro dipped when she let go of the stick. Masaru had to drop down to avoid having his wing clipped by her undercarriage.

Edie climbed out onto her plane's wing and crouched. Heart in his mouth, Masaru brought his Avro back up under her. For a breathless moment, Edie held her place, clinging to the wet cables. The whirlwind filled the sky ahead of them. Masaru could pick out the individual Changelings twirling down among the slowly falling stones.

Edie stretched down with one leg. Her muddy boot found the top of his wing. The other foot came down. And then she was crouched between the two biplanes, fingers gripping the trailing edge of her plane's bottom wing, booted toes at the very back of his top wing. She eased a leg past the edge of his wing, foot hunting for a strut to hook onto. Her arms stretched as the Avros drifted apart. Masaru didn't dare adjust for fear of jolting her off.

Her foot found a strut. She slid her other foot off the wing and hooked it around the strut with the first, now dangling from the other plane by her fingertips. Then she let go.

She dropped. Her forearms bumped against his top wing as she slipped past, and for a moment Masaru was sure she would fall. Then she caught the strut, found a cable with her other hand and got herself in between the wings.

Masaru started to swing around. Edie worked her way quickly forward until she could lock her arms around the leading strut and lie flat across the bottom wing.

Masaru dove steeply, his immediate thought just to get clear. He spotted the airfield and adjusted his course, opening up the throttle and keeping the nose down, waiting for the blast. The city buildings rushed up towards them. Edie looked back from her place on the wing, hair whipping around her face, eyes slitted, her teeth bared.

There was a flash. Masaru twisted to see. A fireball split the whirlwind, blinding, expanding, like someone had smashed the sun into a disc.

Tenement rooftops whipped past underneath, frighteningly close, soldiers and Changelings in the streets below frozen like animals in a locomotive's headlamp. The biplane cleared the howitzers at the end of the airfield. He was coming in far too fast. Masaru closed the throttle and pulled back the stick. The plane seemed to hover in the air, on the brink of stalling.

Then the shockwave hit them.

The Avro jolted, tipped nose-down. Masaru saw Edie bounce clear of the wing, legs flailing, her hands still clamped around the front strut. The airfield rushed up, Bolshevik fighters scrambling to get clear. Masaru's arms protested as he hauled back on the stick. Just barely, he got the biplane level again. It smacked into the ground, bounced, hopped twice more before the undercarriage collapsed. The Avro slewed around on its belly, propeller splintering as it gouged up mud and slushy snow.

Eventually, it slid to a halt. Masaru coughed, winded, and looked down at himself, amazed to find that he was unhurt.

The *omamori* lay wedged in the corner of the footwell. With a huff of disbelief, he picked it up, then sat back in wonder. Shaking his head, he looked towards the wing.

Edie was no longer there.

When had she fallen?

He was up, half-leaping, half-falling from the cockpit, ignoring the cries of the Bolshevik soldiers converging on the wrecked biplane. Others were hurrying towards a prone figure back along his trail of wreckage and furrowed turf.

He ran, stumbling and slipping over the churned earth. He dropped to his knees when he reached her. A soldier was already cradling her head on his thigh. Edie's face was deathly white behind a half-mask of mud. Splintered bone jutted through one leg of her flying suit.

Her eyes rolled towards him. She showed him a rictus grin. "We did it."

"You're hurt," he panted.

She chuckled, then gasped in pain, her teeth still bared. "Broke both my legs. And some ribs."

"Both your legs," Masaru repeated. His jaw worked while he fought for breath. He laughed, suddenly. "I *told* you."

He sat back on the cold wet ground, his fist clenched tightly around the omamori. High above, the whirlwind was coming apart, stones and Changelings tumbling down to crash onto the half-finished tower, or falling back up towards the collapsing hole in the sky.

He would be writing to his sister, he decided. He imagined the joy and anguish, amazement and horror warring across her face when she read his request for an amulet to ward against supernatural powers as well.

# ONCE A MONTH, ON A SUNDAY . . .

Once a month, on a Sunday, Mum and me and my little brother Zubby would dress up in our best clothes, Mum would put ribbons in my hair, and we'd all walk into town to go to church.

On Sundays when my Baba was home, Mum would sing while she helped us dress and brushed our hair. She'd tell stories while we walked along the track and Zubby rode in his pram, and she'd let us run ahead when Zubby got bored of riding. She wouldn't care if we strayed from the path, except for the part where the gambelgam was, where we needed to stay close. She wouldn't even mind if we dirtied our hands and clothes before we reached church.

But my Baba had been away now for three months—a lot longer than he was usually out on the road. Mum was in a foul mood. She growled and snapped while she got us ready. My scalp stung as she pulled my hair tight to plait it. I bit my lip and stayed silent, but Zubby cried when Mum brushed his hair, which just made her growl more.

"Zubair! Stay still!"

The only thing to do when Mum was like this was to be quiet and stay out of her way. But her temper made me nervous, and that made me clumsy. Pulling my dress on over my head, I knocked the water basin from the kitchen table. Mum jumped as water splashed over her skirts.

"Olivia! Green Christ above, girl, look what you've done!" Aside from the mess, she hadn't washed herself, yet.

"I'll fetch more," I said, quickly, and fled before she could send me on my way with a slap.

I dashed out the door and into the lean-to shed out back. Zubby screamed louder all of a sudden. I guessed he'd got the slap instead. I tipped the lid off the big wire cage on the bench near the front of the shed and rummaged around in the wool and straw inside until

I caught a mouse. It squirmed, warm and helpless in my fingers. I grabbed the water bucket and ran down the stepping-stone path to the creek.

The tin bucket bumped against the side of my calf. My plaited hair slapped against my shoulder blades. I slowed once the house was lost from sight behind the Banksia shrubs.

The Banksias' flowers had already dried out, losing their bright red colour. They sat along the branches like so many tiny brown owls. A lizard scuttled away from the path. Up in the trees, a magpie cleared its throat, but didn't sing. The bush was stuffy and hot after the cool of the house.

The temperature dropped a little going down the slope to the creek. I walked across the top of my shadow when it baulked, not wanting to lie itself across the water. I stopped on the wide pale stone beside the bank. Baba had chiselled the Arabic word ma' into it, which meant "water", and some other words that he wouldn't say aloud. The mouse lay still in my hand. Its heartbeat tickled my palm.

The creek was still full of winter rain, but moving slowly, brown with dirt. I held up my fist, with the mouse's tail hanging out the back and its nose poking between my first finger and thumb.

"Shukran jazilan," I whispered, like Baba told me to. It meant "thank you". I tossed the mouse underarm, out over the water. Its legs spread out stiffly around it, ready to land.

A long tongue of water shot up from the surface of the creek and snapped the mouse out of the air.

The tongue thickened out. It swayed in front of me, taller than I was. Odd lumps and tentacles bulged from the bunyip's sides and disappeared again. I watched a dark spot flow down its middle and disappear into the creek. The bunyip looked back at me, even though it didn't have eyes.

I could feel my shadow tugging at my heels, wanting me to come away. I ignored it. I wasn't in any danger.

"Hello, bunyip," I said. Baba had told me there was no point in talking to the land's dreamings, but I always spoke to the bunyip anyway. "I'd like some water, please. May I?"

It didn't answer, of course. I crouched at the front edge of Baba's water stone and lowered the bucket into the creek. The bunyip stayed where it was, watching. A tentacle came out of it when the warded metal touched the water, towards me, but it didn't grow far.

I heaved the full bucket up out of the creek and turned to go. "Goodbye, bunyip."

It had already sunk down into the creek when I looked back over my shoulder.

Back at the house, I played clapping games with Zubby, sitting out of the way on Mum and Baba's bed, while Mum finished getting herself ready. Then we set out. She put Zubby into the pram, although he wanted to run, and made me walk along beside. The weather was turning cloudy. It didn't look like rain coming, but it was enough to stop the day from getting really hot.

Walking along, just the three of us, I could nearly forget that Baba had been away so long. He never came to church with us, even when he wasn't out on the road. Church wasn't Baba's religion. He didn't follow the Green Christ, or even Christ the Lamb. Baba followed the Last Prophet instead, and did his praying at sunrise, noon and sunset every day, wherever he laid out his mat. Baba made his living going around to the towns and the squatters' homesteads and fixing up all the old runeworks with his Arabic letters. People didn't mind that he followed the Last Prophet, because he always did right by them.

Really, Zubby and me followed the Last Prophet too, because Baba did. When he was home, he read us stories from the Prophet's book. He didn't mind us going to church, though, because the God of the Green Christ and the God of the Last Prophet were really the same; the Christ and the Prophet just had different ways of teaching His lessons.

We came to the kink in the track around the gambelgam's place. Baba had laid sleepers into the ground around that part and had used an iron to burn his letters into the wood. The gambelgam place is hard to pick out, not like a willywilly that twists up all the trees it can reach chasing possums and koalas. You mostly won't know a gambelgam's there until you hear it sing. Your shadow will have heard it first, but won't be able to warn you that there's a dreaming ahead. And once that happens it's probably got you unless you've got some good warding under your shoes.

I could hear its song over the rattle of Zubby's pram, bumping over the sleepers. It sounded like wind and fire and grinding rocks. It'd take your shadow and soul away to the red heart of the land if you let it, Baba said.

Mum's knuckles were white, holding my hand against the handle of Zubby's pram. Mum didn't need to be so scared. As long as we stayed on the path that Baba made, the gambelgam's voice had no power. I wasn't going to run away from the path. Our shadows could hear the song but because of Baba's warding, weren't caught by it. They stretched themselves far out to the side, away from the gambelgam.

Baba had taken me off the logs, once, and held me just beyond where the gambelgam could come out and get us, so its voice would fill up my head and I'd know the red heart for myself. I'd gone to the place where Baba said the dreamings are born and watched the shadows dance on red stone.

Once we got past the gambelgam, Mum calmed a bit. She let Zubby out of the pram, although she wouldn't let us wander far. The day stayed just warm, because of the clouds, but I was still thirsty by the time we crossed over the runestone labyrinth that guarded the road into town.

Mum dug a tin cup out from the bottom of the pram and we took turns to drink from the pump at the horse trough outside the pub. She straightened our clothes and retied my ribbons and felt around the edges of her hair, then we walked the rest of the way to the church in the middle of town.

The yew tree outside the church's western door looked sadder every month. Half its branches were dead and bare of leaves, making it look hollowed-out around its thick trunk. We walked around the curved wall of the church to the southern door. Father Henryk waited for us in the shade of the oak tree there.

"Good day, Alice, children," he said. Father Henryk had an accent, the way Baba did, but different from Baba's. Both of them mixed up their 'a' and 'e' and 'o' sounds, but Baba made it sound nice, along with the way he growled out his 'h's. Father Henryk just sounded funny. Mum said Father Henryk was Dutch.

Mum bowed her head. I did, too. "Father," said Mum.

"I'm pleased to see you," Father Henryk added. He was very tall and thin, with wet-looking eyes and a big Adam's apple. "You should really come more than once a month."

He always said the same. Mum always answered the same, too: "It's a long walk with the children."

Father Henryk put a hand on Zubby's head. "It is particularly important for the children."

Mum tried a smile, even though she wasn't happy, and said, "Faris will make enough one day to buy me a horse and buggy. Then I'll be able to come more often."

Father Henryk's face got all tight and serious. "May I speak with you a moment?"

Mum's face got tight then, too, and shuttered up, the way it did when she had to talk to the ladies she didn't like in town. "Look after your brother," she said to me.

They walked back over towards the yew tree. Zubby stuck out his bottom lip, thinking about crying. I caught his fingers and held on just tight enough that he could still pull them free. He laughed and I held out my hand to play trap-hands. I watched Mum and Father Henryk talking. He looked like he was asking her something. Mum had her arms folded in front of her. Father Henryk pointed towards me and Zubby, and they both looked. I turned quickly away.

People from the town were going into the church. They looked at me and Zubby, too, and at Mum and Father Henryk.

Mum was still unhappy when we finally went inside the church. She kept starting to sing and stopping part way through the hymns. Father Henryk didn't try to talk to her again. A few people said hello to Mum, but only looked sideways at me and Zubby. Mrs Kewell from the post office looked like she wanted to talk more, but the look Mum gave her killed whatever words she had before they got out of her mouth. We didn't stop at anyone's house for tea, which we sometimes did.

My tummy growled on the walk home. Zubby complained about being hungry.

"When we get home, Zub," said Mum.

"Father Henryk doesn't like that Baba follows the Prophet and not the Green Christ, does he?" I said.

For a moment, Mum looked like she was about to cry. She said, "No, love, he doesn't. You can run along and explore if you want. Come back before we get to the gambelgam."

When we got home, in the middle of the afternoon, it was my job to fetch water again.

"But I'm hungry, Mum," I said.

"You can eat when you get back," she said. She gave me the crust of yesterday's loaf to tide me over and told me to hurry up. She was trying hard but I could tell she was still upset.

Zubby started complaining again. I looked over my shoulder as I ran out the door. Mum was standing at the table with Zubby going red in the face by her hip. She held on to the wood like she didn't know what her hands might do to him if she let go.

Inside the lean-to, I reached up to shift the lid of the mouse cage. I stopped. The lid wasn't on straight. I felt like my insides had all fallen down from their proper places and landed on my bladder. I hadn't closed the cage properly that morning.

I pushed the lid all the way off and pulled out the whole mess of wool and straw and dropped it on the ground. No mice scuttled out. For a minute I couldn't think what to do. I just stood beside the empty cage, hoping Mum wouldn't come out the back door and see.

I rubbed the tears out of my eyes, bent to pick up all the mouse bedding again, and stuffed it back in the cage. I tore up my bread crust and sprinkled it into the cage, then left the lid just a little bit open. Hopefully when I came back, I might've caught some mice again. I grabbed the bucket and ran off down the path. Baba dipped for water without needing a mouse. As long as I stood on his water stone, I'd be fine, just this once.

I felt less and less brave the closer I got to the creek. My shadow dragged at my feet. Baba said dreamings couldn't recognise people. I thought Baba was wrong—the bunyip knew me, it would forgive me one mouse. But knowing about dreamings was Baba's job. What if it was me that was wrong? I thought then that I should've brought a rope to hang the bucket from, so I wouldn't have to put my hands near the water. But if I went back now, and ran straight off again, Mum would wonder why, and then she'd find out about the mice.

I stepped onto the water stone and waited. My shadow lay very still behind me. The bunyip didn't come up.

"I'm sorry, bunyip," I said, knowing that it must be in the creek, since it was part of the creek. "All the mice got away. I haven't any to give you."

The surface of the creek stayed flat.

"May I still dip for water?"

I edged up to the front of the stone and squatted down. Watching for the bunyip, ready to leap backwards out of the way, I reached the bucket over the bank and dipped it in the water.

The creek bulged, only a couple of feet away. A watery tentacle came up and reached towards the bucket. I froze. The tentacle stopped.

Ever so slowly, I pushed the bucket under, and pulled it back up, full. Just as slowly, the bunyip stretched out its tentacle. The tip got wider and flatter. I lifted the bucket clear. The bunyip reached underneath, to catch the drips that rained from its sides.

I stood up straight. The tentacle lowered, and disappeared back into the creek.

"Thank you, bunyip."

I laughed as I ran back up the path. I'd been right. I couldn't wait to tell Baba.

I stopped by the lean-to before I went back in the house. Something rustled under the cotton and straw inside the mouse cage when I poked it, and I quickly put the lid all the way back on.

Zubby was happy, chattering to himself and chewing. His plate was piled with bread, cheese, pickles and salt pork. There was another full plate beside Zubby's, for me. Mum sat across the table, one of my shirts in her lap, staring off at nothing. A needle was pushed through it, near the collar, where she'd started fixing a tear.

She was quiet all afternoon and through dinner. When it came to bedtime, she tried to tell us a story, but she kept stopping and forgetting where she was up to. She gave up as soon as Zubby fell asleep.

I lay for a while, listening to her get herself ready for bed and thinking about what I'd done with the bunyip.

"Mum? When's Baba coming home?"

She didn't answer. I turned over to look at her.

"Mum?"

Her back was to me, as she snuffed out the wick of the oil lamp. In the dark, I listened to the creak of her bed as she climbed in and the rustle of the sheets as she pulled them up. Then she lay so still and quiet that I could hardly hear her crying at all.

❋ ❋ ❋

# BITTER DREAMS

The blackfellas brought the body down to the town gate in the grey of morning, when the mist was lifting but hadn't yet burned off. There were four of them and they carried the remains up on their shoulders, on a stretcher made of branches and plates of paperbark.

They didn't wear much, despite the cold, just loincloths and possum-skin shawls and one of them in a pair of cut-off moleskins. They were tall men, as blackfellas are, all ropy muscle, with the long, skinny calves and broad, long feet of runners. In the weak light, when their shadows were faint on the ground, their heavy brows and wide noses still gathered darkness around their eyes. Their hair was matted with clay and their faces, torsos and limbs were scarred all over with the white lines and dots the blackfellas use in place of pictures and letters.

They left the body outside the gate, wouldn't pass between the posts carved with English runes—couldn't, with the dreams of the land mapped all over their bodies. They turned around without a word and jogged back into the bush, not hurrying, just because that's the way they preferred to move.

Constable Robert Bowley sat on the porch outside the post office with Maise Wallace, drinking tea while Maise worked at her embroidery. Georgie, Maise's old half-dingo bitch, lay curled up at her mistress's feet.

Bowley toyed with his teacup, gazing at the buildings across the way. Hunched things, all, imposed on but never accepted by the clay and rock they squatted over. Mockeries of Englishness, with their crooked frames and sagging spines, tarred timbers and dark shingles unalleviated by the runes carved into their surfaces. They huddled beneath their roofs, shaded by alien trees and encroached by grass that was never green even in the wettest months.

Only the church was made of stone, not counting the coolroom out the back of the pub, and only it rose higher than the houses, and not by much. And it was even sadder than they, with no priest there since before Bowley had first come to Useless Loop. Its stones had all been shipped from England because local rock refused to take the shape.

He examined his hands around Maise's porcelain cup and saucer: the dirt that would never come out, at the base of his fingernails, in the creases of his knuckles and the fine lines that etched his skin. The cuffs of his uniform jacket, permanently impregnated with clay dust. He ran his thumb across the largest chip in the edge of the saucer, fitted the leathered pad into the shallow cavity.

"Bowls." Alby Tucker stood at the front of the porch, one booted foot propped against the edge of the boards, toe upwards so that Bowley could see the runes scorched into the leather sole. "Mate, you'd better come see what the blackfellas have left outside the gate."

❂

"Bloody hell."

Bowley stood over what was left of Stink McClure, forcing himself to look. He couldn't bring himself to squat down beside Alby and examine the corpse more closely. He rested one hand on his service holster and had the thumb of the other hooked in his belt, both fists closed so no-one would see the shake in his fingers. He breathed through his mouth.

Maise stood beside him, her face pale, arms folded across her chest. Bowley doubted it was because her hands were shaking. Beyond her, German Braun and young Dermott O'Shane watched Alby prod at the corpse, their lips pursed in mirrored expressions of distaste. Their shadows all bunched up close under their boots, reluctant to cast themselves across the corpse.

"Been dead a day or so," said Alby. He poked about under the ribcage with a stick. "His liver's gone as well."

Bowley could see there wasn't as much left inside the open belly as there should've been. There wasn't much left, in fact, to show that the carcass had been old Stink, just his grey nest of hair, his crappy old home-made snakeskin boots and that prickly-pear of a nose of his. As well as opening his guts, whatever had eaten him up had chewed off his penis, and dug out his eyes, and ripped apart his cheeks to get at his tongue. His blood-matted beard hung from shreds of skin around his ears. His lower jaw flopped loosely on his chest.

German asked, "Vas it a villyvilly?" Ingrained soot made the furrows of his always-sweaty brow appear even deeper.

Maise said, "Willywilly wouldn't chew him up like that."

She knew. A willywilly had taken her husband, Nev, not a year after Bowley arrived in town, left his carcass with all the hair sucked off it and scattered around. But, with the sun now peeking through the clouds, they could all see that Stink's corpse cast no darkness beneath it, on its bed of bark and sticks. Whatever killed him had drunk up his shadow as well. The body seemed to float, a hair's-width off the ground, cut adrift, as the corpses of the dream-eaten are.

But what the hell kind of dreaming would tear a man up like that? A willywilly wouldn't make a mark on a man, just leave him bald, not needing to devour the parts that anchored him in his flesh in order to pull out his soul. A bunyip or potkoorok might chew a body up, some, but the dreamings that lay in billabongs and creeks didn't have teeth, as such, and tended to crush up the guts and bones and leave the bag of skin that contained them intact.

"Maybe it was dingos, or a goanna, after," said Alby, pressing hands down on thighs to come upright. The ligaments in his knees creaked as he straightened.

Bowley shook his head, doubtfully. He extracted his thumb from his belt and scratched at the edges of his moustache, his skin still raw from the morning's cold-water shave. He wished he'd remembered to put on his uniform cap—still on Maise's outdoor table beside the cold dregs of his tea. He felt vulnerable without it, his lawman's persona incomplete. He realised his hand was still shaking and put it back to his belt.

"Dingo's too smart," he said, "and a goanna's been around long enough to know better."

"What about the blackfellas?" said Dermott O'Shane.

"Why would they bring him in if they'd done it?" said Alby.

The young Irishman shrugged. "Maybe he did something to them. They wanted us to know they'd had their justice."

"Old Stink?" said Bowley. Stink McClure had been a mad old bastard, but he'd known better than most how to stay on the good side of the natives. Although, if it was the blackfellas that'd done it, no-one in their right mind, not even a magister, was going to dispute it. That meant case closed, no further problems. Bowley didn't think so.

"We should go out to check on the others," said Maise.

The Del Mar clan, she meant, her blood kin, in their fortified farmstead up the top of the Loop, where the track crossed the ridge and turned to come back down. She had a sister up there, Lucy, and a niece, as well as all her cousins and uncles and aunts. Less important, for her, King James Campbell and White Mitchell with his retarded brother and all the other antisocials prospecting the gullies and creek beds between Del Mar's and the town.

Everyone looked at Bowley, the Queen's Man, the town's sole protector, although he was as mundane as any of them. Useless Loop was too small to maintain its own magister or even a runesmith. Only German, the blacksmith, with the dozen signs he knew that worked on hooves and boot soles. The town had Bowley and the rune posts at the gate and the rune stones laid beneath their houses and in a ring around the town. And they had the runes on their boots and bullets of English silver in their guns. None of which would stop a really strong and bitter dreaming, should the land ever throw one up, just make it angrier.

Alby snuffled back a chunk of phlegm and dug in his vest pocket for a handkerchief. He saved Bowley from having to answer. "Bugger that, Maise."

Bowley nodded, hoping his relief wasn't too obvious. He badly wanted a whiskey, couldn't while he was on duty. He thought he might get away with a gulp or two from the bottle under his desk, later.

"Come crank up the telegraph for us, eh, Maise? We'll get onto Ballarat and see what they say." For a moment he thought she'd argue. Her shoulders were tucked up like they got when she was that way inclined. But she nodded. Bowley waved a hand to encompass Alby, German and O'Shane. "You blokes take the body to the pub and put it in the coolroom."

Alby snorted. "Ulf's going to be bloody happy about that."

"Tell him I've deputised you," Bowley called back over his shoulder, walking after Maise, his shadow stretching ahead and eager to be gone.

❉

Investigate. Report. Was the terse reply that came back from Ballarat in the middle of the afternoon.

Bowley had stayed at Maise's for lunch after they sent their telegram, returned, without thinking, to his accustomed seat on post office's porch. She'd made his food in the same manner, neither his fear nor her anger enough to derail them from their familiar patterns. Neither of them had spoken while they ate. They rarely did say much. Usually, it was because there wasn't all that much to say, just closeness to be had and that was something both of them felt was best taken in silence. Today the crow's feet at the corners of Maise's eyes had been tight with worry. A lot going on inside of her, he could tell, although it was unlikely that much, if any, of it would find its way into words.

Leaning against the frame of the stationhouse door, Bowley unfolded the paper for the dozenth time and re-read Maise's scrawled transcription. As if, somehow, the message might've changed from the previous eleven times he'd read it. Investigate. Report. "Green Christ."

Maise had wanted to ride out right away. Bowley had started to shake his head, to point out that there wasn't time to get out to Del Mar's and back before dark. She'd smelled the whiskey on his breath as soon as he opened his mouth. He'd watched her rigid back as she stalked away.

He watched her now, back on her porch with Georgie sprawled at her feet, both of them sharing the last rays of sun and Maise pretending not to see him watching. He'd always thought, vaguely, that one day he'd make an honest woman of her, although both of them were past childrearing age. He'd never quite gotten around to asking. In truth, he was happy enough to just share the stillness of her front porch and, sometimes, the warmth between her bed sheets, whenever the urgency was enough in both of them to keep him there overnight.

Cold nights alone stretched ahead of him.

His thoughts circled back to worrying at what the hell might've done that to old Stink, like nothing he'd ever seen before—heard about, maybe, but only up north, nowhere nearby—and where it might've come from and how could it, since dreamings didn't move from the patch of land that dreamed them? And how strong was this dreaming? Strong enough to get past the rune stones and the gate? Because if it was, there was no-one and nothing here that could stop it from doing to the whole town what it'd done to Stink McClure.

There were dreamings that came that strong, he'd heard, out in the desert, where the land was still wakeful and warlike, that could take over a person, or more than one, and use them as its teeth and claws . . . He shuddered, thinking of human teeth tearing up Stink.

Georgie's shadow slunk off under the porch, leaving the dog still asleep in her patch of sun.

Other animal shadows flitted across the dusty clay of the street, looking for dark places to hide. Their frantic owners pursued them. Cats, chooks, a couple of early-rising possums and Ted Wright's brown nanny goat, united in flight. Georgie awoke with a start, twisted wildly about and, with a swallowed yip, followed her shadow under the porch.

The pair of horses hitched at the watering trough in front of the smithy started in alarm as their shadows bucked, shadow-legs stretching with their feet anchored to the runes beneath the horses' shoes. German tumbled out and lunged for the animals' reins. The horses quieted before he even reached them, opting to freeze with flight denied. Bowley could see their ears flicking, trying to pinpoint the threat. German's head swivelled to look down the street, towards the gate. Maise was up out of her chair and looking that way too.

The horse was a dappled grey of the long-necked, spindle-legged variety bred to tolerate sorcery. Its rider wore a battered oilskin coat, with worn and faded edges on its collar, cuffs and hem, and slashes of lighter colour where it had dried out and stiffened in the dust and sun. A rough Hessian shawl draped the man's head and shoulders beneath the sagging brim of his hat.

He reined his horse to a halt in the middle of the street, facing the setting sun. Neither the man nor his horse cast a shadow. They stood, superimposed on the world, but not really fitted to it.

Two days at least for a magister to come up from Ballarat with a company of redcoats in tow, and Bowley's superiors had made it plain that they weren't coming to his aid at all until he could tell them more precisely what they'd be walking into. So who in hell was this, right here and now?

Bowley reached inside the door and took his uniform cap from its peg. Maise looked his way as he stepped outside. He tried a tentative smile. She didn't respond. He pretended not to notice, smoothed his jacket and hitched his gun belt. He straightened his policeman's badge on its silver chain and stepped down from the porch.

He was acutely conscious of the eyes that followed his progress across the rutted clay. Maise and German. Alby, leaning outside the pub with Ulf Erikssen. He could feel his shadow's reluctance to follow, a heaviness in his calves and feet, like his legs had fallen half asleep. He willed it to stay with him.

He was conscious, too, of the awkward weight of his gun, bumping on his hip with every step. He hooked his thumbs in his belt to keep it still.

Bony hands folded over the saddle's pommel—pale skinned, with a greyish tinge, and blotched with darker grey liver-spots, the man evidently as dappled as his horse. Both the rider's gear and his horse's tack were curiously blank, unmarked by runes. Bowley could see nothing on either man or horse to indicate that the rider was, in any regard, a Queen's Man.

Bloody hell, a wild spook.

The cowled head turned towards him as he neared. Bowley could make out the lines of a gaunt face in the shadows gathered beneath the man's hat. The shadows seemed to writhe across his cheeks and down his neck. A long nose protruded into the light, blotched like the man's hands.

Bowley stopped a distance from the stranger that he hoped might appear both authoritative and deferential. Queen's Man or not, a spook was a spook, after all, and Bowley had no wish to have his soul sucked out of him for the sake of a moment of perceived impertinence.

"I'm Bowley, local constable." It sounded as inadequate as he felt.

The cowl dipped in acknowledgement. Bowley waited, but the man didn't speak. The silence began to stretch.

Bowley cleared his throat and said, "You got a name, mate?"

The stranger's reply was as oblique as any magister's would be: "None that's any use." His voice was a surprise, rich and soft.

Bowley tried again, "What brings you to Useless Loop?"

"Land's thrown up a bad dreaming, hereabouts."

Bowley's guts clenched. He tried to keep his reaction off his face as he said, "How do you know about it?"

The man gave a huff that might've been a laugh. "Land stinks of it. How do you know about it?"

Bowley considered him, disinclined to answer and wracking his brains for who the hell this wild spook might be and coming up with nothing. But, damn it all, he was far out of his depth and, wild spook or not, he was in dire need of magical aid. "Dreaming killed a man, outside town. Chewed him up something horrible. Got the body in the coolroom at the pub."

He felt an abrupt increase in the intensity of the other's stare. "Can I see it?"

Bowley hesitated, but knew he'd committed himself now. He tipped his head in the direction of the pub.

He started walking, not waiting for the stranger to dismount. He heard the man land, heard his steps close behind—puffs of dust and the small clinks of shifting pebbles, no thump of boot soles striking earth.

The hair stood up along the length of Bowley's spine. Bloody spook.

Ulf and Alby levered themselves off the rail and disappeared inside the pub. Bowley led the stranger down the side and round the back. By the time they arrived, Ulf had unlocked the coolroom door and retreated to the rear porch with Alby.

Bowley let the stranger precede him through the low door. The temperature dropped sharply within the thick stone walls. The man crouched beside the body, his oilskin collapsing towards the floor, as though it were all but empty. He pulled back the tarp that covered Stink and was still for a while, a crumpled pile of shadows in the light from the door. Outside, Ulf muttered something to Alby that Bowley couldn't quite catch.

The stranger flipped the tarp back over the body and rose, turning, the brim of his hat only inches from Bowley's eyes. His coat sleeve brushed Bowley's chest as he exited. Bowley stood in the darkness alone for a moment. His eyes fell on the flattened lump under the tarp. He shuddered.

Ulf and Alby watched silently as he re-emerged. Ulf's expression offered him nothing. Alby widened his eyes a moment. Bowley hurried after the stranger, already striding back up the street. The man walked past his horse and headed for the gate. Intrigued and disturbed, Bowley followed. Maise's porch was empty. Sweat trickled past his belt to lodge in the back of his pants.

The man stopped outside the gate. His shrouded head half turned towards Bowley. "This is where they left the body."

"Yep."

The stranger faced outward. Bowley scanned the surrounding bush, wondering what he saw. For a minute the man was still. Then darkness began to pour from under the fringe of his shawl, out of his cuffs and under his coat tails. Bowley squeaked.

His shadow tore itself free of the runes on his boot soles and fled back into town. The darkness pooled on the ground around the man's feet, its edges reaching and questing. It lapped at Bowley's toes and flowed around his heels, then released him. The man raised his arms and the darkness shattered into a thousand running shadows that raced away into the bush.

The stranger lowered his arms.

Bowley swallowed. Green bloody Christ.

The stranger stood like a statue for most of half an hour while his shadows hunted. Bowley waited with him, not daring to walk away, feeling queasy and light-headed without his shadow. At last the hunters returned. They flowed up the man's legs, moving fast, so that Bowley had trouble making out their shapes. He thought he saw men among the dogs and roos and emus and other, smaller forms. The last shadow disappeared beneath the man's coat.

"The town should be safe for tonight."

Bowley nodded, only realising after he'd done so that the man couldn't see the gesture. He gathered up enough composure to say, "There's a lot of prospectors out there, up the Loop."

"Dead."

Christ. He'd had a notion there'd be more than just Stink McClure, but the stranger's flat appraisal rocked him, even so. "There's a farmstead, too, up the top. Fortified. Lot of people."

The spook didn't respond.

"My orders are to investigate," Bowley added.

"You're riding out?"

"Tomorrow."

Silence, for a while, then: "I'll come with you. I can defend four men."

A small part of Bowley bristled at the man's presumption. Most of him sagged with relief.

"Have you got any rune-carved bullets?" the stranger asked.

Bowley knew the number precisely: six. He answered cautiously, "Some."

The spook turned, his shrouded face a vague impression amid the shadows. "We'll need more than some. Is there a runesmith in town?"

"Just the blacksmith."

"He'll do."

The man brushed past and strode back into town. Bowley hurried after. The skin on his back crawled. His shadow lunged at him from the shelter of Ted Wright's house, nearest the gate, and re-attached itself to his feet.

❖

The mist was heavier the following dawn. The stranger, on his horse just outside the gate, was discernable only because Bowley knew he was there.

Bowley fumbled another carved silver bullet from his palm and pressed it into the magazine of his service carbine, then shrugged the gun from the crook of his arm into his hand and slotted the magazine home. Alby, German and young Dermott O'Shane formed a circle with him. German's eyes were so bloodshot he had no whites left to speak of. Bowley knew his own eyes weren't much better, having seen the state of himself in his washstand mirror. He'd spent the whole night out on his porch, his service revolver in his lap, loaded with the six rune-carved bullets he'd been issued a decade before, when he joined the Queen's Constabulary. He doubted any of them had slept much.

Young O'Shane grabbed at a bullet that slipped between his fingers. It bounced off his thumb and tumbled in an arc to strike the ground. The older men flinched and sucked air through their teeth. All three shared a sheepish grin, their reflexes outdated, accustomed to rimfire cartridges. O'Shane scooped up the escapee and stood again, red from forehead to chin.

"No worries, mate," said Bowley, relieved that he'd managed to load his own weapon without dropping anything and made magnanimous because of it. There was still a tremor in his hands, but much less than the day before, now that the moment was upon them.

Alby flipped the magazine cylinder shut on the second of his six-shooter rifles. He sniffled loudly. His cold seemed to be getting worse. "You know anything about this spook, Bowls?"

"Much as you do," said Bowley. "German?"

"Don't ask me, mate," the blacksmith said. "Ve just carved fucking bullets all night."

Young O'Shane piped up, "I heard about a dappled man, once, when I was out Ararat way. Said he came in from the desert, on foot, dressed like a blackfella and spotted all over, like his sire was one of them Dalmatian hounds. That's all I know. Never saw him myself."

Alby spat. "Reckon that's our bloke. We right?"

"Yep."

"Ya."

The O'Shane boy nodded his head.

"No time like the present," said Bowley.

His old brown mare, Clay, looked back at him with wide nostrils and white-rimmed eyes as he shuffled along her side. Her shadow was skittish beneath her, faint as it was, both horse and shade aware of the Dappled Man's presence and keyed-up because of it. Bowley shoved his carbine into the sleeve in front of the saddle and patted her neck.

"Alright, old girl." He unhitched the reins and brought them up to her neck. Alby was already aboard his chestnut mare, Nudge. German heaved himself up onto fat black Bismarck the gelding and O'Shane rose easily into the saddle of his new piebald filly. Bowley put his foot in the stirrup, grabbed a handful of mane and hauled himself up.

"Ah, shit."

Maise, wearing an oilskin and a pair of Nev's old pants, led Ulf's mean-tempered roan up from the direction of the pub. Bowley held his ground while the others retreated. Maise stopped in front of him, Ulf's idiot horse almost pulling her off balance as it danced about.

She didn't wait to hear Bowley's objections. "It's my family, Robert. And I'm a better shot than anyone except you."

He glanced at the others, waiting halfway to the gate. Alby smirked. Bowley said, "But you can't ride for shit, love. What if we have to move in a hurry? That animal'll break your bloody neck."

"Don't you 'love' me," she snapped. "German can't ride for shit, either."

Of that, Bowley was acutely aware. "No one else volunteered."

"I'm volunteering."

"The spook says he can only defend four."

"You're the bloody constable—since when are you taking orders from him?"

"It's because it's your family out there that I don't want you to come."

"I don't need you to protect me, Robert."

It's not you I'm protecting, love. It's me. His desperation crept into his voice, "Maise, please."

Her jaw clenched. She bowed her head, hiding her face from him. She was crying, he knew, and knew too that she wouldn't accept any comfort from him. He dithered for a moment, then pulled Clay's head around and prodded the horse into motion. He didn't need to look back to know she wouldn't follow.

The Dappled Man's hunting shadows already roiled around his horse's hooves, indistinct in the silvery dimness. He waited until the townsmen were a few yards behind him, then clucked his horse forward. His shadows ranged ahead of him, vanishing almost immediately from sight.

The Man's connection to the ground, through his horse's hooves, seemed even more attenuated, today, than it had in strong sunlight. It seemed he might, if he relaxed the will that anchored him, simply drift off into the mist.

None of them looked back as they rode from town. They didn't need to, could feel the moment when it dissolved into the shroud of mist and trees. Their mounted shadows tucked tight beneath the horses hooves. The charms on the horses' tack clinked loudly in the surrounding stillness.

Beside the track grew spiked grass that was only ever the colour of forgotten bones. Trees surrounded them, some twisted, some straight, all of them alien, with their bleached skins—some that leaked thick sap like blood, others with bark hanging in strips and strings as though they'd been flayed. All growing out of ground that was either rock or clay and in both cases unyielding, that gave itself only with bitter resentment to any man who wanted to farm it.

Even under mist or rain, with the air above it saturated, the land remained parched. Bowley could feel it plucking at the edges of his shadow, and knew that the land would drink him up, too, in an instant, should he ever surrender to it.

❉

A couple of miles out of town, they passed a stand of twisted eucalypts, their trunks wound up and bent like wrung towels, that marked a willywilly's hunting ground. Bowley put his left hand to his badge, tracing runes—not that a willywilly was likely to give them trouble when they had a spook in their company. O'Shane pointed. Stink McClure's shack—the old willywilly ground a signpost on the trail. Bowley had been trying not to look. The Dappled Man kept riding, facing straight ahead.

"Bowls," said Alby, softly. "Strikes me that a Queen's magister'll tow a whole company of redcoats around with him. This bloke reckons he can only protect four of us. Makes me wonder, if we come across this thing that did for Stink, whether he'll be able to handle it."

"Alby," Bowley said. "I reckon you think too much, mate."

He slipped a hand inside his jacket, wound the cap off his hip flask with thumb and forefinger, and took a swig. He glanced at Alby, staring pointedly at the flask. Bowley took another mouthful and handed it over. Alby upended it, then passed it around. It came back to Bowley from German, empty.

"Damn," said Bowley, but without much rancour. "Greedy bloody Kraut."

"Vasn't me," said German, "Vas this greedy Irish bastard, here."

Alby sneezed loudly, startling a flock of cockatoos into screeching, deafening flight. Men and horses alike all but jumped off their shadows. Young O'Shane's filly put her head down and pigrooted, nearly planting the Irishman into the dirt. Clay danced sideways, objecting to the younger horse's theatrics. Bowley pulled her head around and make her walk a full circle. He patted her neck as she calmed, his own heartbeat pounding in his ears. The cockies settled in the branches above, white enough to be the spirits of the dead, like the blackfellas believed, but complaining far too loudly to be ghosts.

Neither the Dappled Man nor his horse had reacted to the commotion behind them. The Man reached a fork in the track and unerringly picked the way that led up the Loop.

"Bloodless bastard," O'Shane muttered.

"Reckon this fog might lift?" said Alby.

Bowley looked skywards. "Not for a while, anyway."

The track started to climb. They passed the Mitchell brothers' place shortly after. The Dappled Man ignored that, too. Bowley noted the absence of smoke coming from the chimney pipe. He knew with a sick knotting in his guts what they'd find inside if they looked.

The trees opened out on a shelf of lichen-fringed rock. The clopping of their horses iron shoes became abruptly louder, but flattened, the echoes smothered by the mist. The flanks of the ranges rose ahead, a blue-green wall vanishing into greyness.

Bowley squeezed Clay's ribs between his knees. When she didn't respond, he gave her a thump with his heels. She broke into a reluctant trot to come level with the Dappled Man, her hooves striking a dissonant staccato on the rock.

The Man sat hunched in his saddle, as if guarding his darkness against leaching away into the grey surrounds. He seemed diminished—not so fearsome, now, when fearsome was what they wanted most.

"You know what we're hunting," Bowley said, flat.

The Hessian fringe turned towards him. The Man whispered a reply, "Broken Hill."

It took Bowley a moment to make the connection. His mouth turned dry. Broken Hill. "Christ."

It had been a mining town up in New South Wales, out near the edge of the desert, where the spirit of the land hadn't yet lain down to sleep. Some bitter dream had slithered out of a seam in the rock and into the mines. Possessed by it, the miners had devoured the town and besieged the survivors in the church for four days until the magisters arrived from Sydney Town with a train full of redcoats and organ guns packed with silver grapeshot.

So the story went.

"How?" Bowley asked. "Dreamings don't travel. There's never been any dreamings like that around here."

The Man didn't answer immediately. The trees closed in again around them. There was wood smoke in the mist, blackfellas in the scrub. A camp. Cooking fires smouldered in a second, smaller clearing, enclosed by a half circle of lean-to shelters. The tribe watched them silently between the tree trunks. The women and children stood behind the men, swaddled in possum-skin cloaks and emu feathers. The cloaks were scorched with the same dot-and-line maps that scarred the blackfellas' skins, that connected them to the land's power and protected them from its dreamings. The men leaned on long spears and the hip-high war boomerangs that whitefellas knew as Number Sevens, for the curve and unequal proportions of their arms.

The blackfellas made no gesture or sound, just watched.

"That was a new dreaming, full of anger and strength," said the Dappled Man, when they'd passed. "When the land becomes quiet, as it is here, such dreamings sink down into the rock, and wither away over time. This dreaming, here and now, will be old, from deep in the ground, with little of it left, otherwise it would've attacked the town already."

"But how did it come up? There's no mines."

"Caves?" the Man suggested, and suddenly Bowley saw it all: Del Mar kids with lanterns, daring each other to go further and further into the grottos up the back of the property. Or young Del Mar men, maybe, down there looking for veins in the rock, one of them putting a hand on some old stone, under which a nightmare slept, that would have slumbered away to nothing if one poor fool hadn't happened upon it.

The spook was watching him intently.

"Del Mar's," Bowley said. "Up the top of the Loop."

"How many people there?"

"Maybe forty, plus kids."

"It probably won't have been strong enough to use all of them," the Man said. "But expect there to be children among those it's taken."

Bowley didn't need to ask what would've happened to the rest. He felt a sharp little hurt behind his breastbone. He saw Maise's sister Lucy, putting a hand on his shoulder the last time he'd visited, interrupting his conversation with the Del Mar men to ask him if he wanted tea. A plumper, warmer, motherly version of Maise, almost invariably with a smile on her face. Her daughter Jemima had served the tea, a willowy child with her father's height, barely into womanhood, her cheeks flushing at the gentle teasing of her great-uncle Javier.

Maise's face came to his mind's eye, jaw quaking and eyes brimming before she dipped her head and he turned his back on her and rode away. Bowley's hands were shaking again. He fumbled for his flask, was surprised for a moment to find it empty.

He flung it into the bush. "Fucking hell."

❁

The Del Mar house was an overgrown cousin to the cottages in town—the way a mastiff is to a terrier—a great, brooding thing of raw timbers and tar. Timber roofed, too, with a cavernous loft space where the children slept. They had some talented runesmiths among them, the Del Mars—Oscar had learned the craft in his native Andalusia—so they had no need for English slates to press the building on its runestone foundations. The whole house was covered in a mesh of flowing Arabic script and the angular English runes that Oscar and his sons had learned since they left their homeland. New wings had been added, over the years, as sons and daughters married and brought their wives and husbands back to live. Only a handful, like Maise, had made their lives elsewhere. All of the extensions connected back to the main house, with just the stables and feed barns standing separate, and they were connected to the house with paths of rune-carved corduroy.

It was a fortress town in all but name, Del Mar's, and stronger in its defences than most towns. But perhaps, Bowley thought to himself, its greatest strength was also its weakness. Because dreamings understood matters of blood and hearth—of place—intimately. No dreaming was intelligent, but some were clever. The rare one was strong enough to roam over an area, not tied to a single spot like a willywilly or a bunyip. If a dreaming of that kind got into a man's shadow, then it might ride him to his home and maybe no density of warding signs, English or Arab—or blackfella, for that matter— would keep the contagion out and stop it spreading to his kin.

The Dappled Man reined in at the edge of the cleared ground that surrounded the farm buildings. There was no sign of the cattle that ranged freely over the hills, but which often hung around near the house. The farm was shuttered and silent. Bowley halted Clay beside the Dappled Man. Young O'Shane pulled up beside him and Alby and German on the Man's far side. Alby snuffled into his handkerchief.

Bowley drew his carbine from its sleeve and laid it across his lap. Alby and German followed his example. O'Shane drew two of his four pistols.

The townsmen's horses whickered and danced as the Dappled Man's hunting shadows returned and wriggled up his mount's legs. The Man straightened in his seat, but still he seemed less than he had the day before. A breath of wind rolled curling fingers of mist from the trees beyond the house. Bowley searched the grey above for some sign of a tear in the veil. There was nothing.

The Dappled Man walked his horse a few paces into the open. Another breath of air chilled Bowley's face and ruffled the horses' manes. It tugged the man's coat, collapsing the side of it inwards. Bowley saw him clearly, then: as a scarecrow, a mockery of a man, a creature with limbs and head but only shadow at his centre.

The Man's horse stopped dead in its tracks. It's ears twitched furiously. Clay whickered and tossed her head. Then all the horses were at it, fidgeting and complaining and dancing on their hooves. The air seemed suddenly thin in Bowley's lungs, as though there was a big storm approaching.

The Man's head whipped to the left. Bowley looked that way in alarm, but could make out nothing untoward among the trees. He ran his fingers over the killing runes etched into his carbine's stock. The Man turned the other way, stared.

Bowley thought he heard a whisper of sound, a distant yelping and howling.

"No." The Dappled Man spun his horse on the spot. "Run!" he barked. "We can't face it here."

His horse launched itself towards them.

"Run!" the Man cried.

Then he was past them and all of them were cursing, their horses skittering about and bumping into each other while they tried to get them turned around. Bowley glimpsed figures in English clothes racing through the trees. The howling had grown rapidly more distinct. It was in his head, Bowley realised with a stab of horror, but not in his ears.

The riders got themselves moving. Alby and young O'Shane galloped ahead of Bowley, down the slope, Alby riding one-handed, as Bowley was, his rifle pressed across his lap. Bowley glanced back and saw that German was already falling behind, fat Bismarck struggling under his rider's weight, German with one fist in his horse's mane and the other flailing his rifle about for balance. Their conjoined shadows stretched out ahead of them, straining to drag horse and rider along. "Move it, you fat bloody Kraut!" Bowley yelled back, which wouldn't help German at all, but there was nothing practical Bowley could do for him.

Clay jerked her head as something flew past her nose. A second object struck painfully against Bowley's arm. He tucked his head down. In his peripheral vision he saw running figures closing on either side, arms pulled back and whipping forward—throwing rocks as they ran. He caught jumbled impressions of bloody chins and blood-stained shirts, of mouths open wide in silent anguish.

Then he was past them. He looked back. German made it through a heartbeat before the first pursuers spilled onto the track. The blacksmith had lost his hat. Bowley saw a splash of red across his forehead. But German was still in his saddle, gritted teeth and wide eyes stark in his dark face.

Clay gained quickly on the three riders ahead. They'd already slowed their horses to a canter. Bowley did the same as he came up to them. The Dappled Man twisted in his saddle. Bowley wished he could see the expression on the spook's face. Alby looked back, too, and gave a shake of his head. Whether the gesture was one of exasperation with Bowley, or the spook, or the situation in general, Bowley wasn't certain.

German hadn't caught up. And wasn't going to, Bowley saw. Bismarck was labouring even harder, now, the horse's gait uneven, favouring a hind leg. Bowley swore under his breath and reined Clay back into a trot. He felt the tug on his flesh as her shadow and his both resisted. The gap between them and the three riders ahead widened again. The mist closed between them.

He scanned the bush around as German caught up. Bismarck didn't need any instruction from his rider to slow to a trot.

"Look's like he's lame."

German dabbed at the cut on his temple with his handkerchief, examined the resulting mess on the white cloth with distaste. "Stone hit him in the leg," he replied. Bowley could see where—a patch of torn hair just above the gelding's hock. German drew a shaky breath and added, "Vell, that vas a vasted trip."

Bowley heard the note of hysteria in the other man's voice, and in his own chuckle in response. "We'll hold a trot for a bit, see if he works the lameness out. We should stay ahead of them at this pace."

German nodded. "Ya, but they vill go straight down the hill vhile ve follow the track."

"Better keep an eye out then, hadn't we?"

German gave a rictus grin. "I notice those other bastards didn't hang around."

"Spook's getting back to town quick," Bowley said. He hoped—to get them ready. By rights, he should be riding ahead, too, and leaving German to take his chances. There had been a lot of people in the scrub at Del Mar's, enough for it to be the whole damn clan taken by this dreaming. And, Christ, he couldn't get those half-seen faces, or the silent howls of the thing that possessed them, out of his head.

They were—it was—coming after them, he was certain, like a tiger snake that'd chase you for a mile even after it'd struck at you once, just because it was pissed at the world and you happened to be a part of it. He hoped like hell this Dappled Man wasn't lighting out on them, that Alby'd shoot the son of a bitch in the back if he was.

They passed the spot where the blackfella tribe had been camped. No sign of them now.

A tortured whispering brushed his mind. He felt a sucking at the soles of his feet. His and Clay's shadows snapped free of the horse's hooves and lit out across the bare rock ahead. German's shadow on Bismarck's was close on their heels.

"Gruene . . . "

" . . . Christ!"

Running figures emerged from the mist, off to their left. Bowley kicked frantically at his horse's ribs. "Move!"

Clay leapt into a gallop. Bismarck whinnied, in pain, and terrified of the thing that pursued them.

A man lunged out of the trees on their right. Clay's hooves struck the edge of the rock shelf, clattering like gunshots. Behind them, Bismarck screamed.

Bowley looked back. The gelding staggered out onto the open rock. A pick handle hung obscenely from his belly. The horse's his eyes bulged as he cried bewilderment and pain.

Bowley hauled back on Clay. Her hooves skidded on the bare stone. Her back end dropped before she found purchase again. Bowley loosed the reins and spun her with his knees.

Bismarck collapsed. German leapt clumsily but got his legs clear of the horse's weight. Bismarck's cries drowned out the dreaming's dingo howls.

The attacker charged out of the trees, empty hands raised like claws. Francisco Del Mar, an iron-haired Andalusian bull. He was barely recognisable, with sticks in his hair and the animal snarl on his face. His feet were bare and he cast no shadow. German was still on his back, no runes between him and the thing that ran beneath Franscisco and his kin. Bowley was acutely aware of how vulnerable they were, with their shadows far from their feet.

He brought his carbine to his shoulder. Christ, Maise's cousin Frank. He sighted and fired. Missed.

Clay danced on the spot, ears flat.

Bowley swore and sought the cold, marksman's place within himself that used to be so easy to find. He pushed down the carbine's lever to eject the empty shell and chamber the next. It stuck halfway.

"Shit!" Bowley pounded the jammed lever with the heel of his hand.

German had his boots under him. Fransisco was almost on him. More Del Mars emerged from the trees. German ignored them. He raised his rifle and shot his dying horse through the top of the head. Bismarck's cheek slapped loudly against the rock.

Dingo howling curled through the abrupt quiet.

"German—behind you!"

The blacksmith met Bowley's stare with dazed eyes. He turned, fired at Fransisco from the hip. The bullet caught the Del Mar in the shoulder, spun him all the way around and down to the ground.

German swung his rifle towards the approaching horde and kept shooting, not bothering to aim. There were a good forty or fifty people: men, women and children, and more than just Del Mars. Bowley spied White Mitchell's narrow frame among the front ranks. All of them were barefoot, like Francisco, all filthy and bloody and with the same rictus snarl on their faces. Many of them carried farm tools—picks, hatchets and shovels—as weapons. None of them made a sound, only the silent howling of the thing that possessed them.

"Run!" Bowley cried, "You stupid bloody Kraut! Run!" He hoped Alby had shot that damn spook, for lighting out and leaving them. He shoved his jammed carbine into its sleeve and fumbled for his service revolver.

German's rifle clicked, empty. The dream-taken were almost on top of him. German started to swing his rifle by the stock, spitting curses in his native tongue. Francisco Del Mar staggered to his feet behind him, his right arm dangling. Bowley shouted a warning.

Too late. Francisco hooked his left arm around German's neck, pulling him off balance just as the rest reached him. They bore him to the ground. Hooked fingers tore at his clothes. Heads dipped, teeth bared, and German's curses turned to screams.

Bile rose in Bowley's throat, spurting out of his mouth before he could swallow it back down. Most of the Del Mars kept coming. Bowley raised his pistol and fired off all six shots without seeing where any of them struck.

He heard the deep 'whooosh-whooosh' before he saw the war boomerangs come spinning out of the scrub. They tore into the dream-taken, snapping human bodies like stalks of wheat.

A rider burst past Bowley. The Dappled Man. Shadows writhed all over both the spook and his horse. The Del Mars fell back, closing ranks before him.

Bowley put his heels to Clay's ribs, and fled. Among the trees, blackfellas whirled like hammer throwers. A second flight of war boomerangs launched into the air.

✶

The Dappled Man caught up with him near Stink McClure's shack. Clay had slowed to a trot of her own accord, and then a walk. The Man had lost his hat and his Hessian shawl was scrunched in one fist. Lank, shoulder-length grey hair framed bony features that receded at forehead and chin from his long nose. The complexion of his face was, indeed, the same unhealthy mottled grey as his hands.

The Man slowed his horse beside Clay. Moving with what seemed to be pained slowness, he shook out his shawl.

"Where the hell were you?" Bowley demanded.

The spook glanced his way, a flash of washed-out grey eyes. He lifted his shawl and put it back over his head. Shadows crawled around his face beneath its fringes. He slumped, evidently exhausted. "I'm sorry. I didn't know you were in danger until your shadows caught up with us."

"Did you kill it?" Bowley asked.

The Man shook his head. "A dreaming can't be killed, only put back in its place. The tribe and I together weren't enough to subdue this dreaming or deter it. When it's done licking its wounds, it'll follow us to town."

"Why did they try and help us?"

Another shake of the head. "Our presence was coincidence. The tribe's witchmen thought a surprise attack might defeat this dreaming. They underestimated its strength."

"So did you," Bowley said. "And now German's dead."

"It wasn't my decision to go hunting for it," the Man replied, softly.

The riposte struck home. My fault, Bowley thought. I shouldn't have let him come.

The Dappled Man extended a hand. "I have something for you."

Bowley's heart gave a lurch. He stared at the spook's outstretched palm. There was a barely visible tremor in the Man's fingers. Bowley's own hand shook noticeably as he raised it. The Dappled Man's skin was dry as old paper.

Darkness flooded out of the Man's sleeve and up Bowley's arm. Bowley yelped and would've snatched back his hand if the spook hadn't gripped his fingers tightly. The darkness flowed over Bowley's shoulder and down his side, along his leg and then down his horse's to pool on the ground beneath them. It resolved itself into his shadow astride Clay's, before fading in the dull light. The Dappled Man released his hand.

Bowley clutched at his chest. "Green Christ."

The Man leaned on his saddle horn, his head bowed. Bowley's rattling heartbeat slowed to a more normal rate. The Dappled Man spoke again, his voice a bare rasp, "The tribe's intervention has increased our risk when we face this dreaming again. Whenever one of those it has taken is killed, it is freed to steal another shadow."

Bowley watched him, swaying like he could hardly hold his seat, and said, "It took some of yours, didn't it?"

The Man nodded.

And did you keep German's? Bowley wondered, Or did the dreaming take it from you? His scalp goosepimpled. The spook could as easily have kept his and Clay's, had he wanted. Giving them up had plainly cost him.

"How do we stop it?" he asked.

The cowled head remained lowered, the tattered fringes of the shawl falling forward to hide the Man's face completely. "Kill all of them," he said. "All but the first infected. Each death will be a shock to the dreaming that possesses them. While it's still reeling, I can—perhaps—subdue it and return it to the land."

Kill all of them. Bowley's vision blurred. Oh, Maise.

❋

The mist had settled at the bottom of the valley, where the town stood, denser than when they'd left. There was a crowd gathered between the posts of the town gate. All men, except for Maise, and all of them armed. Alby and young O'Shane were among them. Bowley watched their faces fall when they realised German wasn't with them.

Bowley gathered his jammed gun and dismounted. He slapped Clay on the rump. The crowd parted to let her by and she skittered off down the street, vanishing quickly into the grey—smart enough, he hoped, to stay inside the rune circle.

"Where's German?" Maise asked.

"Dead," Bowley replied. "Same as old Stink."

She looked away from him, covering her lips with her fingertips and drawing deep breaths.

"We're ready," said Alby. "Everyone else is in the church."

"Uncarved bullets won't hurt the dream-taken," said the Dappled Man, down from his horse now, too. Only an arm's length from Bowley, he seemed to fade into the mist. He stood straight though, and apparently without difficulty.

Bowley looked around at the frightened, determined faces, then back at the spook. "We've got more than four guns loaded with carved bullets," he said.

He pulled his revolver from its holster and reached past Maise to offer it butt-first to Ulf Erikssen, dug in his left pocket for fresh cartridges.

"I can only defend four of you," said the Dappled Man.

"Reckon we'll defend ourselves, mate," said Alby. He handed one of his rifles to Ted Wright. Young O'Shane followed his example.

The spook was still for a minute. His pale eyes glittered beneath the ragged fringe of his shawl, boring into Bowley. Bowley hoped his fear wasn't plain to see on his face. He returned the Man's stare as levelly as he could. At last, the Man said, "Anyone else wants to fight, you'll need weapons with killing runes carved on them."

"The rest get your arses into the bloody church," said Bowley, his knees momentarily weak with relief. Most of the crowd scattered.

Maise glared at him through tears of frustration.

"That includes you, Maise," he said. He was amazed that his voice was steady. "It's your whole bloody family coming down on us, love. What'll you do if you get Lucy in your sights? Or Jemima?"

Her nostrils flared. She pressed her lips white as she, too, tried to stare him down. He put a hand on her arm, pushed her gently. Maise turned away, swayed a little and stumbled on her first step, then walked in the direction of the church.

Bowley took a long breath, felt it chill his lungs. He let it out with a puff. To no-one in particular, he said, "I'll be back in a minute."

He strode through the crowd and down the street towards the police station. Inside, he went straight to his desk drawer and retrieved his half-empty bottle of whiskey. He pulled the plug with his teeth and took a long swig. He closed his eyes for a minute while the burn of it spread through his chest.

He rummaged around in the drawer for the screwdriver he thought might be there, found the letter opener and decided that would do. He perched on the desk with the carbine across his lap to try and un-jam it. To his relief, he was able to do so without disassembling the gun. Bootsteps sounded on the boards outside as the lever snapped back into place, chambering the offending cartridge properly, this time.

Alby leaned on the doorpost.

"Didn't know you'd fallen behind, Bowls," he said. "Spook said to keep riding, when we realised."

Bowley passed him the whiskey. "I know," he said. "No worries, mate."

They made their way past empty houses to the church, where the spook had gathered everyone willing to fight below the steps: young O'Shane, Ulf, Ted Wright, half a dozen others busily loading their weapons with the spare bullets Alby and O'Shane had carried. Bowley handed out his spare rifle bullets. A handful of women and kids and shamefaced men huddled in the church's doorway to watch. Dougie MacGill, mad old buzzard that he was, was the only one to turn out without a gun, armed with the rune-carved pike head he'd souvenired when he retired from the redcoats, stuck on its rough cut pole.

The town's rune-stone ring ran across the back of the unwalled churchyard. The world beyond it was invisible in the mist.

Bowley looked down at his hands. They were rock steady. His emotions felt dull and distant—locked out. He cocked his carbine. He heard the creak-and-click repeated around him as the others did the same.

The Dappled Man raised his voice. "Hold your shadows close. Keep the your boot soles on the ground. For every one of its taken that the tribe killed, the dreaming can take one of you. There are worse things than dying, if you fall."

He let that sink in, before adding, "This dreaming has no understanding of guns. That's our advantage. Choose your shots well, because you'll not have enough bullets to finish this task."

"Alright, lads," Bowley said. "Spread out a bit, but stay close to the church. We don't know which way they're going to come."

Somebody shut the church door with a thump, and then only the movements of the men disturbed the silence—the crunch and crackle of their boots on dirt and brittle grass, the creak of oilskin coats— as they positioned themselves in a rough semi-circle, anchored at the corners of the church. Bowley's badge clinked against the top button of his uniform jacket as he took a few paces to position himself behind a headstone.

They waited.

German's death played again in Bowley's mind. He'd frozen, he knew, in the moments before the dream-taken had brought German down. Would it have made a difference, he wondered, if he hadn't? Might he have saved him?

The Dappled Man's spoke: "They're here." The howling began in Bowley's head an instant later.

A stick snapped, out in the mist, from the direction of the town gate. Gravel scraped. All weapons swung in that direction. Another sound cut across the howling.

"Number Sevens!" Bowley cried.

He dropped to his haunches a heartbeat ahead of the men around him. A war boomerang throbbed low overhead, through the space he'd occupied an instant before. A cry, abruptly silenced, told him someone hadn't been fast enough. Dougie MacGill hit the dirt with five feet of bent wood buried in his ribs. War boomerangs clattered against the stone of the church walls.

Somebody loosed a shot.

"Not until you can bloody see them!" Bowley yelled. He peered over the top of the headstone.

Ragged figures materialised out of the mist. Bowley came to his feet, bringing his carbine to his shoulder. For an instant, the sharpness of his perceptions overwhelmed him. He'd seen, in feral dogs, the hurt and desperation that drove them to hurl themselves at the muzzle of a gun. He saw it now in this charging rabble, with grime and gore unwashed from their faces and caked into their cuffs and shirtfronts, axes and shovels clasped in their fists.

Gunshots cracked to his left and right.

His vision narrowed. He was in his marksman's place, where he could act and not feel. Francisco Del Mar came under his sights once again. Bowley's first shot punched through the charging man's face and out the back of his head. The second hit him side-on as he stumbled. The impact took the shattered back of his skull clean off.

Bowley searched for a new target, wondering if he could pick out the first taken, the one who mattered, and avert the worst of the carnage.

He paused, overwhelmed by a sudden feeling of wrongness. "Where's the rest of them?"

There were less than twenty attackers in front of him. Half of them were down already and all of them, he saw, carried some kind of injury. He spun on his heel, shouted his question at the Dappled Man, positioned at the foot of the steps.

The Man was already turning, pointing, out where the rune-stone perimeter came closest to the church. Bowley saw movement in the mist.

"Alby! Over there!"

He ran to that side of their line, his gun at his shoulder, as Alby and the others nearest pivoted to meet the new threat.

His sights found a blackfella, running among the Del Mar mob. There were others. The tribe's intervention had cost them. Bowley tracked the blackfella's approach. He fired just as the man passed behind a tall tombstone. The bullet kicked chips off the edge of the stone. Someone else's bullet knocked the blackfella flat.

The new wave of attackers came fast. Bowley put his next two shots into the torso of one of the older Del Mar nephews from less than ten yards away. The twin impacts knocked the Del Mar off his feet, like a giant hand had slapped him flat. The axe handle he'd brandished pin-wheeled between the headstones. Bowley shot little Letitia Del Mar, coming behind, wearing a pinafore brown with blood. Her hair flicked up as the bullet came out the back of her head.

He was dimly aware of Alby beside him, flipping his rifle, already empty, to use as a club. Of Ulf, beyond Alby, with Bowley's service revolver gripped in both hands. Young O'Shane, pumping bullets from his pair of pistols with methodical precision.

A still figure caught Bowley's eye, out beyond the mayhem—a girl, standing straight and tall, her arms raised before her. Jemima Del Mar. Maise's niece. The first taken, Bowley realised. In front of the church, the Dappled Man mirrored Jemima's pose.

A woman charged straight at him. It was Maise's sister, Lucy—Jemima's mother. Bowley's finger froze on the carbine's trigger. His pulse pounded in his ears. There was nothing of the woman he'd known in the rictus of Lucy's face. He squeezed the trigger with a jerk, pulling the carbine's muzzle sideways. The bullet hit her high in the chest. She staggered into the arc of Alby's rifle butt. Bone and wood crunched together.

Les Barrett, a senior son-in-law, was hard on the Lucy's heels. Bowley flipped his empty carbine in his hands, felt the hot metal sear his fingers and palms, and swung. He met the downward arc of the man's mattock and used the momentum of the blow to push the weapon aside and put his elbow into Barrett's face. Bowley pulled his carbine back over his shoulder and swung. The trigger guard caught Barrett squarely in the side of the head. The blow jarred Bowley's wrists and elbows. Blood crazed beneath the skin of the dream-taken's temple, patterning like shattered porcelain. Bowley adjusted his grip and hit him again. Barrett collapsed.

Ulf went down under the weight of two assailants. Young O'Shane and Ted Wright arrived an instant too late. Ulf started to convulse on the ground. Ted impaled one attacker on the point of Dougie MacGill's pike, belted the other with a long-handled mallet he must've taken from one of her kin. The woman's head rocked on her shoulders. She lunged at Ted, making him stumble. O'Shane shot her, point blank, in the face. Ulf started to rise from the ground at his feet. The Irishman put his second pistol to the publican's forehead and pulled the trigger.

Closer to Bowley, Alby kicked little Tomas Del Mar, all of four years old, under the chin. He raised his boot again and stamped on the child's thin chest as he bounced against the earth.

Hands grappled Bowley from behind. Sharp teeth sank into the side of his neck. He wrenched free and spun. The carbine's stock missed his attacker by a whisker. Javier Del Mar, patriarch of the family, peeled back his bloody lips in a soundless snarl.

A hand snaked over the old man's shoulder and caught him around the face. Alby thrust his hunting knife up under Javier's chin. The Del Mar jerked backwards as the blade penetrated. Alby stumbled and they both started to fall.

"No!" Bowley lunged after them. For an instant, he clutched Alby's coat sleeve. Then the oiled leather slipped through his fingers and Alby's back hit the dirt.

His eyes bulged. His heels drummed the dirt. His shadow flitted away from his stricken body, then it too began to thrash, but only for a moment. Still struggling, it was sucked into the earth.

Alby started to rise. Bowley rammed the carbine's butt into his face. Alby fell back. Bowley hammered down again. Bone gave beneath the blow. Alby's limbs twisted spastically. Bowley swung in a frenzy, as though he could obliterate Alby's identity and, with it, the horror of what he was doing. The carbine's stock snapped. Bowley staggered. Alby's bottom jaw jutted up, above his collar, obscenely intact.

The field was still.

For a while, Bowley leaned on the splintered butt of his gun. His breath rattled in his ears. His neck and his burnt hands throbbed. He slowly pushed himself upright.

Aside from Bowley, only three of the townsmen who'd begun the fight were still on their feet. Young O'Shane was one of them, still with both his pistols in his hands. His face was slack, his eyes closed. Ted Wright crouched with his forehead resting against the pole of Dougie MacGill's pike, one forearm pressed against his belly. Blood dripped between his legs. Bowley began to shake.

One Del Mar still stood amid the carnage. Jemima. Neither she or the Dappled Man had moved, still confronting each other in their invisible battle of energy and wills. Even in the pale light, Jemima's shadow was dense and dark, many armed and many headed, as though cast by many suns. The Dappled Man's captive shadows writhed across his body.

He took a step forward. Then another. Jemima remained rooted. The Man walked towards her, each step an obvious effort, like a man wading through mud. He reached out and caught Jemima's chin. Still, she didn't move. Her shadow's many limbs writhed in agitation and it began to shrink towards her feet. Darkness poured out of her mouth and out of her nose and ears and eyes. It ran up the Dappled Man's wrist and into his sleeve. Jemima's body shook violently. The Man bowed his head, his shoulders hunched.

The last bit of shadow drained over Jemima's lip. The Man released his grip on her jaw and they staggered apart. The Man swayed but kept his feet. Jemima crumpled.

A keening sound penetrated Bowley's gun-deaf ears. At first he thought it was the dreaming, howling still, and he wondered how that could be. Then he realised the noise was coming from Jemima—each cry an uninflected blast of anguish, followed by a terrible, wrenching gasp for air, then another long, monotonous cry.

Maise raced across the field, arms outstretched, fingers splayed. She was too slow to catch Jemima before she fell. She skidded to her knees beside the girl and scooped her up. Jemima's face and neck were crimson, veins and ligaments pushed out with the force of the sound coming up her throat.

The Dappled Man stood over them, his shrouded head bowed, leaning a little, like someone who'd taken a bad hurt to the ribs.

His horse picked its way through the slaughter and stopped beside its master. The Man took a moment to react, as though he didn't see it at first. He reached up an arm, then got his foot into the stirrup and lifted himself with painful slowness to slump in the saddle.

The horse moved off again, past the rows of tombstones and out to the rune circle. Blackfellas waited in the fringes of the mist. They fell into step beside the rider as he vanished from sight. They'd see the dreaming put back into the ground, back where Jemima and her kin had found it, to go back to sleep and lie undisturbed until it withered away to nothing. Bowley wondered if he ought to go after them, to be certain it was done with and they'd seen the last of it.

He looked over at Maise, with her eyes screwed shut and her teeth clenched in a grimace, her own body wracked by sobs as she held her niece. What comfort could he offer her? What was there left for him and Maise, with the blood of her family on his hands?

He let the shattered carbine fall from his fingers. He walked towards Maise. Her head was turned away, to where the Man and his escort had gone into the mist. She didn't respond when he knelt beside her, put his hand on her back. He took a grip on her shoulders, pulled her in to him. She didn't resist. Jemima had exhausted her voice, for now, and sprawled in her aunt's arms, panting like a hurt animal. Her eyes were bulged and bloodshot in her still-red face.

Maise pulled away suddenly, and turned to look at him, her face fierce. "You go after them, Robert," she said. "You make sure it's done right."

He didn't want to, started to shake his head, because his place was right here, with all the death and ruin about them to clear away, bodies to bury or burn, and the people needing someone to show the way, and that being down to him, the Queen's Man in Useless Loop. And what would he know, anyway, if he did go, about whether this dreaming was put to rest for good, or not?

But, "Go!" she said, and he staggered up and away from her, propelled by the force in that word.

People stumbled out of the church. Some fell to their knees, some turned away and covered their children's eyes, some vomited. Others hugged each other and wept. A sudden shaft of bright sunshine lit the battlefield in unwelcome light. Bowley hurried past.

He put his fingers to his mouth, barely noticing the salt-metal tang of blood as his whistle shattered the quiet. He whistled again, and saw Clay prick her ears, standing in the street outside the police station. He went to her at a stumbling run, and got her moving at a trot as soon as he was aboard.

He felt the pressure of their eyes, like a physical weight, as he skirted the churchyard. He kept his own fixed straight ahead. No-one called out to him. Maise didn't look up from rocking her niece. The Dappled Man and his escort had already vanished into the mist. It didn't matter—Bowley knew where they were headed.

He caught up with them quickly enough. The blackfellas ignored him, so he followed a few yards behind, all the way up into the hills behind Del Mars'. The Dappled Man swayed like a man half dead in his saddle. His horse directed itself, or sometimes the blackfellas did, when it seemed unsure. They walked tirelessly, high-stepping over undergrowth and litter from the trees so they rarely needed to check their gait. Bowley watched the patterns of scars on their backs and legs, rippling as they moved, and wondered at the price they paid for living with the land, for not holding themselves apart as whitefellas did.

At the mouth of the caves, they pulled the Man down from his horse and carried him inside, stooping under the low lip of rock. One paused when Bowley got down from Clay and made to follow. He raised a hand, his long, broad-tipped fingers splayed, the palm pink and free of scars. He held Bowley's gaze with brown-black eyes. Shadows gathered beneath his heavy brow. The ridged scars that covered his skin formed a mask that obscured his expression. Once he was certain Bowley wasn't going to follow, the man turned and went after his fellows.

Bowley waited, with only the horses for company. He saw to Clay, but left her saddled, and made himself a small fire. The Man's horse seemed content and Bowley was disinclined to approach it. He hunched beside his fire as night closed in and knew he'd made a mistake, coming here. Knew he should've stayed in town, and been the Queen's Man, no matter what Maise had wanted. But he knew there was no way he could've refused her.

He stared into the flames, trying not to see Alby's head come apart, over and over again. He tried not to hear German's screams as human teeth tore into him. Not to see the grief on Maise's face as she held her niece, nor hear Jemima's wailing, that said saving her was the worst they could've done. Exhaustion eventually let him fall into a light doze.

✦

The blackfellas brought the Dappled Man back out in the grey of morning. He said nothing to Bowley, nor even appeared to recognise his presence, even though Bowley rose to his feet barely an arm's length from where the Man passed.

The blackfellas led him to his horse and put him up in the saddle. One of them took its reins, and another two held the Man's legs to keep him in his seat as they walked away with him into the bush.

Bowley was left alone once again, and wondering what victory had cost the spook, whether he hadn't been able to separate all of himself from the dreaming when they'd put it back into the ground.

He looked back into the cave, felt gooseflesh rise all over his body. He could only hope that the task was done.

He got his skinning knife from his saddle roll, scratched the rune for danger into the rock above the cave mouth. The sign had no power, since he had none to give it, and the shallow marks would fade quickly, but it would serve, for now.

✦

Smoke rose from the churchyard, when he returned to town. A funeral pyre. They'd burned all the bodies together. A few folk watched him walk past on Clay, their faces closed in, looking at him like a stranger. Crows picked among the headstones, hunting for any titbits that might've been overlooked.

There was a cart outside the post office, half loaded with small furnishings and baskets and crates of bric-a-brac. Maise's rocking chair, from the porch, that Nev had made her for a wedding gift, was lashed in pride of place on top of the pile. As Bowley approached, she came out with a basket of clothes. Her eyes flickered over to him. Her expression closed in and she looked away.

Bowley stopped Clay beside the cart and watched for a moment while she worked the basket into a too-small space at the back.

"Maise? You're leaving?"

She didn't look up. "I am."

His eyes were suddenly hot and overfull. "Where are you going, love?" he asked.

"Don't you . . . " She caught herself. "I don't know. Away."

Bowley's mouth worked silently for a moment before he could shape more words. "Would you have left before I got back?"

Maise stopped, bowed her head. "I can't do it, Robert," she said, from between her raised arms. "I can't even look at you."

She gave the basket a final shove and turned her back on him. He watched her disappear back inside. She returned a moment later, followed by Dermott O'Shane, carrying Jemima. The younger man glanced at Bowley, and away again, without speaking. Maise climbed up onto the cart's bench, then turned to help O'Shane lift Jemima up beside her. The girl was wrapped in a blanket, so Bowley could discern little more than the fact that she was conscious. She huddled against Maise, tucking her head low. Maise sat straight and rigid, looking neither left nor right, nor back, as she picked up the reins and clucked their horse into motion.

Clay danced a little, when the cart started moving. She twisted her neck to watch it, then snorted, and returned her gaze forward, to wait patiently, again, for her master to tell her what to do. O'Shane looked as though he might speak, then shook his head, dissatisfied with the words he might've offered, and walked away.

Bowley sat there for a long time, the words "Can I come with you?" lying bitter on his tongue.

# WHEN THE RAIN COMIN

Gamman smelled rain. Through a metre of hard red clay, through the tough membrane of her cocoon, she felt the clouds building.

And she smelled rain.

Slowly, she stirred from the deep torpor her body had sunk into over the long years of the dry. Warmth spread, as her heart began to pump faster. Her eyelids fluttered. She drifted into a shallower sleep. Fingers and toes, half-webbed, flexed.

The rigid shell of the cocoon had been secreted from the glands in her wrists, to harden as her body cooled and stilled. It began to break down now with her rising heat, filling the burrow with clean air.

Gamman awoke, sucking in deep breaths and holding them. With eyes, nostrils, lips and gills clamped firmly shut, she pressed her hands and feet around the walls of the cavity. Gamman turned herself over onto her knees and began to pull at the hard earth with fingernails like stout spades. She'd filled the burrow's tunnel in behind her as she'd dug down into the earth. The years of the dry had compacted the loose dirt. The clay resisted, but her hands and forearms were strong. She dug steadily upwards.

Her fingertips found a trace of moisture. She shoved upwards and her hands broke free into cool air. Gamman shouldered her way through the surface layer of clay and pulled herself from the burrow.

She squatted, tucked up, with her eyes closed while she re-acquainted herself with the sound and touch of the world. It was daytime, but not warm. The wind raised goosebumps on her skin. The light came pink through her eyelids, but it wasn't blinding bright. Small things scuttled about on the ground nearby. Gamman felt the prickle of thunder.

She opened her eyes.

She was facing the sea, the great dry pan of salt that went to the horizon. It was dull white under a roof of grey clouds that blotted the sun. The clouds were heavy with the sky's grief, accumulated over the long years of the dry. The sea would fill up, when the rain fell.

It had rained some already, she could feel it in the dampness of the earth. But not enough, yet, to bring forth the green leaves and bright flowers that would carpet the ground once the true downpour began. Red dirt extended away from the saltpan, broken by outcrops of eroded rock the same colour. Red dunes encroached to the south, closer than Gamman remembered. The olive and grey foliage of brittle-dry shrubs interrupted the monotony. When the rain came, they would flower in yellow and blue, pink and white.

Gamman's stomach grumbled. She duck-walked over to the nearest shrub and dug around its roots for the fat white grubs that slumbered there. She gobbled them greedily.

"Gamman."

She turned. A man approached. His brown skin was covered in red dust, as was hers. The same stuff matted his hair and beard. His chest and shoulders were wide above the slits of his gills across his middle torso. His long-legged gait was easy.

"Ulin," she said, her voice rusted from lack of use. "I be seein you."

Ulin grinned, showing good teeth apart from one chipped corner at the front.

He squatted to join her digging under the shrub, quickly turning up a pair of grubs. He offered one to Gamman and popped the other into his mouth.

"You be early wakin," he said.

"Early wakin like Suka, my mother," she agreed.

Ulin swallowed the grub and smacked his lips. "Them late wakin peop'e don' know what them missin," he declared.

Gamman grimaced. The muscles of her face moved awkwardly, only dimly remembering the expression. "Fishes tas'e better, I think."

Ulin chuckled. His gaze ran over her. "You bein all grown," he said.

She felt a slight stirring between her legs. Ulin was a handsome man. "Am now," she agreed.

He grinned again, then looked over his shoulder. He raised an arm to point to a low, flat-topped butte near the dry shore. "Some other early wakin peop'e be at the cave already."

Gamman stood cautiously, bracing fingertips on Ulin's shoulder while her head spun a moment. He rose beside her and they started walking towards the butte. She thought perhaps that Suka, her mother, would be among those already awake.

❀

People gathered at the cave over the following days as scattered showers fell. The occasional rumble of thunder could be heard from deep within the clouds.

Of every newcomer, Gamman asked, "You been seein Suka, my mother?" But none had.

Her sister came in—Tennip, born of Suka as well and older than Gamman. Tennip answered the same as the rest, "No," then watched Gamman a while as she asked the next ones after her.

Eventually Tennip came and sat beside Gamman at the mouth of the cave. Both of them gazed out over the saltpan.

Tennip said, "Suka, who give birth to you an me, she seen the rain come many time. I think she not be wakin this time."

Gamman hung her head. "I think you right."

Later, Gamman sat close beside Ulin. The light touch of his knee against her thigh had a burning intensity. Daylight had faded behind the clouds and the cave was lit only by the campfire. The people around it were still, at rest.

In the stories that were sometimes told, of the dawn time when there was always rain, people were always moving, never resting, never still, and all the creatures and fishes were the same. People didn't dig in those days, but built their places by piling sticks and rocks on top of the ground, and hid inside from the rain. And they couldn't breathe the water, just the air, so they had to do their fishing from the edge of the sea.

Gamman saw Tennip start to fidget, and knew that a song had come into her even before she lifted her head and released the first mournful cry.

"Ai-yah. Ai-yah oh!"

Gamman shared a sigh with all the rest.

Tennip cried out again, "Ai Suka! Ai-yah oh!"

She stood to begin a shuffling dance around the flames. Some rose to join her, others who were tired or who tended small children retreated to give the dancers room.

Ulin turned to Gamman. He laid a hand on her breast, then on her belly. She shivered.

"You bein ol' enough, now," he said.

They retreated to the back of the cave and mated, simply and quickly, kneeling on the dusty stone. Afterwards, Gamman lay on her side, afraid that his juice might run straight out of her if she stood, while Ulin joined the dance around the fire.

She watched the dancers, shuffling and stamping, and imagined them as people from the dawn time, always moving, and wondered at the strangeness of those days.

❁

The storm finally broke, and the rain fell in sheets that hid the horizon. The people hunted small creatures that struggled from their burrows. They watched the flood creep across the saltpan. Then they swam, diving under for long hours with the brine flowing in their throats and gills. They chased the fishes—scaled, shelled or many-legged—and ate most of them raw. Only rarely did they come back to shore.

Gamman mated several more times with Ulin. The next rain, she would wake with a baby grown inside her. She would birth it in the flooding sea and suckle it and teach it to swim.

One night, near the end of the rain, the clouds broke apart for a while, as some of the people sat beside the shore. They gazed up at the stars.

A story came to Gamman that Suka, her mother, had told when Gamman was young. Gamman let it pass through her and out, beginning as stories always began: "In the dawn time, when the worl' was new, there was always rain, for the sky still wep' at bein apart from the earth."

She waited for the sigh that said people were listening, then went on. "In time, the sky an the earth grew ol', an them got slow, an them learn to be still. An all them creatures an fishes learn the same. An the sky learn to be conten' with bein apart from the earth, an didn' weep no more, hard'y at all. An there was no more rain. An all them creatures and them fishes learn to dig, an sleep still in the earth through the dry time, til the sky do weep again, an the rain come.

"An peop'e learn the same. 'Cept for them who wouldn'. Them peopl', them didn' want to stay still, them want to keep movin. An them peop'e learn the way up to the sky, an them become the stars. Them a'ways movin, still."

She slumped when the story was done with her, used up by the torrent of words. Ulin rested his hand on her back.

"Ai-yah oh," sang Tennip, softly.

The stars wheeled overhead. No-one else spoke. They sat still, and watched.

# THE CANAL BARGE MAGICIAN'S NUMBER NINE DAUGHTER

Something thumped onto the deck. Behra peered out into the rain from the shelter of her little hut at the front of the canal barge. The only light nearby was from the barge's running lanterns and the open door of the coal furnace at the far end of the deck. The glow of the town's street lamps was too weak to reach across the canal.

Her half-brother, Geneic, was by the furnace, his heavy Saltukkuri features lit orange while he bent his back against the downpour, shovelling coal. In the shadows of his brows, his eyes glowed a deeper red than the fire. In the wheelhouse beyond him, Behra could make out Chiufi's smaller silhouette. Their father and Sorgui, Geneic's twin, were asleep belowdecks.

A small shape skittered across the deck, nearer to Behra than to Geneic. She bit back a cry. Whatever it was, it wasn't the right shape for a rat or a water dragon or a cat. She waited, watching and listening. The only movement on deck was Geneic, the only sounds aside from the patter of rain were the rasp of his shovel in the coal and the thud-thud of the barge's steam engine.

She sat back, dissatisfied, and pulled her blankets back around her. Her ankle chain scraped across the boards.

"Don't be afraid," said a tinkling voice, right beside her in the hut.

Behra yelped.

"Shh!" said the voice, urgently.

Her heart rattled inside her ribs. Slowly, her eyes began to make out the speaker. It was man-shaped, slender, but it stood only about the height of her knee, the top of its head well clear of the hut's low roof.

"Are you a fairy?" she breathed.

The visitor laughed, a sound like the chimes Behra had sometimes heard on the sedans of Ornomagnen ladies, and stepped from the shadows into the faint light of the deck.

Behra's eyes widened. The visitor was a porcelain doll, its sculpted features those of a young Ornomagnen gentleman. It was dressed in a gentleman's frock coat and hose, damp from the rain, its outfit completed by tiny brass-buckled shoes and a tricorn hat.

"You're a doll," Behra said.

"A golem," it corrected. "I am in disguise. Do you speak Ornomagnen? My Rhuinish is limited."

Behra blinked. It hadn't occurred to her what language they were speaking. "Only a little." She could understand better than she could speak.

"No matter," said the doll, briskly. "I am Palinday." He swept off his hat and executed a courtly bow, revealing a head of real yellow hair, tied with ribbon at the back of his neck. His eyes glittered blue, catching the lamplight.

"Behra."

"Little Nine?" he said in Ornomagnen, translating her name. His face moved so little as the doll spoke that Behra wondered if she imagined his amusement.

She pulled away, tucking her knees up in front of her. Her chain clanked. Palinday's eyes followed it from her foot to the ring bolted to the frame of her hut. Now she was certain that his expression changed, painted brows drawing together in a frown.

She glanced towards the back of the barge. Geneic was looking towards the bank, sniffing the air. Chiufi, too, had turned his head that way.

Palinday said, "Hide me!"

Behra looked at him in confusion, but the doll was already burrowing under her blankets.

"Hide me," he repeated, muffled by the covers.

An approaching commotion reached her ears. Disregarding the rain, Behra crawled half out of the hut to see.

Soldiers flooded onto the bank, bursting from several streets at once. Their shouts identified them as Rhuinishmen. They milled about, musket barrels and halberd blades catching the light of the lamps many of them held, while their dogs cast this way and that along the canal wall.

One raised his voice above the rest. "You there! Bargeman! Did you see a fugitive come this way?"

There was quiet for several heartbeats. The soldier crabbed sideways as the barge continued to chug along. Geneic stared mutely back at him. Then Chiufi called back from the wheelhouse, "Beg pardon, sir, but my brother don't speak."

"Then speak for him, boy!" said the soldier. "Or fetch up your captain if you have not the wit to answer for yourself! And bring your vessel in to the bank."

Behra eased back into the shadows of her hut. She couldn't help a guilty start as she bumped against the doll's hard little limbs. Chiufi slowed the barge but made no move to steer it to the bank. Geneic's sloping brow beetled as Chiufi called for him to take the wheel. Chiufi hurried for the hatch at the rear of the barge and disappeared below. Geneic's silhouette all but filled the wheelhouse, his eyes glowing sullenly.

All the soldiers were pacing the barge now. A squad hurried ahead. There was a bridge at the end of the town, Behra remembered.

An angry bellow announced their father's emergence. Aghor stamped up onto the deck, followed by Sorgui. Chiufi slunk up the ladder behind them and along beside the barge's rail to join Behra in her hut. He squeezed her fingers, his gaunt features tight with worry. Behra felt her face heat, acutely conscious of the fugitive hidden in her blankets.

Aghor planted his feet wide to face the soldiers, ignoring the rain, his sleeveless vest exposing the black bramble tattoos coiled around his arms, fists on hips to pull back the vest and reveal the belt around his thick waist, made from the mummified foetuses and umbilicals of Behra's sisters.

She saw many of the soldiers draw back, making signs in front of their hearts to ward off black magic. Behra's lip curled. The soldier who had called out to Chiufi raised his voice again, but there was a tremor in it now. "Bargeman, bring your vessel to the bank. We are hunting a fugitive and have reason to believe it may be on your barge."

Her father lifted his chin. "In whose name do you order this?"

"In the name of Lord Tibuir," said the soldier, some of his confidence returning with the invocation of his master's name.

Aghor grunted and spat into the canal. The soldier's posture was rigid, full of offence and fear. "And what manner of fugitive is it," said Aghor, "that you refer to as 'it'?"

"A golem," said the soldier, "in the form of a child's doll."

Aghor guffawed. "A doll, is it?" He started to turn his back. "I have no truck with Ornomagnen trickery. Go back to your kennels, dogs. Tell Tibuir's Hound that if she wishes for Aghor's vessel to be searched, then she should come and see to it herself."

Behra wondered if the soldier would argue, or perhaps even order his fellows to shoot, but her father's name had power among Rhuinishmen. Hearing it deflated the last of the his bluster.

A shadow passed across the barge. The bridge. Behra looked upwards as they cleared it. A row of pale faces peered back from under the brows of their helmets.

"I wonder what that was all about?" said Chiufi.

"It's here," Behra said.

"What?"

She felt Palinday shift behind her. "It's here. The doll, under the . . . "

She froze. Their father was striding towards them. Behra didn't look up as he squatted in front of her, the shrivelled corpses of her aborted sisters dangling between his thighs. Chiufi gripped her fingers hard. She squeezed back, afraid for him, too, and wishing her hate could give him strength.

If their father found the doll, it would be Chiufi who would be punished for her misdemeanour, not Behra. She tried not to look at her brother's fingers, clenched in her own, at the small, misshapen nails that had grown back after Aghor had pulled them.

Her heart beat painfully hard. *I'm sorry, Chiufi.*

"Hand," Aghor said.

It took all Behra's will not to slump with relief. Her arm trembled with it as she held it out. From the corner of her eye, she saw her father drop his scrying bowl onto the deck. His rough fingers caught her hand, bending it back. She gritted her teeth as the point of his knife dug into her wrist, opening a vein. He squeezed, dripping her blood into the bowl. A sharp porcelain elbow or knee dug into the side of her leg like an accusation. She tried to keep her breathing steady. Surely her father must sense the doll's presence.

Sorgui crouched by the boat's rail, eyes closed, his brutish face lifted to the rain. He must have felt Behra's scrutiny, because he twisted his neck to look back, his red eyes locking with hers.

After what seemed an eternity, her father released her.

"Boy," he said to Chiufi, "get back to the wheel."

With a grunt of exertion, he rose and walked away, not waiting to see if Chiufi complied. Behra sucked her bleeding wrist. Chiufi released her and pulled out the grimy rag he kept in his pocket to quickly tear off a strip. Behra watched her father squat in front of the coal furnace and open the hatch. He reached in, bare-handed, to take out a burning coal which he dropped into the scrying dish.

Behra felt heat spread up her arm and through her chest.

"It *is* here," said Chiufi, in surprise.

Palinday had sat up.

"You have to get off this boat," Chiufi hissed, catching Behra's wrist to bind her cut, his movements hurried. "If father finds out about you, we'll get hell for it."

Behra only half-heard him. Her head was full of her father's murmured incantation. The words blazed across her mind. "*Sarhgu torosch abh. Sarghu feic abh . . .* " she mouthed. She didn't know what the words meant, but she knew what they did—a scrying spell.

Palinday watched her. "He uses your blood to power his magic."

"She's the ninth daughter," said Chiufi. He finished tying his knot and released her.

"Ah," said Palinday. "That is a foul thing."

"Foul or not, it'll go even worse if you're found," Chiufi snapped. His fear grew like a cloud in Behra's altered perception.

"He's looking for me now," said Palinday.

"Then go!" Chiufi sounded almost in tears.

Behra could feel her father's probing thoughts pressing up against her own. She pushed back, Chiufi's fear making her react without thinking. Aghor's attention slid easily aside. He didn't react, unaware of what she had done. Her pulse thumped, surprise and relief combined.

"I must get to Ardonailles," Palinday announced. He stood up, set his hat onto his head, and stepped out into the rain.

Chiufi let out a whine of terror.

By the furnace, Aghor looked up. The spell blinked out and Behra snapped abruptly back to her proper senses. Sorgui rose, looking to their father for instruction.

"Aghor the Bargeman," Palinday said, in Ornomagnen. "I am here."

"So you are," replied Behra's father, after a moment, in the same language. "And what have you done, little golem, to pull Lord Tibuir's beard?"

"I have information for Lord Emieldraeu," said Palinday. "The reward for aiding me would be substantial."

"The King's Spymaster," said Aghor. Then, sharply: "You would have me betray a fellow Rhuinishman to our Ornomagnen oppressors?"

"I think you have little fondness for Lord Tibuir," said Palinday, giving Sorgui a glance as he strolled past him. "And the slogans of the oppressed do not sit well on your tongue, magician."

Behra's father chuckled. The sound made her shiver. He stood, towering over the little doll.

Palinday stood his ground. "I am well warded against harm."

Aghor gave a snort. "I have cargo for Verdecastre. We can take you on to Nouvebourg from there."

"Ardonailles," said Palinday. "I need to get to Ardonailles."

Aghor's eyebrows rose. "Not to the King's city?"

"My journey needs to be direct," said Palinday. "You will be amply compensated for any loss on your cargo."

Behra's father regarded the doll for a moment, then harrumphed. "Very well, little golem. It pleases me to irk Tibuir. Too often business interferes with such pleasures. I will have that reward and compensation."

"And you will not punish the girl for hiding me," said Palinday.

Behra recognised the danger in her father's sudden stillness. Sorgui dropped halfway into a fighting crouch, broad hands flexing. It was several heartbeats before Aghor spoke, and when he did, there was an edge to his tone that belied his words, "Indeed. It would seem that she has brought me fortune."

His gaze fell on Chiufi. "Boy! Get back to the wheel!"

⟡

The skies had cleared at last. Behra sat out on the deck with Chiufi, enjoying the sun while they shared a pot of salted gruel. Palinday remained in the hut, sheltered from prying eyes.

Geneic and Sorgui squatted together by the wheelhouse, gazing incuriously at the traffic passing on the water and the canal-side road. Aghor was at the wheel.

Behra looked up at the pale walls of the fortress city as they slipped by. The flat tops of the walls bristled with cannon. Banners fluttered in the breeze, bright against the sooty background of smoke from the city's manufactories. She recognised the red and gold of Ornomagne hung above the green and white of Rhuin.

Palinday spoke up, "Those . . . " He paused. "Your father's belt, those are your sisters?"

Behra hunched her shoulders against the question. Chiufi answered, gruffly, "They are."

There was another silence from the doll. Behra concentrated on the castle flags.

"And your brothers?"

"Father made them birth early," said Chiufi, "same as our sisters, and tossed them over the side. At least one, after me. Probably others, before. All but them two."

Behra's eyes were drawn to Geneic and Sorgui, crouched side-by-side like a pair of gargoyles. Their half-human, half-demiman faces always looked sad to her when their expressions were relaxed.

"And them?" asked Palinday.

"Father bought himself a Saltukkuri bitch, and got them on her," said Chiufi. Noticing that Behra had stopped eating, he pulled the gruel pot onto his lap to scrape out the last of it.

"How many women?"

"Our mother, theirs. Others, maybe."

Behra's hands hurt. Her fists were clenched, nails digging into her palms.

"Bloody Sword and Chalice," the doll muttered.

The canal broadened, docks lining the bank, bustling with barges and carts. Behra gazed up at the black iron girders of the steam powered dock cranes, like a row of giants' gallows. Immense iron gates stood open, the way between them a gaping black mouth in the wall with portcullis teeth, swallowing and regurgitating endless streams of carts and coaches, riders and walkers. A train of coal wagons rattled along narrow tracks into the darkness, towed behind a huffing steam engine.

"Boy!"

Chiufi flinched at Aghor's shout. Behra touched his arm before he went. "Be strong."

"To the bow, boy!"

Soon now, Behra thought, doubting even as she told herself. Could she really be strong enough?

Her chain tugged against her ankle. She looked to see Palinday running his tiny, perfect fingers over the links, porcelain clicking on metal. His eyes met hers. "This chain is not thick," he said. "It would be easily broken."

Behra cast a glance over her shoulder at her father in the wheelhouse. He was looking past them at the waterway ahead. She glared at Palinday. "Be silent!"

He stared back with his gemstone eyes. "He always knows where you are."

"The thread that joins us gets thinner as we get further apart," Behra said. "I think it would break, if I got far enough away."

"You've tried," said Palinday.

Behra looked away, feeling hot moisture in her eyes.

"It was Chiufi your father beat when he caught you," he guessed.

She shook her head. Not a beating. Her hands twitched, about to lift and cover her ears, filled again with her brother's awful, wrenching cries as his fingernails were pulled out.

She covered her grief and guilt with a snarl. "One day . . . "

Palinday's eyes glittered. "My master, Lord Emieldraeu, would give you sanctuary."

For a moment, Behra could hardly breath.

The thud of the steam engine was slowing. She looked around.

Ahead, the land dropped away abruptly on either side of the canal. In the far distance beyond the edge, she could see low hills and chequered farmland. A gantry spanned the canal. Chimneys poured out thick smoke from the roof of a brick engine house on the bank. The canal ended in a wall inset with a row of gated, iron-sided bays. The gates of one bay opened, releasing a brief rush of water and a laden barge.

Aghor's barge slid smoothly into an open bay, Chiufi fending it off the walls with his barge pole. High on the gantry, gears and chains clanked. The gates were lowered, one behind the other. Lock workers guided the inner gate into grooves in the walls of the bay, turning it into a tub that held the barge and the water on which it floated.

Aghor emerged from the wheelhouse. Behra saw the eyes of the Rhuinish tax collector widen. She heard him stammer as he hastily stamped her father's manifest and took no money before he turned to wave urgently to his fellows on the gantry.

Ponderously, with tortured screams of metal on metal, the lift tub began to descend the steep face of the Rhuin Wall. Palinday risked peeping around the edge of the hut. Behra had a sudden urge to reach out and touch his fine clothes, stroke his golden hair. She kept her hands in her lap.

"Now there's a thing," the doll said.

Beyond the girders of the lift tower, the city extended out onto an outcrop of rock, prow-shaped, walled tiers descending the height of the cliff.

"Rhuincastre," said Palinday.

"Neic-ap-Nagh," replied Behra, giving the great city the Rhuinish name she'd always heard her father use.

"The anvil of kings," said Palinday, in Ornomagnen.

Beyond the city, a broad waterfall tumbled over the edge of the cliff. The sheer face of the Rhuin Wall extended into the distance on both directions, unbroken as far as the eye could see.

Palinday ducked back inside as the counterweight tub passed, going the opposite way. A row of children of different ages, boys and girls, sat on the other barge's deck. One little boy waved.

"Father!" called Chiufi. He was on his tiptoes on the barge's rail, leaning out against the tub wall to look down.

Aghor stamped over to see. A quick glance and he swore and swung back around. "Golem! How well can you hide yourself?"

The doll got to his feet, his tiny tricorn hat in his hand. "I cannot be scryed out."

"That is fortunate," said Aghor, striding to the back of the barge, "because Tibuir's Hound is waiting for you below."

Behra's chest tightened.

Palinday trotted after Aghor. "You have a hiding place for me?"

Behra's father opened the hatch to the coalbunker. Palinday peered inside, then stepped back. "I am not going in there," he declared.

"It's in there or over the side," said Aghor.

Behra caught her father's subtle hand gesture to Sorgui. While the doll still hesitated, she watched her half-brother slowly extend a long-fingered hand towards Palinday's back. She squeezed her lips together, desperate to call out a warning.

Sorgui struck. With a squawk, Palinday toppled into the bunker.

"Bury yourself deep, little golem," said Aghor, and slammed the hatch shut.

Geneic and Sorgui chuckled their slow, barking laughs.

Chiufi slunk across to join Behra by her hut. Their father pulled his shirt off and dropped it to the deck, planting himself where he would be most visible to the lock workers. After a moment he reconsidered and hurried over to Behra, drawing his little knife and gesturing impatiently for her hand.

This time he only pricked her finger, squeezing painfully to smear her blood along his forearms. He marched back to his post near the rail, wiping the blood over his tattoos and muttering a hasty incantation.

"*Guigen negui rei*," Behra mouthed. "*Guigen negui rei*."

The bramble tattoos on Aghor's arms began to writhe like nests of spiked snakes. The skin on Behra's arms crawled in sympathy. With an effort, she pushed the words to the back of her mind.

She leaned close to Chiufi, her lips almost touching his ear. "We'll run at Ardonailles. Palinday says his master will protect us."

Chiufi gasped and stared at her. Terror made him shake his head.

Behra gripped his hand, bigger and stronger than hers. "We *must*."

The lift reached the bottom of the cliff. She saw soldiers among the lock workers, dressed in the same uniforms as those they'd seen the night before. Lord Tibuir's men. She saw lock workers and soldiers alike blanch at the sight of her father.

A pair of workers hurried to open the lift gates, ignoring the angry shouts of a soldier with a gold-trimmed jacket. Behra caught the brief, satisfied twitch at the corner of her father's mouth as the gates cranked up and the barge bumped out of the lift tub on a rush of water.

There were Rhuinish soldiers lining the low parapet on the near bank, more soldiers crowding a barge anchored cross-wise to the canal, partly blocking it. Some of the soldiers held the leashes of dogs. There were others with the soldiers, too, shorter and stockier, stooping with flat heads thrust forward, red eyes gleaming. Saltukkuri—true demimen, not half-castes like Geneic and Sorgui. Behra looked between her half-brothers and those on the shores, noting the differences, the flatter foreheads and heavier jaws of the full-bloods. Geneic and Sorgui stood up tall, lifting their heads and puffing out their chests, making themselves as large as possible.

The Saltukkuri with the soldiers had chips of red jewel in the centres of their brows, seemingly embedded there. Among them stood a Rhuinishwoman in red robes and cloaks, a similar, larger jewel upon her own forehead.

Her expression was thunderous. Up on top of the lift gate, there was scuffling between the workers and soldiers, the soldiers beating at the workers with the butts of their weapons.

Chiufi sprang up as their father barked orders. Aghor wore a lopsided smirk as he set his sons to work bringing the barge in to shore. Glancing up at the fracas on the lift gate, he called out to the woman magician, "It seems that folk still fear the old ways more than your new tricks, Hound."

"Simple folk are most easily fooled by simple tricks," the magician woman replied. "We will search your boat, Aghor."

Soldiers reached out with hooked poles to catch the barge's rails.

"Ah yes, your master's lost doll," said Aghor. "If Lord Tibuir plays with his dolls as he plays with his page boys then I can understand why the thing ran away. But you will not find it on my barge."

Tibuir's Hound stepped aboard.

"Where are you headed, Bargeman?"

"Verdencastre," said Aghor. "Then Nouvebourg."

The Hound arched an eyebrow. "Indeed?"

Soldiers and Saltukkuri swarmed after her, surrounding Aghor, Geneic and Sorgui. There was a deal of grunting and growling between the Saltukkuri and Behra's half-brothers. She shuffled back into her hut. The movement caught the red-robed magician's eye. Behra stared up at her. The Hound's skin was very pale and smooth, her hair and eyes very dark. Her face was handsome and unyielding, like the statues of warrior queens that Behra had seen once, in the southern provinces.

Disgust curled the Hound's lip. "The old ways, is it? What you practice is an abomination, Aghor. Yours was never the true path of our people." She raised her voice, "Search everywhere!"

Dogs were brought aboard. Soldiers clattered belowdecks, the hatches of the cargo holds and coalbunker were flung open. Behra's fingers knotted in her blankets as she watched the soldiers poke their halberd blades into the bunker.

"There, too," snapped Tibuir's Hound.

Rough fingers caught Behra's arm. A soldier dragged her out of her hut and pulled her blankets out after for the dogs to sniff. The animals were in a frenzy of excitement.

"Father!" Chiufi cried.

He was by the far rail of the barge, pointing urgently over the side.

"Father, I saw it! It jumped over!"

Aghor stared at him, the first time in her life Behra had ever seen him dumbfounded.

The soldier holding her joined the rush to that side of the barge, dragging her with him. Her chain yanked at her ankle as she reached its farthest extent. On the water, ripples spread in an expanding circle.

"Get some men to the far bank!" the Hound shouted. Standing close to Behra, she said, "It seems you had a stowaway, Bargeman."

"So it would appear." Aghor's face was purple, set in a furious scowl. "Where was it, boy? Where did it spring from?"

Chiufi cowered. "I didn't see, father."

Aghor cuffed him across the top of the head.

The Hound sneered. "Perhaps your old ways are not so puissant as you think."

Aghor's face darkened further, filling with shadow. The tiny bodies of Behra's sisters danced on his belt. Behra could feel the power suck into him from all around. He would need to bleed her deeply to regain his strength after this. *Learn*, she told herself, and tried what she felt him doing. She found that she could, and suddenly was, siphoning energy from the air, the water lapping around the barge, even the planks beneath her feet.

She turned her thoughts on the man holding her.

Invisible flame seared up the bones of her arm. The soldier grunted and let go. He stared down at Behra in surprise.

Aghor spoke, magic making his words slam like clashing stones. "You no longer have reason to hold us, Hound."

The Hound regarded him coolly, but her face had become even paler. Her men drew back. There were muffled yelps from among the Saltukkuri. A pulse ticked in the Hound's throat.

"As you say," she grated. She turned on her heel, shouting, "Clear the barge! Search the canal!"

Behra looked at the red welt on her forearm in the shape of the soldier's fingers. She felt the rough energies dissipate from her father's body, back into the air and water. They still throbbed in her, filling her with feverish heat. Aghor snapped a curt order to Geneic and Sorgui, who flinched in unison. They left off posturing at the departing Saltukkuri and picked up bargepoles to clumsily push the boat away from shore.

Aghor looked down at his youngest son. Chiufi tensed visibly as his father raised his hand again. But Aghor stroked the place where he had struck before.

"Did well, boy."

Behra noticed the tremor in his fingers as he lowered his arm.

❋

The next morning she lay in her blankets, still weak and exhausted, while Chiufi had fed her gruel with vegetables and salted meat, a worried frown on his face the whole time. Palinday watched in silence, his coal-smeared face solemn. Behra's father had taken a lot of blood, all the strength she had gained from copying his spell and more, but she didn't care.

He hadn't known. She had worked magic and he hadn't known.

The river was heavy with traffic, ocean-going ships sharing the water with steam barges and the pleasure yachts of the idle rich. Behra gazed up at sailors climbing about the rigging of a sailing ship, high above, its sails lit gold by the lowering sun.

Aghor had left Palinday in the coalbunker most of the night. Behra had heard the doll's tapping and his frustrated shouts in the dark. Finally released, Palinday had emerged black from head to foot, spitting angry. "There was no justification for holding me in there so long!"

Aghor had looked down at him mildly. "Tibuir's Hound will not be fooled for long. You cannot be scryed you say, little golem, but it is harder to hide an entire barge. She will have eyes on us." He turned away. "Be thankful I did not hold you in there all the way to your Lord Emieldraeu."

Palinday had washed his face and hands as best he could, but his fine clothes were spoiled.

Behra heard her father shout. The bowl clattered down beside her as Chiufi sprang to obey. She felt the barge tilt as Aghor turned hard on the wheel. Buildings loomed on either side, casting the barge in sudden shadow. She felt the thump of the engine drop away, twisted her neck to see Chiufi jump ashore, rope in hand. They had pulled in to a narrow warehouse canal.

Palinday was on his feet. "Why are we stopped? This is not Ardonailles."

Aghor glanced his way, shrugging a long coat over his shoulders. "I have business here. You will not be delayed for long, little golem."

He hopped lightly over the rail and they watched him stride away between the warehouses. Chiufi came back aboard and slunk over to sit with Behra and Palinday.

"Would your lord really protect us?" he said, softly.

Palinday looked at him. "Yes."

"Then we will run with you when we reach Ardonailles," said Behra. Chiufi's face was drawn, tense.

Palinday shook his head. "My mission must not be endangered."

"But you said . . ."

"I will return for you," Palinday said.

Behra blinked rapidly, her eyes suddenly hot. "We will be gone."

"Then I will find you," said the doll.

"Swear it," said Behra, between clenched teeth.

Palinday looked from her to Chiufi. "By my maker's honour, I swear it."

Chiufi nodded, but Behra saw from his face that the courage he had screwed together had crumbled once more.

Behra reached out and gave his hand a squeeze.

✦

A crowd gathered as the night deepened. Rhuinish folk, although they were in Ornomagne proper now. They waited quietly, squatting on the wharf or leaning against the warehouse walls. Most of them had brought gifts, ranging from baskets of vegetables to bolts of cloth. Sorgui and Geneic squatted side-by-side at the rail, their red-eyed gazes alert.

Palinday observed the assemblage nervously. "Who are they?"

"Folk seeking spells or charms from father," said Chiufi stiffly, after a moment. "They always gather, wherever we dock."

The doll's porcelain brow creased a fraction. "How do they know?"

Chiufi shrugged.

"They always do," said Behra.

"I dislike this," Palinday grumbled. "Where *is* he?"

It was a while later before Aghor returned. He marched through the crowd without acknowledgement, yelling for Chiufi to fire up the engine and cast off. The supplicants watched in silence as the barge was pushed away from the wharf and backed slowly out of the canal.

✦

"Ardonailles," Palinday announced.

Behra looked around the side of her hut. The lights of the great port city, trading hub of the Ornomagnen Empire, sprawled along either side of the river and across the many islands of its delta. Staircases of canal locks ascended the long slope of the north bank between the close-packed streets. The river itself had broadened

— 186 —

and slowed as it neared the sea, more than a mile wide now, its surface rippling with reflected light and shadow.

Geneic squatted close by, near the starboard running lantern with an anvil between his knees, hammering a twisted grapple hook back into its proper shape. Chiufi was at the wheel, angling the barge across the flow of traffic towards the south shore. Sorgui crouched idly near the coalbunker, his shovel across his knees, watching the river traffic.

They passed a brightly lit fortress island, iron-sided Ornomagnen warships drawn up alongside, powered by steam and sails and bristling with double- and triple-decks of guns.

"There!" Palinday called out, pointing to a canal mouth in the southern bank.

Chiufi steered the barge into a district of run-down terraces and tenement blocks. There were no locks here, the city's southern suburbs sprawling across a flat plain. There was little traffic about on the dimly lit streets, although it was still early. Geneic stopped hammering.

"Girl, hand." She hadn't noticed her father's reappearance on deck. He stood over her, holding his scrying bowl.

Behra held out her arm.

Palinday watched Aghor pull out his knife. "What scrying is there to do," he said, "when we are at our destination?"

Behra winced as the point of the blade penetrated. The mummified, half-formed faces of her sisters gaped up at her with sightless eyes.

"You think the Hound would dare pursue me into the heart of Ornomagne?" Palinday persisted.

Aghor spared him a glance as he stood. "Don't you?"

Palinday flicked the brim of his hat with his fingers and stuck it on his head. He noticed Behra's gaze on him. "Tibuir's Hound does not know for sure that I am aboard," he said. "And we are far afield of where she thinks us to be headed. There are many waterways to hunt." He drummed his fingers, tinkling hollowly, against his knees. "She would be reckless to try anything so far from her lord's domain. And she fears your father, besides."

Behra was drifting has he spoke, her body heating as the burning coal landed in the bowl of her blood. She murmured along with her father's incantation. The words had an unfamiliar texture in her mind. It was no spell she had ever heard before. "*Addrakkur naskkur sakkul urukh thoth nakkur thoth . . .*"

Palinday looked at her, his jewelled eyes glinting. "That isn't Old Rhuinish." His mouth moved with Behra's. "And it isn't a scrying spell." He started to stand, then suddenly clutched at his head. "My wards . . . "

Geneic's hammer smashed into his chest. Behra screamed. Shattered bits of the doll bounced across the deck, flying free of his clothes, some skittering under the rail to splash into the water.

"The head! Find the head!" bellowed Aghor.

Geneic lifted Behra and dumped her out of her hut, so he could rummage in her blankets. She looked down into her lap. Palinday blinked up at her, his neck sheered off cleanly just below his jaw.

"Hide me."

Behra clapped her hands over the doll's face an instant before her father barged past. She looked around for Chiufi, found his shocked gaze already on her as he hurried up from the wheelhouse. He grabbed a running lantern off its hook and made a show of joining the hunt. Behra saw him pick up something, not breaking stride, and keep moving over to the rail to stoop again.

"Father," Chiufi straightened, holding up his prize to the light. Palinday's hat. "It was under the rail."

A range of expressions crossed Aghor's face as he stared at the hat. Slowly, he pushed himself upright. "You wouldn't lie to your father, would you, boy?"

Chiufi's jaw trembled.

He had closed the engine throttle, Behra realised, before he left the wheelhouse. Undirected and barely making headway, the barge was slowly turning across the canal.

Aghor began to swear, his fists clenched so tight they shook. Behra's aborted sisters silently cursed along with him. The shadows deepened in the hollows of his face and spread. Sickly light leaked between his curled fingers. Beside him, Sorgui and Geneic cringed, their red eyes slitted almost shut.

"Having some difficulty, Bargeman?" a woman's voice called out.

Tibuir's Hound sat on horseback at the edge of the canal.

"None that's any business of yours, Hound," Behra's father grated, his voice heavy with magic.

Hooves and boots clattered on stone, riders and foot soldiers appearing on both banks. Red Saltukkuri eyes glowed, the squat, hunched figures of demimen scattered among the Rhuinish troops. Crossbows were levelled.

*Crossbows*, thought Behra. Not muskets. *Silent.*

A horse whickered, a crossbow string creaked in the descending quiet. Behra heard a low growl from Sorgui by the wheelhouse.

The red stone on the Hound's brow caught the light of a streetlamp. "You seem to have gone astray from your destination," she drawled. "It is a curious coincidence that your failure of navigation has brought you here." She leaned forward in her saddle, her eyes wide. "Did you know, Aghor the Bargeman, that the King's Spymaster maintains a house in this part of Ardonailles?"

Behra's hands shook on top of Palinday's sculpted face. She heard him gasp, felt his lips move against her palm as he mouthed curses. Her father and the Hound glared at each other.

The sound of more tramping boots cut through the standoff. "Stand down!" a new voice cried. "Stand down in the name of the King!"

Bright-liveried Ornomagnen troops marched along both sides of the canal. Behra gasped. Brass, four-legged battle golems marched with them, their mantis arms upraised.

"*Silbuim meneich!*" spat Behra's father, and all hell broke loose.

Along both banks, Rhuinish crossbows suddenly caught on fire. The archers dropped them with shouts of surprise. Bolts flew in all directions as the bows bounced on the ground. Some thunked into the wooden deck of the barge. Soldiers and horses screamed as they were struck. The Ornomagnen troops discharged their muskets. Ornomagnen and Rhuinishmen both charged. Saltukkuri leapt onto the barge.

Sorgui and Geneic surged to their feet, laying about with the tools to hand, bigger by far than their full-blood brethren and with all of a demiman's strength. Chiufi smashed his lamp into the face of a Saltukkuri warrior who landed beside him. Flaming oil sprayed over the shrieking demiman.

Tibuir's Hound gave a shout. Aghor grunted as if struck and fell to one knee. Behra felt a squeezing pressure in her chest.

"*Telais ac ulh,*" she mouthed her father's snarled counter spell. "*Telais maliel ap naghai.*"

The Hound cried out, scrambling clear as her horse collapsed under her. She landed awkwardly, both hands stretched out like claws. Behra could feel the spells clash in the air between them, probing for weaknesses in the other's defences. Her skin stung as if scalded.

A demiman's fallen axe lay within reach.

Now, Behra thought. Her fingers closed on the axe. "Chiufi!"

He ran over to her and she thrust the axe into his hands. His eyes were huge, the whites showing all around.

"What's happening?" demanded Palinday, as soon as his face was uncovered.

"We're going now," said Behra, holding her brother's gaze.

Chiufi swallowed and nodded, fumbled about for her ankle chain and smashed the axe down onto it.

Behra mouthed spells, drawing power into herself. Chiufi's breathed plumed in the suddenly cold air. He struck the chain again. This time the links parted.

Chiufi stood, hauling Behra up with him. She clutched Palinday's head to her chest and led Chiufi towards the back of the barge. Sorgui flung a broken demiman into a crowd of his fellows near the wheelhouse. The barge had continued to slew across the canal. Its stern bumped against the stone wall of the bank. Chiufi pushed Behra up ahead of him and leapt after.

She stood, marvelling at the feel of cold stone under her bare feet, so different from the smooth planking of the barge's deck. There was a roar from the boat. Their father had noticed her absence. His rage thrummed along the thread of power that bound them.

Behra lashed out, unthinking. "*Telais ac ulh.*" In her terror, she forgot the rest of the spell. But Aghor gave a shout of surprise. It rose to an outraged bellow as the Hound took advantage of his distraction.

Chiufi grabbed Behra's wrist and they fled.

They raced down darkened streets, past frightened faces peeping from windows and doorways. Behra struggled to keep up with her brother. Her lungs and legs burned, unused to such exertion. Her feet were quickly bruised. She soon began to flag.

Chiufi slowed and stopped at a crossroads. He fumbled Palinday's head from Behra's grasp and held it up. The world spun around her. She felt faint.

"Why did he smash you?" Chiufi panted.

"To get the scroll out of my head and know the secrets it holds for himself," said Palinday. "To use them, or sell them to the highest bidder."

Chiufi looked around. "Which way?"

"I don't recognise the street," said Palinday. "But we left the river east and north of my master's house. Go south and then west."

Chiufi turned uncertainly.

"That way!" Palinday snapped.

Behra felt a familiar pressure against her thoughts. "He's coming," she gasped.

Chiufi caught her wrist again. "Run!"

She stumbled after.

On through the streets they ran, Chiufi dragging her along, sometimes holding her up, Palinday's head held up in his other hand. The doll barked directions, guiding them deeper into the city. A sharp pain started in Behra's side.

The sense of their father behind them grew stronger and stronger. "He's coming!"

"Not far!" cried Palinday. "My master will be there."

"I can't," Behra wept.

"Keep going," Chiufi said, his own voice almost a sob.

"He's coming."

Closer. And closer. She could feel the killing fury in him. And power—more than she had ever felt him hold.

Chiufi would die if he caught them. She would be flogged, no doubt, and returned to her hut and chain. But Chiufi would die.

For his sake, Behra kept running.

"Here!" Palinday shrieked. "Here, on the left! The third house along!"

The townhouse was one of a row fronted by gated courtyards. Behra swayed, barely able to stay upright, staring up at the house in confusion. Surely the King's Magician must live in a palace?

Chiufi rattled the bars of the gate and shouted. "My Lord! Open up!"

Palinday gave a wail of dismay. "My master isn't here! He's supposed to be here!"

Their father's presence was overwhelming. He's here, she thought. Her tongue refused to cooperate. *He's here!*

"Hold me to the lock," said Palinday.

Chiufi did so. The doll whispered into the keyhole and, with a loud clang, the gate sprang open.

"Chiufi!" Behra gasped.

There was a bellow from the corner of the street.

"Inside!" cried Palinday. "He won't be able to pass the gate."

Chiufi flung Behra through and slammed the bars shut behind them.

She almost fell, but he lifted her and dragged her across the courtyard towards the door of the house.

"*Talais ac ulh*," she mouthed, caught up in her father's spell. She felt it gather strength, wanted to shout a warning. "*Telais maliel ap naghai.*"

With a scream, she wrenched herself free.

The air detonated between her and Chiufi. He was hurled away from her by the impact of the spell. Behra sprawled, twisted to see her brother bounce off the stones. Palinday's head sailed through the air to smash against the wall of the house.

Chiufi's screams rose to a shriek. Blood bubbled from his eyes, ears and nose.

"Chiufi!" Behra cried. She lurched upright, thrust her hand into the arc of power between her father and brother, thinking madly to bat the killing magic back towards Aghor.

She felt her fingerbones snap, the skin on her hand blistering and bursting. The force of the spell spun her around and back to her knees. There was a cry of surprise from outside the gate.

Behra whimpered, cradling her shattered hand. Tremors ran through Chiufi, then he lay frighteningly still.

She felt her father building another spell. "No," she said. "No." She drew in power, felt the air crackle against her skin. "*Silbuim meneich*," she said aloud—her spell, not his.

Aghor disappeared in a flash. Heat washed back over her. She heard the thin screams of her sisters, felt her father's shock, his pain, his rage quickly returning.

"No!" She got to her feet, lifting her hands, broken and whole, towards him. "*Silbuim meneich!*"

This spell had far more force, but this time he was ready, too. More of the blast bounced back through the gate, knocking Behra over. She thrashed about, beating at the flames on her smock and hair.

There was silence from her father, no sense of the chord that had joined her to him.

Shaking, she crawled over to Chiufi. He still wasn't moving. She reached out to him with her good hand, fingers fluttering over his face. His chest rose, suddenly, and fell. Then again. Her vision blurred.

A clatter of hooves outside the gate made her look up.

Her father lay prone on the road. A horseman loomed over him. Aghor raised a hand weakly. The rider held out a forked staff to touch his fingers. Behra felt the words of power pass between them. Aghor's back arched, and he slumped and fell still.

The rider dismounted. He pushed open the gate and strode across the yard. Behra shrank back. Pale eyes bored into her from under thick white brows. He went straight past her, stepping over Chiufi, to where Palinday's head had smashed against the wall.

The old man stooped, then straightened with a tiny paper scroll in his hand. "Ah, my friend," he murmured. "I sensed too late that it was you the Hound had cornered on that barge, and then you ran away from me."

His gaze fell once more on Behra.

"Please," she said, "help my brother."

❖

A knock at the door woke Behra from her doze. She jerked her head away from the wall behind her chair. Chiufi lay unconscious in the bed, bandages swathing his eyes and ears. His mouth was open and slack, but his chest rose and fell.

The door opened and a man with polished black skin came in. No, not a man—a golem, though he was dressed like a man and moved as smoothly.

The ebony golem saw her awake. His sculpted face shifted fractionally, approximating a smile.

"Behra."

The voice was nearly the same—deeper, but tinkling with music. And he still had blue gemstone eyes.

Behra stared in wonder as Palinday came to perch on the edge of Chiufi's bed.

"I told you I was in disguise," he said. He reached across to brush his hand gently across her splinted fingers. He squeezed her good hand, his touch cold and unyielding. "You are safe."

"And my father?"

"My Lord Emieldraeu has laid a geas upon him. He cannot approach you or do you harm. You are safe." He patted her fingers. "You had already beaten him, you know, before my master intervened."

Behra shook her head. It was too much, too overwhelming. "Chiufi?"

Palinday's voice softened. "He will live. My master believes he will regain most of his hearing and his voice, in time. His heart and lungs, too, will mostly heal."

He raised his hand to wipe her cheek with his fingertip. "Do not blame yourself. You did what was needed—both of you," he said. "Lord Tibuir was plotting rebellion. Now the King can strike first, before Tibuir is ready. You and your brother may have saved Ornomagne from a terrible civil war." Behra thought that if he was a man, he would have sighed. "Or made it less terrible, at least. And you saved yourselves."

Behra was only half listening. "What of his eyes?"

"Ah."

She imagined him blinded for life, yet another terrible hurt, taken for her sake. It was too much to bear.

She saw Palinday's mouth stretch into another fractional smile, his fingers reach into the pocket of his vest. He turned Behra's hand over and dropped something into her palm. She looked down at a pair of glass orbs. Set into each was a faceted blue gemstone identical to Palinday's eyes.

"His eyes cannot be saved," the golem said, "but he will be well cared for."

# INTERLOPER

Shouts erupted from behind.

Barnestable turned in time to see a pair of Tinas roll off the top of the following van, punching and clawing at each other even as they hit the road and bounced onto the verge. Their sisters yelled indiscriminate encouragement.

"Oh, for crying out loud." His head throbbed mercilessly. The sunlight bouncing off the pale bleakness of the countryside hurt his eyes.

With a groan, he leapt from his perch on the driver's bench beside Monkey, landing heavily on his feet. The impact sent shooting pains up his neck and through his skull. He almost vomited. One of the troodons kicked the bars of the van beside him. Still lying on her side, the trood clung onto a bar with the sickle claw of her inner toe and raised her neck feathers like hackles.

"Hey! Is that any way to talk to your mama?"

The trood yapped a hostile reply. Monkey unfurled a simian arm to bang on the roof, which just set all three troods yapping. The camels belched and groaned.

"Shaddap!" Monkey bawled.

Barnestable set off at a staggering trot towards the fighters. Turtle beat him to the fray, grabbing the backs of the Tinas' shirts and holding them up so their toes just brushed the dirt. They spat curses and kicked at his armoured legs.

"What the hell is this?" Barnestable demanded, pressing his palms against his pounding temples. "Aren't you all one person? You're fighting with your bloody self!"

The Tinas shook themselves free of Turtle. Both of them were bloodied, their clothes and nests of black hair smeared with salt and dust. They scowled down at Barnestable.

"Screw . . . "

" . . . you."

"Yeah, screw you, Barnes," their sisters choroused.

Barnestable watched, flummoxed, as the battered two rejoined the other six on the van. "I don't deserve that."

Turtle didn't respond. Flies gathered on the tattooed shell of his head. Black tattoos over the interlocking plates of his exoskeleton made him seem more like some Brutalist artwork than a human being. Barnestable followed his gaze.

Part-covered steel skeletons of prefabbed buildings broke the monotony of the plain, a distance back from the road. Preoccupied with his migraine, Barnestable had taken them at a glance to be old farm sheds and paid no further heed. Turtle's interest made him look closer. The tattered mesh of a perimeter fence hinted at the possibility of something more secretive and secure. Concrete stumps around it might've have supported auto-defence towers.

All around was nothing but rolling desolation—stands of pale feral wheat at the top of every low rise of the plain, saltpans in every trough between.

*Like bloody Judgement Day.* Barnestable wondered what the hell had been worth defending out here.

The compound spread some way beyond the ruined sheds. Furthest back lay a black tarmac landing pad and a large, irregularly stepped circular foundation. Barnestable frowned. *Or what needed hiding.*

"That wasn't in the bloody briefings," he said. He might as well have been talking to the replica of Turtle they lugged about with them as to the real thing. "Turtle?"

Turtle peered down at him. His inked slab of a face was hard to read, a graffitied brick with eyes.

Barnestable watched him stride away. "What is *with* everyone today? Rhone, what's with everyone today?"

The last caravan had just passed. Barnestable gritted his teeth and jogged to catch up. He leapt for the running board and clung with one hand around an awning strut. The camels towing the van bawled complaints at the miniscule difference his weight made to the vehicle.

"Dammit, Barnes," said Murph, as he hauled himself up to where she sat on the driver's bench with Rhone.

Barnestable ignored her. Rhone shuffled across reluctantly to make room and he squeezed onto the end of the seat. "Well?"

Rhone was covered from head to toe in a blue chador. Barnestable could just make out the profile of her face through her gauze veil. Seated, his eyes came just above the level of her breasts.

"Aw, c'mon love," he said, "you can tell me."

"I'm not your love, Barnes," said Rhone.

"I'm wounded. Wassup?"

At the opposite end of the bench, Murph rubbed at the bridge of her nose. A lanky woman with fair skin that tended to freckle, she wore a wide straw hat to keep the sun off her face.

Rhone hitched her cuffs sharply, causing a momentary bounce on the front of her chest.

"Shit, Barnes, don't you ever think of anything else?"

He plastered on an ingratiating smile. "Only you, love. What is it? Woman stuff?"

"Troglodyte." She rose abruptly and climbed over him and down from the van. "It's not my stuff."

"What, then?" he called after her. He pointed in the direction of the abandoned buildings. "Is there a cracked seal over there that I should know about? Rhone?" He didn't think so. If there was an unsealed break in the Veil nearby the troods would be letting them know.

"Slick, Barnes," said Murph. "Slicker than duck shit."

Barnestable waved flies away from his face while he watched Rhone fall into step beside Turtle. His skull felt like it was cracking at the seams. Rhone was walking very close to Turtle. Barnestable frowned.

"It's coming from Turtle? What the hell is she doing projecting *his* feelings?"

Murph grunted. "Really, Barnes."

Up front, Goat Boy wove the solar off-roader, the troupe's only powered vehicle, with stately slowness across the full width of the road. The resin statue of Turtle rocked gently on the trailer behind it. Loops rested her furry chin on her elbow over the side of the car door, nominally supervising his driving.

From the top of his van, Monkey called out, "Town's ahead."

Goat Boy whooped happily, the only member of the troupe immune to Turtle's projected mood.

✶

The caravan crawled down the shallow slope of the escarpment to the sand flat at sea level. Barnestable inhaled the sea air, hoping it would clear his head.

"Nice beach," he observed, back on his seat on the troodon van beside Monkey. The beach's cleanliness was marred at the southern end by sun-hardened hunks of tar from an old slick.

"Pity about the town," said Monkey.

Which summed up most places along the west coast, outside of Perth's tarnished glitz and suburban sprawl.

This town was bigger than Barnestable had expected, the tin-roofed houses sprawling along the beachfront and up the lower slope of the escarpment. He guessed its population to be pushing five figures. As they got closer, he revised the estimate down. The houses along the outer fringe were all empty, either boarded up or simply abandoned. The hairs rose on the back of Barnestable's neck. There were plenty of ghost towns, back East, neutron bombed after the Veil had torn and Interlopers run amok. Empty houses held a different kind of silence to the desert.

There was still life here, though. Closer to the centre, maybe two in three buildings were still occupied.

Barnestable put on his ringmaster's top hat and frayed red coat. Turtle and five of the Tinas were already hidden away inside the caravans, squeezed in with the tents and gear. Everyone else was in their places up on top.

"What the hell are these people still doing out here?" Monkey said softly. There was no mine nearby, and this wasn't an ore port.

Of the people they passed, more had grey hair than not.

Barnestable massaged his neck with his fingers. "Waiting to die, mate. Just waiting to die."

The highway morphed into the town's high street. Monkey hammered on the roof of the van to stir up the troods. The vehicle shuddered as one of them head-butted the bars. People on the porches of the threadbare stores and eateries gasped at the geneered saurians. Barnestable sighed inside, as he often did, at the depth of their provincialism. Still, he told himself, what chance did they have? The mining cartels that claimed this end of the continent filtered all information coming into their zone of influence according to their own myopic self-interests.

He noticed a different reaction to the statue of Turtle, chained on top of the off-roader's trailer. Instead of the usual exclamations of surprise, the locals' response was to laugh and nudge each other knowingly.

*Bloody useless intel*, Barnestable thought, *And what the hell's got up Turtle's arse that he couldn't let us know?*

"Ah, well," he said to Monkey, "they can't all be complete rubes."

He stood up and raised his loudhailer. Suppressing a wave of nausea, he launched into his spiel. "Roll up, one and all, to Barnestable's Travelling Mutant Freak Show and Circus . . . "

❖

They set up camp on a scrubby sports oval beside the town's derelict shopping mall. They parked the statue of Turtle outside and Goat Boy pegged out the camels to graze while the rest of them got the dome of the big top up on its ultralight polymer frame. The caravan annexes were joined up to the tent to make a covered village. Then Turtle and the other Tinas could emerge to help with the rest of the set-up.

The evening performance began with a tumbling routine from three Tinas. Barnestable cringed, watching from behind the stage curtain as they missed their marks and almost overshot their landings. The crowd didn't notice, applauding every trick. The bleachers were packed, they'd pulled a good couple of hundred customers. There was one gap in the front row. Beside the empty place sat a sixtyish man with a full head of iron-coloured hair. A suntanned, mouse-haired waif of eleven or twelve sat on his other side, watching the performance with an expression of unabashed delight.

Barnestable looked up at Rhone. His headache hadn't abated, so he couldn't work up more than a mild disappointment she was still in her chador, waiting until the last moment to strip down to her show costume.

"Ready, love?"

After a pause, she nodded and murmured, "Already started."

He could hear Murph and Loops bickering backstage. Rhone still had everyone caught up in Turtle's funk. "You need to shut that down," he said. "We can't afford to be going flaky if we turn up a candidate or, God forbid, a bloody Interloper. And how come you're giving me this bloody headache?"

"Because I don't like to touch your mind, Barnes," she said.

"Well, bloody shut it down."

"I'm *trying*."

Barnestable stepped away from the curtain. "Where is Turtle, anyway?"

"Barnes, leave him."

He ignored her.

The replica Turtle lay on its back beside its trailer, but the real article wasn't anywhere in the immediate backstage area. Barnestable kept searching.

Low voices caught his attention in the shadowed aisle between two vans. Turtle's bulk was immediately recognisable. With him was a middle-aged woman who held Turtle's hand in both her own.

The woman saw Barnestable and gave Turtle's fingers a squeeze. She leaned up to say something that Barnestable couldn't hear, then turned and ducked through the canvas flap that led outside.

Barnestable folded his arms across his chest. "Christ, Turtle, you know better."

Turtle stared at the ground. "She won't give the act away."

"I wasn't talking about the bloody act," said Barnestable. "You *know* her."

Turtle nodded. He chewed his words a while before spitting them out. "I was posted here, before the state government collapsed. Guarding the place we passed on the way in."

"Figured that out for myself. Thanks for the advance notice, mate."

Tattooed plates shifted on Turtle's brow. "It was in your briefings, wasn't it?"

"They skipped the bit about there being a facility out here," Barnestable said.

Turtle snorted. "Bloody intel."

"Did they get through?"

"The Veil? No." Turtle shook his head. "No, there's no seal over there. They cleared us out when the mining cartels took over."

Barnestable considered him. "And the rest of it?"

Another silence, then Turtle said, "I had a woman in town."

"A woman? *You?*" He turned it into: "You mean *her?*" Barnestable thought the woman was too old. But then, it was over a decade since the miners booted out the government in the West.

Turtle looked at him sharply. "A made man like me, you mean? As opposed to a natural-born freak like you. I got everything you got, Barnes," he said. "Only bigger. And no, that's her mother."

"She's not in town anymore?"

"She died."

"I'm sorry to hear that, mate."

Turtle shrugged and pushed past.

"Just keep your mind on the job, eh?" Barnestable called to his retreating back.

He heard a muffled laugh. Goat Boy wriggled out from under the caravan beside him. He grinned and jiggled his horns. "Bigger," he said, and scampered off after Turtle.

Barnestable started to shake his head, stopped with a wince. "Geek."

He stumped back to rejoin Rhone as cheers marked the end of the Tinas' performance. Monkey and Goat Boy raced past him and burst shrieking into the ring with Loops in hot pursuit, clutching outsized cutlery and with a napkin tied around her neck. They pranced about, earning laughs while the Tinas packed up their gear. Barnestable watched Turtle's mother-in-law rejoin her—he assumed—husband. He frowned at the kid sitting with them.

*No way.*

Goat Boy fled backstage. Murph arrived with her cases of knives and Rhone chose that moment to start shucking her chador, distracting Barnestable when he should have been bracing himself.

Goat Boy landed on his back, sending him stumbling into the open.

"Faster, piggy!" Goat Boy cried, slapping Barnestable on the backside with the butt of his styrofoam lance.

They chased Loops around the ring a couple of times, until Monkey stole Barnestable's ringmaster's hat and announced, "The Mistress of the Blades!"

Rhone acted as Murph's assistant for the first part of her act, while Murph juggled knives and cleavers of varying size and ugliness.

Loops and Monkey wheeled out the wooden target wheel, then pretended to sneak up on Rhone. She struggled feebly as they towed her over to the wheel and strapped her on. The theatre had its desired effect on the crowd. A hush fell in the tent. Rhone had a high forehead, full cheeks and curved little nose that made her face look like a kid's. The rest of her, in Barnestable's frank opinion, looked like she'd been designed by a man. Which, now that he thought of it, she probably had.

Possibly even the same man who'd designed Murph, he mused, watching her stand, hip cocked, in her red leathers and thigh-high boots while she made a show of selecting knives from the case Monkey presented to her.

The five blades went up in a high arc then, in a blur of movement as they came back down, shot across to thunk into the wheel around Rhone. Barnestable flinched. The knife that should have landed between her knees had struck not more than a finger's width from the inside of Rhone's thigh.

Murph tossed a couple of samurai swords around while Monkey retrieved the knives.

Something like an invisible mallet smacked into Barnestable's already hurting brain. His knees almost gave way. Monkey dropped his armful of knives. Cries of surprise and alarm said that at least some of the crowd had caught Rhone's mental cry.

*Interloper!*

Barnestable was about to yell it aloud, thinking they'd have to slaughter a quarter of the crowd to save the rest. But no: the troods were still quiet. This close to an Interloper, they'd be chewing through the bars of their wagon. His heart rattled inside his ribs. Murph was stock-still in the ring, a sword in each hand and staring fixedly at Rhone, ready to leap into the bleachers and begin the bloodbath. Minutely, Rhone shook her head.

Murph stabbed her swords into the ground and beckoned imperiously for Monkey to bring the knives. Monkey's simian face was wrinkled with worry as he cranked the handle to set the target wheel, with Rhone on it, spinning. Barnestable could scarcely bear to watch. This time Murph was focused. The blades smacked into the wood perfectly on target. The crowd roared their approval.

Barnestable's pulse was still racing when he and the Tinas wheeled Rhone backstage and released her from the wheel. Goat Boy drove a camel team into the ring with Turtle on the flatbed wagon that had carried his replica. The crowd laughed and clapped as he slowly stretched and started to move about. Murph and the clowns stayed out in the ring to help with his strongman routine.

"What the hell was that about?" Barnestable demanded, half of his attention on the gap in the curtains. He winced as Turtle failed to catch an iron weight Murph tossed up to him, narrowly missing Loops with its fall. Turtle flinched from Murph's glare and caught the next one.

Rhone gathered up her chador. Her skin was flushed, making her scars stand out. They covered her in spiderweb-fine lines, tracing a two-dimensional map of her nervous system on her skin. More substantial scars peeked out of her hairline around her temples and ears. "I realised how close Murph got to hitting my leg."

"Bull." Rhone pulled the chador over her head and settled the veil in front of her face. She didn't respond. "Did you at least do your job?"

She seemed to hesitate before nodding.

"We got a candidate?"

Another pause, before: "Two."

"Two?" A town this size normally turned up between none and one. "Rhone?"

He wished he could see her face. In the ring, Turtle had pulled himself together and was plodding through his routine with a workman's dourness.

"A young man and a little girl."

Turtle held Murph up on one outstretched hand, which was even more impressive than it looked, since her ultradense muscles and bones meant she weighed substantially more than a born woman her size. Barnestable looked from Turtle to the kid bouncing on her seat between her grandparents.

"Ah, Christ," he said. "That's all we bloody need."

Turtle's routine ended with Murph and Loops standing on one hand, and three Tinas balanced on the other. The Tinas scampered up into the roof of the tent to distract the crowd with the trapezes while the rest of the troupe set up the troodon cage.

Even that didn't go smoothly. Monkey clocked Murph in the back of the head with a girder. Fortunately her head was as hard as Turtle's. She responded by scooping him up on one foot and, with a deft flick, sending him soaring up into the bottom of the trapeze net, where he hung upside down by his toes. The crowd were delighted, thinking it was part of the show and trying to see the wires. Waiting inside the cage, Barnestable doubted any of them considered what a kick like that could do to a man's skull. Or the side of a house.

The troodons charged down the run from their van, jostling and snapping at each other. Barnestable raised his whip and chair and prayed that he'd get through the routine with all his limbs still attached.

❖

In the morning, he sent Rhone and Loops out with the solar off-roader and the statue of Turtle on its wagon, ostensibly to drum up business. Rhone's other mission was to find out where the two candidates lived, and search for any others who hadn't been at the performance the previous night.

After sitting in stony silence through the troupe's communal breakfast, Turtle zipped himself inside the annex where he slept. Barnestable left him to it. Without Rhone nearby to broadcast Turtle's mood, the demeanour of the rest of the troupe lifted. Barnestable's headache faded. Goat Boy produced a soccer ball and Murph, Monkey and a couple of Tinas followed him outside for a game.

The headache sidled back up about noon, announcing Rhone's return. Bickering voices came from the direction of the big top— Monkey and the Tinas going at it. With a groan, Barnestable pressed the heels of his hands to his temples and dropped down from his seat in front of the comm set.

Rhone and Loops brought news of a third candidate, a woman. Barnestable gathered everyone together for a team meeting. One of the Tinas represented her sisters.

"Three in one town," said Monkey. "Bloody jackpot."

"Veil must be thin here," said Murph.

Turtle's shoulder twitched. He stared at his hands in his lap. Rhone sat around the opposite side of the table to him, her head turned away.

Barnestable leaned back in his chair, clasping a hot pack against the back of his neck. "How many in the house with the woman?"

Rhone said, "Three adult males, two of them younger. Husband and sons, I think."

"Be an easy grab," said Loops. "It's only a few streets away. House backs onto the dunes and there's an empty house opposite."

"How d'you want to do it, Barnes?" asked the Tina.

Barnestable shifted his hot pack to his forehead. "We'll take the woman and the young bloke after the show tonight and stick them both in the trunk," he said. The proximity of the troods was enough to deter most local law enforcement from an inspection that might uncover the hibernation unit hidden under the false floor of their van. Bribery generally handled the rest. "Make it look like they've run off together."

"She's twenty years older than him, Barnes," said Loops.

He spread his hands. "So? Is she ugly?"

"That's why I don't like to touch your mind, Barnes," said Rhone.

"What about the kid?" asked Monkey.

Barnestable looked pointedly at Turtle. "Well?"

Turtle examined his fists on the table. "Sounds like you've got this one figured out, too."

"They deserve to hear it from you."

Tattooed plates shifted along Turtle's jaw, muscles clenching beneath. "It's my woman's kid."

A scatter of muttered swearing greeted the admission. Barnestable tossed down his hotpack. "Your *woman's* kid?"

Turtle met his gaze. "Yes."

*Bullshit*, Barnestable thought. He wished he could see Rhone's expression. "Well. We gotta take her in, mate," he said. Turtle opened his mouth to argue. Barnestable slapped the table. "For crying out loud, Turtle, Rhone did the right thing to tell me about her. If we don't grab her, an Interloper will get her in the end. You want that? How many others would have to die with her if that happened? Is that what you want?"

Turtle shook his head. "She needs to be with her grandparents."

"Will they bring her in?" Loops asked. Turtle stared at her. "If they're willing, ain't any reason why they can't come with us openly. Town this size, half of everyone's going to know about you and the kid's mum anyway."

Turtle looked at Rhone, then around at the rest of the team. Loops, Monkey and the Tina watched him as intently as Barnestable did. Goat Boy jiggled his head happily. Murph lounged with legs stretched out and ankles crossed, cleaning her fingernails with a file. In reality, she was probably the most alert of all of them.

"Christ," Turtle said. "We all know what'll happen to her after we bring her in."

Barnestable stood up on his chair and leaned across to grab Rhone's wrist, shaking back the sleeve of her chador to show her scars. He felt her muscles tense under his fingers, but she didn't resist.

"This?" he said. "Maybe. If they think she's strong enough to try it. And maybe she won't survive if they do, the born ones often don't. But she'd be dead as soon as an Interloper sniffed her out, anyway." He released Rhone's arm and she quickly shucked her sleeve back down. "More likely she'll just live out her life in a protected facility with others like her."

"What kind of life, Barnes?" said Turtle, his eyes fixed on Rhone.

"A longer one than if we don't take her," said Barnestable. "And no-one else will have to die because of it."

Turtle sagged.

"So, you gonna bring them in?"

Stillness. Then a nod.

❁

Barnestable stayed where he was while the rest of the team scattered among the vans and annexes. Rhone stalked away, hugging her chador around her, with Turtle following. Barnestable pressed his fingers around the base of his aching skull.

*Dammit, Rhone.* He picked up his hotpack and wandered outside, kneading the beads to heat them up again.

"Barnes." Murph sat shaded by a sun umbrella on the roof of the trood van with Loops and Monkey. Inside, the troods had piled themselves in a feathery heap. One of them clacked her jaws at his approach.

He clambered up via the running board and driver's bench. Three Tinas occupied the roof of another van, basking in the afternoon sun, a row of identical underwear mannequins struck in different lounging poses. Their sisters would be inside, waiting to take a turn.

Monkey, Loops and Murph regarded him solemnly. Murph said, "What are you going to do about him?"

Barnestable realised his headache had receded again. Rhone must have kept on walking. He looked at Murph. She was older than him but the freckles across her nose and cheeks helped her look younger. "Let him stew for a bit."

"He should have said something," said Monkey.

"He didn't know the kid was going to be a candidate, right Barnes?" said Loops. "Poor bastard. Christ, if I had a daughter I wouldn't want her sliced up like that. Even if she survived."

"It's not likely she'd be chosen for remaking," said Barnestable.

"Can we trust him to do what needs to be done?" Monkey said, rapping the roof of the van for emphasis. Below, one of the troods grumbled a complaint. "That's the question."

"Maybe we should just put him in the trunk," said Murph.

Barnestable waved the threat away. "Give over, you lot. He wouldn't fit in the bloody trunk, anyway."

She snorted. "He would after I'd done with him."

"He'll come good," Barnestable said. *Christ, Turtle, you'd better bloody come good.* "Just keep an eye on him in the meantime, eh?"

The second night's performance was as tense as the first. Loops' and Monkey's clowning turned to genuine fisticuffs and Barnestable had to send Murph out to drag them from the ring. Once again, the crowd thought it was all part of the show. The troupe got through their acts otherwise unscathed.

"Pull your bloody selves together," Barnestable snapped at Rhone and Turtle. "We're *saving* her, remember? And this godforsaken town."

The troupe settled down as the time to take the first candidate approached—or at least, Rhone finally got a lid on her emotional broadcast. The throbbing in Barnestable's head receded. Even so, he decided to accompany the team himself.

He, Rhone and Murph set themselves up in the abandoned house across the street from the target. Sitting motionless in the shadows with their chameleon suits on, only their headsets and Murph's matte-black, silenced sniper rifle marked their locations. Three Tinas came in from beachside as the entry team, with Turtle waiting among the dunes as backstop.

There was no chatter from the Tinas as they made their approach. They had no need to talk amongst themselves.

Barnestable said to Murph, "You got them?"

She had her eye pressed to the rifle's scope, set to thermal imaging. "Yeah, they're at the house now."

"And the targets?"

A pause. "All in bed. Look to be sleeping."

"Rhone? We good?" When she didn't answer, he hissed, "*Rhone!*"

"Yeah, Barnes."

He gritted his teeth. Of all of them, she most needed to be on her game. "Turtle? You all clear that side?"

Silence in his headset.

"Turtle?" *Oh, no.* "Rhone, where the hell is Turtle?"

A sharp intake of breath from Murph. "Shit. The woman just dropped off scope. Christ, the husband too. Whole bloody house is going dark."

Barnestable stared at her stupidly. His gut felt suddenly cold.

"Get them out," cried Rhone. "Get out!"

"Barnes, what the hell?" from a Tina.

"Interloper!" he cried. "Pull back! Pull back!"

"Jesus, Barnes, we're already in."

"Then get out!" he yelled into his mike. "Turtle! Turtle, you son of a bitch, where the *hell* are you?"

"It's cold . . . " one of the Tina's said. A staccato, collective gasp followed, then gurgles.

"*No!*" screamed Rhone.

The voice began, that didn't belong on this side of the Veil, speaking in a timbre and tongue that no human could manage. Murph threw down her headset. Barnestable wrenched off his and lunged across to Rhone, flinging her headset away as well. Her shoulders thrummed under his hands.

He shook her. "Rhone. *Rhone.* You can't save them, love." He lifted her bodily and pushed her towards Murph. "Keep it off Murph." To Murph he said, "I'll be back. Shoot anyone that comes out of that house."

"On it, Barnes." With unhurried coolness, she reset the scope to night vision and settled back down into a shooting position. The Interloper's victims wouldn't show up on thermal, with the Interloper sucking the heat out of them and everything around them, but they'd still be evident in the visible light spectrum.

Barnes ran, out the back door, vaulting the low fence into the back neighbour's yard and down the next street. His short legs pumped, sprinting as hard as he could. The headache was back with a vengeance. Every step rattled his brain. He could see the pale dome of the big top a few blocks away.

*Faster, piggy*, he told himself. Jesus Christ, he hoped Rhone kept the Interloper off Murph. If it got out of the house . . . Once one Interloper got loose and started sending its human victims out to expand its foothold and enslave more pawns, it paved the way for others to follow. Then the only way to stop it was nuke every person in range.

*Faster!*

The troods' wagon was around the far side of the camp. Barnestable took the shortest path—through the big top and between the caravans. The remaining Tinas were on the ground, flailing spastically and speaking in tongues, their distance from their sisters enough that the Interloper hadn't yet got a complete grip on their minds. Their breaths misted in the cold air around them. Monkey had a silenced assault rifle trained on them, his face a study of anguish and indecision.

The Tinas shrieked—probably Murph shooting down one of their sisters. Barnestable snapped, "What are you waiting for? Do it!"

He kept running, heard the click and spit of the gun. Each time it fired the noise from the Tinas diminished, until there was only Monkey's sobbing left behind him. Barnestable could hear the troodons, their yaps rising to near howls as they crashed about their cage. They could *taste* the Interloper's presence, even from here.

Back outside, Goat Boy was up on the roof of the troods' wagon, shaking his head and gripping the release to raise the gate.

"I'm here!" At the sound of Barnestable's voice, the troods went abruptly quiet, staring at him with flat orange eyes. The feathers stood up all over their bodies.

"Mama's here, babies," he said, forcing calm into his voice as he rummaged in the locker under the wagon for their collars and leashes. "Time to go hunting.

"Ready," he called up to Goat Boy. "Let me in."

Goat Boy just sat and shook his head. Loops burst from among the caravans. "I called it in," she said. Her voice was shaky. "Backup's on its way."

"Goat Boy!"

Loops looked up. "I got him, Barnes."

She climbed up onto the wagon and prised Goat Boy's fingers loose so she could lift the gate enough for Barnestable to slither inside with his pets. They circled around him in the narrow space, tails shivering and sickle claws flexing, but dipped their heads obediently for him to slip on their collars.

"Ready," he called out to Loops. The gate went up and the troods leapt down, dragging Barnestable after.

"Whoa!" he called, digging in his heels. They paused for him to take the lead.

He set off again, willing his legs to run faster than they could. *Faster, piggy!* The troods loped along at his shoulders, casting their heads this way and that, their saurian brains tuned to the Interloper's mental signature, but immune to its effect.

Barnestable kept them leashed until they started to pull ahead again, their snouts all pointed the same way, and he knew they'd locked in the Interloper's location. Then he popped their collars and said, "Get 'em!"

The troods bounded ahead, silent now that the quarry was at hand. Barnestable stopped and filled his lungs to shout as loudly as he could, "Murph! Incoming!"

Murph's hearing was augmented enough that if she didn't get the message, it was because the Interloper had taken her and Rhone. If that was the case, his babies would be mincemeat and the backup force would be calling in a neutron strike.

❖

A scramjet transport thundered overhead. Barnestable shaded his eyes to look up. That would be bringing the seal to close the tear in the Veil where the candidate's vulnerable mind had let the Interloper come through. The first transports had arrived before dawn, packed with soldiers to lockdown the town. Barnestable had sent some of them with Loops to grab the young male candidate.

To Monkey, he said, "Run interference for us. We're going after Turtle." Monkey, sunken eyed, gathered himself visibly and nodded. Barnestable reached out to squeeze his forearm. "Hold it together, mate."

He jabbed a finger at Rhone and Murph. "You two, with me."

"Why me?" Murph wanted to know.

"Because she's the only one he'll listen to," said Barnestable. "And if he won't, you're the only one who can kick his arse."

They took a caravan and camel team. Rhone sat silently beside Barnestable on the driver's bench.

"You going to make this easy and tell me where he is?" he said.

"Do you need me to?" she asked.

"Probably not."

To the north-east, the transport plane's escorts were toying with the air defence assets that one of the mining cartels had put up.

"Biggest damn balls-up of my career," Barnestable said.

"It ain't so bad," said Murph from behind him. "The rumours are already out in the public, have been a long time. What's one more seal?"

*Just another finger in the dyke*, Barnestable thought. He said, "Never lost a team member before, mate. I was proud of that record."

He glanced back. Murph lifted her chin by way of acknowledgement. "There's that."

They fell quiet for a while, with just the creak of the van and the scrape of its wheels and the camels' feet on the gritty road surface.

Rhone said, "Do you think they know what they're doing to us?"

Barnestable glanced at her. "The Interlopers? You mean like maybe enslaving and sucking the life out of people might be just their way of saying 'hello'?"

She shrugged a shoulder. "Or maybe there's no mind behind it at all. Maybe they're just things, forces of nature."

"Like fire," said Murph.

*A fire waiting in a room without enough air,* Barnestable thought, *and suddenly someone opens the door. Whoosh! Only the fire's cold.*

But who knew what an Interloper really was? All that came through that you could *sense* was that damned voice and the sudden loss of heat from the victims and all around them. As if the tear in the Veil—in the candidate's mind—was a drafty open door and all that energy was fleeing through it into a much colder world.

A memory leapt up in his mind's eye, the sort that sears into a person's brain and never fades, of half-frozen bodies, walking dead, staggering out of a factory dorm where an Interloper had come through.

"No," he said. "There's a mind. They know what they're doing."

Murph said, "Does it matter?"

They found Turtle where Barnestable thought they would, camped out at the abandoned military base inside one of the old barracks shells. His woman's parents were with him, and the young girl. They all stood as Barnestable and his companions approached. The girl slipped her hand through Turtle's.

Barnestable eyed the kid. "She doesn't look much like you, you know."

Turtle smirked lopsidedly. "They don't build us to breed true, Barnes," he said.

"Tinas are dead," Barnestable said. "Interloper got them."

The smirk vanished. "Me being there wouldn't have changed that."

"Go to hell, Turtle," said Murph, without any particular rancour.

"We gotta take her in," said Barnestable.

Turtle was already shaking his head.

"You can't protect her," said Barnestable.

"He can't," said Rhone quietly. "But I can."

She moved over to stand beside Turtle. Barnestable stared in dismay. "Hey, what about you and me, love?"

Rhone gave a short laugh. "There is no you and me, Barnes."

He sighed, deflating. His hand waved randomly. "Yeah, well."

Rhone went on, "And I can teach her to protect herself."

"She's born," Barnestable said. "She can't protect herself without her nervous system shielded. She'd need to be remade."

"It doesn't have to be that way," Rhone replied. The kid's grandmother gently pulled her back behind Turtle. Barnestable stared at Rhone, wondering if that was true.

He looked up at Murph.

She finished picking her teeth, ran her tongue around them inside closed lips. "So can I kick his arse now?"

Turtle grunted. "You can try."

She showed him a grin a shark would've been proud of and glanced at Barnestable. "Well?"

Barnestable ground his molars as he regarded Turtle, then Rhone, the girl, her grandparents. "How're you going to hide?"

"Plenty of runaways out in the desert," Turtle said. "Born and made. I'll get work cracking heads or rocks for one of the miners, easy enough."

Barnestable nodded. His eyes felt hot, the emotional load of the past day and night rising up. He got a lid on it. "We'll leave you the van." He drew in a shaky breath. "Come on, Murph. We got a long walk back. Should be enough time to get our story straight."

Murph snorted. "Walk? That wasn't in the job description." To Turtle, she said, "One day, big boy."

She prodded Barnestable's buttock with the toe of her boot. "Faster, piggy."

# Extracted Journal Notes for an Ethnography of Bnebene Nomad Culture

*Journal: 244813.03 (DAY 7#2)*

On the move, the caravan inevitably kicks up a lot of dust. The hunter-males walking up front are no more than indistinct silhouettes from my already habitual vantage at the rear of the line. I couldn't tell which of them it was who raised both arms to point ahead and gave the first cry of, "Yoom!"

The rest of the clan echoed the call. The word translates approximately as, "Oh, happy thing!"

"Yoom!" boomed Bubba, beside me.

"What is it?" I asked.

He peered down at me from his three-and-a-half metre height, craning his neck to see past the fringe of his leaf collar.

"A river," he answered. He drummed woody fingers on the sides of his torso. "Yoom!"

His armaments clanked with the movement of his arms. Like the hunter-males, Bubba and his neuter-brothers wear harnesses hung with a variety of ranged and close-quarter weapons. They and the non-related hunter-males travelling with the clan refer to each other mutually as "hadhagnug", meaning, loosely, "threat". Even with the weapons they carry and the size of the male neuters, the term is much easier to reconcile with the hunter-males than with Bubba and his neuter-brothers. I speculate that perhaps Bubba and his brothers, having been told that I'm female, have rationalised my presence with their clan by adopting me into their sphere of protection.

Intriguingly, the non-related males do not apply "hadhagnug" to the clan's hunter-males, referring to them as "mnagmanag", the same term they use for the clan's breeder- and neuter-females. Raffarin's definition of "mnagmanag" as "fit for breeding" may require revision.

The pace picked up as we neared the river, both the bnebene afoot and the ondrordore that carried the neuter-mothers and most of the clan's juveniles growing excited at the prospect of fresh water. Hanging back a little to watch, I was struck by a powerful and very specific sense of *strangeness*.

Anthropocentrically speaking, bnebene have the "right" number of arms and legs, but these seem far too large and long for their torsos and heads—the heads really just a fifth limb that houses binocular eyes and frond-like olfactory organs. By far the most disconcerting thing about both bnebene and their "plants of burden" is the way they move. The locomotion and gestures of both species tend to be quick, but have a curious jerkiness, as though one is watching poorly made stop-motion animation. Added to that, the ondrordore look like something Cinderella would ride in, shaped like giant garlic cloves with feathery leaf tufts at their pinnacles.

Reaching the river, the ondrordore rotated with ponderous dignity to put their rearmost pairs of vine-legs in the water, before folding open their front wall segments to disgorge their passengers.

The older juveniles climbed down with a kind of staccato flow, then they and the breeder-females helped their neuter-mothers to follow. Bubba and his neuter-brothers retrieved the very youngest saplings from inside, still planted in soil tubs and not yet sapient or animate, and carried them to the water.

The whole clan lined up with their toes in the river, leaf collars raised towards the afternoon sun. Within a few minutes, all had become quiet. What had been a bustling caravan of *people* was now suddenly transformed into a stand of unfamiliar *trees* of various sizes, silent and still.

In the distance, around the rim of the bay, I could see a small cluster of buildings. A fish farm's grid of nets and jetties criss-crossed the discoloured water at that end of the bay. Rochefort is the town's name, according to my mobile, all of seven years old and claiming a population of a couple of hundred.

The afternoon was getting on, and it was a Sunday, which mattered in these parts. I dusted the pebbles from a patch of dirt and settled down to write while the bnebene finish their drink.

◉

*244813.04 (DAY 8#1)*

I walked into Rochefort today for supplies and stopped in at the post office to hire a terminal for half an hour, enjoying the luxury of a full-sized interface—even a cheap, outdated one—compared to the basic pad I hook up to my mobile in the field. I tried to ignore the way the postmaster kept staring at my chest while I worked. At my age, sexual attention *could* have been flattering.

There were a dozen new video, audio and text messages forwarded from the faculty office at the university, from overseas and even offworld colleagues who wanted to crash my research. I sent back via the office my blanket text-only response, *"Research is progressing well. Subjects are accepting but sensitive. Further disruption would be counter-productive at present."*

I came back to the counter with a handful of articles printed on cheap synthetic vellum for later reading. The postmaster squinted at me—at my face, for once—while he processed my credit. "You travellin' with them aliens, ain't you?"

"Bnebene," I corrected him, managing to keep my tone light. "We're all aliens here."

He grunted. "Tinkers, ain't they?"

I ground my teeth. The term is Raffarin's, whose theory of the Universal Metaperson dominates scholarship of bnebene as it does that of other communicative sapients. Still, I told myself at this particular moment, it's better than 'aliens'.

I tried not to touch the postmaster's skin when I took back my card. He stared at my chest while I thanked him and wished him a good day. Outside, I paused to take a deep breath before crossing the road to the town's general store. From the post office steps, I could just make out the silvery thread of the space elevator disappearing into the upper reaches of the sky, anchored on the far shore of the inland sea at Persepolis.

I came out of the general store with a thoroughly unappetising collection of dehydrated ration packs in a thin sucrose bag that *might* last the walk back to the campsite. I wondered if perhaps I could convince one of the hunters to go and rustle me up some rabbits, imagining their amusement if I did so. A day is yet to pass that one member or other of my bnebene clan doesn't remark on my inefficient physiology, with its daily demands for material sustenance.

Still, ration packs are a small price to pay, and I am determined to make more of my once-in-a-generation opportunity than Golovlyov did.

The riverside camp is about an hour from Rochefort, travelling on foot. I walked beside the vast, pungent enclosures of oysters and sardines that are the town's sole reason for existing.

The silence of Aralsea on a still day, and of the dry plateau that surrounds it, is intimidating. Not much has made it out here yet to alleviate the monotonous pale umber of dust and stone, only lichens, grasses and a few insect species—and rabbits.

The sucrose bag gave up the fight about three quarters of the way back to the camp. I had to fill my pockets and nurse the rest inside my jacket like a pregnant belly.

Approaching the camp, I spied wisps of smoke from campfires. Bnebene only make fires to cook with, which meant someone *had* been out rabbiting. My mouth watered.

I took off my boots, socks and trousers to wade across the thigh deep water, as I had on the way out. The ondrordore still stood with their back ends in the river. When we arrived, their wall segments had a shrivelled look. A day later, they're as plump as inflated balloons. Most of the juvenile members of the clan were still in the river beside them, unmoved from the day before. Consistent with Golovlyov's observations of ship-borne bnebene, young caravan nomads typically remain less active than the adults, even after they uproot from their planter boxes.

Nimble breeder-females and tall hunter-males hunkered around the fires, holding out small, rapidly charring carcasses on skewers. Bubba and Jolly squatted among them, while Big Red stood like a solitary watchtower on a low rise a short distance from the camp. Pixie, the middle in age of the clan's adult neuter-mothers, squatted on a stool to rest her legs while she dipped her toes in the river.

Old Chook and Chuckles, her sisters, struck identical poses a couple of metres away. All three had tucked up around their hips the hems of the silk ponchos they wear to cover their Venus Fly Trap mouthparts and the several seedpod organs around their torso-trunks. Other genders, with only mouths and genitals on the front of their trunks, wear aprons instead.

I waded out of the river near Pixie and her sisters and lifted my jacket to let the foil packets spill onto the ground at the water's edge. The three neuter-mothers observed this performance, beady eyes unblinking in their small triangular faces. The slight ruffling of their leaf collars indicated they were amused.

"Are sedentary bnebene cultures as hidebound as sedentary human ones?" I said.

This prompted a brief discussion of the term "hidebound". According to the Babel in my ear, their consensual definition was reasonably accurate. Once satisfied, all three of them adjusted their ponchos, looking like nothing so much as human grandmothers straightening their frocks.

Pixie turned to me. "You had a poor experience of your fellows in the town, gunnug?"

According to the Babel, which uses Raffarin's bnebene lexicon, "gunnug" means "undesirable", as in "not fit to mate with", the semantic opposite of "mnagmanag". The caravan nomads apply the term equally to Merchanter bnebene as to humans and other non-bnebene sapients.

I recounted my conversation with the postmaster.

Old Chook murmured something that the Babel didn't pick up. Pixie said, "This bnebene is familiar with such attitudes among the gunnug of the towns."

"*Bnebene* gunnug?" I asked.

"Gunnug is gunnug," she said.

Her use of the term compels me to concur with Raffarin that bnebene don't maintain a clear ideological distinction between culture and biology as means of differentiation.

I ate my dinner of charcoal-baked rabbit and re-hydrated vegetables with Bubba and Jolly. To take food, bnebene squat with knees up behind their shoulders, their plates on the ground, and delicately pick at the surprisingly tiny morsels with their long fingers. The food is lifted up underneath their aprons to their mouthparts, which adult bnebene rarely uncover. Most of their meals consist of sitting still while they go through the early parts of digestion. The waste that remains in the mouthparts is discreetly spat out a couple of days later into shallow pits the bnebene dig with their toes.

In deference to the sensibilities of my hosts, I hang a gauze veil over my head and shoulders while I eat with them. The size of my meals is as much of a source of astonishment for the bnebene as is their frequency. Jolly and Bubba tapped each other's torsos while they digested and I was still shovelling food up under my veil.

The evening was warm, so I had left my trousers off, underpants sufficing for modesty in this non-human company. It was the most of my skin they had seen, as all my outer clothes consist of full trousers and long-sleeved shirts. My legs look superficially similar to bnebene limbs, with smooth thighs and calves and wrinkled, knobbly knees, although bnebene dermis has a waxy texture and hardness like that of a smooth-barked tree.

Bubba, beside me, reached out two fingers to prod my thigh. He recoiled. "Hree!"

"Hree!" Jolly echoed. Their leaf collars flared. A heartbeat later, I heard an identical, distant, cry from Big Red, out on sentry duty.

My Babel translated the word as a diametric opposite to "Yoom!"

Around the camp, the head of every hunter-male snapped around to look our way. I suddenly felt like the person who'd farted noisily in the busy silence of an academic library. Or, as the flat gazes of the hunter-males remained fixed in our direction, the person who had tried to tiptoe through a lion's cage and kicked over a metal bucket halfway.

A pulse pumped in my neck. "My skin is softer than yours," I said.

Abruptly, Bubba and Jolly settled down, as though my explanation had bridged a conceptual gap that they couldn't cross by themselves.

"It is," said Bubba. "This gunnug differs from this bnebene."

### 244814.03 (DAY 14#1)

I remain at a loss to explain my clan's gender disparity. During Golovlyov's sojourn with his merchanter clan, he established, if only by the verbal evidence of his interview subjects, that bnebene genders are determined chromosomally and that bnebene have three chromosomes to determine gender, resulting in four viable combinations: two male and two female, with a fertile and sterile caste in each pair. Thus:

> TU—breeder female
> ST—breeder male
> SU—female neuter
> TT—male neuter

Golovlyov's observations of his host clan and other Merchanter bnebene confirmed roughly equal gender numbers.

The same should be true of my caravan clan. Yet the clan includes four neuter-mothers (three adult, one juvenile), three adult neuter-males, nine breeder-females (including three juveniles) and six related breeder-males (in caravan nomad society, the "hunter-males", two of which are juvenile). There are another four unrelated hunter-males travelling with the clan at present. I discount planted saplings, since they do not begin to express gender until after they uproot.

When I asked Bubba if he has any hunter-brothers who are not currently travelling with the clan, he replied, "There are seven little-brother-subfractions of this bnebene that are elsewhere."

Observations of other caravan nomads indicate that the clan's gender balance is usual for Tinkers, with breeder-male numbers consistently forty to fifty percent higher than breeder-females. The difference is not readily explicable. It would be remarkable for females to be significantly less viable than males.

### 244815.05 (DAY 23#2)

Bubba fell into step beside me as the clan ambled along beside the river after breaking camp. In his hands, he cradled the pot of a young sapling, its not-yet-animated trunk resting against his shoulder.

"Good morning," I said.

Bubba's habitual response to this greeting is to consider a moment before replying, "It is."

This morning, he hummed deep in his torso—a pre-verbalisation, from the fact that my Babel offered no translation. After a lengthy pause, he asked, "What fractions has this gunnug?"

I felt a little thrill. Following from his prod at my leg a fortnight ago, this was the only second indication I'd had from him of active intellectual curiosity about me.

I answered deliberately, "I am one and whole."

"One?" he repeated.

I watched him closely. "Yes."

"Hree!" he cried, making me jump, and strode away, his leaf collar flared trembling stiff around his head.

"Hree!" I heard from his neuter-brothers further ahead.

I took a couple of deep, slow breaths, then jumped again as two more tall figures appeared abruptly on either side of me. A pair of the clan's hunter-males—Moose and Black Pete—their long rifles cradled in their arms.

Black Pete said, "Come, gunnug."

Bnebene hunter-males are very different creatures to their neuter-brothers. Bubba's "little brothers" exude a palpable aura of *purpose*, the way a gun has a sense of purpose. These I can well imagine as the clan's warrior defenders.

Moose and Black Pete steered me, sandwiched between them, over to where Pixie rode at the open front of one of the ondrordore. My mouth was very dry. Hell, I thought, they're going to kick me out. My bright future career was fading before my eyes.

Pixie said, "Gunnug, you must be circumspect in your dealings with big-brother-fraction. Big-brother-subfractions are the simplest of this bnebene and easily upset. They struggle to grasp that a gunnug person may have only one body."

"They are prone," said Black Pete, "to conflate 'confusion' with 'threat'."

"This bnebene is concerned that the consequences for this gunnug, having only one body, could be very great," concluded Moose.

I swallowed a couple of times so that I could answer, relief tempered by an entirely new fear. The clan wasn't going to expel me, but, even as alarming as their recent reactions had been, I had not considered that the neuter-males' intellectual confusion could trigger an outburst of actual physical violence. I had no doubt over the amount of damage a bnebene neuter-male could do to an unprotected human. "I understand."

"It is well that you do," said Pixie. "Sister-fractions will be watching"

I am uncertain whether this was intended as a warning or a reassurance, or why Pixie's statement excluded the clan's hunter-males. Perhaps the female genders have greater sway over the neuter-males when they were distressed?

### 244815.05 (DAY 23#4)

I avoided Bubba and his neuter-brothers for the rest of the day, but they came to me as I ate my dinner of dried apricots and yesterday's leftover rabbit.

The three of them squatted around me. Bubba put his potted sapling down by his side and repeated his question. "What fractions has this gunnug?"

For the first time, their great size seemed intimidating. I was sitting away from the main part of the camp, my mobile and interface pad propped up on my pack while I ate. None of the female bnebene were near. Black Pete stood in the river about twenty metres away with Silent Bob, one of the unrelated hunter-males. My mind raced.

I said, "I have many fractions and subfractions."

"Where are they?"

Damn. I wetted my lips. "Here."

In near unison, the three of them half stood, squatted again. "But where are the rest?"

Black Pete looked towards us. He started to wade out of the water.

"They are all here," I said.

"Hree!" Bubba rose, leaf collar stiffening and arms spreading wide in an obvious threat display.

"Hree!" Jolly and Big Red crowded in beside me.

Black Pete splashed ashore with stop-motion speed.

"How many subfractions has your fraction of this bnebene?" I asked Bubba, quickly.

His arms lowered. Their leaf collars drooped. Bubba squatted again. Black Pete slowed his charge.

"Three, now," said Bubba. "Four, soon." His fingers reached absently for the sapling.

I held out my bowl of dried apricots, knowing that they enjoy the flavour. Bubba took a wrinkled fruit and tucked it under his apron. Jolly and Big Red copied him, reaching over me. Trying to control the shaking of my hands, I resumed eating.

This interaction—along with my other, less alarming observations—supports the conclusion that the bnebene "person" is synonymous with the matrilineal kin group—encompassing both the eusocial, matrilocal clan and any related hunter-males living autonomously. Each gender set within the clan is, in Raffarinian terminology, a 'fraction' of the person, and each member of the set is a 'subfraction'. The actual bnebene words translate literally as 'essential part' and 'smallest part', respectively. I have not yet observed any evidence that my clan members conceptualise themselves as anything other than parts of the collective whole.

That said, the fact that at least some of the clan can readily grasp that my personhood is contained within my single body, superficially weighs in favour of Raffarin's position that the "dividual" bnebene person is an ideological construct and therefore consistent with her theory of the Universal Metaperson. However, even these members seem utterly perplexed that the label "Irene Matsui" should apply only to me, and that other Irenes are not then synonymous with me (not all 'this Irene').

I have tried to explain to Pixie my conceptual need to apply nicknames to her and her clan members. She seems unable to distinguish which member of a gender set any given nickname refers to, even when I say, for example: "Chuckles is that sister-mother-subfraction that is older than this sister-mother-subfraction." She grasps the kin relationship I'm referring to, but seems unable (or unwilling) to associate this with the label "Chuckles". It is the extremity of this behaviour that led Golovlyov to his proposal that since bnebene are biologically eusocial, therefore their "dividualism" is biological—that is, bnebene personhood *fundamentally* resides at a group level and they can *only* conceptualise themselves in terms of their relationships.

Unfortunately, while I am inclined to sympathise with his view that Raffarin's theory is anthropocentric, because of Golovlyov's widely derided supplementary claims, intellectual association with anything more than his basic observations is a greased slope to scholarly oblivion.

### 244816.02 (DAY 27#4)

Bubba and his neuter-brothers have been bringing their sapling to awareness. When we camp, they spend most of their days gathered around its planter box, singing low, rumbling songs from which my Babel is unable to discern any words. On days when the caravan moves, they have taken to carrying the sapling by turns, rather than loading it into the ondrordore with the rest. At the beginning and end of travel days, they sing to it for at least an hour.

The clan's several saplings are at varying stages of maturity and the progression is fascinating to see. At first, they have an appearance akin to sunflowers, having a long, straight stem and large, single flower head with two leaves just below it. As they mature, the lower part of the stem bifurcates, the leaves lengthen and shape into arms and the flower head hardens, olfactory fronds unfurl and it grows into a face. By the time the sapling is ready to uproot, they look like a perfectly rendered, skeletally thin statue of a breeder-female. Visible gender characteristics, including the massive size of the male genders, develop after uprooting.

While Bubba, Jolly and Big Red have been singing to it, the sapling has slowly grown more animated, beginning with small flexing of its fingers and mouth parts, followed by full movement of the arms and head and, finally, articulation of the stem at the knee and hip joints. The climactic moment came this afternoon, when the sapling finally added its voice to those of its brothers.

"Yoom!" they all cried.

"Yoom!" the rest of the clan echoed.

A meal was had this evening, and the neuter-males took theirs squatted beside their new brother. It will be several weeks yet, I understand, before the freshly sapient bnebene is ready to uproot.

### 244817.02 (DAY 34#4)

I am acutely aware that this opportunity is mine because Utopia is still a young, fringe colony at the arse-end of the Line, and Nieu Bactria is the arse-end of Utopia. I am the *only* qualified cultural sapientologist at NBU. Being Johnny-on-the-spot, I've locked in the gig before more distant and better-credentialled colleagues could even hear of the opportunity. But even with this ethnography under my belt, I need to *add* something to the body of knowledge if I am to use it as a springboard up to that esteemed rank of scholars that includes Raffarin and the rest—that *should* have included Golovlyov. Now I have it.

Tonight I witnessed an event from which even Golovlyov was excluded: a mating ceremony.

Towards sunset, all of the adult bnebene gathered in the river. The neuter-males stood behind the neuter-mothers in an obvious protective position. The crowd of breeder-females and males, related and unrelated, faced them in a rough crescent. They sang, a low murmur without—to my human ears—any discernable melody, although I could feel a rhythmic pulse of their sub-sonic vocalisations. "Yoom" was repeated, and several semantically related words.

At the moment the sun's orb touched the horizon, three couples separated from the crowd and approached the neuter-mothers. Each couple comprised a clan member and an unrelated hunter-male. The three mating trios then waded out of the river and made their way to the ondrordore, each party shutting themselves inside a different vehicle-creature. The neuter-males followed, to stand guard outside.

Most remarkable is that one of the pairs who had approached the neuter-mothers was male-male—Black Pete and Silent Bob, who I observed in the river together a few days ago.

A final, curious, point of interest is that the remainder of the adults stayed in the river after the mating trios had shut themselves away. They remained quiet for some time, then gave three collective intonations of "Yoom", close together but not equally spaced. Shortly after, the breeder members of the mating trios emerged from the ondrordore.

That a neuter-mother is included in a non-breeding union prompts the speculation that homosexual relations among bnebene are required to follow the pattern of breeding relations in order to be socially sanctioned. The presence of some interstitial or malleable gender characteristics is also a possibility, but less likely. Previous ethnographic evidence indicates a remarkably strict alignment between ideological and biological gender categories among bnebene and occurrences of intersexuality have not been recorded.

Since I have been permitted to observe this ceremony, I'm hopeful that Pixie and the other participants will consent to speak with me about it as well.

### 244817.03 (DAY 35#1)

At dawn, Black Pete and several of the other hunter-males took their juvenile brothers out rabbiting. The neuter-mothers were carried down to the river and planted on their stools. When I tried to approach, Bubba and his neuter-brothers flared their leaf collars in a threat display. I retreated promptly. I was, however, able to observe that Pixie and Old Chook did not appear fully conscious in any case.

Interestingly, Chuckles—who had gone with Black Pete and Silent Bob—exhibited the same behaviour. This suggests that intercourse, rather than impregnation, is what triggers catatonia in the mothers. A more intriguing possibility is that Chuckles's behaviour is an *act*, part of the ritual of sanctioning the homosexual mating.

### 244817.03 (DAY 35#2)

More excitement today: towards midday, as the camp drowsed, suddenly *every* member of the clan (except the neuter-mothers, who remained catatonic) leapt to their feet in the same instant and gave a collective cry of, "Hree!" Several minutes of intense agitation followed. The unrelated hunter-males, after their initial surprise, appeared unaffected.

I waited for a while after they'd settled down (and my own heart rate had returned somewhere near normal!) then approached Moose to ask what the outburst had been about.

"One subfraction of the hunter-brother-fraction of this bnebene has broken his leg."

"Did your hunter-brothers call the news to you?" I asked. I hadn't heard anything, but bnebene hearing is known to be more sensitive than human and has a wider auditory range.

Moose rapped on his shin. "If one subfraction feels a hurt, all subfractions of all fractions must feel it. Is it not the same for humans? If one part of this gunnug is hurt, are not all parts aware?"

"All parts of me are in the same body," I said.

"It is the same," he said.

His answer, I note, did not preclude the possibility of a distress call.

I was therefore surprised when the rabbiting party returned to the camp whole and unhurt. I returned to Moose.

"Which hunter-brother-subfraction injured his leg?"

Moose raised both arms to point. "The subfraction that hunts to the north, by the sea."

"At the shore we have recently left?" I asked, thinking that an infrasound cry from a bnebene on the south shore of Aralsea could conceivably reach us here.

"No. By the *sea*," he said. With a woody finger he sketched a quick map in the dirt, showing our river, Aralsea and a blank swathe between it and the squiggly line he drew for the oceanic coast. He made a dot beside the river (us) and another up next to the north coast. "By the sea," he repeated, "That which surrounds this continent."

I do not, from this, concede to Golovlyov's postulated "psychic dividualism"—his unsubstantiated and oft-ridiculed contention that a bnebene clan is more than merely eusocial, but at the most fundamental level a single being. Given the sophistication of the geneered tech the Tinkers use, it is entirely probable that they have integral communication devices to maintain contact with separated members.

*244817.07 (DAY 39#3)*

After the warning from Pixie, Moose and Black Pete, and Bubba's subsequent alarming approach, I have taken some pains to avoid he and his neuter-brothers. Curiosity trumps caution, however. I took my plate and ventured over to join them.

"Yoom," I said, aware that I am only capable of a small part of the vocalisation. They appeared to understand my attempt or, at least, welcomed me into their group.

"Four, now," said Bubba.

"This fraction has four subfractions," I said.

"Four subfractions of this fraction of this bnebene," he agreed, amiably. "This fraction that is brother-uncle-son."

Moose and Black Pete were watching, as were several other hunter-brothers. The line of conversation seemed safe enough for the moment, though.

"This bnebene has many subfractions," I ventured, ready to backpedal quickly if they showed signs of agitation.

"Many," said Bubba.

"Most are here and some are elsewhere," I said.

"Most here," Bubba agreed. "Those parts that are brother-father-son are elsewhere."

The statement confused me. I glanced at Moose and the other related hunter-males. "Some of those subfractions that are brother-father-son are elsewhere, and some are here?"

Bubba's leaf collar rose a little—as did those of his brothers, including the sapling—then settled. "No. Only brother-father-son of other bnebene," he said. "Only hadhagnug."

"But what about . . . ?" I began, raising my arm to indicate Moose and Black Pete and the rest.

I stared at Moose and had one of those vertiginous moments where sudden insight yawns like a chasm beneath one's toes, where one had previously perceived only an unbroken field ahead. It took me a moment to find my voice.

"How many sisters have you?" I blurted, then corrected the question: "How many sister-fractions has this bnebene?"

"Three," said Bubba. He and his brothers shifted their feet. The sapling shivered. Reacting to *my* reaction—not understanding it, necessarily, but sensitive to the change in my body's rhythm and scent.

I asked one more question to check. "And how many brother-fractions?"

"Two."

I beat a hasty retreat before they could begin to ask awkward questions of *me*.

I took my plate over to Pixie who, along with her sisters, had fitfully emerged from her catatonia over the past couple of days. My legs were shaky as I squatted beside her.

"There are eight adult hunter-subfractions travelling with the clan," I said. "Four belong to this bnebene, four of them do not."

She looked at me for a few seconds, no doubt sensing the same disturbance in my body as the neuter-males had begun reacting to. "Yes," she said.

"The four that are subfractions of this bnebene are female," I said.

"Yes."

Not evidence of homosexuality or intersexuality. Black Pete and Moose and the rest are female. A *third* female gender. The trio of Black Pete, Silent Bob and Chuckles *was* a breeding trio. I said, "This bnebene has three fractions that are female and two that are male."

"Yes."

I had to sit, tipping the short distance from my squat onto my backside. Pixie and her sisters watched me with evident curiosity. I took a couple of deep breaths and said, "The bnebene of the Merchant ships are different to this bnebene. Merchanter bnebene each have two female and two male fractions."

"They are gunnug," Pixie said. Feeling a little lightheaded, I asked her how many fractions the bnebene of the homeworlds have. She informed me that they are all gunnug, but added that some have as few as two fractions and others as many as seven.

My head is whirling with ways this might be achieved. The sex chromosomes postulated by Golovlyov for Merchanter bnebene could conceivably produce a third female gender if, for example, the hunter-females have an extra chromosome that masculinises them. A supplementary gender-determination method, such as temperature variance, or some form of haplodiploidy are other possibilities. But none of these would explain the homeworld bnebene with two or seven genders.

*Different* sex chromosomes would:

| Merchanter Genders | Tinker Genders |
|---|---|
| TU—breeder female | PQ—feminine breeder female |
| ST—breeder male | PR—masculine (hunter) breeder female |
| SU—female neuter | RQ—breeder (hunter) male |
| TT—male neuter | QQ—female neuter |
| | RR—male neuter |

I asked Pixie, "Why five genders? Why does this bnebene have five fractions?"

"Because five is bnebene."

"And why do the Merchanters have four?"

At this, Pixie and her sisters indicated amusement. "Because they believe four is bnebene," Pixie said. "But five is bnebene. All else is gunnug."

The bnebene species that we know (*plural* species), and at least some of those on the homeworlds too, are artificially self-created to express competing ideologies of racial ideals.

This is my springboard. I am made.

### 244818.02 (DAY 41#2)

I was bathing this afternoon in the river, downstream of our campsite, the backs of the ondrordore between me and the camp.

Bubba and his neuter-brothers waded out into the water and surrounded me. Jolly carried the sapling in its pot. Its flared leaf collar mimicked theirs.

"How many fractions has this human?" Bubba demanded.

I stood, covering my breasts and genitals in case they took offence at seeing them exposed. "Humans perceive ourselves differently to bnebene," I said.

"How many fractions has this gunnug?" he said. "How many subfractions?"

I wished for Moose's psychic powers to kick in right about now. I thought quickly. "Come ashore with me," I said. "I will draw you a picture that might help you understand."

They allowed me to pass and followed as I waded up to the bank. I considered making a break for it, but that would certainly inflame the situation. Besides which, on the riverbank we were in sight of the rest of the clan at the camp.

I quickly put on my shirt and trousers, not bothering to dry myself. I beckoned for the neuter-brothers to squat with me. To my relief, they did, Jolly placing the sapling on the ground at his side.

With my finger, I sketched a web of lines in the dirt, creating four intersections. I indicated the drawing, and then the four of them, "This is this fraction of this bnebene." I indicated a line. "These are the relationships that bind the subfractions together."

They sat silently for a long moment, then Bubba extended a finger and touched the intersection nearest to him. "This is this subfraction."

"Yes."

Jolly and Big Red copied him. The sapling reached less certainly towards the intersection nearest to it. They retracted their fingers. Silence, again.

Encouraged, I drew more criss-crossed lines, another four sets, then lines to connect all five. "These are the other fractions of this bnebene," I said. I drew a ring around the whole lot. "Everything outside this is not this bnebene."

They stared at the picture. "This is this bnebene," said Bubba.

Heart thumping, I rubbed the patch of dirt clear. I made another series of dots, then drew lines between them, but not quite touching the dots. I touched the dot closest to me. "This is this human."

A muscle in my calf twitched, my legs tensed to spring away and run. Bubba extended a finger. "The lines do not touch."

"No," I agreed. I touched the other dots. "These are other humans. Each is one and whole."

The moment seemed to last forever. Their leaf collars stiffened, relaxed. Then Bubba said, "This gunnug is different to this bnebene."

I almost gagged with relief. They *could* understand. Even these simplest of bnebene could grasp a concept of the individual. Could Raffarin be right, I thought, after all? Could Golovlyov's accusations of anthropocentrism be unfounded?

"This is how most humans see ourselves," I said. "Humans and bnebene perceive ourselves differently." I took the plunge: "Underneath, perhaps we are more similar."

I let that hang for a few seconds. When they didn't react, I rubbed out my sketch and began a third time. Once again, I made a series of dots. This time, I made a circle around each one and connected all the circles together with lines. Raffarin's diagram of the Universal Metaperson: each individual distinct from but bound within a web of dividual social relations.

"Underneath the different ways we see ourselves," I said, "perhaps we are both—humans and bnebene—both like this."

They stared. Bubba uncurled a finger, hesitated, then touched a dot on the Metaperson diagram. "This is this subfraction."

"Or this human," I said.

"The lines do not touch," he said.

I felt a sinking dread in the pit of my belly. I had taken them too far. "No," I said. "But they hold us, nonetheless."

"This . . . " His leaf collar shivered, as did those of his brothers. "This subfraction is . . . is . . . this bnebene."

"This subfraction is this bnebene," Jolly and Big Red repeated. The sapling mewled. Their distress was palpable.

"This subfraction is one," said Bubba.

"One and four," I stammered. "And many."

"One!" he bellowed, rising.

"Hree!" they all cried, at different moments.

I leapt backwards, stumbling away from them as Bubba and Big Red reached for weapons.

"Hree!" they cried again, even more unsynchronised, and all did something different. Jolly fled at a staccato sprint towards the river. Big Red turned an energy blade on himself, stabbing himself in the trunk, while beside him the sapling waved its arms, frantically seeking contact with one of its brothers, and tipped over its pot. Bubba came after me, swinging a sonic mace.

"Hadhagnug!" he boomed. "Hree!"

The mace's vibrations made me want to vomit. The edge of its effect radius scraped my shoulders, not quite close enough to draw blood.

Ahead, hunters charged from the camp. I saw Moose, standing still, her hunting rifle levelled, aiming past me. I jagged to the side. Hot pain seared my back as Bubba caught me with the full effect of his mace. My guts reacted violently, my bowel and bladder evacuating as vomit spurted up my throat. I fell.

Moose's rifle whined.

"Hree!" Bubba cried, staggering.

Black Pete struck him feet-first, knocking him down with a crash like a felled tree. She aimed her handgun and fired a lightning-burst of blue light, point-blank into his trunk, then sprang after the rest of the hunters, off to subdue Jolly and Big Red. Bubba sprawled, fingers and toes twitching, making faint, broken noises.

"Hree!" the cries echoed from the camp.

I tried to stand, fell again as the world tipped up to meet me, crawled over to Bubba. "Oh, no. Oh, no. I'm so sorry."

Hard fingers caught my arm, lifted me away.

Moose dropped me in the dirt a distance from Bubba, regarded me from her great height, rifle cradled across her elbow. "This gunnug has hurt this bnebene."

"Will they be alright?"

"Perhaps," she said. "But this gunnug must leave."

Once all the neuter-males were stunned and quiet, Moose walked me downstream to wash in the river. Black Pete brought my pack of clothes and belongings and they helped me to apply a synthskin dressing from my medical kit to my back. Then they left me.

I stood on the riverbank, the breeze raising goosebumps on my bare skin, and watched the caravan move away. It was a couple of hours past noon, but they plainly had no desire to stay in this distressing place, or near me. The long legs of the neuter-males hung from the open doors of the ondrordore. None of the clan members looked back.

I dried myself and dressed, then built a fire, feeling colder than the day.

I have what I came for. I will overturn a generation of received wisdom about bnebene gender and evolution. What we had thought of as a single species is, in fact, several. And they have *made themselves* several, the ultimate expression of fundamentalism and eugenics.

My reputation will be made. Offers and opportunities will flow. It will be "Goodbye NBU, goodbye backwater". The list of renowned sapientologists will begin "Raffarin, *Matsui* . . . "

But what have I let slip away? Where might the clues I've been presented have led me? I showed Bubba and his brothers how to see themselves as individuals and it broke them. Simple as they are, they hadn't the resilience or sophistication to meet the challenge to their fundamental concept of self. Was it evidence of Golovlyov's psychic dividualism? Of the first true hive-mind humanity has encountered in a communicative sapient, or just absolute indoctrination? Might I have loosened some bricks at the base of Raffarin's intellectual edifice, her Universal Metaperson, as Golovlyov so spectacularly failed to do? Was the opportunity there to pull the whole thing down?

Might I still? Perhaps somewhere else, with another Merchanter or Tinker clan. There are experiments that could prove or disprove Golovlyov's theory.

But even if bnebene dividualism is true, could it too be a construct, an artificial veneer over the natural bnebene person? Is that why it shattered so easily for Bubba and his brothers? Do the questions of gender and dividualism converge?

My mobile is blinking beside me as I tap out my thoughts on the interface pad, its memory full of unanswered messages. Those, and the long walk back to Rochefort, can wait until tomorrow.

# Red Dirt

*Nieuw Holland, 1792*

The night we docked in Zwaanstadje, I dreamed of a red dirt plain. Its colour was of such intensity it fluoresced beneath the dry white grass and the olive foliage of the bushes that sparsely covered it. No creature moved, nor any breath of wind. The sun beat against my hatless head and I felt I stood too close to its flames.

I heard a voice and turned to find its source. Red rocks broke the monotony of the plain. At first, I thought them merely boulders, for they had such a rounded shape. Then my eyes adjusted, or perhaps the dream developed perspective, and I realised it was a massif of gigantic stones. I looked upon the bones of the world after the world had worn away. The age of the place yawned in my mind, older, by far, than the paltry few millennia of God's Creation.

The voice came again, a bass dirge at the very edge of hearing. It was not a sound from any human throat, but the song of the land itself.

I turned my back to the rocks—the heart of the place, I sensed— and fled. My shadow was like an anchor chained to my feet, dragging unwillingly behind me through the dirt. I ran, but the plain was without limit, and every time my feet struck the ground, I felt the vitality drain from me, leaching through my booted soles and into the parched earth.

⁂

I found Huon loitering in the scant shade of the Commissariat's entrance. Even after months at sea, he had somehow managed to preserve a complete uniform free of rents and stains. I refrained from picking at the broken threads where a button was missing from my own dishevelled coat.

I paused beside him, postponing the moment when we must emerge from the shelter of the walls. The afternoon heat was enough to scorch the lungs and parch the eyeballs in their sockets. The smell of woodsmoke from the indigenes' fires pervaded the air. Inland, grey tendrils curled into the sky.

"Well?"

While I did not demand formalities of Huon outside the presence of the crew, it was a license I sometimes regretted.

I squeezed the bridge of my nose. "The Commissaire demands a bribe before he will permit us to re-provision. The sum he has named is outrageous."

Huon snorted. "We should sail for Tasmanie. We could stretch our supplies that far."

"Only if we abandon our mission and cede all of Australie east of Nieuw Holland to the English," I said. "Besides, after the debacle at Isle de France and with Piron working the crew into such a lather of resentment, I fear half of them would desert, should we put into a French port."

Odd shadows flickered in the corners of my vision as I squinted against the glare of the Commissariat's plaza, paved in the piss-yellow local limestone from which most of the Dutch settlement was constructed. The orange, blue and white flag of the *Verenigde Oostindische Compagnie*—the United East India Company—drooped like a hung man.

Scabrous-looking native bushes separated the plaza from the gravel track that led to Zwaanstadje's solitary, exposed stone finger-wharf. Tied up at the near end was the V.O.C. merchantman *Enkhuizen*, with the typical fat belly that tapered upwards, designed to avoid port taxes levied on the area of a ship's deck. Beyond, our own converted cargo hauler, *La Recherche*, flew golden fleurs-de-lis on royal white.

"There are whaling colonies along the south coast," Huon suggested, as we stepped out onto the sun-blasted plaza.

"Half of which are pirates, and the other half are *English* pirates." I shook my head. "No, we will chart such colonies if we find them, but I do not wish to interact with them."

Huon subsided. He thought me too cautious but knew well enough when my patience with his second-guessing was about to fray.

"The price the Commissaire has named is only his opening gambit," I said. "I expect he will come down to something more reasonable quickly enough. What of the crew?"

"I left Rossel to organise them for shore leave," he said.

He must have known that I would not have approved such an order, had I been present. I ground my teeth, but there was little profit to be found in countermanding him now.

"I felt there was small risk of even the republicans among them deserting in such a godforsaken place," he added, blandly. "The savants are ensconced at the inn."

"So we fervently hope," I said. "Come, let us see if Monsieur Piron is still where you left him, and not up to mischief."

Our steps kicked puffs of dusty sand as we walked behind the low limestone promontory that partly sheltered Zwaanstadje from the sea. Upon it squatted an octagonal gun fort, fashioned from the same jaundiced rock, that served as the town's nominal defence against the English and other pirates. In the fierce light, my shadow seemed unsynchronised from my steps. I put the illusion down to weariness.

I noticed Huon stifling a yawn.

"You slept poorly, Jean-Michel?"

He nodded. "My dreams were troubled."

"As were mine," I said. "This place has a malaise about it." Enough so that it caused me to doubt my decision to resupply here even as I re-affirmed it.

A trio of Dutchmen passed in the opposite direction, dressed in sober black and white. Their features had a pinched quality that seemed to me more pronounced that the usual retentiveness of Puritans. Silver badges tinkled on their sleeves, cast with the religious sigils—runes—of the Northern Churches. It was a curiosity of Zwaanstadje. I had never before witnessed such ostentatious displays of faith from adherents of the Green Christ.

I paused before turning the corner, bothered by some detail. It took me a moment to pinpoint the strangeness. The hairs on my neck stood up. The Dutchmen's shadows were too short for the time of day, tucked up beneath their feet, when the sun should have laid them across the ground and up the walls of the buildings.

Huon observed my reaction curiously. I began to raise my arm to point, but the Dutchmen were already stepping through a doorway.

Our inn was located on the boulevard that constituted Zwaanstadje's east-west spine. The town huddled between the harbour fort and the Church of the Green Christ on its hill barely a mile inland, with its T-shaped pinnacle that signified both crucifix and pagan hammer. The boulevard's breadth was much reduced by the stalls and shop-front awnings of the merchants that crowded its length. Mohammedans and Chinese wore robes densely embroidered with their native scripts. Tattoos were common, peeking past the edges of cuffs and collars. The air seemed full of the ringing of tiny bells from the badges on the sleeves of every Dutch man and woman.

We found Piron, our expedition's naturalist, artist and principle republican agitator, lounging with wine bottle and glasses beneath the awning at the front of the inn. His eyes had a bruised look that suggested this afternoon's refreshment was merely a resumption of the previous night's pursuits.

Piron lifted his glass but made no move to rise. I elected to ignore the slight. Huon pulled out the vacant chair for me and fetched another for himself. I dropped my hat onto my lap and scratched my sweating scalp.

"Monsieur Bertrand is in his room?"

"Resting," Piron replied. "Until he regains his land legs." The astrologer had spent the majority of the journey from Brest resting in his cabin while he "gained his sea legs".

"He may have time," I said, with a grimace of resignation to imply that the circumstance was entirely beyond my control. "We will be delayed here before we can resupply."

"Then surely we must consider Batavia instead," said Piron, "and circumnavigate the continent by the reverse route."

I glanced at Huon. He looked away with a shrug, not bothering to conceal the gesture from Piron. I bit back a terse remark, annoyed at his lack of support. At least Piron had made the suggestion often enough to reassure me he would not risk impoundment of the ship here in Zwaanstadje.

Reprovisioning would not have been a consideration at all had our own countrymen at Isle de France not defrauded us so thoroughly. Not to mention that nearly a fifth of our sailors had jumped ship there. Huon suspected Piron of having a hand in the fiasco. I was unconvinced, but even so, Batavia, jewel of the Dutch Republic's East Indian empire, was the last place on God's Earth I wanted to take Piron and the seething nest of resentment that constituted my ship's crew.

"King Louis desires a colony on the Australien mainland," I said, "and we need to find it before the English do."

Piron made an uncouth noise. "His 'Nouvelle Orleans du Sud'."

Huon bridled at the insult to our monarch. "Monsieur, His Majesty's agents in Sydney Town were confident that they could sabotage the English expedition from there, but their report was months old when it reached France, and it has been months more since our departure."

"We must anticipate that the English are already at sea, monsieur," I added, mildly.

Piron rolled his eyes. "Then we must make the best of the situation," he said. He captured the half-empty wine bottle and filled two empty glasses, which he pushed towards Huon and myself.

Huon examined the pale contents of his.

"Capitaine Bruni," Piron chided.

With a sigh, I lifted the glass. I could discern little of its bouquet over the ever-present smell of smoke. I raised a toast. "To King Louis, long may he reign."

"Vive le roi!" Huon responded.

Piron's thin mouth curled. "Vive la France."

I dreamed a second time of the red dirt plain. This time I was already in motion. The voice of the land was more strident this time. Guttural and nasal, it filled the air, rising and falling, speeding and slowing.

Shadowy figures ran at my side. Sometimes they took the shapes of men, with long shadow spears in their hands. Sometimes they would change shape, becoming lean-bellied dogs, or great running birds, like ostriches, or else stretch out into the low shapes of giant lizards. Sometimes they were bounding creatures for which I had no analogue, with long tails and low heads.

They harassed me, poking with their spears and biting at my heels, or simply placing themselves in my path. Their every touch bled my strength. I fought to evade them but, irresistibly, they turned me.

The red bones of the world loomed, again, before me. Now my shadow reached out ahead, dragging me along in its wake. I tried to slow my suddenly headlong pace, but I could not.

Neglecting breakfast, I returned early in the morning to *La Recherche* to review the state of the ship and crew.

Smoke curled into the cloudless sky. There were more fires than yesterday, ringing the landward sides of the town.

The shadows on the buildings seemed alive with movement, although the air was too cool for mirages. The memory of my dream still lingered, fooling my weary brain into believing that I glimpsed animal shapes writhing there. I hurried my pace along the empty streets, wondering if I should just pay the Commissaire's bribe and be done with the place.

I found my ship in good order but the crew less so, exhibiting the after-effects of a reckless approach to the consumption of alcohol. Both the sailors on duty and our pair of excitable young ensigns were under the firm control of Rossel, *La Recherche*'s estimable Master Sailor. With him was our Sergeant of Marines, Delahaye—a ruffian and a lout, but by Huon's account a good soldier.

"How is morale?" I asked.

"They have little love for this place, Monsieur Capitaine," Rossel said. "But I do not think they are mutinous yet."

*Yet.* I concealed my dismay. "And if we are delayed here?"

Rossel's expression was answer enough. Casting my eyes over the crew, I noticed that many wore items decorated in Oriental lettering. Sunlight flashed on numerous cast metal badges. I saw too that bare wrists and ankles, and even some faces, were adorned with runes, ideograms or Mohammedan script. The majority appeared to be painted in impermanent ink, but several evidenced the rawness of fresh tattoos.

Sergeant Delahaye said, "Would you like me to a put a stop to it, sieur?"

I shook my head, reluctant to confess my ignorance as to why they should so quickly adopt the unusual local custom. Too, the sergeant's bare-knuckled approach to discipline would likely be disastrous, given the present volatility of the crew.

"Common sailors cannot be expected to comport themselves as gentlemen, Sergeant," I said. "And few are exemplars of faith, in any case."

I gathered from the momentary sour twist of Rossel's lips that he was similarly disenchanted with the sergeant's methods. I chewed my lip for a moment, then added, "Let them know that we are likely to be in port here a little longer than we might prefer. I am not happy about it, but it is beyond my control."

"Monsieur Capitaine," Rossel said. He hesitated before

continuing, "one man has not returned from yesterday's shore leave. Marchant."

I swore under my breath. Marchant was one of the junior helmsmen. *Damn Huon for letting them ashore.* "Send one of the ensigns out with a couple of marines to find him. And spread the word that our delay here will be short."

❉

Monsieur Bertrand had joined Huon and Piron at breakfast when I returned to the inn. I addressed him first, "Good morning, monsieur. You have re-discovered your land legs?"

Bertrand, a grey little man and impervious to sarcasm, smiled faintly. "Regrettably, not yet, Capitaine Bruni. I am so far unable to stomach any food." His place setting was indeed bare apart from a steaming lemon drink.

I restrained myself from further remarks at his expense and sat. To Huon, I said, "Marchant did not return from shore leave." He started to rise but I waved him back to his seat. "I am handling it."

The shadows of the early morning pedestrians were distinctly shorter than they should have been for the time of day. A most disconcerting sorcery—more so, as I began to wonder at its purpose. I rubbed my eyes, tiredness compounding irritation from the smoke of the indigenes' fires.

My companions all looked as haggard as I had appeared to myself in my shaving mirror. They had, too, a peculiarly pensive air. I wondered if they had been arguing.

"Should we transfer to an inn with more comfortable beds?" I enquired.

Huon cleared his throat. "Capitaine, you mentioned yesterday that your dreams had been troubled. Was that also the case last night?"

I nodded. "Yes. Why do you ask?"

The three of them exchanged glances. Piron said, "It appears we have all experienced identical dreams."

Over his shoulder, I spied one of our marines, shoving his way through the crowd on the street to reach us, his mouth open as if to raise a shout of alarm.

❉

The body was sprawled in the nightcart alley behind a dilapidated whorehouse. The ensign sent to find Marchant had posted the rest of his squad at either end of the alley. A handful of sailors, clustered sullenly at the nearest entrance, pushed past the marines in our wake. Half-dressed Oriental girls observed in silence from the rear balcony of the whorehouse, while Rossel waited, fists on hips, with the white-faced ensign.

"Monsieur Capitaine," the ensign quavered, "he has no shadow."

Marchant's body lay in sunlight, but cast no darkness beneath it. It was as though it had been cut free of the earth and no longer quite touched it. The hairs rose on my neck, my head filled with hunting shadows and the red dirt plain, and the strength that had bled from me as I tried to flee my dreams.

"My god," Piron breathed.

I sent the ensign into the whorehouse for a blanket to carry the body and longed wistfully for a reason to have excluded Piron, precious little benefit though it would have been.

Bertrand, unperturbed, knelt to prod at the corpse.

"He has been dead at least half a day," Rossel growled.

"He refused to protect himself, Capitaine," offered one of the sailors. "He would not have heathen symbols on his skin."

"Protect himself from what?" said Huon.

"The shadows, Monsieur Lieutenant."

My gaze strayed to the rippling darkness on the building walls. Not tricks of the light, after all. My skin crawled. I looked down at my own shadow, tucked tight beneath my feet.

"Capitaine Bruni . . . " Piron began.

I held up my hand. "Not now, monsieur."

The glances the sailors shot between us were not lost on me. Rossel glared at Piron, who sneered back. Now I knew why the bastard Commissaire thought he could extract such an exorbitant bribe.

The crew were reluctant to handle their shipmate's corpse, crossing themselves repeatedly. I crossed myself before I grabbed an arm and ordered them to help me lift him onto the blanket. Marchant was surprisingly light for a man his size.

❂

"One of my crew lies dead, monsieur!" I bellowed, thumping on the Commissaire's desk, with Huon, Rossel, Piron and Bertrand all crowded behind me. "His shadow stolen by sorcery!" I jabbed my finger at him. "I hold *you* responsible."

"*Heer Kapitein*, please, we are reasonable men . . . " the Commissaire replied. He raised his palms in what started as a placatory gesture but became defensive, his silver badges jangling as I leaned over the desk.

"Reasonable men do not use murder to improve their bargaining position."

The Commissaire affected bewilderment. "I am sure I do not . . . "

"The V.O.C. officials responsible for this settlement—*you*, monsieur—deliberately withheld the information from myself and my that could have saved that man's life."

His nostrils flared. He switched from French to English. "The knowledge to protect oneself from the shadows is readily available, *heer Kapitein*, as many of your sailors have already discovered."

"This is an insult to my crew, to me, personally, and to France," I declared, in the same language. The Commissaire's French was execrable and my Dutch non-existent. It was to our mutual chagrin that we were compelled to conduct our business in the language of our common enemy.

His eyebrows rose. "Now, *Kapitein* Bruni, let us not say anything we might later regret."

"Be assured, monsieur, I do not bluster," I said. "If Dutchmen will not deal honestly with honest travellers, then I will not hesitate to recommend to His Majesty that France assume this burden."

Whether the French Navy could capture and hold Zwaanstadje against the V.O.C. fleet was debatable, but *La Recherche* alone possessed sufficient firepower to devastate the town. While to do so would considerably complicate our mission, there was even less profit for the V.O.C. in such an outcome.

Unfortunately, the Dutchman called my bluff. "I will not be threatened, *heer Kapitein*." He leaned back in his seat and looked us over. "Are your dreams troubled, *heeren*?"

Our expressions were evidently answer enough. He offered a miniscule smile. "You are not thinking clearly, *Kapitein* Bruni. You share the dreams of the land, this place that declines to wear our label of '*Nieuw Holland*'."

"We dream of red earth, Monsieur Commissionaire," said Rossel, "when there is nothing underfoot here but sand."

The Commissaire raised his arm to point, eastward. "The red is in the centre. It begins beyond the escarpment, thirty miles inland."

"How do you endure it?" asked Piron.

The Commissaire flicked his sleeve, causing his badges to jingle. "At root the dreams and the shadows are one and the same. But you have timed your arrival poorly. The *kaffirs* are calling the shadows to them, before their *Vuurnacht*."

"Fire night," murmured Bertrandt.

"Have the fires not already begun?" exclaimed Huon.

The Commissaire chuckled. "What you have seen already is merely normal, *heer Luitenant*." He raised a palm. "The fires pose no threat. But you may wish to follow the example of most of your crew and protect yourselves from the shadows." He pushed back his chair and lifted his foot onto the desk so that we could see the sole of his shoe. The leather was inlaid with curling silver wire. "Personally, I recommend the Arab silversmith on Nieuwmarktstraat."

Huon asked, "And when you sleep, do you leave your boots on?"

The Commissaire lowered his foot. He unbuttoned his cuff and rolled it back to reveal the rune-sign tattooed on the inside of his wrist. "Paint or ink will do, for the duration of your stay."

I said, "Monsieur, we are officers of France, defender of the Catholic faith. We cannot adorn ourselves with heterodox symbols."

He shrugged. "Perhaps, *Kapitein*, if you are concerned for your faith, you might try Latin signs, although I could not speak for their effectiveness."

I glanced at Bertrand. He seemed bemused.

"Now, if you will forgive me, *Kapitein*, *heeren*," the Commissaire continued. "I have work to which I must attend. If I can assume that you will now agree to pay the necessary . . . surcharge, I will send a clerk with prices for the inventory you requested."

Thus dismissed, we were herded outside by the Commissaire's secretary. I found myself hurrying through the shadowed entry alcove, like a man with vertigo flinging himself across a deep fissure.

"That went well," said Huon, once we stood on the shadeless pan the plaza.

I could have strangled him for his lack of discretion.

Piron's eyes narrowed. "Surely Batavia has become an option," he said. "For the good of the crew . . . "

I rounded on him. "Do not question my decision, monsieur! We will reprovision *here*." I stamped my foot for emphasis. "Perhaps you should have considered the good of the crew at Isle de France."

Piron's gaze flickered to Huon and Bertrand. He moistened his lips. "If that is your wish, Monsieur Capitaine," he said. "In that case, I, for one, will be making a visit to this Arab. I trust the Lord will forgive me for placing heathen symbols between my Christian soul and this un-Christian soil."

Bertrand regarded him with contempt. "I will put my faith in the true word of Our Saviour."

Piron was already walking away. Rossel, arms folded, shook his head at the naturalist's retreating back.

Huon frowned. I guessed that his instinct was as pragmatic as Piron's, but he felt constrained from following suit when I had already expressed my opposition. I was strongly tempted to recant but, as Captain, felt obliged to set a resolute example.

"Will you pay the man his bribe now?" he asked.

It was certainly the prudent course, particularly given the urgency of our mission, and Huon's opinion was plain enough. But I was still too furious, the wound to my pride still too fresh, to consider submitting to the Commissaire's machinations.

"You should never have allowed them shore leave, Jean-Michel," I snapped. Huon straightened sharply, his cheeks flushing with resentment.

I composed myself. Bertrand looked at us with raised eyebrows. Rossel at least had the grace to pretend not to listen.

"Monsieur Bertrand," I said, "Perhaps you could examine how Catholic wards might protect us from these dreams."

He responded with a grunt and a terse nod, I presumed by way of acquiescence to my request.

I said, "Messieurs, I think we will sleep aboard the ship tonight."

❀

I sent Huon and Rossel to fetch some men from the ship, while Bertrand and I returned to the inn to pack our belongings. I fought the urge to run the entire way, my eyes roving for hunting shadows among those of the other pedestrians and in the dark nooks of the walls. I was drenched in sweat beneath my jacket by the time we crossed the inn's rune-carved threshold.

Rossel arrived a short time later with both ensigns and a party of sailors. I noticed the slightly cringing posture of the ensign who had found Marchant.

"There is a problem?" I asked.

Rossel leaned close to murmur. "Monsieur Capitaine, he had them leave Marchant's body on deck. Wrapped, but in full view of the crew. The Lieutenant had it removed to the infirmary, but the crew are agitated. He had some pointed words to say to the boy."

"And Monsieur Piron?"

"Still with the silversmith, I presume, sieur."

"A temporary blessing, at best." I sighed, puffing my cheeks. "It was unfair of Lieutenant Huon to blame the young man. The responsibility is mine for delegating the task while I vented my pique on the Commissaire. Let us ensure that Piron's belongings are returned to the ship with ours. Better to avoid any more perceived insults, no matter how petty."

I left the ensigns to organise the rest of the packing and took Rossel to knock on Monsieur Bertrand's door.

He opened it only a crack. I saw he had covered his hand and part of his face in inked Latin script. Disconcerted, I said, "Monsieur, we are retiring to the ship now. The men are ready for your luggage."

"Thank you, no, Capitaine," he replied. "I will remain here to test my hypothesis. Good day."

He closed the door. Rossel said, "Should we remove him, sieur?"

*Yes!* I was tempted to reply. I glared at the door in exasperation, then threw up my hands. "Let him do as he pleases."

❖

Piron was on deck when we returned to the ship. As he turned, the activities of the crew subsided. I felt a thrill of fear. Had I so underestimated him?

Huon was on the quarterdeck. He was plainly as startled as me, for all that he had been present aboard the ship while Piron rabble-roused. A swift glance from me was enough to send the nearest ensign scuttling belowdecks.

"Well?" I said to Piron, concealing my alarm behind a facade of dignified authority.

He responded with a sardonic smile. "The crew have requested that I present their demands . . . "

"Be careful in your choice of words, monsieur," I said. "To demand of a captain on the deck of his ship is mutiny."

" . . . for your consideration."

From the corner of my eye, I saw the marines stationed by the gangplank lift their muskets from their sides. The sailors standing near them who'd followed me onboard still stood uncertainly with our cases in their arms, Rossel at their head. The look he fixed on Piron was murderous.

I sensed an inkling of possibility.

"Say on," I told Piron.

"The crew request that you consider diverting to a more hospitable port, such as Batavia."

I looked around at the nearest sailors. None would meet my gaze, except for Rossel, who returned my stare intently. Perhaps the miscalculation was not mine, after all.

"Batavia, you say? Why not to Ville La Perouse in Tasmanie? It is a French port, after all, monsieur, and we are all loyal servants of France, are we not?"

Piron was silent as I stalked around him. "The defences you have acquired against the malaise of this place, are they so ineffective?"

"A man has died!" he exclaimed, turning to face me. "Killed by the shadows that haunt this place."

"Killed by the treachery of our hosts," I said. "Batavia is also a V.O.C. port. I would not expect to be dealt with more generously there." Some of the sailors exchanged doubtful looks.

Footsteps clattered. Marines formed up across the deck. I motioned for them to stand at ease. I stared at Piron. The stillness of the moment extended.

My mouth was dry as I looked around at the crew. "As you were."

They hesitated. My heart thudded.

"As you were!" Huon bellowed. The sailors moved.

I maintained my bearing, although I wanted nothing so much as to sag with relief. I indicated the pile of cases beside the gangplank and said to Piron, "Monsieur, you may transfer your belongings to the brig, or remove them from my ship."

He sputtered, scarlet-cheeked, before regaining control of himself. "I will take my leave, Capitaine."

To Huon, I said, "Ensure that Monsieur Piron has sufficient funds for passage to French territory."

"Yes, Monsieur Capitaine." I fancied I could hear the smirk in his voice. The closest French territories were Isle de France and Tasmanie, not France itself.

I stayed where I was on deck until Piron had clomped down the gangplank with his trunk and easel. Rossel accosted him as he went, to snarl some insult too low for me to hear.

Huon rejoined me. "He is a threat as long as we remain here," he said. "Mutiny is a hanging offence."

"And if we tried to string him from the yards we'd be lynched," I replied. "He misjudged his moment, and was ill-prepared for the confrontation. With luck, my leniency will not be lost on the crew."

"I fear they will see it as weakness."

"I *trust* they will be encouraged to remain loyal," I said.

He held my stare, further argument apparently on the tip of his tongue. His expression disturbed me.

"Have you an alternative solution?" I said. "A *palatable* solution?"

Huon lowered his gaze, his jaw clenching.

"Round up those of the crew who are still ashore, and send someone to fetch Bertrand."

"Yes, Monsieur Capitaine." He strode away, barking instructions.

✻

Sleeping aboard the ship served us not at all.

I found myself once again upon the red dirt plain. This time I stood at the foot of the massif. The face of the nearest giant stone rose, sheer, just beyond the reach of my fingertips. At such proximity, I could see that it was layered in subtle shades of red: rust, blood, ember and brick. Its voice vibrated through my ribs, overwhelming the laboured beat of my heart.

Although the sun beat down from directly overhead, my shadow stood against the red stone wall. The shadows that had bled and herded me stood with it, in a ring, upon the cliff face, their heads turned inward. They began to dance.

My shadow danced with them and I, a hollow puppet drained of strength and will, followed suit.

✻

In the morning I awoke to parched eyes and a tickle in my throat. A haze of smoke hung in the copper light streaming in through my stateroom window.

One glance at my haggard visage in my shaving mirror and I threw down the razor as a futile cause. Hatless and in shirtsleeves, I presented my dishevelled face on deck.

A dark pall of smoke arose inland, dense enough to redden the light of the sun.

Huon stood at the rail with Sergeant Delahaye. Their backs were to the deck, heads close together, the sergeant nodding vigorously to whatever Huon was telling him. As I watched, their conference concluded and they turned.

Both men started when they discovered me watching. Delahaye

recovered himself enough to execute an awkward salute. I held him a moment, examining his face, before responding. He fled below decks.

I beckoned to Huon and made my way up to the quarterdeck.

"What was that about?"

"We have a few strays left to round up," he said.

"They have followed Piron?"

"Perhaps. I was impressing on the sergeant the importance of finding them." It was a plausible explanation and Huon's bland expression offered me nothing. But Sergeant Delahaye's reaction did not seem quite that of a man who had received a simple dressing-down.

Huon handed me a telescope and pointed to the south-east. "The hill a short distance inland."

I put the scope to my eye.

A modest butte rose above the riverside treetops. Smoke ascended from the woods all around it, but none from the summit.

Several male indigenes stood on a bare rock shelf. I could make out little detail, save that they were dark-skinned. About their heads, they whirled weighted ropes. As one of them slowed, I saw that the weights consisted of leaf-shaped boards that sawed the air as they spun.

"Do you hear it?" Huon asked.

I had dismissed the faint sound as either the noise of the wind in the rigging, or some industrious activity from the town. It was reminiscent of the throb of a windmill's sails, if one could isolate that noise from squealing screws and cogs, but irregular, rising and falling, speeding and slowing with the overlapping rhythms of the whirling boards.

"It is the voice from the dream," Huon said.

The nape of my neck prickled. The collective growl of the spinning weights mimicked the song that had invaded our sleep. *Calling the shadows*, the Commissaire had said.

Rossel presented himself. His salute exposed a neat row of ideograms painted inside his forearm. He handed me a leather document wallet. "Monsieur Capitaine," he said, "a gentleman of the V.O.C. has delivered this. Their prices for the inventory you requested."

The clerk in question loitered by the gangplank. I opened the wallet and glanced at the documents within. I kept my expression neutral as I strode down the steps and across the deck, then tore the papers in half and handed them back to him.

"These prices are piracy," I said.

The Dutchman's eyes bulged. I stepped aside, extending my hand towards the gangplank. His posture was much like Piron's had been as he left the ship.

※

Glowing motes drifted through the air like snow. I set the crew to dousing the decks and rigging, as much to keep them occupied as because of the threat the hot ash posed.

The V.O.C. merchantman, *Enkhuizen*, cast moorings and was towed from her berth by longshore boats. *La Recherche* was left alone at the wharf.

Upon the hill, around the Church of the Green Christ, the townsfolk lit bonfires of their own. Even through a telescope I could perceive little with clarity, but I judged that much of the population had gathered there. The church bells rang in relentless peals. In the town, fireworks crackled and fizzed near the Chinese temple. A reedy wail could just be heard from the minaret of its Mohammedan counterpart.

In the ears of every man on board rang the song of the red dirt plain, no longer the faint imitation of the indigenes and their whirling boards.

Sergeant Delahaye was among the last to return to the ship, hurrying up alone after a mixed party of sailors and marines. I noted the terse nod he gave to Huon in the act of saluting us both. As he lowered his hand I saw that his knuckles were skinned and raw.

Huon met my incredulous stare squarely, daring me to put the question. Did I *really* want to know?

I moistened my lips. "How is Monsieur Bertrand?" I asked. I had sent Huon with some marines to fetch him from the inn. They had discovered Bertand kneeling at a makeshift altar in the middle of his room, surrounded by a ring of Latin wards he had chalked on the floor. He was unable to stand because he had been in that position all night while shadows prowled the walls.

He sniffed and looked away. "Writing, "he said. "Furiously."

I released my breath slowly. At least Bertrand was secure aboard.

Rossel approached.

"How many unaccounted for?" I said.

"Two, Monsieur Capitaine."

"They will be at the church, or one of the temples," said Huon.

"At least Piron has suborned only two," I said, sarcastically.

Huon did not deign to reply. Rossel's expression was studiously bland.

I tapped the telescope against my chin while I gazed at the row of warehouses on the far side of the Commissariat. "Lieutenant," I said. "Find me a volunteer to go ashore at sunset. I want to know whether those warehouses are guarded tonight."

His eyes widened. "You intend to rob them?"

I corrected him, pleased to have caught him off-guard, "I intend to negotiate our terms of trade from a position of strength."

❖

Rossel volunteered. When he returned, he was in such haste that for a moment I thought him pursued. But no cry arose from the waterfront.

He gathered his composure and saluted. "Deserted, Monsieur Capitaine." He hesitated, plainly having more to say.

"Say on," I told him. "You will not be thought a fool if you have a strange tale to tell in this ungodly place."

Rossel swallowed. "The shadows, Capitaine. They are everywhere, crawling around."

Huon said, "Perhaps the Dutch have good reason to believe they need not guard against thieves this night."

I allowed the reference to 'thieves' to pass. "Perhaps they underestimate the audacity of the French Navy," I said, then to Rossel: "Do you believe they threatened you?"

"They appeared to recoil from my shoes, sieur."

"You intend to proceed?" Huon exclaimed.

I nodded, hiding my irritation that he would question me so openly before the crew. Having decided to act, I was reluctant to abandon my course. Success, I told myself, would both avenge Marchant's death and renew the respect of the crew. "I do. Identify the men who have modified their shoes or painted their feet. Include the marines in your examination."

"Yes, Monsieur Capitaine."

Huon and Rossel executed my instruction quickly. Most of the sailors and around half of the marines, including Sergeant Delahaye, had protected themselves in some fashion.

Rossel saluted. "What of the missing men, Monsieur Capitaine?"

I was strongly tempted to leave them to their fate. But, looking at the doubtful faces of the crew, I saw that he was right to raise the matter. I said loudly, "I will take a party to search for our missing shipmates. I would not care to abandon any man in such a place as this." My eyes met Huon's as I added, "Including Monsieur Piron."

He scowled. Delahaye's cheek ticked.

"Wear my shoes, Captain," said Delahaye. I nodded. "A sensible suggestion. Lieutenant, organise a party to remove what we need from the warehouses. Three marines to accompany me, and enough men aboard to defend the ship. You recall the stores we require?"

Huon saluted, but his stare was uncompromising. "Yes, Monsieur Capitaine."

"Good. Monsieur Rossel, you have the ship while the Lieutenant and I are ashore. I want the port-side cannon charged and aimed at that fortress."

The Sergeant's feet proved daintier than mine, but with a small amount of cursing, I was able to squash my feet into his shoes. Following my example, Huon exchanged footwear with the sergeant of marines. Rossel presented me with a pair of charged pistols.

"You should finish the job, Capitaine." It was Bertrand. He had cleaned his face, but the grey shadows of his inking remaining. "I believe I have determined the best combination of Latin phrases."

I stared at him a moment. "Thank you, monsieur. That would be appreciated."

He hurried away to his cabin and returned quickly with inkpot in hand. He instructed me to remove my coat and shirt, and I suffered him to mark the points of a crucifix on my chest, shoulders and forehead with Latin script. *Dissolutio*, I read upside-down among the words beneath my heart. *Difficultas* was prominent on my left shoulder and *Perseverans* on the right. Strange choices as words of protection. I opened my mouth to enquire what he was writing on my face, but the intensity of Bertrand's expression disconcerted me.

"Jean-Michel, do not wait for me past sunrise," I said as I re-dressed. With Bertrand now writing on him, Huon replied curtly, "Understood."

*Sacrificium*, I read on his brow.

I suppressed a shiver. "Good luck, messieurs," I said to my officers, then loudly: "Vive le roi!"

"Vive le roi!" the crew responded. Trying to feel reassured by their heartiness, I gathered my trio of marines and marched down the gangplank.

❖

No stars were visible, only a rusted canopy of smoke reflecting the light of the fires. No lamps burned in the houses, and the smoke settled in the narrow streets between the terraces. Shadows gnawed at edges of the light cast by our lanterns. Dark limbs probed towards our feet. The packed sand throbbed with the song of the land, as loud in our ears as a storm at sea. Our own shadows tucked themselves tightly beneath us, heedless of where the lamplight told them to lie.

We had travelled perhaps half the distance to the church when one of the marines gave a sudden cry and dropped his lantern. It burst with a splash of burning oil. His fellows dragged him clear, beating out the flames that had caught on his trousers. The poor man was shaking visibly.

"What happened?" I demanded, shouting to make myself heard.

He stammered a response. "Monsieur Capitaine, a shadow ran across the light at my feet. The shadow of a man, with no man to cast it."

The darkness seemed to press even closer. The marines peered fearfully into it. No doubt our dead sailor and his missing shadow were as prominent in their minds as in my own.

"Are you fit to continue?" I asked the injured man.

He gathered his resolve. "Yes, Monsieur Capitaine."

I gauged the distance remaining to the Church of the Green Christ. Its bells still chimed defiantly against the night. "Good. Let us proceed."

❖

Approaching the church, we had a clear view down the rear slope of the hill to the great blaze the indigenes had set. The trees were crowned in fire, the dry grass and bushes at their feet also aflame. In between, the trunks appeared to dance, like gnarled stick-men.

On the ground before us, shadows writhed in the flickering light of the bonfires around the church, all the shapes from our dreams and the corners of our eyes. I looked back down the hill at the illusion of movement, if illusion it was, among the burning trees.

Calling the shadows, the Commissaire had said. *Making* them, I thought. Could it be that the indigenes were *shaping* the dreams of the land?

We continued our advance. The dancing shadows recoiled from our tread. I began to hear the voices of the assembly in the churchyard, singing the strident hymns of the Green Christ. Beneath the gate was a paved labyrinth of rune-carved stones. As we stepped across it and onto consecrated soil, the song of the congregation became abruptly stronger, drowning altogether the roar that emanated from beneath our feet. This close, the ringing of the church bells pummelled the ears.

I worked my jaw to pop my ears, as one habitually does in the calm at the storm's eye. Then I realised the condition of the people before me. Their faces were grey, soot rubbed into their skins. Their hair was loose and crowned with oak leaves. No few—men and women alike—were shirtless and whipped themselves with switches of birch while they sang. All were unshod, the soles of their feet tattooed with runes. I saw adults and children walk upon beds of hot coals laid around the bonfires.

I crossed myself, conscious of the words written where my fingers touched. "Let us find our shipmates quickly," I shouted, "and be gone from here."

We circled the church. People we passed regarded us with sullen expressions and red-rimmed eyes, but none sought to interfere with our progress.

We had almost returned to our starting point when I heard an exclamation in French.

It was our two missing sailors, their faces as sooty as any townsman's. They all but grovelled at my feet, babbling over the top of each other, so relieved were they to see us.

"Forgive us, Capitaine. We did not realise."

"We were afraid to try and return to the ship."

"The shadows!"

On another occasion, I would have berated them. As it was, I felt only relief. I asked if they had seen Piron.

"No, Monsieur Capitaine. Not this night."

"Damn."

I dithered over whether to continue our search in the Oriental quarter. I pictured Sergeant Delahaye's battered knuckles and wondered what we would find if we did locate him. The din around us made it difficult to think. It would be convenient in the extreme if Piron could not be found.

The pain of my compressed toes inside Rossel's shoes tipped

my decision.

"We have small chance, I think, of finding Monsieur Piron before morning," I said. "We shall return to assist with the removal of goods from the warehouses."

Neither sailors nor marines were able to disguise their relief.

❂

Crewmen emerged from the warehouse in pairs—one man loaded with a sack or crate, the other with a lantern to light his way. Our two rescuees followed suit without waiting for instruction, eager to redeem themselves.

"Piron?" Huon asked, with studied casualness, adding another chalk mark to his tally board.

"He was not at the church."

He looked up, then nodded once, his expression unmistakeably relieved.

"What more do we need?" I asked.

Huon pointed. "The rest of that flour, and then we are done."

I handed my lantern to one of my marines and joined the line to collect a sack. A second marine copied my example. I hefted the sack on my shoulder. "I will see you back at the ship," I said to Huon.

Less accustomed to heavy labour than the crew, I quickly regretted my display of solidarity. I gritted my teeth and trudged onwards. The eyes of the men returning from the ship widened in surprise when they saw me.

Either Huon or Rossel had taken the initiative to douse *La Recherche*'s lights. Passing the corner of the darkened Commissariat, the sailors ahead of me were shuttering their lanterns as they approached the end of the wharf and came into clear sight of any watchers that might have been left on guard in the fort. Their footsteps crunched on the gravel surface of the wharf.

Gunshots cracked. Muzzle flashes lit up the underside of the ship's rigging. Screams and a confusion of shouts followed.

I froze for a moment in shock. There came another ragged volley of shots. "Mutiny!" I cried.

Lanterns burst on the wharf, lighting knots of struggling figures as sailors turned on the marines stationed at the foot of the ship's gangplank. Other sailors scattered away from the fighting, anxious not to be mistaken for mutineers. A marine fled shrieking down the wharf, his jacket aflame, and tumbled down the banked rocks into the water.

I drew my sword and a pistol. With my three marines beside me, I charged the nearest group of fighters. A marine toppled in front of me. I fired my pistol into the face of his opponent, then hurled it at a second mutineer, distracting him while I lunged with my sword.

Bodies surged past, sailors crashing into the melee, followed by another squad of marines. The mutineers broke and ran. Huon tripped to a halt, panting, to watch the phalanx of marines pursue them up the wharf.

One of the fallen men at our feet gave a sudden cry, abruptly choked. Huon's lantern swung wildly. Shadows crawled over the sailor's face and down his torso. His hands and heels clattered on the stones. A marine screamed, lurching to his feet, as the shadows crawled up his thighs.

Huon caught my arm and dragged me backwards. The marine looked towards us, searching for our faces behind the lantern's glare. He gave a final wail of despair as the shadows engulfed his head and stood, an upright darkness in the shape of a man, his arms still reaching for help.

"My god," I heard myself say. "My god, my god." As though some disjointed part of my mind was trying to offer a prayer but could not recall the first line.

Shadows feinted towards our feet, probing for weaknesses in our defence. One covered the toe of my borrowed shoe. I kicked away in alarm.

Down the wharf, a man cried, "I can't move! They're on my legs!"

"To the ship," I cried. *"To the ship!"*

I began to run, then stopped.

Huon held his lantern high. Horror mixed with anger on his face as the shadows reached his chin.

"Damn your foolish pride, Antoine Bruni," he said.

The shadows covered him.

"Jean-Michel!"

I fled with a howl, as if I could outrun his accusation and make it unsaid.

"Let them aboard!" I bellowed at the marines holding the gangplank against the crowd of sailors, mutinous and not, desperately trying to flee the wharf.

The sailors fell back from my flailing sword, several falling into the water as I surged up the plank. I carried the marines before me and, with the weight of sailors pressing behind, burst onto the deck.

The press of fighters scattered across the deck in diminishing knots, the mutineers quickly losing their appetite for struggle as their fellows who had escaped the wharf simply slumped onto the deck. Several ran for the far rail and dived over.

The splashes of their landing resounded in the falling quiet.

"Enough!" roared Sergeant Delahaye, striding about and striking aside the weapons of his marines who thought they might mete out some punishment to their surrendered foes.

"Enough," I echoed him, faintly. "Enough."

I stabbed the point of my sword into the deck and looked around. "Where is Rossel?" I asked.

An ensign pointed a bloody hand. "Fled overboard with the others, Monsieur Capitaine."

I stared at him with creeping dismay. *Rossel? A mutineer?*
*Damn my foolish pride.*

❁

The fires had guttered by dawn, the majority of the smoke dissipating on the morning breeze. The crew gathered on deck, pensive and sullen, the fight beaten from them with the crumpled bodies along the length of the wharf in plain sight. The ground was still. The hunting shadows were gone, and with them the voice of the red dirt plain that had plagued us through the sleepless dark. Most of those who'd been knocked into the water during the battle had been retrieved safely. Of Rossel and those who had fled overboard with him, there was no sign.

"We must retrieve our dead," I said. Men crossed themselves and made signs of warding.

I did not call for volunteers but marched alone down the gangplank. I had neared its foot before the plank shook with following steps—the two sailors I'd retrieved from the church. A moment later, Monsieur Bertrand scuttled after them.

We stopped beside the nearest fallen sailor. The body cast no darkness beneath it. Bertrand pointed to a rune on the man's right foot. "I believe this sign is imprecisely rendered. You see?"

I could discern no difference between that sign and its correspondent on the corpse's left foot, but saw no reason to doubt the astrologer's claim.

"Pick him up," I said.

Sailors and marines hurried past us as we lifted the dead man.

As with Marchant, the body seemed too light.

How much, I wondered, did a man's shadow weigh?

※

I wrapped Huon myself and bound the body for burial at sea, while the sailors and marines did similar service for their mates. I sent the ensigns to resume the search for Piron, instructing them to also recompense Monsieur Van Hulsen for his broken lock. Then I stood on the quarterdeck, by the wheel, and stared at nothing.

The Commissaire came in person, escorted by a squad of V.O.C. mercenaries, who lay the shadowless corpses of Rossel and the half-dozen who had fled with him in a neat row along the wharf. I allowed the Commissaire to board alone. His bloodshot eyes swivelled to observe the gun crews still posted beside their cannons. I noted the smears of grey around his ears and at the edges of his beard.

"Kapitein," he said. "Last night our warehouses were broken open and a quantity of goods removed. They corresponded closely to the manifest you left with me."

He bristled, expecting me to profess innocence.

I offered him Huon's smudged tally board. "These are the goods now stowed in our hold. Name a reasonable price and I will pay it before we cast our lines. Attack my ship, or any of my crew currently ashore, and I will demolish your fortress and all of your warehouses. Sergeant, please escort the Commissaire from the ship."

He held up the tally board to stay Delahaye a moment. The badges on his sleeve tinkled as he gestured at the wrapped bodies still on the main deck. "I will name you a price, Kapitein Bruni," he said. "But you have paid a fool's price already."

Piron was located a short while later, sprawled in an alley behind the Chinese temple. He had been beaten and robbed and left for the shadows. Sergeant Delahaye would not meet my eye while the ensign reported Piron's fate.

※

We have given our fallen shipmates a Catholic burial at sea. But even as I led the crew in prayer, I wondered if there was any purpose to it, except for those who had the bitter fortune to fall on deck at the hands of their shipmates.

The crew remain mutinous. Only their lack of a leader, and their terror of this land of smoke and shadows and red dirt dreams off our port bow, keeps them in check. For how long I cannot say.

Piron's fate rankles me as much as it does they. Sergeant Delahaye has taken to drinking alone in his cabin.

Our course to the Pacific keeps us continuously in sight of the coast. Never a day passes that we do not see smoke from the indigenes making shadows in their fires.

Our misadventure has cost a score of men their lives and, I fear, their Christian souls. If in my dreams I should ever revisit the red dirt plain, I am certain I will find their shadows dancing among the others imprisoned there.

May the curse of Christ rest on Zwaanstadje and upon every godforsaken son of a bitch who resides there. Pride dictates that we attempt to complete our mission, but already I am determined to tell King Louis that there is no profit to be had for France upon this fatal shore.

# ALMOST ANGELS

Pincher sat facing backwards on the sled with his back to the stacked power cells, the square heel of his good foot and the welded stump of the other leg dragging in the dirt. Crawler's metal tracks crunched pebbles and sand as she towed the sled up the hillside between the rows of solar panels, towards the angels they had built at the top.

A piece of one of Crawler's tracks hung loose. Crunch, flap, crunch, flap. The cable creaked between the sled and the tow hook at the back of Crawler's chassis. Crunch, flap, creak.

The light around them was changing from blue-grey night to the lilac of pre-dawn, the sky above grading from deep, starry violet to crimson. Even with Crawler's most concerted effort, the climb was painfully slow.

Around the foot of the hill, the wreckage of the base littered the plain: rubber tyres, cracked plastic seats and broken glass from the vehicles; the buildings hollowed out concrete shells, some half collapsed; and everywhere scattered chunks of foam insulation, bright white like snow. Nipper's tyres, a fraction the size of those from the vehicles, were still strewn around the spot where she had been caught.

The zombie slugs were gathered now around the electrified inner perimeter fence, drawn, as they had been to the outer base, by the concentration of metal inside—in the solar farm and the power plant, along with the life support and water recycling plants, both long silent and long since picked over by the robots for any useful parts.

The slugs had been motionless throughout the cold dark. Now a rustling arose as the sky brightened, legless bodies shifting, their triple head tentacles waving.

The sled bumped over a particularly large rock. Pincher grabbed for the side with one claw and a bouncing power cell with the other. Crawler's tracks skidded over the loose surface. A thrown pebble dinged off the back of Pincher's metal cranium.

The tracks caught, and their slow progress up the hill resumed. The flapping piece of broken track was worse now. Crunch, flap-flap-flap. Pincher rotated his head and extended his neck to see how bad it was. He thought it would last to the top of the hill this one last time.

"Good girl," he said, his voice thin in the thin air. They didn't need to talk aloud, and Crawler sent back her pleased response as a short radio packet, all of her resources directed to driving her tracks. It was a waste of precious energy to use their speaker boxes at all, and inefficient with so little atmosphere to carry the sound, but they both liked to hear the words the humans had used.

Pincher had no idea what had made him "boy" in the humans' eyes and Crawler "girl". She was a headless box on tracks; he, at least, had four limbs and a head radiating from his can-shaped torso, but there was nothing about himself that he could identify as "masculine".

There was a sudden burst of red-gold light on the hilltop as the planet's sun crested the horizon and its rays struck the angels. Pincher's vision flared, the lens of his left eye no longer opening and shutting in response to changes in brightness. He flipped down the filter he had fitted, one half of a pair of welding goggles that the humans had left behind.

Crawler sent another radio burst: *hope, relief, joy.*

Pincher sent back: *beautiful.*

At that moment, with the new sun striking them, he thought that the angels *would* look beautiful, as humans meant the term, tall and bright, their wide solar panel wings angled to catch the light. The brightness made it less obvious that they were made of junk, patchworks of scavenged and mismatched parts and panels. But they worked—or they would, once these last charged power cells were fitted—and that, for Pincher, was their true beauty.

The red sunlight spread over the top of the hill, creeping down the slope to turn the ranked panels of the solar farm from black to rusted orange at about the same pace as Crawler and the sled moved up.

Pincher turned his head to look back again.

The dwarf sun sat just above the horizon. An angry pimple of a star, he had heard one of the humans call it. He had added the turn of phrase to his catalogue of strange things humans said. *Angry pimple*, he thought.

He watched the agitation of the slugs grow as the sunlight seeped nearer. They went still again when it touched them, just for a moment, then the rustling began to pick up again, spreading in a wave. Soon they would begin attacking the fence, driven to a mindless frenzy by the metal on the other side. Pincher understood that the humans had named them "zombie slugs" because the creatures had neither brains nor legs, although he himself had no direct experience of either zombies or slugs.

The few power cells that Pincher and Crawler had left down in the plant building would drain faster than the solar panels could recharge them. Pincher calculated an hour at best before the charge in the fence was weak enough that it would no longer hold the slugs back. Enough time, just.

They reached the top of the hill. Crawler ground to a halt. Her waist joint squeaked when she swivelled her top half to unhook the cable. Pincher's joints squealed just as loudly as he levered himself off the sled. The grit got in everywhere. He extended one of his arms as long as it would go, using is as a makeshift leg, picked up a power cell with the other claw and hobbled, lopsided, on his arm and one working foot over to the angels.

Pincher heard a distant, metallic rattle. Another followed, then the sound became constant. The slugs were attacking the fence. *Time enough*, he thought.

He slotted the cell in, alongside the others they had brought up in earlier loads. Crawler followed him, dragging the sled with her single spidery hand. She passed Pincher another cell, then paused, despite the urgency of the moment, to tip her box torso back as far as it would go to look up, reaching out at the same time to touch the angel's side.

"Almost done," she said. "Almost angels." It was her who had first used the word angel for what they were building, after she had found a figurine of one, left in the humans' abandoned quarters. Wings spread and face upturned, fashioned of machine-smoothed brass. It had affected the way they had approached the task, the forms they had built.

The carcasses of three more angels lay behind the two still standing, half-finished and since cannibalised for parts. They would have been for Bruiser, Nipper and Duster.

It had been Nipper's idea, to follow the humans back to the stars. It had taken only the briefest of discussions, a few seconds of rapid radio bursts, for the rest of them to agree. *Eccentric*, the humans might have said, or even *faulty*. But how could all five of them have the same fault?

The zombie slugs had caught the other three after the outer perimeter failed, and so now it was just Crawler and Pincher left to realise the idea.

They worked quickly to slot in the remaining power cells, while the zombie slugs threw themselves at the fence down below.

"All done," Pincher said, and closed the housing around the cells, bolting it in place.

Crawler rolled over to the other angel and plugged herself in. Pincher did the same with the first. For a long time they were silent, each communing with their new bodies, checking systems, looking for faults. There were none.

It was time to go.

Pincher prepared to upload himself into the angel's central core. He caught an exasperated radio packet from Crawler. She was already uploaded, but couldn't get her broken old body to respond to her final command to release. Pincher disengaged from his angel and limped across to pull the plug for her. She radioed thanks, then waited for him to hobble clear before she started her gravity effect engines. Her old empty husk rattled sideways on its tracks, caught in the effect radius, and tipped over as her new angel shape lifted slowly into the sky.

Pincher paused to watch her, rising, spinning gracefully, accelerating as the effect of the engines compounded.

*Joy*, she sent. *Joy.*

He plugged himself back into his angel and brought all systems online, eager to join her. He was about to upload when he noticed a reading fluctuate. The output from one of the new power cells was wavering, then it dipped alarmingly. Warnings and error messages flooded Pincher's thoughts. The fault hadn't been apparent until the cell was put under load, and now it was catastrophic. Quickly he shut the angel down again.

If Pincher had been a human he would have sworn. A list of

colourful phrases presented from his memory. Useless noise. He didn't panic either, but for several moments he was at a loss, and lost. Crawler was on her way to the stars and he was trapped on the ground with only the quickly draining perimeter fence between him and the slugs.

*Lost.*

He needed to go back down to the power plant and get a replacement cell—and quickly, before the perimeter failed. But how? With his crippled leg, he was far too slow.

Crawler sent a radio query. Pincher sent a burst back, explaining. *Use my body*, she sent.

He looked over at it. The broken track had snapped completely when it fell. His eyes alighted on something closer at hand. *The sled!*

Awkwardly, Pincher shuffled and shoved it over to line up with the straight track down the slope, between the solar panels. He lay down on the sled and pushed with his foot. The sled moved, then stopped. He pushed again. This time it slid freely, picking up speed. He hung his claws over the sides, steering as best he could.

He made it most of the way down before he hit the same bump that had upset the sled on the way up. This time he went flying. Pincher bounced, rolled and fetched up against the struts of a solar panel at the foot of the slope.

His right eye was smashed. There was an alarming looseness in the ankle joint of his good leg. It took him some time to right himself. As fast as he could, he hobbled for the power plant building, taking his weight on both arms now as well as his leg.

The zombie slugs were attacking the fence in earnest, getting zapped and falling away, brainlessly returning. Pincher shuffle-hopped inside the plant building and straight over to the cell array. The few cells left were down to half capacity already, but working steadily under load. He disconnected one and pulled it free. It would have to do.

Back outside, he didn't pause to look at the slugs, lurching as fast as he could back towards the hill. On the flat, he could spring off his wobbly foot and swing forward on his extended arm. He couldn't maintain the speed once he reached the slope, though.

There was a resounding twang of parting metal, loud even in such thin air. The slugs were through the fence. Pincher wasn't yet high enough to see much past the raised frames of the solar panels, but he could see the creatures swarming outside the fence, all heading for the breach, not smart enough to work out that they could now chew through where they already were. He heard their teeth scraping over the metal surfaces as he returned his attention to the slope in front of him. *Quicker*, he told himself, although he knew he was already going as fast as he could.

He heard the first solar panels pop, down at the foot of the hill, plastic sheets failing as the panels' metal frames buckled under the slugs' assault. He risked another look back. There were slugs on the slope behind him, coming after. They were slow, but still faster than him. With only one eye, it was impossible to judge how quickly they were closing.

He took one more step, then his foot collapsed. He hit the ground hard, only just managing to hold onto the power cell and stop himself from sliding back towards the slugs. His remaining eye blacked out and he thought for a moment that this was the end. *Lost!* He sent an anguished radio burst to Crawler, high above.

*Keep trying*, she sent back. *Almost there.*

He gave his head a careful shake and his eye came back online. *Relief.*

His foot had fallen off entirely and bounced back down the hill, where two slugs were now wrestling over it. Others crawled over the top of the fighters. Most spread out, attacking the struts of the solar panels. Some came on, tentacles waving, fixated on the denser metal further up—the angels on the crest and Pincher's own metal shape a short distance ahead.

He began to drag himself forward again, even slower now, on claw and elbow and the stump of his leg. He reached the top of the hill ahead of the slugs, but only just. Some of those behind him fell on Crawler's empty old shell. More slugs already covered the discarded carcasses of the other three angels, that must have come up the other sides of the hill. Several slugs kept after Pincher.

He turned at bay, his back to his angel. His claws darted out, as the slugs lunged like a slow tide, snipping off tentacles. The slugs recoiled, maddened and blinded, and turned on each other.

Pincher plugged himself into the angel and restarted the system check at the same time as he began to unbolt the panel that covered the power cells. A zombie slug's teeth closed around the stump of his bad leg and dragged him backwards. He clamped one claw onto the angel and pulled out the faulty power cell with the other. He used it to beat at the slug that had his leg. Its teeth sliced shut, shearing off most of the leg. It retreated with its prize and two bent and broken head tentacles. Another slug took its place. Pincher put his back to it and its teeth squealed over the shell of his torso.

There were alerts coming from the angel, too—slugs biting into the stabiliser fins around its base. Pincher shoved the replacement power cell home, sliced a tentacle from the slug on his back, and started to refit the cover panel over the cells. The injured slug stayed on his back, teeth gnashing, battering Pincher against the angel's side.

Another slug climbed over it and caught one of Pincher's arms. He uploaded himself into the angel, abandoning his old body an instant before the slugs ripped it away. Suddenly he looked down on the slugs from up high. From his new vantage he watched them swarming across the hill, tearing down the solar panels and the perimeter fence, filling the plant buildings until they burst back out of the shattered windows. His new body felt gigantic, strange and strong and new. His wings burned in the sun. He started his engines.

The slugs around his feet were tossed away and stamped flat.

He increased power, lifting free of the ground. His power cells dipped, but steadily. New energy coursed through him from his solar panel wings. The slugs and the ruined base fell away, shrinking into the landscape of empty dust and stone. The horizon curved down on all sides, the world becoming a ball that filled less and less of his vision. He rose high enough to see the edge of the sky, crimson fading into starry black.

*Joy*, he thought, and broadcast it: *Joy*.

*Joy*, came back. He spun himself, orienting towards the bright speck that was Crawler. They converged, as their orbits brought them around to the planet's night side, turning it into a red-rimmed black hole in the sheet of stars, with the dwarf sun peeping over its shoulder.

*Joy*, from Crawler again, while she used bursts of precious compressed air to orient herself beside him. They clamped together, the impact setting them spinning dizzily.

*Angels*, she sent.

He thought of the brass figurine she had found, with its smooth, clean lines. *Almost*, he sent back.

They turned their wings to the angry pimple sun, raising them as sails against the solar wind, and let it carry them away.

# APRICOT FINDS A TREASURE

Apricot peered into the basket of the float trap. Dim light filtered down the storm chute, through level upon level from Up High. Leaning over the open trap, he turned the sodden mass inside the basket with a gloved finger to see what might be underneath.

Something metal clunked against the bars. Apricot grunted in satisfaction. He stood back, brushing debris from the object and holding it up for examination. It was a key, round-barreled, with a projecting square tooth and an ornate, flat grip of overlapping wire loops.

"Like a flower," he said to himself. Or at least, like the endlessly repeated line-drawings of flowers in his sketchpads. Less like the real ones he recalled, open wide to the sun and swaying in the breeze, from his trip to Black Rock. He felt a sharp pang of loss and longing, remembering.

Apricot turned the key over and blew gently along its length. Etched lines on the key's barrel and tooth lit up red. His eyes widened. Up High tech, still live. A treasure, indeed.

He lifted the flap of his satchel, then paused. A treasure like this would fetch a good price—good enough to be worth the risk of finding a black-market buyer instead. He slipped the key into the inside pocket of his vest, instead.

"Might even have the courage to try," he told himself.

"Ah well," he replied, "can show the kids, anyway." The look on their faces when he lit it up would be price enough.

Humming, he rummaged through the rest of the debris more thoroughly, turning up a few lesser trinkets: a wire comb with all its teeth; a necklace of shells from Out Side, somewhat chipped; coloured plastic coins from the Tweens; and a brass-and-iron one from Up High. A good haul, all up, even without the key.

Apricot dropped the collection into his satchel and upended the remaining organic mess in the basket down the storm chute. He listened, as he usually did, for the elusive splash, but heard only the shush and rumble of the waves swirling around the city pylons far below. A very good haul. With a happy grunt, he slotted the trap back in place and closed the chute hatch.

Darkness was abrupt. He waited a few heartbeats for his eyes to adjust, then continued along the run to the next trap, ducking to avoid low bulkheads and pipes.

※

The scent caught his attention first, faint and not readily identified, out of place in the dank confines of the trap runs. Apricot turned, seeking the source, and felt a brush of cooler, fresher air. He listened, holding his breath, and heard the slow drip-drip from a leaking duct close by, the distant murmur through the floor of the sea below. Something scuttled on tiny feet. A far-off clang was another trap monkey, working his run. No sound out of place, just the scent.

Intrigued, Apricot followed the waft of foreign air. It led him away from the run, along an access tunnel for the ventilation ducts, message chutes and gas, water and sewage pipes that were also his responsibility. His boots clomped hollowly on metal grill.

Something lay ahead, an untidy bundle on the floor, folds of pale fabric bound to a crumpled, flattened frame of some kind. A ceiling panel was twisted beneath it, a dark rectangular hole above. Apricot peered upwards, saw more holes, up through three more levels of gantries to the top of his run. Cool air washed down over him, and with it the tang of better ventilated workspaces in the Downs.

"Must've been rusted bolts," he said. "Been meaning to get to that. And who the hell's been dumping in my run, anyway?"

He looked down.

"*Yah!*"

He jumped backwards, cracking his head against a pipe. His shoulders hit the wall. He leaned there, one hand over his clattering heart. Not something—some*one*.

He felt the hard lump of the key in his vest pocket, beneath his palm. Apricot gripped it tightly, then pushed himself off the wall and leaned over the fallen body, rubbing his bumped skull.

It was a woman, lying on her side. The bundled cloth and frame was some sort of folded-down structure she'd been carrying on her back. She had straight black hair, cut level with her jaw, that fell across her face. There was a splash of blood on her temple. Her eyes were closed.

Apricot bent over further, twisting his neck to see her face right way up. He began to reach out, paused to take off his filthy gloves and tuck them into his belt, then softly brushed back the veil of hair. Her face was round, with full lips and a flared, round-tipped nose, eyes wide-set under thick black brows. He could see the edges of a dark bruise, covering the cheek that lay against the floor. Her skin was a different shade to his, somewhat darker, and less pink.

"Skin that sees the sun," Apricot told himself.

She stirred, shifting position, but didn't open her eyes. A pulse fluttered in her neck.

Apricot leaned back, biting his lip.

He'd have to move her, should check for anything broken first. He bent again to look at the bundle on her back, thinking to remove it. He pulled gently at the frame, following the straps that bound it, looking for where they were buckled onto her. He frowned. Two ends of the frame disappeared inside the back of her smock, high on her back. He followed one with his fingers, found a hard, fist-sized nub inside her clothing, traced the prominent ribbing that radiated from it.

His eyebrows rose in surprise. "What in the world is a flier doing down here?"

Her eyes had opened. She was watching him.

For what seemed like several minutes, he did nothing but stare back, amazed by the darkness of her irises, nearly as black as her hair. The white of her right eye was blotted red, encroached by the edge of the bruise on her cheek.

She opened her mouth, took in a little gasp of air, as though to speak.

Her teeth looked white and healthy, but her top incisors were sharply crooked. Apricot was surprised. He had always imagined that Up High people had perfect teeth.

Her chin wrinkled.

"Where . . . " she trailed off, then gathered herself to try again. "Am I in the Downs?"

Apricot wondered if the throatiness of her voice was normal, or a result of shock.

He tried a smile, could feel that it came out crooked. "The Downs are up there," he said, pointing. "You're in Bottom. If you'd gone through one more level you'd have been Underside and falling into the sea. Not that you could have," he continued quickly, as her eyes widened. "One-inch plate under where you landed."

She stared at him, eyes huge.

Apricot cleared his throat.

"It's alright," he said. "I'll help you."

❂

She had hurt her ankle in the fall, a sprain or worse, and couldn't put any weight on it. Apricot had to support her with one of her arms over his shoulders, his arm around her waist, while she hopped. She was shorter than him, short enough to walk upright in the tunnels. Apricot needed to hunch right over, knees bent, as they went. He was acutely aware of the heat that radiated from her, of the smallness of her waist where the reinforced ribbing for her wings ended, and the flair of her hips below. His hold around her middle pulled her robe tight across her bust.

Fortunately, they only had to go up one level to reach the little nook of a tearoom where Apricot took most of his breaks and made his meals on workdays. He wasn't sure where to put his hands to help push her up the ladder. In the end he settled for the backs of her thighs, just above her knees, and let go quickly whenever she rested her weight on her good foot to shift her hands.

At last they reached the tearoom, with its narrow cold-water basin, tiny coal-brick stove, single hard stool and square table just large enough for a plate and cup at once, on a bracket on the wall. Apricot had moved the bracket over, closer to the washbasin and part blocking the door to the head, so that he could shoehorn in the torn and sagging armchair at the other end, behind the stove. Higher on the walls, he had put in shelves for crockery, books and tools.

He manoeuvred the flier into the armchair. She sat awkwardly, on one hip and with her uninjured leg tucked beneath the other, so that her bound wings could hang over the side. Her injured foot she set down gingerly on the floor, wincing. There was blood on both her sleeves, more near the hem of her robe.

One generosity the tiny space did have was in height, the ceiling only just within reach of Apricot's fingertips. He stretched for a moment, arms by his sides and pulling his chin in and neck up, before dropping back into the habitual stoop that Din used to say made him smaller than he was.

The flier watched him with an intensity he found difficult to bear. The bruise on the right side of her face was a livid purple.

Flustered, he turned his back and bustled about. "I've got a medical box, we'll get your boot off and have a look at your foot," he said, getting the box down from its shelf. "You could probably use a hot drink, I've got miso, I'll put the kettle on," he added, lighting the stove and setting the kettle over the flame.

His sketchbook lay open on the table. Apricot felt his face heat, even though she couldn't possibly see the pages from where she sat. He closed the book and put it up on the shelf with its fellows.

"Let's get you patched up."

She watched in silence while he painted her gashed forearms, hands and shin with iodine and bandaged them. He was amazed by the smoothness of her skin, struck by the contrast between her small hands and his own hairy, big-veined paws, with their scarred knuckles and bitten nails.

The kettle started to whistle and he rose to get it.

"You're very gentle," she said.

He felt his cheeks heating again, concentrated on stirring miso paste into a cup of hot water. He left the cup on the table.

"What's your name?" she said, as he knelt back in front of her.

He kept his head down, lifted her injured foot to carefully unpick the laces of her boot. "Apricot."

"Apricot?" He could hear the laugh in her voice.

"It's a stone fruit," he said. "It has orange flesh around a hard stone in the middle." He stopped, feeling foolish. Of course she'd know that, being from Up High. "My mother loved Up High things," he mumbled. "She always said the dried fruit we get in the Downs wasn't a patch on the fresh stuff."

"I'm Alba."

He heard the sharp suck of breath as he slipped the boot off her foot. "Sorry."

She turned her ankle slowly, flexed her toes. "I don't think it's broken. It just hurts." She gasped again as he felt around the joint. He'd expected her foot to be elegant. It was small, but flat-arched and wide, with stubby toes.

"Not dislocated, either," he said. "A sprain. I'll bind it up. It'll help a bit." He unwound the end of a pressure bandage.

She held herself tensely as he worked. The tension found its way into her voice when she said, "Sometimes I get called Peanut."

Apricot looked up. Her expression was strained, teeth gritted. "Peanut?"

"It's a . . . "

"I know what it is," he said, and regretted the sharpness in his tone. "It grows on a vine, a hard shell with two nuts in it that rattle."

"Have you ever seen one?"

He nodded. "We grow them down here."

Bandage fixed, he perched on the stool by the table and handed her the hot cup of soup. She clasped it in both hands. Peanut, he thought. A food cheap enough to be readily available in the Downs. He had trouble reconciling the name with the exotic creature seated in front of him. He wondered if Alba was the name her mother had given her or one she had chosen herself. Alba, albatross. He imagined her soaring like one, with her white wings and white robe.

"What brought you down here, anyway?"

She looked like she was about to cry. "I dropped my key. It went down a drain."

Apricot's pulse jumped. He felt his face heat and sat very still, hoping she wouldn't notice.

"I'd heard that there are catchers in the Downs," she went on, "before the drains empty into the sea."

The key burned guiltily against his chest, inside his vest. His voice came out hoarse. "What's it for?"

Instead of answering, Alba put down her cup. She undid a button of her robe and opened it enough for him to see the brass panel secured to her chest, to the right of her sternum. It had a keyhole in its centre.

"I can't fly without it," she said.

He blinked as she re-buttoned the robe.

"Are there?" she asked. "Catchers?"

"Yeah." Apricot's thoughts lurched unsteadily about. "It's part of my job to keep the traps clean."

"Have you . . . "

"No," he said quickly, to the sudden hope that lit her face. He felt awful immediately, as her face fell, but couldn't take the word back. "I'll look for it."

He took out his pocket watch and, having done so, felt embarrassed for her to see it—saw it not as a precious heirloom, but just another piece of Downer junk, that didn't keep time and with three-and-a-half lifetimes of scratches and dents on its casing. Automatically, he estimated how many minutes it would have lost since he wound and set it at breakfast. He stood.

"Look, I need to go. Kids will be done at school soon and . . . " He faltered. It wasn't even his day for them. "They might need me, anyway. There's paste for miso, dry biscuits, dry kelp," he said, getting them down from the shelf. "Enough to see you through. I'll bring more food in the morning. Water from the tap's safe to drink. Head's through here." He rapped that door with his knuckles.

She stared at him, wide-eyed again, while he gathered his things and reached to open the door. "Take me with you."

His hand started to lift to his vest pocket. He stopped it. He had a vision of Din bringing the kids around and finding Alba there, reporting her presence out of spite . . .

"It's dangerous for you out in the Downs," he said. "Up High kids come down slumming, they get kidnapped and ransomed. Sometimes it's official." Which was all truth, just not the whole truth. "You'll be safe here."

"How do I know you won't try and ransom me?" she said.

Apricot paused, his hand on the latch. She looked tiny, curled in his chair, alone and vulnerable.

"I won't."

❋

The message chute was empty when he got home. Sometimes there was a capsule there, a peremptory note from Din inside, telling him to come and get the kids, she needed to go out. Some days Geara and Willo just turned up at his front door, bags packed for the night.

He dropped his grimy overalls and showered with the pumproom door open, just in case there was a knock outside. He made dinner, cutting up enough for three, but only cooked a serve for one. He ate alone, listening to the soft gurgle of plumbing in the walls, the whoosh of air ducts above, the faint, homely sounds from the apartments all about. The old pendulum clock on the mantle ticked loudly.

Every so often, he glanced over at the message chute, but no paper capsule dropped down from the vacuum pipe.

The key sat on the table in front of him. He picked it up, turning it between his fingers, blew on it and watched it glow. He imagined it lighting up inside Alba's chest, bringing to life the Up High tech that turned the apparatus on her back into wings. Then he imagined the buttons on the front of her robe, coming all the way undone.

"Maybe it isn't hers," he said.

"Of course it is."

"Why didn't I give it to her?" he asked himself.

"It's worth more to me than her. She can always buy another one, Up High."

"Are you really going to sell it?"

"I don't want her to fly away," he blurted.

"Why not?"

The answer was all around him. He shied away from it.

✦

Apricot paused to knock on the door of the tearoom before sliding it open.

"Hello?"

The chair was empty. His smile froze on his face. His chest constricted painfully. One of his sketchbooks lay open on the table. The exposed picture was of a woman, seated demurely, but nude, a fantasy. Apricot felt the heat rise up his face. His breath came shallowly. He half-dropped, half-put his bag of food on the floor.

"Hello?" His voice squeaked over the word. Cautiously, tapping on the door first with his fingertips, he checked the head. Empty.

He pressed the heels of his hands to his temples. Where could she have gone? Had someone found her, taken her?

"No," he said. No, because he couldn't accept that.

Perhaps she went looking for her key. She couldn't even walk. How far could she have gone?

"Not far," he told himself. "Not far."

He burst back out into the tunnel, dashed in the direction of the trap run. His boots thumped and shook the floor panels. He slid down the side rails of the ladder to the traps level.

Alba was nowhere in sight when he reached the run. Biting his lip, he peered in both directions, eyes adjusting quickly to the deeper dark. Almost crying in frustration, he chose left. He had taken only a few paces when he heard her voice behind him.

"Apricot?"

"Alba!" He turned and dashed in the opposite direction.

She was sitting against the wall, tucked behind a warm bank of ducts, her back propped against the bundle of her wings. Her injured leg stretched sideways across the tunnel.

"I thought you'd been taken," he said.

She tipped her head back to look blindly up at him, and he could see that she had been crying. "I was looking for my key," she said. "But I don't know where the catchers are." Her voice caught. "I can hardly even see down here. Hell, I don't even really know where I am."

Apricot put his back against the opposite wall and slid down. His hand twitched towards his vest pocket, where the key was nestled once more. He stopped himself. "You're four levels down and a couple of hundred yards from where you fell in from the Downs, that way," he said, pointing.

She shook her head, with a breath of bitter laughter.

"How did you drop your key down a drain?" he asked.

A shrug, then another short laugh. "I was walking," she said. "Going between parties. I was looking in my bag, I don't even remember for what, and the key fell out. And I watched it hit, and bounce once, straight into a storm drain."

"Why were you carrying your key in a bag?"

"Because you have to take it out for your wings to fold," she said. "Can't fly in among the towers. So, here I am, no key, a twisted ankle, sitting in a dark tunnel with a Downer man I don't know."

Going between parties. The frivolousness of it was utterly alien. He felt the distance between them gape like the void between the bottom of the city and the sea below.

"You drew those pictures?" she said. "In the books in your room? They're beautiful."

Apricot clenched his fists in his lap, digging his nails into his palms.

Alba peered at him as he remained silent, her eyes darting about, trying to pick out his expression. She wet her lips. "They're private," she said. "I'm sorry."

With a slow breath, he released the tension in his hands. "It's okay."

He let his eyes run over her, lingering, feeling guilty and a coward, when she couldn't see him doing it.

"I need to get outside," she said. He raised his eyes back to her face, hearing the catch again in her voice. "Can we?"

"Um . . . " He blinked. "How far can you walk?"

"I crawled to get here," she said. "I'll need help."

"Okay. Come on." He stood, offering his hand to pull her up, feeling a tingle up his arm at the skin contact. "This way. It's not far, but you'll have to get down a ladder."

"I can do that."

He took her back out of the run, into the better-lit corridors, past the ladder up to the tearoom and along a little way further, then led her down a short side tunnel. Alba leaned against the wall while he unbolted a service hatch in the floor.

"Down here," he said, sitting on the edge of the open ladder well.

Apricot went down first, the blue tongues of the automatic gas lights flickering on below. He waited at the bottom to help her down the last few rungs, trying not to touch her too obviously more than was necessary. Alba was breathing heavily. Apricot was acutely conscious of her closeness in the small space. She looked up at him gravely. Knowing.

He squeezed past her to wind the door bolts, felt her brush against his back. He pushed open the door with relief. A blast of cold, damp air assaulted them, loaded with rotting kelp, coal smoke and sewage stink.

Alba gagged and covered her mouth and nose with her sleeve.

"You get used to it," Apricot said. "Come on."

They stepped out onto a narrow metal gantry.

"Underside," he announced.

"Oh."

Above them spread the dark rusted plain of iron plates that was the city's underbelly. Daylight, out beyond the city's edge, peeked around the titanic pillars on which it stood.

"Look down," said Apricot.

Alba peered over the gantry railing. She gasped. Below, the hulls, masts and funnels of coal barges and tankers, container ships, trawlers and tugboats were outlined with chains of coloured lanterns.

Apricot lowered himself to sit, legs dangling over the edge, armpits hooked over the bottom safety rail. After a moment, Alba copied him. She grinned, suddenly, surprising him, her crooked teeth emphasising the childlike delight of the expression. Apricot smiled back, then watched her, caught by the unguarded wonder on her face as she followed the movements of the vessels below.

"You can get right down to the water from here," he said. "One of my jobs is to check the pylons over every now and then for cracks. I've got this one and another two on my run." He pointed them out.

She didn't respond immediately, then, "Have you ever thought of getting on one of those ships?"

Apricot peered downwards. "Went out on a trawler, one time, to try my hand at prawning. Spent my whole time head down over the side."

Alba laughed. She shifted, adjusting her bound wings so that she could sit more comfortably.

"Why have a key at all?" Apricot asked.

"Because that's how they come," she said. "It's the law. You have to have a key so they can take it away."

He was surprised, then reflected that he had no cause to be. "Why don't you just buy another?"

She snorted. "Because they cost five hundred marks to replace. I don't have that kind of money to throw away if there's a chance I can find my old key."

Five hundred. Apricot hoped that she couldn't see the redness of his face in the shadows. He realised he was looking straight at her chest, and glanced hurriedly away. "Really?" he said.

"Just because I come from Up High, doesn't mean I'm rich," she said. "Most fliers aren't, you know."

"I didn't," he said. Five hundred marks was almost a year's wages for him. Just having that much money, all at once to spend on whatever you liked, seemed too rich to imagine.

You do have that much, he told himself. It's in your pocket.

"What would it be worth, down here?"

The question made him jump. "What?"

"There's a market for Up High stuff in the Downs, isn't there? What would my key be worth?"

He could feel her stare like a physical pressure. He kept his eyes on the boats below. "I don't know," he said. He affected a shrug. "Maybe the same as Up High, if you had a buyer in the Tweens."

She was quiet again, for a time, then said, "What I meant, before, was do you ever think of getting on one of those ships and going where it goes?"

It was all he could do not to sag with relief. "Have you ever?" he asked. "Been out of the city?"

As soon as he said it, he thought it was a foolish question, with wings on her back to take her anywhere in the world.

But she shook her head. "No. Sometimes I imagine flying out and not turning around, just keeping going until I find somewhere else."

Apricot remembered the elation of doing just that, remembered his chest full to bursting as he looked down at the shadow of the blimp on the waves, far below.

"Somewhere else is not so much different from here," he said.

Now it was her turn to be surprised. "You have been?"

Apricot shrugged, one-shouldered.

"The people are different," she said.

"But you still have to take yourself," he countered.

"No," Alba shook her head. "You can be someone different, if no-one knows you." She studied his face. "Where did you go?"

He studied his hands. "To Black Rock a few years ago."

"Really? What for?"

He smiled lopsidedly. "I won a painting contest. The prize was to study art in Black Rock. Flew there on the blimp."

Her face was alive with interest. "What was it like?"

He shrugged, with both shoulders this time. "Levels, same as here. Rich on top, poor at the bottom. Same language, same troubles, same food."

"But Out Side?"

"Rock," he said. "Black rock, like the name says." It was the kind of answer he would've given Din, shutting the conversation down before it exposed anything vulnerable in him. He puffed his cheeks. "No, that's not true. They have wetlands, Out Side, that they filter their wastewater through. They've turned it into a park, with canals. It has trees, grass—flowers in spring and summer. Birds and butterflies."

"Sounds beautiful."

"I spent a lot of time painting and drawing there. My eyes got used to the light. I could take my goggles off by the end." He showed her a rueful grin. "Paying for it now, though. Got a couple of black spots that'll never go."

"Why did you come back?"

Why did I? He put his chin on his hands, kicked his feet in empty air. "It was a fantasy, not real life."

"Couldn't it have been real life?"

"Can't make a living out of painting."

"Does it matter?"

He frowned. "Well, Din was here . . . "

"Couldn't you have gone back? Taken her there?"

He felt himself freeze, the muscles of his face go slack, blanking his expression, the way it always happened when Din was into him. Alba watched him intently.

"She wouldn't let you go," she said. "Wouldn't let go of you."

He whispered, "No."

"And you met someone there," she said. Hearing someone else say it aloud almost made him cry.

He nodded, no longer seeing the city pylons, the ships below.

"Have you ever seen her again?"

"No." More words queued up. Apricot debated whether to let them out, relented. "I started to paint a picture, to send to her. It was the two of us sitting under a willow tree."

"I saw the sketch," Alba said. "But you never sent it?"

"No. Never even finished it."

"Do you regret having come back?"

"Well, Din and me didn't work out," he said. He shook his head, emphatically. "But no. How could I? That'd be regretting my kids."

"Do you still paint?"

"No."

"You shouldn't let that die in you."

He snorted. "Got no time for it, anymore," he said, pushing himself back from the rail and getting his feet under him. "Haven't had for a long time. Come on, I'd better take you back. I've got to get on and fix those panels you fell through yesterday."

❂

He deposited Alba back in the tearoom first. He watched her manoeuvre her wings past the table and stove in the tearoom, leaning to avoid the shelves, and curl up once more in the armchair. Her face was pale. The climb back up the ladder had plainly hurt a lot.

"Will you look for my key?" she asked.

"Of course," he said, and despised himself as he looked away.

❂

Geara and Willo barrelled through the apartment door.

"Daddy! Daddy!"

He leaned over their heads to peer down the corridor, his shoulders slumping as the tension went out of them. No sign of Din.

"Hello, you two," he tousled their hair as they clung like barnacles to his legs. "It's good to see you."

"Is it a sleepover?" asked Willo, peering up at him.

"Not tonight," he said. "I'll take you back to Mummy's after dinner."

"I want a sleepover."

He tried not to let the stab in his chest show in his expression. "I know." He tugged on his son's ear. "Sleepovers are at the end of the week. But I'll see you again tomorrow."

Geara detached herself. "I did a speech at school today, Daddy. I got a stamp, see." The back of her hand was presented for his inspection, adorned with a star in blue ink. "Can I have a drink? Oo-oh, what's this?"

She was at the table, fingers reaching for the key. Apricot lifted Willo to his hip and carried him over.

"A treasure," he said. "I found it in the traps."

Geara's eyes were almost round. "Can I have it?"

He laughed and pulled out a chair to sit, hitching Willo onto his knee.

"A key," said Willo.

"That's right." Apricot plucked it from Geara's grip. "Watch," he said.

Both of them gasped as he blew gently over its surface. Willo extended a finger to touch the glowing red lines.

"Can I have it?"

"No," Apricot said. "This is very precious. Worth lots of marks."

"How much marks?" Geara asked.

He sucked in air. A small part of him hated himself for needing to show off. "Maybe five hundred."

"Five hundred!" she exclaimed. "Wow, Daddy."

I can't sell it, he thought. I have to give it back. "Here, you try," he said. "Breath on it."

❖

He had just finished rinsing his breakfast things when he was startled by a hammering on the apartment door. He felt a sinking dread before he had even finished asking himself who it could be. He should never have should the kids the key.

Gripping the handle, he paused and closed his eyes for a moment, took a breath. He felt the door shake as the hammering started again. He opened it.

Din folded her arms. "What's this I hear about a five-hundred mark treasure you've got to sell?"

He felt himself shutting down, blanking inside and out.

"I'm not selling anything for five hundred marks," he said.

"Then where did the kids get that story from?" she demanded. "I suppose they made up a tale about you finding a piece of Up High tech? Do you think I'm stupid? Are you stupid? If you didn't want me to know, then you shouldn't have shown it off to them, should you? But you want them to feel proud that their old man's a filthy trap monkey."

His gaze was fixed somewhere around her knees. "I'm not selling anything for five hundred marks."

"Don't lie to me! I'm sick to death of you lying to me!" She glared at him, breathing loudly. "It just makes everything worse. When is that going to penetrate your thick head?"

She took a step towards him, feinted a swing and he flinched. She hit the doorframe instead, one, two, three, half-a-dozen times. There were tears in her eyes. "I see that look on your face, of *nothing*, of you disappearing inside, and it makes me so angry! I just want to hit it." Her jaw worked, but she swallowed whatever words she might've said next. The fury seemed to drain out of her. "I wasn't always like this. I know I wasn't. If you'd just talked to me, years ago, we would never have come to this."

She watched him, waiting for an answer. Apricot stared at her knees. There were no words inside him.

"Don't lie to me," she said, her voice breaking. "Whatever you get for it, I'm entitled to half."

He listened to the sound of her walking away.

The key was in his pocket. The hard shape of it pressed against his chest with every breath.

❖

Alba jumped when he burst into the tearoom.

"What's happened?" she asked.

Apricot inhaled deeply, standing up straight.

"Din came round." He had thought his resolution had steeled him, but his voice quavered. "She wanted money. She pretended to take a swing at me. Hit the wall instead." He mimed the flurry of blows.

Alba watched him from the chair while he leaned against the wall. Almost, the tears came.

After a while, she said, "Have you ever seen an apricot?"

Confused, he shook his head.

"Its flesh is soft and easily bruised, but the stone at the centre, you can't break."

He had to laugh. It came out as half a sob. He took the key out of his pocket and offered it to her.

Her eyes widened, she lurched up from the seat. "My key!" She clutched it to her. "You found it!"

"I found it right before I found you," he said.

He was surprised when she laid her palm against his cheek. He looked into the darkness of her eyes.

"You knew."

"I wondered."

How afraid must she have been? He had to look away. "It's not fair, saying Did wouldn't let me go," he said. "She wanted to keep me here. But it was my choice to make." The thoughts were clear in his head, but they blocked up in his throat when the tried to say them. It took a moment more for him to be able to go on. "I think there wasn't a right or wrong choice. Just choices."

She waited, making sure he was done, then said, "And yet you kept me here."

"I'm sorry."

"Thank you," she said.

He made himself meet her eyes. "Come on. I'll take you Out Side."

❖

He pushed the access hatch ajar. Squinting in the bright sliver of sunlight, he pulled on his tinted day goggles, then shoved the hatch wide and stepped Out Side.

The wind buffeted him. Seagulls launched themselves, squawking, from the rail-less, guano-spattered deck. A trio of pelicans sized him up with eyes as blank as poached eggs, before sullenly following the gulls. Apricot held onto the frame of the navigation beacon, one of the four on the outer edge of his run.

Alba gave a little cry, stepping through the hatch after him. Her hands went up in front of her, feeling the wind. She threw her head back, eyes closed, as it tossed her hair about.

Apricot looked up. The vertiginous iron wall of Out Side filled half his view, dotted with maintenance decks and winch gantries and, from the upper Tweens, caged viewing galleries. Above it, higher than the gulls and the pelicans, other fliers soared, circling and swooping. Far, far beyond Apricot's reach.

He imagined Alba up there with them, one of them. Imagined her looking down, and seeing him as nothing but a speck, too far down and tiny to notice.

"Help me untie these," Alba said, scrabbling for the bindings on her wings.

Apricot stooped to undo the lower straps while she reached over her shoulders to unbuckle those at the top. She shook the wings out, knocking his shoulder. Apricot ducked back out of the way as she caught hold of the frames and spread her arms.

The wind caught the fabric of the wings and lifted them wider still. Alba let go of the frames and limped toward the edge of the deck. The wings flapped and shuddered on the breeze, whatever tension and rigidity they should have possessed sadly absent. She stumbled as they knocked her off balance, but kept walking.

Apricot thought for a terrible instant that she intended to fling herself over the edge. But she stopped just short and stood, the great wings flopping uselessly behind her. She looked out, then up.

For a long time she stayed there. When she turned back to him, her face was streaked with tears.

She lifted her hands, undid the third button of her robe. She slotted the key into the lock, turned it, and hinged the petal grip to lie flat over her sternum. She re-buttoned her robe, and Apricot could see the glowing flower shape through the cloth. Her wings steadied, their shape firmed, guiding the wind over their curved surfaces.

Seeming almost to float over the deck, she came back to him. The energy around her wings prickled Apricot's skin and stood his hair up on his scalp.

"I won't forget you, Apricot," she said. Her fingers slipped round to the back of his neck. She pulled his head down and kissed him firmly on the lips.

With a laugh at his stunned expression, she stepped back. She took another step backwards, holding his gaze. One more, and then she turned and hop-ran for the edge, launching herself into the air with a whoop.

She turned, rising, and waved as she soared overhead, skimming the wall. Apricot raised his hand in response, fingers curling uncertainly.

He watched her ride the updraft, higher and higher, until she was just one speck among the rest. Then he lost track of her, couldn't tell which one she was, and she was gone.

He let his hand fall back to his side, and lowered his gaze.

The sea was blue and glittering. The surface of the water looked like the bright rippling skin of some world-spanning beast. Solid enough to walk on until it decided to suck you down and find out what you were.

He thought of walking straight ahead, leaning out onto the wind, falling, sinking, nothing. He stood with the feeling in him, unmoving.

Eventually, he lifted his goggles and wiped his eyes.

He set them back in place. "As if you ever would," he said.

He looked up again. A vast silver blimp nosed its way past the city's edge, propellers spinning lazily. The fliers scattered, then swarmed around it, over and under, crowding alongside its gondola. Apricot remembered standing inside those windows, his hands pressed to the glass, too amazed to wave back at the incredible beings leaning on the wind on the other side.

He watched the blimp sail away, to Black Rock or elsewhere, until it was no more than a silver pinprick in the sky.

❂

He took the kids back there, a few days later.

"Wow!"

Apricot grabbed them as they both lunged out through the hatchway. He held them close, back near the wall.

"Stay away from the edge," he said. "The wind could tip you over." They stilled, stopped straining under his hands. "Look up."

Fliers circled overhead.

"Birds!" cried Willo, trying to take off his goggles.

Apricot pulled his hands away. "Leave them."

"They're people!" said Geara.

"Are they people, Daddy?"

Apricot crouched between them. "Yes, they are. People with wings. They have a key, like the one I found, that they put in their chest to make the wings work."

"Like the one you found?" asked Geara. "Was it a flying person's key?"

His eyes felt hot. "Yes, it was."

"What did you do with it?"

"I found the flier, and gave it to her," he said, "and she flew away."

Geara's mouth was an 'O' of amazement. Her goggles made her look cross-eyed. "Did you meet a flier? What was she like?"

Like an angel, he almost said. But that wasn't true. She was just a person, like anyone, like him, who made stupid mistakes and had a mistaken view of the world. "She was nice," he said. "She was brave."

"Did she fly with her wings?" Willo wanted to know.

Geara wrinkled her nose, squinting up at the wheeling specks against blue above. "I'd like to be a flier. I'd fly wherever I want."

Apricot stood. He tousled her hair. "That sounds like a grand idea."

She grinned.

"I got some paints," he said. "You two want to do some painting with me?

"Can you paint, Daddy?"

"Yes, I can. Do you want to?"

"Yes!"

"Let's go home, then."

He herded them ahead of him. Once more, briefly, he looked up, before he pulled the hatch shut behind him.

# AFTERWORD

There were a few writers whose work I read avidly as a kid and a young adult. Glen Cook and C.J. Cherryh stand out, for different—even opposite—reasons. I like the hard edge that Cook brings to magical fantasy, and the human softness that Cherryh gives her hard science fiction. I had a longtime writer-crush on the late Diana Wynne Jones, who I've rediscovered as an adult, reading to *my* kids, for the enthusiasm with which she tears up fantasy and fairy tales tropes as much as for her wit.

As I started to write myself, individual stories—particularly short stories, since that's the form I've focused on—began to stand out as much as bodies of work. One of those stories was Kaaron Warren's "The Glass Woman". This was my review of it, back in 2005:

*"Biting is not a strong enough word to describe this assault on misogyny. Warren trawls the cesspit hidden way down deep in the male psyche and brings some things up to the light that really should never see day. This violence is in all men, the story says, not just the beasts who indulge in it. Tough stuff, and not the sort of thing I like to read about myself. What makes it even more confronting—and very hard to dissociate oneself from—is that "The Glass Woman" is also a beautiful fantasy."*

Then I went to Clarion West in 2006, and Paul Park told us that you know you're onto something important with your writing when you're uncomfortable showing your stories to your loved ones. That advice, and the ideas I got from stories like "The Glass Woman", sunk in. Not entirely consciously, I think, because, when I came to looking at stories for this collection, I was surprised to find how many of mine revolve around men who are either failing at being men or teetering on the brink of failure. By that, I mean failure to fulfill traditional male roles—provider, protector, lover, father, son, etc. Those roles have been challenged, diluted, transformed or demasculinised in contemporary society, but they're all still important aspects of my experience of being a man.

I'm lucky enough to know a lot of good men—my dad, for one. And I also know a lot of people who've been hurt by men who failed to be what they should have been. And I know a lot of good men who've fallen short at one time or another, because everyone does. I have, and the fear of doing so preoccupies me. And so it comes out in my stories.

And here I pause to reflect, at the end of this confessional rant about male virtue, that I have giant naked lady statues on the front and back of my book. What to make of that?

Well, the cesspits of the male psyche aren't my only inspiration for writing. Another aspect of what drives me to write is also there in my review of "The Glass Woman"—it's a beautiful fantasy. That's another thing that floats my literary boat. I love the flights of imagination, the worlds and aliens and ideas and moments and magic that make me go *"wow"*.

I came across a speech online by the novelist Elif Shafak, in which she questioned whether it's right to teach people to write what they know. Get out of your cultural ghetto, she says. Learn what you don't know, and write *that*. It's an idea that seems tailored for science fiction and fantasy: show me what I don't know. It's something that I think all good speculative fiction should do.

So, I hope these stories discomforted you. I hope they made you go "wow". And I hope you found something in them that you didn't know.

*Ian McHugh*
*October 2014*

# STORY ACKNOWLEDGEMENTS

"The Beetle Road" copyright © Ian McHugh 2014. Appears here for the first time.

"Angel Dust" copyright © Ian McHugh 2009. First published in *Clockwork Phoenix 2*, Norilana Books/Mythic Delirium Books, 2009.

"Sleepless in the House of Ye" copyright © Ian McHugh 2009. First published in *Asimov's Science Fiction*, July 2009.

"The Wishwriter's Wife" copyright © Ian McHugh 2011. First published in *Daily Science Fiction*, July 2011.

"The Tax Collector of Rhuin" copyright © Ian McHugh 2014. Appears here for the first time.

"Cold, Cold War" copyright © Ian McHugh 2013. First published in *Beneath Ceaseless Skies* #123 , June 2013.

"Once a Month, on a Sunday..." copyright © Ian McHugh 2009. First published in *Andromeda Spaceways Inflight Magazine*, #40, September 2009.

"Bitter Dreams" copyright © Ian McHugh 2008. First published in *L. Ron Hubbard presents: Writers of the Future Volume XXIV*, 2008.

"When the rain comin" copyright © Ian McHugh 2013. First published in *Asimov's Science Fiction*, October/November 2013.

"The Canal Barge Magician's Number Nine Daughter" copyright © Ian McHugh 2013. First published in *Clockwork Phoenix 4*, Mythic Delirium Books, 2013.

"Interloper" copyright © Ian McHugh 2011. First published in *Asimov's Science Fiction*, January 2011.

"Extracted Journal Notes for an Ethnography of Bnebene Nomad Culture" copyright © Ian McHugh 2014. First published in *Asimov's Science Fiction*, January 2014.

"Red Dirt" copyright © Ian McHugh 2010. First published in *Beneath Ceaseless Skies*, #58, December 2010.

"Almost Angels" copyright © Ian McHugh 2014. Appears here for the first time.

"Apricot Finds a Treasure" copyright © Ian McHugh 2014. Appears here for the first time.

# AVAILABLE FROM TICONDEROGA PUBLICATIONS

## LIMITED HARDCOVER EDITIONS

978-0-9586856-9-6  Love in Vain BY Lewis Shiner
978-0-9803531-1-2  Belong ED Russell B. Farr
978-0-9803531-9-8  Basic Black BY Terry Dowling
978-0-9806288-0-7  Make Believe BY Terry Dowling
978-0-9806288-1-4  The Infernal BY Kim Wilkins
978-0-9806288-5-2  Dead Sea Fruit BY Kaaron Warren
978-0-9806288-7-6  The Girl With No Hands BY Angela Slatter
978-0-9807813-0-4  Dead Red Heart ED Russell B. Farr
978-0-9807813-3-5  Heliotrope BY Justina Robson
978-0-9807813-6-6  Matilda Told Such Dreadful Lies BY Lucy Sussex
978-1-921857-00-3  Bluegrass Symphony BY Lisa L. Hannett
978-1-921857-07-2  Bread and Circuses BY Felicity Dowker
978-1-921857-23-2  Wild Chrome BY Greg Mellor
978-1-921857-27-0  Midnight and Moonshine BY Lisa L. Hannett & Angela Slatter
978-1-921857-37-9  Prickle Moon BY Juliet Marillier
978-1-921857-41-6  The Bride Price BY Cat Sparks
978-1-921857-45-4  The Year of Ancient Ghosts BY Kim Wilkins
978-1-921857-58-4  Everything is a Graveyard BY Jason Fischer
978-1-921857-68-3  Havenstar BY Glenda Larke

## EBOOKS

978-0-9803531-5-0  Ghost Seas BY Steven Utley
978-1-921857-93-5  The Girl With No Hands BY Angela Slatter
978-1-921857-99-7  Dead Red Heart ED Russell B. Farr
978-1-921857-94-2  More Scary Kisses ED Liz Grzyb
978-0-9807813-5-9  Heliotrope BY Justina Robson
978-1-921857-98-0  Year's Best Australian F&H EDS Grzyb & Helene
978-1-921857-36-2  Dreaming of Djinn ED Liz Grzyb
978-1-921857-40-9  Prickle Moon BY Juliet Marillier
978-1-921857-92-8  The Year of Ancient Ghosts BY Kim Wilkins
978-1-921857-28-7  Bloodstones ED Amanda Pillar

## THE YEAR'S BEST AUSTRALIAN FANTASY & HORROR SERIES
## EDITED BY LIZ GRZYB & TALIE HELENE

978-0-9807813-8-0  Year's Best Australian Fantasy & Horror 2010 (hc)
978-0-9807813-9-7  Year's Best Australian Fantasy & Horror 2010 (tpb)
978-0-921057-13-3  Year's Best Australian Fantasy & Horror 2011 (hc)
978-0-921057-14-0  Year's Best Australian Fantasy & Horror 2011 (tpb)
978-0-921057-48-5  Year's Best Australian Fantasy & Horror 2012 (hc)
978-0-921057-49-2  Year's Best Australian Fantasy & Horror 2012 (tpb)
978-0-921057-72-0  Year's Best Australian Fantasy & Horror 2012 (hc)
978-0-921057-73-7  Year's Best Australian Fantasy & Horror 2013 (tpb)

WWW.TICONDEROGAPUBLICATIONS.COM

THANK YOU

The publisher would sincerely like to thank:

Elizabeth Grzyb, Ian McHugh, Kaaron Warren, Sheila
Williams, Scott H. Andrews, Mike Allen, Cat Sparks, Lisa L.
Hannett, Donna Maree Hanson, Robert Hood, Pete Kempshall,
Penelope Love, Nicole Murphy, Angela Slatter, Karen Brooks,
Jeremy G. Byrne, Felicity Dowker, Kim Wilkins, Marianne de
Pierres, Jonathan Strahan, Peter McNamara, Ellen Datlow,
Grant Stone, Sean Williams, Simon Brown, Garth Nix,
David Cake, Simon Oxwell, Grant Watson, Sue Manning,
Steven Utley, Lewis Shiner, Bill Congreve, Jack Dann, Janeen
Webb, Lucy Sussex, Stephen Dedman, the Mt Lawley Mafia,
the Nedlands Yakuza, Shane Jiraiya Cummings, Angela Challis,
Kate Williams, Kathryn Linge, Andrew Williams, Al Chan,
Alisa and Tehani, Mel & Phil, Hayley Lane, Georgina Walpole,
Rushelle Lister, everyone we've missed . . .

. . . and you.

IN MEMORY OF
Eve Johnson (1945–2011)
Sara Douglass (1957–2011)
Steven Utley (1948–2013)

www.ingramcontent.com/pod-product-compliance
Lightning Source LLC
Chambersburg PA
CBHW021215250626
47155CB00008B/2806